Gothic Horror
Short Stories

GOTHIC HORROR

SHORT STORIES

SIRIUS

Disclaimer
Throughout the text readers may find that some of the language used and sentiments expressed are unacceptable by today's standards. These reflect the attitudes and usage common at the time the book was written. In no way do they reflect the attitude of the publishers.

SIRIUS
This edition published in 2022 by Sirius Publishing, a division of Arcturus Publishing Limited,
26/27 Bickels Yard, 151–153 Bermondsey Street,
London SE1 3HA

ISBN: 978-1-3988-2463-8
AD007964UK

Printed in China

Contents

Introduction

The Classic Gothic Horror Collection

The publication of *The Castle of Otranto* by Horace Walpole in 1764 marked the emergence of a new genre of literature: the gothic horror story. The success of the novel spawned a number of imitators, including Clara Reeve's *The Old English Baron* (1777), Anne Radcliffe's *The Mysteries of Udolpho* (1794) and Matthew Lewis' *The Monk* (1796). When they first appeared, they shocked and horrified the reading public, and many of their scenes remain an uncomfortable read today.

Gothic stories featured foreboding and oppressive landscapes, supernatural manifestations, flawed heroes and doomed romances. Set in looming castles and abandoned abbeys, it is often not the supernatural that proves most terrifying but the people themselves. At the heart of these tales are disturbed families and they do not shy away from describing the scandalous relations between them.

While the gothic is often associated with weighty tomes, a number of writers attempted to evoke the same experience in the short story. This collection begins with 'Leixlip Castle', a story from one of the best-known practitioners of gothic literature, Charles Maturin. His 1820 novel *Melmoth the Wanderer* is now recognised as one of the greatest English gothic novels of all time, but during Maturin's lifetime it proved more influential in France, where Honoré de Balzac was so impressed by the novel that he decided to write a sequel.

It features all of the essential elements of a gothic story – an ominous castle, a demon lover and a family filled with unresolved tensions.

Around the same time Maturin was writing, Mary Shelley completed one of the greatest ever works of horror fiction in *Frankenstein* (1818). Shelley was also an accomplished short story writer, and in her fiction she drew deeply on gothic influences. Included here are two of her most explicitly gothic stories: 'The Dream' and 'The Invisible Girl.'

By the middle of the 19th century, the boundaries of the gothic horror story had been firmly established, and a new generation of writers took up their pens. Edgar Allan Poe became one of the new masters of the genre and he brought with him an unmatched ability to create suspense. Included here is 'The Fall of the House of Usher' telling the story of a family's decline and fall in the classic gothic manner, while 'Berenice' is a dark tale of obsession, malice and psychosis. Sheridan Le Fanu, one of Ireland's most established writers in the genre, steered away from the shock and gore that had marked many of the early gothic stories, and instead used his exceptional prose to create atmospheric tales. Here you will find two of his stories, 'A Chapter in the History of a Tyrone Family' and 'Strange Event in the Life of Schalken the Painter'.

As the 19th century progressed, the motifs of gothic fiction began to merge with the newly emerging popularity of the ghost story. Stories by Elizabeth Gaskell, Ambrose Bierce, Henry James and Edward Frederic Benson brought the supernatural element to the fore in their stories while retaining many of the elements that had made gothic fiction so popular over the years.

In the pages that follow, you will find many more brooding tales of terror. They will leave behind a lingering malaise that will keep you wondering long after you finish the final page.

Leixlip Castle

Charles Maturin

The incidents of the following tale are not merely founded on fact, they are facts themselves, which occurred at no very distant period in my own family. The marriage of the parties, their sudden and mysterious separation, and their total alienation from each other until the last period of their mortal existence, are all facts. I cannot vouch for the truth of the supernatural solution given to all these mysteries; but I must still consider the story as a fine specimen of Gothic horrors, and can never forget the impression it made on me when I heard it related for the first time among many other thrilling traditions of the same description.

C.R.M.

The tranquillity of the Catholics of Ireland during the disturbed periods of 1715 and 1745, was most commendable, and somewhat extraordinary; to enter into an analysis of their probable motives, is not at all the object of the writer of this tale, as it is pleasanter to state the fact of their honour, than at this distance of time to assign dubious and unsatisfactory reasons for it. Many of them, however, showed a kind of secret disgust at the existing state of affairs, by quitting their family residences and wandering about like persons who were uncertain of their homes, or possibly expecting better from some near and fortunate contingency.

Among the rest was a Jacobite Baronet, who, sick of his uncongenial situation in a Whig neighbourhood, in the north – where he heard of nothing but the heroic defence of Londonderry; the barbarities of the French generals; and the resistless exhortations of the godly Mr. Walker, a Presbyterian clergyman, to whom the citizens gave the title of 'Evangelist'; – quitted his paternal residence, and about the year 1720 hired the Castle of Leixlip for three years (it was then the property of the Connollys, who let it to triennial tenants); and removed thither with his family, which consisted of three daughters – their mother having long been dead.

The Castle of Leixlip, at that period, possessed a character of romantic beauty and feudal grandeur, such as few buildings in Ireland can claim, and which is now, alas, totally effaced by the destruction of its noble woods; on the destroyers of which the writer would wish 'a minstrel's malison were said'. – Leixlip, though about seven miles from Dublin, has all the sequestered and picturesque character that imagination could ascribe to a landscape a hundred miles from, not only the metropolis but an inhabited town. After driving a dull mile (an Irish mile) in passing from Lucan to Leixlip, the road – hedged up on one side of the high wall that bounds the demesne of the Veseys, and on the other by low enclosures, over whose rugged tops you have no view at all – at once opens on Leixlip Bridge, at almost a right angle, and displays a luxury of landscape on which the eye that has seen it even in childhood dwells with delighted recollection. – Leixlip Bridge, a rude but solid structure, projects from a high bank of the Liffey, and slopes rapidly to the opposite side, which there lies remarkably low. To the right the plantations of the Vesey's demesne – no longer obscured by walls – almost mingle their dark woods in its stream, with the opposite ones of Marshfield and St Catherine's. The river is scarcely visible, overshadowed as it is by the deep, rich and bending foliage of the trees. To the left it bursts out in all the brilliancy of light, washes the garden steps of the houses of Leixlip, wanders round the low walls of its churchyard, plays, with the pleasure-boat moored under the arches on which the summer-house of the Castle is raised, and then loses itself among the rich woods that once skirted those grounds to its very brink. The contrast on the other side, with the luxuriant walks, scattered shrubberies, temples seated on pinnacles, and thickets that conceal from you the sight of the river until you are on its banks, that mark the character of the grounds which are now the property of Colonel Marly, is peculiarly striking.

Visible above the highest roofs of the town, though a quarter of a mile distant from them, are the ruins of Confy Castle, a right good old predatory tower of the stirring times when blood was shed like water; and as you pass the bridge you catch a glimpse of the waterfall (or salmon-leap, as it is called) on whose noon-day lustre, or moon-light beauty, probably the rough livers of that age when Confy Castle was 'a tower of strength', never glanced an eye or cast a thought, as they clattered in their harness over Leixlip Bridge, or waded through the stream before that convenience was in existence.

Whether the solitude in which he lived contributed to tranquillize Sir Redmond Blaney's feelings, or whether they had begun to rust from want of collision with those of others, it is impossible to say, but certain it is, that the good Baronet began gradually to lose his tenacity in political matters; and except when a Jacobite friend came to dine with him, and drink with many a significant 'nod and beck and smile', the King over the water – or the parish-priest (good man) spoke of the hopes of better times, and the final success of the right cause, and the old religion – or a Jacobite servant was heard in the solitude of the large mansion whistling 'Charlie is my darling', to which Sir Redmond involuntarily responded in a deep bass voice, somewhat the worse for wear, and marked with more emphasis than good discretion – except, as I have said, on such occasions, the Baronet's politics, like his life, seemed passing away without notice or effort. Domestic calamities, too, pressed sorely on the old gentleman: of his three daughters the youngest, Jane, had disappeared in so extraordinary a manner in her childhood, that though it is but a wild, remote family tradition, I cannot help relating it: –

The girl was of uncommon beauty and intelligence, and was suffered to wander about the neighbourhood of the Castle with the daughter of a servant, who was also called Jane, as a nom de caresse. One evening Jane Blaney and her young companion went far and deep into the woods; their absence created no uneasiness at the time, as these excursions were by no means unusual, till her playfellow returned home alone and weeping, at a very late hour. Her account was, that, in passing through a lane at some distance from the Castle, an old woman, in the Fingallian dress, (a red petticoat and a long green jacket), suddenly started out of a thicket, and took Jane Blaney by the arm: she had in her hand two rushes, one of which she threw over her shoulder, and giving the other to the child, motioned to her to do the same. Her young companion, terrified at what she saw, was running away, when Jane Blaney called after her – 'Good-bye, good-bye, it is a long time before you will see me again.' The girl said they then disappeared, and she found her way home as she could. An indefatigable search was immediately commenced – woods were traversed, thickets were explored, ponds were drained – all in vain. The pursuit and the hope were at length given up. Ten years afterwards, the housekeeper of Sir Redmond, having remembered that she left the key of a closet where sweetmeats were kept, on the kitchen table, returned to fetch it. As she approached the door, she heard a childish voice murmuring – 'Cold – cold – cold how long it is since I have felt a fire!' – She advanced, and saw, to her amazement, Jane Blaney, shrunk to half her usual size, and covered with rags, crouching over the embers of the fire. The housekeeper flew in terror from the spot, and roused the servants, but the vision had fled. The child was reported to have been seen several times afterwards, as diminutive in form, as though she had not grown an inch since she was ten years of age, and always crouching over a fire, whether in the turret-room or kitchen, complaining of cold and hunger, and apparently covered with rags. Her existence is still said to be protracted under these dismal circumstances, so unlike those of Lucy Gray in Wordsworth's beautiful ballad:

> Yet some will say, that to this day
> She is a living child –
> That they have met sweet Lucy Gray
> Upon the lonely wild;
> O'er rough and smooth she trips along.
> And never looks behind;
> And hums a solitary song
> That whistles in the wind.

The fate of the eldest daughter was more melancholy, though less extraordinary; she was addressed by a gentleman of competent fortune and unexceptionable character: he was a Catholic, moreover; and Sir

Redmond Blaney signed the marriage articles, in full satisfaction of the security of his daughter's soul, as well as of her jointure. The marriage was celebrated at the Castle of Leixlip; and, after the bride and bridegroom had retired, the guests still remained drinking to their future happiness, when suddenly, to the great alarm of Sir Redmond and his friends, loud and piercing cries were heard to issue from the part of the Castle in which the bridal chamber was situated.

Some of the more courageous hurried upstairs; it was too late – the wretched bridegroom had burst, on that fatal night, into a sudden and most horrible paroxysm of insanity. The mangled form of the unfortunate and expiring lady bore attestation to the mortal virulence with which the disease had operated on the wretched husband, who died a victim to it himself after the involuntary murder of his bride. The bodies were interred, as soon as decency would permit, and the story hushed up.

Sir Redmond's hopes of Jane's recovery were diminishing every day, though he still continued to listen to every wild tale told by the domestics; and all his care was supposed to be now directed towards his only surviving daughter. Anne, living in solitude, and partaking only of the very limited education of Irish females of that period, was left very much to the servants, among whom she increased her taste for superstitious and supernatural horrors, to a degree that had a most disastrous effect on her future life.

Among the numerous menials of the Castle, there was one withered crone, who had been nurse to the late Lady Blaney's mother, and whose memory was a complete Thesaurus terrorum. The mysterious fate of Jane first encouraged her sister to listen to the wild tales of this hag, who avouched, that at one time she saw the fugitive standing before the portrait of her late mother in one of the apartments of the Castle, and muttering to herself – 'Woe's me, woe's me! how little my mother thought her wee Jane would ever come to be what she is!' But as Anne grew older she began more 'seriously to incline' to the hag's promises that she could show her her future bridegroom, on the performance of certain ceremonies, which she at first revolted from as horrible and impious; but, finally, at the repeated instigation of the old woman, consented to act a part in. The period fixed upon for the performance of these unhallowed rites, was now approaching – it was near the 31st of October – the eventful night, when such ceremonies were, and still are supposed, in the North of Ireland, to be most potent in their effects. All day long the Crone took care to lower the mind of the young lady to the proper key of submissive and trembling credulity, by every horrible story she could relate; and she told them with frightful and supernatural energy. This woman was called Collogue by the family, a name equivalent to Gossip in England, or Cummer in Scotland (though her real name was Bridget Dease); and she verified the name, by the exercise of an unwearied loquacity, an indefatigable memory, and a rage for communicating, and inflicting terror, that spared no victim in the household, from the groom, whom she sent shivering to his rug, to the Lady of the Castle, over whom she felt she held unbounded sway.

The 31st of October arrived – the Castle was perfectly quiet before eleven o'clock; half an hour afterwards, the Collogue and Anne Blaney were seen gliding along a passage that led to what is called King John's Tower, where it is said that monarch received the homage of the Irish princes as Lord of Ireland and which was, at all events, the most ancient part of the structure.

The Collogue opened a small door with a key which she had secreted, about her, and urged the young lady to hurry on. Anne advanced to the postern, and stood there irresolute and trembling like a timid swimmer on the bank of an unknown stream. It was a dark autumnal evening; a heavy wind sighed among the woods of the Castle, and bowed the branches of the lower trees almost to the waves of the Liffey, which, swelled by recent rains, struggled and roared amid the stones that obstructed its channel. The steep descent from the Castle lay before her, with its dark avenue of elms; a few lights still burned in the little village of Leixlip – but from the lateness of the hour it was probable they would soon be extinguished.

The lady lingered – 'And must I go alone?' said she, foreseeing that the terrors of her fearful journey could be aggravated by her more fearful purpose.

'Ye must, or all will be spoiled,' said the hag, shading the miserable light, that did not extend its influence above six inches on the path of the victim. 'Ye must go alone – and I will watch for you here, dear, till you come back, and then see what will come to you at twelve o'clock.'

The unfortunate girl paused. 'Oh! Collogue, Collogue, if you would but come with me. Oh! Collogue, come with me, if it be but to the bottom of the castlehill.'

'If I went with you, dear, we should never reach the top of it alive again, for there are them near that would tear us both in pieces.'

'Oh! Collogue, Collogue – let me turn back then, and go to my own room – I have advanced too far, and I have done too much.'

'And that's what you have, dear, and so you must go further, and do more still, unless, when you return to your own room, you would see the likeness of someone instead of a handsome young bridegroom.'

The young lady looked about her for a moment, terror and wild hope trembling at her heart – then, with a sudden impulse of supernatural courage, she darted like a bird from the terrace of the Castle, the fluttering of her white garments was seen for a few moments, and then the hag who had been shading the flickering light with her hand, bolted the postern, and, placing the candle before a glazed loophole, sat down on a stone seat in the recess of the tower, to watch the event of the spell. It was an hour before the young lady returned; when her face was as pale, and her eyes as fixed, as those of a dead body, but she held in her grasp a dripping garment, a proof that her errand had been performed. She flung it into her companion's hands, and then stood, panting and gazing wildly about her as if she knew not where she was. The hag herself grew terrified at the insane and breathless state of her victim, and hurried her to her chamber; but here the preparations for the terrible ceremonies of the night were the first objects that struck her, and, shivering at the sight, she covered her eyes with her hands, and stood immovably fixed in the middle of the room.

It needed all the hag's persuasions (aided even by mysterious menaces), combined with the returning faculties and reviving curiosity of the poor girl, to prevail on her to go through the remaining business of the night. At length she said, as if in desperation, 'I will go through with it: but be in the next room; and if what I dread should happen, I will ring my father's little silver bell which I have secured for the night – and as you have a soul to be saved, Collogue, come to me at its first sound.'

The hag promised, gave her last instructions with eager and jealous minuteness, and then retired to her own room, which was adjacent to that of the young lady. Her candle had burned out, but she stirred up the embers of her turf fire, and sat, nodding over them, and smoothing the pallet from time to time, but resolved not to lie down while there was a chance of a sound from the lady's room, for which she herself, withered as her feelings were, waited with a mingled feeling of anxiety and terror.

It was now long past midnight, and all was silent as the grave throughout the Castle. The hag dozed over the embers till her head touched her knees, then started up as the sound of the bell seemed to tinkle in her ears, then dozed again, and again started as the bell appeared to tinkle more distinctly – suddenly she was roused, not by the bell, but by the most piercing and horrible cries from the neighbouring chamber. The Cologue, aghast for the first time, at the possible consequences of the mischief she might have occasioned, hastened to the room. Anne was in convulsions, and the hag was compelled reluctantly to call up the housekeeper (removing meanwhile the implements of the ceremony), and assist in applying all the specifics known at that day, burnt feathers, etc., to restore her. When they had at length succeeded, the housekeeper was dismissed, the door was bolted, and the Collogue was left alone with Anne; the subject of their conference might have been guessed at, but was not known until many years afterwards; but Anne that night held in her hand, in the shape of a weapon with the use of which neither of them was acquainted, an evidence that her chamber had been visited by a being of no earthly form.

This evidence the hag importuned her to destroy, or to remove: but she persisted with fatal tenacity in keeping it. She locked it up, however, immediately, and seemed to think she had acquired a right, since she had grappled so fearfully with the mysteries of futurity, to know all the secrets of which that weapon might yet lead to the disclosure. But from that night it was observed that her character, her manner, and even her countenance, became altered. She grew stern and solitary, shrunk at the sight of her former associates, and imperatively forbade the slightest allusion to the circumstances which had occasioned this mysterious change.

It was a few days subsequent to this event that Anne, who after dinner had left the Chaplain reading the life of St Francis Xavier to Sir Redmond, and retired to her own room to work, and, perhaps, to muse, was surprised to hear the bell at the outer gate ring loudly and repeatedly – a sound she had never heard since her first residence in the Castle; for the few guests who resorted there came, and departed as noiselessly as humble visitors at the house of a great man generally do. Straightway there rode up the avenue of elms, which we have already mentioned, a stately gentleman, followed by four servants, all mounted, the two former having pistols in their holsters, and the two latter carrying saddle-bags before them: though it was the first week in November, the dinner hour being one o'clock, Anne had light enough to notice all these circumstances. The arrival of the stranger seemed to cause much, though not unwelcome tumult in the Castle; orders were loudly and hastily given for the accommodation of the servants and horses – steps were heard traversing the numerous passages for a full hour – then all was still; and it was said that Sir Redmond had locked with his own hand the door of the room where he and the stranger sat, and desired that no one should dare to approach it. About two hours afterwards, a female servant came with orders from her master, to have a plentiful supper ready by eight o'clock, at which he desired the presence of his daughter. The family establishment was on a handsome scale for an Irish house, and Anne had only to descend to the kitchen to order the roasted chickens to be well strewed with brown sugar according to the unrefined fashion of the day, to inspect the mixing of the bowl of sago with its allowance of a bottle of port wine and a large handful of the richest spices, and to order particularly that the pease pudding should have a huge lump of cold salt butter stuck in its centre; and then, her household cares being over, to retire to her room and array herself in a robe of white damask for the occasion. At eight o'clock she was summoned to the supper-room. She came in, according to the fashion of the times, with the first dish; but as she passed through the ante-room, where the servants were holding lights and bearing the dishes, her sleeve was twitched, and the ghastly face of the Collogue pushed close to hers; while she muttered 'Did not I say he would come for you, dear?' Anne's blood ran cold, but she advanced, saluted her father and the stranger with two low and distinct reverences, and then took her place at the table. Her feelings of awe and perhaps terror at the whisper of her associate, were not diminished by the appearance of the stranger; there was a singular and mute solemnity in his manner during the meal. He ate nothing. Sir Redmond appeared constrained, gloomy and thoughtful. At length, starting, he said (without naming the stranger's name), 'You will drink my daughter's health?' The stranger intimated his willingness to have that honour, but absently filled his glass with water; Anne put a few drops of wine into hers, and bowed towards him. At that moment, for the first time since they had met, she beheld his face – it was pale as that of a corpse. The deadly whiteness of his cheeks and lips, the hollow and distant sound of his voice, and the strange lustre of his large dark moveless eyes, strongly fixed on her, made her pause and even tremble as she raised the glass to her lips; she set it down, and then with another silent reverence retired to her chamber.

There she found Bridget Dease, busy in collecting the turf that burned on the hearth, for there was no grate in the apartment. 'Why are you here?' she said, impatiently.

The hag turned on her, with a ghastly grin of congratulation, 'Did not I tell you that he would come for you?'

'I believe he has,' said the unfortunate girl, sinking into the huge wicker chair by her bedside; 'for never did I see mortal with such a look.'

'But is not he a fine stately gentleman?' pursued the hag.

'He looks as if he were not of this world,' said Anne.

'Of this world, or of the next,' said the hag, raising her bony forefinger, 'mark my words – so sure as the – (here she repeated some of the horrible formularies of the 31st of October) – so sure he will be your bridegroom.'

'Then I shall be the bride of a corpse,' said Anne; 'for he I saw tonight is no living man.'

A fortnight elapsed, and whether Anne became reconciled to the features she had thought so ghastly, by the discovery that they were the handsomest she had ever beheld – and that the voice, whose sound at first was so strange and unearthly, was subdued into a tone of plaintive softness when addressing her or whether it is impossible for two young persons with unoccupied hearts to meet in the country, and meet often, to gaze silently on the same stream, wander under the same trees, and listen together to the wind that waves the branches, without experiencing an assimilation of feeling rapidly succeeding an assimilation of taste; – or whether it was from all these causes combined, but in less than a month Anne heard the declaration of the stranger's passion with many a blush, though without a sigh. He now avowed his name and rank. He stated himself to be a Scottish Baronet, of the name of Sir Richard Maxwell; family misfortunes had driven him from his country, and forever precluded the possibility of his return: he had transferred his property to Ireland, and purposed to fix his residence there for life. Such was his statement. The courtship of those days was brief and simple. Anne became the wife of Sir Richard, and, I believe, they resided with her father till his death, when they removed to their estate in the North. There they remained for several years, in tranquillity and happiness, and had a numerous family. Sir Richard's conduct was marked by but two peculiarities: he not only shunned the intercourse, but the sight of any of his countrymen, and, if he happened to hear that a Scotsman had arrived in the neighbouring town, he shut himself up till assured of the stranger's departure. The other was his custom of retiring to his own chamber, and remaining invisible to his family on the anniversary of the 31st of October. The lady, who had her own associations connected with that period, only questioned him once on the subject of this seclusion, and was then solemnly and even sternly enjoined never to repeat her inquiry. Matters stood thus, somewhat mysteriously, but not unhappily, when on a sudden, without any cause assigned or assignable, Sir Richard and Lady Maxwell parted, and never more met in this world, nor was she ever permitted to see one of her children to her dying hour. He continued to live at the family mansion and she fixed her residence with a distant relative in a remote part of the country. So total was the disunion, that the name of either was never heard to pass the other's lips, from the moment of separation until that of dissolution.

Lady Maxwell survived Sir Richard forty years, living to the great age of ninety-six; and, according to a promise, previously given, disclosed to a descendant with whom she had lived, the following extra-ordinary circumstances.

She said that on the night of the 31st of October, about seventy-five years before, at the instigation of her ill-advising attendant, she had washed one of her garments in a place where four streams met, and performed other unhallowed ceremonies under the direction of the Collogue, in the expectation that her future husband would appear to her in her chamber at twelve o'clock that night. The critical moment arrived, but with it no lover-like form. A vision of indescribable horror approached her bed, and flinging at her an iron weapon of a shape and construction unknown to her, bade her 'recognize her future husband by that.' The terrors of this visit soon deprived her of her senses; but on her recovery, she persisted, as has been said, in keeping the fearful pledge of the reality of the vision, which, on examination, appeared to be incrusted with blood. It remained concealed in the inmost drawer of her cabinet till the morning of the separation. On that morning, Sir Richard Maxwell rose before daylight to join a hunting party – he wanted a knife for some accidental purpose, and, missing his own, called to Lady Maxwell, who was still in bed, to lend him one. The lady, who was half asleep, answered, that in such a drawer of her cabinet he would find one. He went, however, to another, and the next moment she was fully awakened by seeing her husband present the terrible weapon to her throat, and threaten her with instant death unless she disclosed how she came by it. She supplicated for life, and then, in an agony of horror and contrition, told the tale of that eventful night. He gazed at her for a moment with a countenance which rage, hatred, and despair converted, as she avowed, into a living likeness of the demon-visage she had once beheld (so singularly was the fated resemblance fulfilled), and then exclaiming, 'You won me by the devil's aid, but you shall not keep me long,' left her – to meet no more in this world. Her husband's secret was not unknown to the lady, though the means by which she became possessed of it were wholly unwarrantable. Her curiosity had been strongly excited by her husband's aversion to his countrymen, and it was so – stimulated by the arrival of a Scottish gentleman in the neighbourhood some time before, who professed himself formerly acquainted with Sir Richard, and spoke mysteriously of the causes that drove him from his country – that she contrived to procure an interview with him under a feigned name, and obtained from him the knowledge of circumstances which embittered her after-life to its latest hour. His story was this:

Sir Richard Maxwell was at deadly feud with a younger brother; a family feast was proposed to reconcile them, and as the use of knives and forks was then unknown in the Highlands, the company met armed with their dirks for the purpose of carving. They drank deeply; the feast, instead of harmonizing, began to inflame their spirits; the topics of old strife were renewed; hands, that at first touched their weapons in defiance, drew them at last in fury, and in the fray, Sir Richard mortally wounded his brother. His life was with difficulty saved from the vengeance of the clan, and he was hurried towards the seacoast, near which the house stood, and concealed there till a vessel could be procured to convey him to Ireland. He embarked on the night of the 31st of October, and while he was traversing the deck in unutterable agony of spirit, his hand accidentally touched the dirk which he had unconsciously worn ever since the fatal night. He drew it, and, praying 'that the guilt of his brother's blood might be as far from his soul, as he could fling that weapon from his body,' sent it with all his strength into the air. This instrument he found secreted in the lady's cabinet, and whether he really believed her to have become possessed of it by supernatural means, or whether he feared his wife was a secret witness of his crime, has not been ascertained, but the result was what I have stated.

The separation took place on the discovery: – for the rest.

I know not how the truth may be.

I tell the Tale as 'twas told to me.

Sir Bertrand: A Fragment

Anna Laetitia Aiken

After this adventure, Sir Bertrand turned his steed towards the woulds, hoping to cross these dreary moors before the curfew. But ere he had proceeded half his journey, he was bewildered by the different tracks, and not being able, as far as the eye could reach, to espy any object but the brown heath surrounding him, he was at length quite uncertain which way he should direct his course. Night overtook him in this situation. It was one of those nights when the moon gives a faint glimmering of light through the thick black clouds of a lowering sky. Now and then she suddenly emerged in full splendour from her veil; and then instantly retired behind it, having just served to give the forlorn Sir Bertrand a wide extended prospect over the desolate waste. Hope and native courage a while urged him to push forwards, but at length the increasing darkness and fatigue of body and mind overcame him; he dreaded moving from the ground he stood on, for fear of unknown pits and bogs, and alighting; from his horse in despair, he threw himself on the ground. He had not long continued in that posture when the sullen toll of a distant bell struck his ear – he started up, and turning towards the sound, discerned a dim twinkling light.

Instantly he seized his horse's bridle, and with cautious steps advanced towards it. After a painful march he was stopt by a moated ditch surrounding the place from whence the light proceeded; and by a momentary glimpse of moon-light he had a full view of a large antique mansion, with turrets at the corners, and an ample porch in the centre. The injuries of time were strongly marked on everything about it. The roof in various places was fallen in, the battlements were half demolished, and the windows broken and dismantled. A drawbridge, with a ruinous gateway at each end, led to the court before the building – He entered, and instantly the light, which proceeded from a window in one of the turrets, glided along and vanished; at the same moment the moon sunk beneath a black cloud, and the night was darker than ever. All was silent – Sir Bertrand fastened his steed under a shed, and approaching the house traversed its whole front with light and slow footsteps – All was still as death – He looked in at the lower windows, but could not distinguish a single object through the impenetrable gloom. After a short parley with himself, he entered the porch, and seizing a massy iron knocker at the gate, lifted it up, and hesitating, at length struck a loud stroke. The noise resounded through the whole mansion with hollow echoes. All was still again – He repeated the strokes more boldly and louder – another interval of silence ensued – A third time he knocked, and a third time all was still. He then fell back to some distance that he might discern whether any light could be seen in the whole front – It again appeared in the same place and quickly glided away as before – at the same instant a deep sullen toll sounded from the turret. Sir Bertrand's heart made a fearful stop. – He was a while motionless; then terror impelled him to make some hasty steps toward his steed – but shame stopt his flight; and urged by honour, and a resistless desire of finishing the adventure, he returned to the porch; and working up his soul to a full steadiness of resolution, he drew forth his sword with one hand, and with the other lifted up the latch of the gate. The heavy door, creaking upon its hinges, reluctantly yielded to his hand – he applied his shoulder to it and forced it open – he quitted it and stept forward – the door instantly shut with a thundering clap.

Sir Bertrand's blood was chilled – he turned back to find the door, and it was long ere his trembling hands could seize it – but his utmost strength could not open it again. After several ineffectual attempts, he looked behind him, and beheld, across a hall, upon a large staircase, a pale bluish flame which cast a dismal gleam of light around. He again summoned forth his courage and advanced towards it – It retired. He came to the foot of the stairs, and after a moment's deliberation ascended. He went slowly up, the flame retiring before him, till he came to a wide gallery – The flame proceeded along it, and he followed in silent horrors, treading lightly, for the echoes of his footsteps startled him. It led him to the foot of another staircase, and then vanished – At the same instant another toll sounded from the turret. Sir Bertrand felt it strike upon his heart. He was now in total darkness, and with his arms extended, began to ascend the second staircase. A dead cold hand met his left hand and firmly grasped it, drawing him forcibly forwards – he endeavoured to disengage himself, but could not – he made blow with his sword, and instantly a loud shriek pierced his ears, and the dead hand was left powerless in his – He dropt it, and rushed forwards with a desperate valour. The stairs were narrow and winding, and interrupted by frequent breaches, and loose fragments of stone. The staircase grew narrower and narrower and at length terminated in a low iron grate. Sir Bertrand pushed it open – it led to an intricate winding passage, just large enough to admit a person upon his hands and knees. A faint glimmering of light served to show the nature of the place. Sir Bertrand entered – A deep hollow groan resounded from a distance through the vault – He went forwards, and proceeding beyond the first turning, discerned the same blue flame which had before conducted him. He followed it. The vault, at length, suddenly opened into a lofty gallery, in the midst of which a figure appeared, compleatly armed, with a terrible frown and menacing gesture, and brandishing a sword in his hand. Sir Bertrand undauntedly sprung forwards; and aiming a fierce blow at the figure, it instantly vanished, letting fall a massy iron key. The flame now rested upon a pair of ample folding doors at the end of the gallery. Sir Bertrand went up to it, and applied the key to a brazen lock – with difficulty he turned the bolt – instantly the doors flew open, and discovered a large apartment, at the end of which was a coffin rested upon a bier, with a taper burning on each side of it. Along the room on both sides were gigantic statues of black marble, attired in the Moorish habits, and holding enormous sabres in their right hands. Each of them reared his arm, and advanced one leg forwards, as the knight entered; at the same moment the lid of the coffin flew open, and the bell tolled. The flame still glided forwards, and Sir Bertrand resolutely followed, till he arrived within six paces of the coffin. Suddenly, a lady in a shrowd and black veil rose up in it, and stretched out her arms towards him – at the same time the statues clashed their sabres and advanced. Sir Bertrand flew to the lady and clasped her in his arms – she threw up her veil and kissed his lips; and instantly the whole building shook as with an earthquake, and fell asunder with a horrible crash. Sir Bertrand was thrown into a sudden trance, and on recovering, found himself seated on a velvet sofa, in the most magnificent room he had ever seen, lighted with innumerable tapers, in lustres of pure crystal. A sumptuous banquet was set in the middle. The doors opening to soft music, a lady of incomparable beauty, attired with amazing splendour entered, surrounded by a troop of gay nymphs far more fair than the Graces – She advanced on the knight, and falling on her knees thanked him as her deliverer. The nymphs placed a garland of laurel on his head, and the lady led him by the hand to the banquet, and sat beside him. The nymphs placed themselves at the table, and a numerous train of servants entering, served up the feast; delicious music playing all the time. Sir Bertrand could not speak for astonishment – he could only return their honours by courteous looks and gestures. After the banquet was finished, all retired but the lady, who leading back the knight to the sofa, addressed him in these words: ——

The Dream

Mary Shelley

'Chi dice mal d'amore
Dice una falsità!'
— Italian Song.

The time of the occurrence of the little legend about to be narrated, was that of the commencement of the reign of Henry IV of France, whose accession and conversion, while they brought peace to the kingdom whose throne he ascended, were inadequate to heal the deep wounds mutually inflicted by the inimical parties. Private feuds, and the memory of mortal injuries, existed between those now apparently united; and often did the hands that had clasped each other in seeming friendly greeting, involuntarily, as the grasp was released, clasp the dagger's hilt, as fitter spokesman to their passions than the words of courtesy that had just fallen from their lips. Many of the fiercer Catholics retreated to their distant provinces; and while they concealed in solitude their rankling discontent, not less keenly did they long for the day when they might show it openly.

In a large and fortified château built on a rugged steep overlooking the Loire, not far from the town of Nantes, dwelt the last of her race, and the heiress of their fortunes, the young and beautiful Countess de Villeneuve. She had spent the preceding year in complete solitude in her secluded abode; and the mourning she wore for a father and two brothers, the victims of the civil wars, was a graceful and good reason why she did not appear at court, and mingle with its festivities. But the orphan countess inherited a high name and broad lands; and it was soon signified to her that the king, her guardian, desired that she should bestow them, together with her hand, upon some noble whose birth and accomplishments should entitle him to the gift. Constance, in reply, expressed her intention of taking vows, and retiring to a convent. The king earnestly and resolutely forbade this act, believing such an idea to be the result of sensibility overwrought by sorrow, and relying on the hope that, after a time, the genial spirit of youth would break through this cloud.

A year passed, and still the countess persisted; and at last Henry, unwilling to exercise compulsion, – desirous, too, of judging for himself of the motives that led one so beautiful, young, and gifted with fortune's favours, to desire to bury herself in a cloister, – announced his intention, now that the period of her mourning was expired, of visiting her château; and if he brought not with him, the monarch said, inducement sufficient to change her design, he would yield his consent to its fulfilment.

Many a sad hour had Constance passed – many a day of tears, and many a night of restless misery. She had closed her gates against every visitant; and, like the Lady Olivia in 'Twelfth Night,' vowed herself to loneliness and weeping. Mistress of herself, she easily silenced the entreaties and remonstrances of underlings, and nursed her grief as it had been the thing she loved. Yet it was too keen, too bitter, too burning, to be a favoured guest. In fact, Constance, young, ardent, and vivacious, battled with it, struggled, and longed to cast it off; but all that was joyful in itself, or fair in outward show, only served to renew it; and she could best support the burden of her sorrow with patience, when, yielding to it, it oppressed but did not torture her.

Constance had left the castle to wander in the neighbouring grounds. Lofty and extensive as were the apartments of her abode, she felt pent up within their walls, beneath their fretted roofs. The spreading uplands and the antique wood, associated to her with every dear recollection of her past life, enticed her to spend hours and days beneath their leafy coverts. The motion and change eternally working, as the wind stirred among the boughs, or the journeying sun rained its beams through them, soothed and called her out of that dull sorrow which clutched her heart with so unrelenting a pang beneath her castle roof.

There was one spot on the verge of the well-wooded park, one nook of ground, whence she could discern the country extended beyond, yet which was in itself thick set with tall umbrageous trees – a spot which she had forsworn, yet whither unconsciously her steps for ever tended, and where now again, for the twentieth time that day, she had unaware found herself. She sat upon a grassy mound, and looked wistfully on the flowers she had herself planted to adorn the verdurous recess – to her the temple of memory and love. She held the letter from the king which was the parent to her of so much despair. Dejection sat upon her features, and her gentle heart asked fate why, so young, unprotected, and forsaken, she should have to struggle with this new form of wretchedness.

'I but ask,' she thought, 'to live in my father's halls – in the spot familiar to my infancy – to water with my frequent tears the graves of those I loved; and here in these woods, where such a mad dream of happiness was mine, to celebrate for ever the obsequies of Hope!'

A rustling among the boughs now met her ear – her heart beat quick – all again was still.

'Foolish girl!' she half muttered; 'dupe of thine own passionate fancy: because here we met; because seated here I have expected, and sounds like these have announced, his dear approach; so now every coney as it stirs, and every bird as it awakens silence, speaks of him. O Gaspar! – mine once – never again will this beloved spot be made glad by thee – never more!'

Again the bushes were stirred, and footsteps were heard in the brake. She rose; her heart beat high; it must be that silly Manon, with her impertinent entreaties for her to return. But the steps were firmer and slower than would be those of her waiting-woman; and now emerging from the shade, she too plainly discerned the intruder. Her first impulse was to fly: – but once again to see him – to hear his voice: – once again before she placed eternal vows between them, to stand together, and find the wide chasm filled which absence had made, could not injure the dead, and would soften the fatal sorrow that made her cheek so pale.

And now he was before her, the same beloved one with whom she had exchanged vows of constancy. He, like her, seemed sad; nor could she resist the imploring glance that entreated her for one moment to remain.

'I come, lady,' said the young knight, 'without a hope to bend your inflexible will. I come but once again to see you, and to bid you farewell before I depart for the Holy Land. I come to beseech you not to immure yourself in the dark cloister to avoid one as hateful as myself, – one you will never see more. Whether I die or live, France and I are parted for ever!'

'That were fearful, were it true,' said Constance; 'but King Henry will never so lose his favourite cavalier. The throne you helped to build, you still will guard. Nay, as I ever had power over thought of thine, go not to Palestine.'

'One word of yours could detain me – one smile – Constance' – and the youthful lover knelt before her; but her harsher purpose was recalled by the image once so dear and familiar, now so strange and so forbidden.

'Linger no longer here!' she cried. 'No smile, no word of mine will ever again be yours. Why are you here – here, where the spirits of the dead wander, and, claiming these shades as their own, curse the false girl who permits their murderer to disturb their sacred repose?'

'When love was young and you were kind,' replied the knight, 'you taught me to thread the intricacies of these woods – you welcomed me to this dear spot, where once you vowed to be my own – even beneath these ancient trees.'

'A wicked sin it was,' said Constance, 'to unbar my father's doors to the son of his enemy, and dearly is it punished!'

The young knight gained courage as she spoke; yet he dared not move, lest she, who, every instant, appeared ready to take flight, should be startled from her momentary tranquillity; but he slowly replied: – 'Those were happy days, Constance, full of terror and deep joy, when evening brought me to your feet; and while hate and vengeance were as its atmosphere to yonder frowning castle, this leafy, starlit bower was the shrine of love.'

'*Happy?* – miserable days!' echoed Constance; 'when I imagined good could arise from failing in my duty, and that disobedience would be rewarded of God. Speak not of love, Gaspar! – a sea of blood divides us for ever! Approach me not! The dead and the beloved stand even now between us: their pale shadows warn me of my fault, and menace me for listening to their murderer.'

'That am not I!' exclaimed the youth. 'Behold, Constance, we are each the last of our race. Death has dealt cruelly with us, and we are alone. It was not so when first we loved – when parent, kinsman, brother, nay, my own mother breathed curses on the house of Villeneuve; and in spite of all I blessed it. I saw thee, my lovely one, and blessed it. The God of peace planted love in our hearts, and with mystery and secrecy we met during many a summer night in the moonlit dells; and when daylight was abroad, in this sweet recess we fled to avoid its scrutiny, and here, even here, where now I kneel in supplication, we both knelt and made our vows. Shall they be broken?'

Constance wept as her lover recalled the images of happy hours. 'Never,' she exclaimed, 'O never! Thou knowest, or wilt soon know, Gaspar, the faith and resolves of one who dare not be yours. Was it for us to talk of love and happiness, when war, and hate, and blood were raging around? The fleeting flowers our young hands strewed were trampled by the deadly encounter of mortal foes. By your father's hand mine died; and little boots it to know whether, as my brother swore, and you deny, your hand did or did not deal the blow that destroyed him. You fought among those by whom he died. Say no more – no other word: it is impiety towards the unreposing dead to hear you. Go, Gaspar; forget me. Under the chivalrous and gallant Henry your career may be glorious; and some fair girl will listen, as once I did, to your vows, and be made happy by them. Farewell! May the Virgin bless you! In my cell and cloister-home I will not forget the best Christian lesson – to pray for our enemies. Gaspar, farewell!'

She glided hastily from the bower: with swift steps she threaded the glade and sought the castle. Once within the seclusion of her own apartment she gave way to the burst of grief that tore her gentle bosom like a tempest; for hers was that worst sorrow which taints past joys, making remorse wait upon the memory of bliss, and linking love and fancied guilt in such fearful society as that of the tyrant when he bound a living body to a corpse. Suddenly a thought darted into her mind. At first she rejected it as puerile and superstitious; but it would not be driven away. She called hastily for her attendant. 'Manon,' she said, 'didst thou ever sleep on St Catherine's couch?'

Manon crossed herself. 'Heaven forefend! None ever did, since I was born, but two: one fell into the Loire and was drowned; the other only looked upon the narrow bed, and returned to her own home without a word. It is an awful place; and if the votary have not led a pious and good life, woe betide the hour when she rests her head on the holy stone!'

Constance crossed herself also. 'As for our lives, it is only through our Lord and the blessed saints that we can any of us hope for righteousness. I will sleep on that couch to-morrow night!'

'Dear, my lady! and the king arrives to-morrow.'

'The more need that I resolve. It cannot be that misery so intense should dwell in any heart, and no cure be found. I had hoped to be the bringer of peace to our houses; and is the good work to be for me a crown of thorns? Heaven shall direct me. I will rest to-morrow night on St Catherine's bed: and if, as I have heard, the saint deigns to direct her votaries in dreams, I will be guided by her; and, believing that I act according to the dictates of Heaven, I shall feel resigned even to the worst.'

The king was on his way to Nantes from Paris, and he slept on this night at a castle but a few miles distant. Before dawn a young cavalier was introduced into his chamber. The knight had a serious, nay, a sad aspect; and all beautiful as he was in feature and limb, looked wayworn and haggard. He stood silent in Henry's presence, who, alert and gay, turned his lively blue eyes upon his guest, saying gently, 'So thou foundest her obdurate, Gaspar?'

'I found her resolved on our mutual misery. Alas! my liege, it is not, credit me, the least of my grief, that Constance sacrifices her own happiness when she destroys mine.'

'And thou believest that she will say nay to the gaillard chevalier whom we ourselves present to her?'

'Oh, my liege, think not that thought! it cannot be. My heart deeply, most deeply, thanks you for your generous condescension. But she whom her lover's voice in solitude – whose entreaties, when memory and seclusion aided the spell – could not persuade, will resist even your majesty's commands. She is bent upon entering a cloister; and I, so please you, will now take my leave: – I am henceforth a soldier of the cross.'

'Gaspar,' said the monarch, 'I know woman better than thou. It is not by submission nor tearful plaints she is to be won. The death of her relatives naturally sits heavy at the young countess's heart; and nourishing in solitude her regret and her repentance, she fancies that Heaven itself forbids your union. Let the voice of the world reach her – the voice of earthly power and earthly kindness – the one commanding, the other pleading, and both finding response in her own heart – and by my fay and the Holy Cross, she will be yours. Let our plan still hold. And now to horse: the morning wears, and the sun is risen.'

The king arrived at the bishop's palace, and proceeded forthwith to mass in the cathedral. A sumptuous dinner succeeded, and it was afternoon before the monarch proceeded through the town beside the Loire to where, a little above Nantes, the Château Villeneuve was situated. The young countess received him at the gate. Henry looked in vain for the cheek blanched by misery, the aspect of downcast despair which he had been taught to expect. Her cheek was flushed, her manner animated, her voice scarce tremulous. 'She loves him not,' thought Henry, 'or already her heart has consented.'

A collation was prepared for the monarch; and after some little hesitation, arising even from the cheerfulness of her mien, he mentioned the name of Gaspar. Constance blushed instead of turning pale, and replied very quickly, 'To-morrow, good my liege; I ask for a respite but until to-morrow; – all will then be decided; – to-morrow I am vowed to God – or' –

She looked confused, and the king, at once surprised and pleased, said, 'Then you hate not young De Vaudemont; – you forgive him for the inimical blood that warms his veins.'

'We are taught that we should forgive, that we should love our enemies,' the countess replied, with some trepidation.

'Now, by Saint Denis, that is a right welcome answer for the novice,' said the king, laughing. 'What ho! my faithful serving-man, Dan Apollo in disguise! come forward, and thank your lady for her love.'

In such disguise as had concealed him from all, the cavalier had hung behind, and viewed with infinite surprise the demeanour and calm countenance of the lady. He could not hear her words: but was this even she whom he had seen trembling and weeping the evening before? – this she whose very heart was torn by conflicting passion? – who saw the pale ghosts of parent and kinsman stand between her and the lover whom more than her life she adored? It was a riddle hard to solve. The king's call was in unison with his impatience, and he sprang forward. He was at her feet; while she, still passion-driven, overwrought by the very calmness she had assumed, uttered one cry as she recognised him, and sank senseless on the floor.

All this was very unintelligible. Even when her attendants had brought her to life, another fit succeeded, and then passionate floods of tears; while the monarch, waiting in the hall, eyeing the half-eaten collation, and humming some romance in commemoration of woman's waywardness, knew not how to reply to Vaudemont's look of bitter disappointment and anxiety. At length the countess' chief attendant came with an apology: 'Her lady was ill, very ill The next day she would throw herself at the king's feet, at once to solicit his excuse, and to disclose her purpose.'

'To-morrow – again to-morrow! – Does to-morrow bear some charm, maiden?' said the king. 'Can you read us the riddle, pretty one? What strange tale belongs to to-morrow, that all rests on its advent?'

Manon coloured, looked down, and hesitated. But Henry was no tyro in the art of enticing ladies' attendants to disclose their ladies' counsel. Manon was besides frightened by the countess' scheme, on which she was still obstinately bent, so she was the more readily induced to betray it. To sleep in St Catherine's bed, to rest on a narrow ledge overhanging the deep rapid Loire, and if, as was most probable, the luckless dreamer escaped from falling into it, to take the disturbed visions that such uneasy slumber might produce for the dictate of Heaven, was a madness of which even Henry himself could scarcely deem any woman capable. But could Constance, her whose beauty was so highly intellectual, and whom he had heard perpetually praised for her strength of mind and talents, could *she* be so strangely infatuated! And can passion play such freaks with us? – like death, levelling even the aristocracy of the soul, and bringing noble and peasant, the wise and foolish, under one thraldom? It was strange – yet she must have her way. That she hesitated in her decision was much; and it was to be hoped that St Catherine would play no ill-natured part. Should it be otherwise, a purpose to be swayed by a dream might be influenced by other waking thoughts. To the more material kind of danger some safeguard should be brought.

There is no feeling more awful than that which invades a weak human heart bent upon gratifying its ungovernable impulses in contradiction to the dictates of conscience. Forbidden pleasures are said to be the most agreeable; – it may be so to rude natures, to those who love to struggle, combat, and contend; who find happiness in a fray, and joy in the conflict of passion. But softer and sweeter was the gentle spirit of Constance; and love and duty contending crushed and tortured her poor heart. To commit her conduct to the inspirations of religion, or, if it was so to be named, of superstition, was a blessed relief. The very perils that threatened her undertaking gave a zest to it; – to dare for his sake was happiness; – the very difficulty of the way that led to the completion of her wishes at once gratified her love and distracted her thoughts from her despair. Or if it was decreed that she must sacrifice all, the risk of danger and of death were of trifling import in comparison with the anguish which would then be her portion for ever.

The night threatened to be stormy, the raging wind shook the casements, and the trees waved their huge shadowy arms, as giants might in fantastic dance and mortal broil. Constance and Manon, unattended, quitted the château by a postern, and began to descend the hill-side. The moon had not yet risen; and though the way was familiar to both, Manon tottered and trembled; while the countess, drawing her silken cloak round her, walked with a firm step down the steep. They came to the river's side, where a small boat was moored, and one man was in waiting. Constance stepped lightly in, and then aided her fearful companion. In a few moments they were in the middle of the stream. The warm, tempestuous, animating, equinoctial wind swept over them. For the first time since her mourning, a thrill of pleasure swelled the bosom of Constance. She hailed the emotion with double joy. It cannot be, she thought, that Heaven will forbid me to love one so brave, so generous, and so good as the noble Gaspar. Another I can never love; I shall die if divided from him; and this heart, these limbs, so alive with glowing sensation, are they already predestined to an early grave? Oh no! life speaks aloud within them. I shall live to love. Do not all things love? – the winds as they whisper to the rushing waters? the waters as they kiss the flowery banks, and speed to mingle with the sea? Heaven and earth are sustained by, and live through, love; and shall Constance alone, whose heart has ever been a deep, gushing, overflowing well of true affection, be compelled to set a stone upon the fount to lock it up for ever?

These thoughts bade fair for pleasant dreams; and perhaps the countess, an adept in the blind god's lore, therefore indulged them the more readily. But as thus she was engrossed by soft emotions, Manon caught her arm: – 'Lady, look,' she cried; 'it comes – yet the oars have no sound. Now the Virgin shield us! Would we were at home!'

A dark boat glided by them. Four rowers, habited in black cloaks, pulled at oars which, as Manon said, gave no sound; another sat at the helm: like the rest, his person was veiled in a dark mantle, but he wore no cap; and though his face was turned from them, Constance recognised her lover. 'Gaspar,' she cried aloud, 'dost thou live?' – but the figure in the boat neither turned its head nor replied, and quickly it was lost in the shadowy waters.

How changed now was the fair countess' reverie! Already Heaven had begun its spell, and unearthly forms were around, as she strained her eyes through the gloom. Now she saw and now she lost view of the bark that occasioned her terror; and now it seemed that another was there, which held the spirits of the dead; and her father waved to her from shore, and her brothers frowned on her.

Meanwhile they neared the landing. Her bark was moored in a little cove, and Constance stood upon the bank. Now she trembled, and half yielded to Manon's entreaty to return; till the unwise *suivante* mentioned the king's and De Vaudemont's name, and spoke of the answer to be given to-morrow. What answer, if she turned back from her intent?

She now hurried forward up the broken ground of the bank, and then along its edge, till they came to a hill which abruptly hung over the tide. A small chapel stood near. With trembling fingers the countess drew forth the key and unlocked its door. They entered. It was dark – save that a little lamp, flickering in the wind, showed an uncertain light from before the figure of Saint Catherine. The two women knelt; they prayed; and then rising, with a cheerful accent the countess bade her attendant good-night. She unlocked a little low iron door. It opened on a narrow cavern. The roar of waters was heard beyond. 'Thou mayest not follow, my poor Manon,' said Constance, – 'nor dost thou much desire: – this adventure is for me alone.'

It was hardly fair to leave the trembling servant in the chapel alone, who had neither hope nor fear, nor love, nor grief to beguile her; but, in those days, esquires and waiting-women often played the part of subalterns in the army, gaining knocks and no fame. Besides, Manon was safe in holy ground. The countess meanwhile pursued her way groping in the dark through the narrow tortuous passage. At length what seemed light to her long-darkened sense gleamed on her. She reached an open cavern in the overhanging hill's side, looking over the rushing tide beneath. She looked out upon the night. The waters of the Loire were speeding, as since that day have they ever sped – changeful, yet the same; the heavens were thickly veiled with clouds, and the wind in the trees was as mournful and ill-omened as if it rushed round a murderer's tomb. Constance shuddered a little, and looked upon her bed, – a narrow ledge of earth and a moss-grown stone bordering on the very verge of the precipice. She doffed her mantle, – such was one of the conditions of the spell; – she bowed her head, and loosened the tresses of her dark hair; she bared her feet; and thus, fully prepared for suffering to the utmost the chill influence of the cold night, she stretched herself on the narrow couch that scarce afforded room for her repose, and whence, if she moved in sleep, she must be precipitated into the cold waters below.

At first it seemed to her as if she never should sleep again. No great wonder that exposure to the blast and her perilous position should forbid her eyelids to close. At length she fell into a reverie so soft and soothing that she wished even to watch; and then by degrees her senses became confused; and now she was on St Catherine's bed – the Loire rushing beneath, and the wild wind sweeping by – and now – oh whither? – and what dreams did the saint send, to drive her to despair, or to bid her be blest for ever?

Beneath the rugged hill, upon the dark tide, another watched, who feared a thousand things, and scarce dared hope. He had meant to precede the lady on her way, but when he found that he had outstayed his time, with muffled oars and breathless haste he had shot by the bark that contained his Constance, nor even turned at her voice, fearful to incur her blame, and her commands to return. He had seen her emerge from the passage, and shuddered as she leant over the cliff. He saw her step forth, clad as she was in white, and could mark her as she lay on the ledge beetling above. What a vigil did the lovers keep! – she given up to visionary thoughts, he knowing – and the consciousness thrilled his bosom with strange emotion – that love, and love for him, had led her to that perilous couch; and that while dangers surrounded her in every shape, she was alive only to the small still voice that whispered to her heart the dream which was to decide their destinies. She slept perhaps – but he waked and watched, and night wore away, as, now praying, now entranced by alternating hope and fear, he sat in his boat, his eyes fixed on the white garb of the slumberer above.

Morning – was it morning that struggled in the clouds? Would morning ever come to waken her? And had she slept? and what dreams of weal or woe had peopled her sleep? Gaspar grew impatient. He commanded his boatmen still to wait, and he sprang forward, intent on clambering the precipice. In vain they urged the danger, nay, the impossibility of the attempt; he clung to the rugged face of the hill, and found footing where it would seem no footing was. The acclivity, indeed, was not high; the dangers of St Catherine's bed arising from the likelihood that anyone who slept on so narrow a couch would be precipitated into the waters beneath. Up the steep ascent Gaspar continued to toil, and at last reached the roots of a tree that grew near the summit. Aided by its branches, he made good his stand at the very extremity of the ledge, near the pillow on which lay the uncovered head of his beloved. Her hands were folded on her bosom; her dark hair fell round her throat and pillowed her cheek; her face was serene: sleep was there in all its innocence and in all its helplessness; every wilder emotion was hushed, and her bosom heaved in regular breathing. He could see her heart beat as it lifted her fair hands crossed above. No statue hewn of marble in monumental effigy was ever half so fair; and within that surpassing form dwelt a soul true, tender, self-devoted, and affectionate as ever warmed a human breast.

With what deep passion did Gaspar gaze, gathering hope from the placidity of her angel countenance! A smile wreathed her lips; and he too involuntarily smiled, as he hailed the happy omen; when suddenly her cheek was flushed, her bosom heaved, a tear stole from her dark lashes, and then a whole shower fell, as starting up she cried, 'No! – he shall not die! – I will unloose his chains! – I will save him!' Gaspar's hand was there. He caught her light form ready to fall from the perilous couch. She opened her eyes and beheld her lover, who had watched over her dream of fate, and who had saved her.

Manon also had slept well, dreaming or not, and was startled in the morning to find that she waked surrounded by a crowd. The little desolate chapel was hung with tapestry – the altar adorned with golden chalices – the priest was chanting mass to a goodly array of kneeling knights. Manon saw that King Henry was there; and she looked for another whom she found not, when the iron door of the cavern passage opened, and Gaspar de Vaudemont entered from it, leading the fair form of Constance; who, in her white robes and dark dishevelled hair, with a face in which smiles and blushes contended with deeper emotion, approached the altar, and, kneeling with her lover, pronounced the vows that united them for ever.

It was long before the happy Gaspar could win from his lady the secret of her dream. In spite of the happiness she now enjoyed, she had suffered too much not to look back even with terror to those days when she thought love a crime, and every event connected with them wore an awful aspect. 'Many a vision,' she said, 'she had that fearful night. She had seen the spirits of her father and brothers in Paradise; she had beheld Gaspar victoriously combating among the infidels; she had beheld him in King Henry's court, favoured and beloved; and she herself – now pining in a cloister, now a bride, now grateful to Heaven for the full measure of bliss presented to her, now weeping away her sad days – till suddenly she thought herself in Paynim land; and the saint herself, St Catherine, guiding her unseen through the city of the infidels. She entered a palace, and beheld the miscreants rejoicing in victory; and then, descending to the dungeons beneath, they groped their way through damp vaults, and low, mildewed passages, to one cell, darker and more frightful than the rest. On the floor lay one with soiled and tattered garments, with unkempt locks and wild, matted beard. His cheek was worn and thin; his eyes had lost their fire; his form was a mere skeleton; the chains hung loosely on the fleshless bones.'

'And was it my appearance in that attractive state and winning costume that softened the hard heart of Constance!' asked Gaspar, smiling at this painting of what would never be.

'Even so,' replied Constance; 'for my heart whispered me that this was my doing; and who could recall the life that waned in your pulses

– who restore, save the destroyer! My heart never warmed to my living, happy knight as then it did to his wasted image as it lay, in the visions of night, at my feet. A veil fell from my eyes; a darkness was dispelled from before me. Methought I then knew for the first time what life and what death was. I was bid believe that to make the living happy was not to injure the dead; and I felt how wicked and how vain was that false philosophy which placed virtue and good in hatred and unkindness. You should not die; I would loosen your chains and save you, and bid you live for love. I sprung forward, and the death I deprecated for you would, in my presumption, have been mine, – then, when first I felt the real value of life, – but that your arm was there to save me, your dear voice to bid me be blest for evermore.'

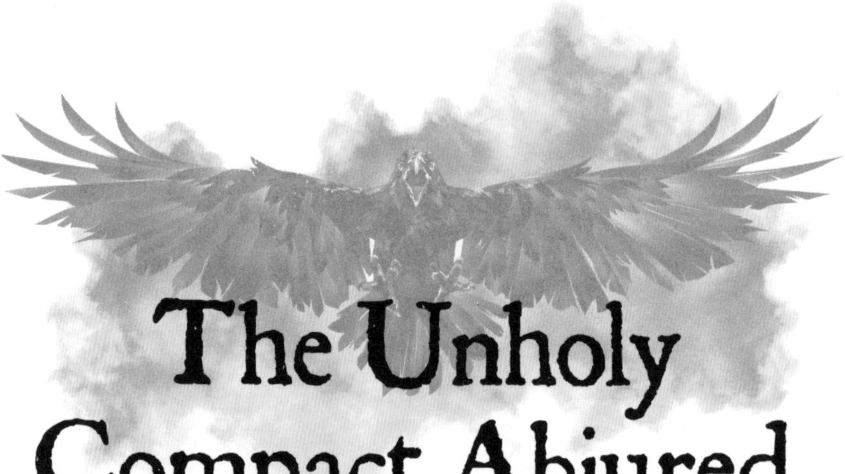

The Unholy Compact Abjured

Charles Pigault-Lebrun

In the churchyard of the town of Salins, department of Jura, may still be seen the remains of a tomb, on which is sculptured in figures as rude as the age in which they were carved, a representation of a soldier, firmly clasped in the arms of a maiden; near them stands the devil in a menacing attitude. Though the inhabitants of the town are all ready to swear to the truth of the story, they are not agreed as to the time when it happened; so that we can only say, that some centuries have rolled away, since a young soldier named St Amand, a native of Salins, was returning after a long absence to the bosom of his family. He walked with quick and cheerful steps, carrying with ease, in a small knapsack, the whole of his worldly goods. Never since he quitted the paternal roof, had he felt so happy; for he hoped ere night, to see his pretty cousin, Ninette, whom he loved with all his heart, and whom he intended to make his wife.

He walked on, gaily carolling, till he saw a cross-road before him, and uncertain of his way, he called to an old woman, with her back towards him, to direct him. She was silent: and, as he approached, he repeated the call, and she raised her head to answer it. The stout heart of the young soldier quailed, as he cast his eyes upon a countenance, such as never before had met his gaze.

He had indeed, reason to tremble; for he had just disturbed in the middle of an incantation, one of the most powerful witches in the country. She regarded him with a demoniac smile, and said in a tone which froze his blood, 'Turn where thou wilt, thy road is sure, – it leads to death!'

For some moments, he stood as if rooted to the spot; but, soon, fear of the sorceress, who remained gazing upon him, gave him strength to flee. He ran forward, nor stopped till he had completely lost sight of the fearful being, whose dreadful prediction had struck him with such horror. Suddenly a frightful storm arose; the thunder growled, and the lightning flashed round the weary traveller, who, drenched with rain, and overcome with fatigue, had hardly strength to proceed. How great was his joy, when he saw at a distance, a magnificent château, the gate of which stood open. He exerted all his remaining strength to reach it, and precipitately entered a large hall. There he stopped, expecting every moment to see some domestics, but no one appeared. He remained some time, watching the progress of the storm: at length it began to abate, and he determined to pursue his way; but as he approached the door, it closed with a loud noise, and all his efforts to open it were vain.

Struck with astonishment and dismay, the young soldier now believed that the prediction of the witch was about to be accomplished, and that he was doomed to fall a sacrifice to magic art.

Exhausted by his vain efforts to open the ponderous door, he sank for a moment in helpless despondency, on the marble pavement; put his trust in providence, and soon revived. He said his prayers, and rising, waited with firmness the issue of this extraordinary adventure. When he became composed enough to look round him, he examined the hall in which he was: a pair of folding doors at the further end, flattered him with the hope of escape that way; but they too, were fastened. The hall was of immense size, entirely unfurnished; the walls, pavement and ceiling, were of black marble; there were no windows, but a small sky-light faintly admitted the light of day, into this abode of gloom, where reigned a silence like that of the tomb. Hour after hour passed; this mournful silence remained still undisturbed; and St Amand, overcome with fatigue and watching, at length sunk into a deep, though perturbed slumber.

His sleep was soon disturbed by a frightful dream: he heard all at once, the sound of a knell mingled with the cries of bats, and owls, and a hollow voice, murmured in his ear, 'Woe to those who trouble the repose of the dead!' He started on his feet, but what a sight met his eyes! The hall was partially illuminated by flashes of sulphureous fire; on the pavement was laid the body of a man newly slain, and covered with innumerable wounds, from which, a band of unearthly forms, whose fearful occupation, proclaimed the hellish origin, were draining the yet warm blood.

St Amand uttered a shriek of terror, and was in an instant surrounded by the fiends: already were their fangs, from which the remains of their horrid feast still dripped, extended to grasp him, when he hastily made the sign of the cross, and sank senseless upon the ground. When he regained his senses, the infernal band had vanished, and he saw bending over him, an old man, magnificently but strangely dressed: his silken garments flowed loosely around him, and were embroidered with figures of different animals, and mystic devices. His countenance was majestic, and his venerable white beard descended below his girdle: but his features had a wild and gloomy expression: his eyes, above all, had in their glance, that which might appal the stoutest heart. St Amand shrunk from this mysterious being, with awe, mingled with abhorrence, and a cold shudder ran through his veins, as the old man bent upon him his piercing eyes.

'Rash youth,' cried he in a severe tone, 'how is it that thou hast dared to enter this place, where never mortal foot save mine has trod?'

'I came not willingly,' replied St Amand, trembling; 'an evil destiny, and not vain curiosity brought me hither.'

'Thou wouldst not the less have expiated thy presumption with thy life, but for my aid.' returned the old man, austerely. 'I have saved thee from the vampires who guard it, and it depends upon me, whether thou shalt not still become their prey.'

'Oh! save me, then, I pray thee!'

'And why should I save thee?' demanded the venerable magician. 'What price art thou willing to give me for thy life?'

'Alas! I have nothing worthy of thy acceptance,' sighed St Amand.

'But thou may'st have; and it is only through thee that I can obtain what I most desire.'

'How?'

'The blood of a dove, for me, would be a treasure, but I may not kill one; she must be slain for me, by one whose life I have saved. Should I liberate thee, a dove will fly to thy bosom; swear that thou wilt instantly sacrifice her for me, and thou shalt be free.'

'I swear it!'

Hardly had St Amand uttered the words, when he found himself in the chamber of Ninette, who, with a cry of joy, rushed into his arms. He pressed her with transport to his breast; but scarcely had he embraced her, when he saw the magician standing by his side.

'Wretch!' cried he, 'is it thus thou keepest thine oath? Pierce her heart – she is the dove that thou must instantly sacrifice, if thou wilt not become a feast for the vampires!'

'Sacrifice her? Never! Never!'

'Then, thou art my prey!' and the fiend assuming his own form, sprang towards his victim; but he stopped suddenly – he dared not seize him: for the maiden held him firmly clasped in her arms, and the little cross of gold, which night and day she wore upon her bosom, had been blest by the venerable priest, whose gift it was. Thus, nought unholy dared approach the maiden, and the baffled fiend fled with a tremendous yell, as the crowing of the cock, announced the approach of dawn.

The cries of the maiden soon brought the neighbours to her chamber, and among them was the pastor, to whom St Amand related his adventure. 'Oh, my son!' said the good priest, 'what have you done? See you not, that you have entered into a contract with the powers of darkness? Unable to wreak their vengeance on you, when you had guarded yourself with the blessed sign of our redemption, the fiend has had recourse to craft to draw you into his power. You have promised a sacrifice, to the enemy of God and man, but you have done it in ignorance. Abjure then, solemnly, the cursed contract, and dread no longer the vengeance of the fiend.'

The young soldier made the required abjuration, during which, the most dreadful noises were heard: it was the last effort of the demon's vengeance; for, from that time, he was never seen, nor heard of. St

Amand married Ninette, who had given him such a courageous proof of her love; and the cross transmitted from her, to her descendants, was always considered by them as the most precious part of their inheritance. In process of time, the family became wealthy, and a great grandson of St Amand erected the monument we have described, to commemorate the miraculous escape of his ancestor.

Eveline's Visitant

Mary Elizabeth Braddon

It was at a masked ball at the Palais Royal that my fatal quarrel with my first cousin André de Brissac began. The quarrel was about a woman. The women who followed the footsteps of Philip of Orleans were the causes of many such disputes; and there was scarcely one fair head in all that glittering throng which, to a man versed in social histories and mysteries, might not have seemed bedabbled with blood.

I shall not record the name of her for love of whom André de Brissac and I crossed one of the bridges, in the dim August dawn on our way to the waste ground beyond the church of Saint-Germain des Prés.

There were many beautiful vipers in those days, and she was one of them. I can feel the chill breath of that August morning blowing in my face, as I sit in my dismal chamber at my château of Puy Verdun tonight, alone in the stillness, writing the strange story of my life. I can see the white mist rising from the river, the grim outline of the Châtelet, and the square towers of Notre Dame black against the pale-gray sky. Even more vividly can I recall André's fair young face, as he stood opposite to me with his two friends – scoundrels both, and alike eager for that unnatural fray. We were a strange group to be seen in a summer sunrise, all of us fresh from the heat and clamour of the Regent's saloons – André in a quaint hunting-dress copied from a family portrait at Puy Verdun, I costumed as one of Law's Mississippi Indians; the other men in like garish frippery, adorned with broideries and jewels that looked wan in the pale light of dawn.

Our quarrel had been a fierce one – a quarrel which could have but one result, and that the direst. I had struck him; and the welt raised by my open hand was crimson upon his fair womanish face as he stood opposite to me. The eastern sun shone on the face presently, and dyed the cruel mark with a deeper red; but the sting of my own wrongs was fresh, and I had not yet learned to despise myself for that brutal outrage.

To André de Brissac such an insult was most terrible. He was the favourite of Fortune, the favourite of women; and I was nothing, – a rough soldier who had done my country good service, but in the boudoir of a Parabère a mannerless boor.

We fought, and I wounded him mortally. Life had been very sweet for him; and I think that a frenzy of despair took possession of him when he felt the life-blood ebbing away. He beckoned me to him as he lay on the ground. I went, and knelt at his side.

'Forgive me, André!' I murmured.

He took no more heed of my words than if that piteous entreaty had been the idle ripple of the river near at hand.

'Listen to me, Hector de Brissac,' he said. 'I am not one who believes that a man has done with earth because his eyes glaze and his jaw stiffens. They will bury me in the old vault at Puy Verdun; and you will be master of the château. Ah, I know how lightly they take things in these days, and how Dubois will laugh when he hears that Ca has been killed in a duel. They will bury me, and sing masses for my soul; but you and I have not finished our affair yet, my cousin. I will be with you when you least look to see me, – I, with this ugly scar upon the face that women have praised and loved. I will come to you when your life seems brightest. I will come between you and all that you hold fairest and dearest. My ghostly hand shall drop a poison in your cup of joy. My shadowy form shall shut the sunlight from your life. Men with such iron will as mine can do what they please, Hector de Brissac. It is my will to haunt you when I am dead.'

All this in short broken sentences he whispered into my ear. I had need to bend my ear close to his dying lips; but the iron will of André de Brissac was strong enough to do battle with Death, and I believe he said all he wished to say before his head fell back upon the velvet cloak they had spread beneath him, never to be lifted again.

As he lay there, you would have fancied him a fragile stripling, too fair and frail for the struggle called life; but there are those who remember the brief manhood of André de Brissac, and who can bear witness to the terrible force of that proud nature.

I stood looking down at the young face with that foul mark upon it, and God knows I was sorry for what I had done.

Of those blasphemous threats which he had whispered in my ear I took no heed. I was a soldier, and a believer. There was nothing absolutely dreadful to me in the thought that I had killed this man. I had killed many men on the battlefield; and this one had done me cruel wrong.

My friends would have had me cross the frontier to escape the consequences of my act; but I was ready to face those consequences, and I remained in France. I kept aloof from the court, and received a hint that I had best confine myself to my own province. Many masses were chanted in the little chapel of Puy Verdun, for the soul of my dead cousin, and his coffin filled a niche in the vault of our ancestors.

His death had made me a rich man; and the thought that it was so made my newly-acquired wealth very hateful to me. I lived a lonely existence in the old château, where I rarely held converse with any but the servants of the household, all of whom had served my cousin, and none of whom liked me.

It was a hard and bitter life. It galled me, when I rode through the village, to see the peasant-children shrink away from me. I have seen old women cross themselves stealthily as I passed them by. Strange reports had gone forth about me; and there were those who whispered that I had given my soul to the Evil One as the price of my cousin's heritage. From my boyhood I had been dark of visage and stern of manner; and hence, perhaps, no woman's love had ever been mine. I remembered my mother's face in all its changes of expression; but I can remember no look of affection that ever shone on me. That other woman, beneath whose feet I laid my heart, was pleased to accept my homage, but she never loved me; and the end was treachery.

I had grown hateful to myself, and had well-nigh begun to hate my fellow-creatures, when a feverish desire seized upon me, and I pined to be back in the press and throng of the busy world once again. I went back to Paris, where I kept myself aloof from the court, and where an angel took compassion upon me.

She was the daughter of an old comrade, a man whose merits had been neglected, whose achievements had been ignored, and who sulked in his shabby lodging like a rat in a hole, while all Paris went mad with the Scotch Financier, and gentlemen and lacqueys were trampling one another to death in the Rue Quin-campoix. The only child of this little cross-grained old captain of dragoons was an incarnate sunbeam, whose mortal name was Eveline Duchalet.

She loved me. The richest blessings of our lives are often those which cost us least. I wasted the best years of my youth in the worship of a wicked woman, who jilted and cheated me at last.

I gave this meek angel but a few courteous words – a little fraternal tenderness – and lo, she loved me. The life which had been so dark and desolate grew bright beneath her influence; and I went back to Puy Verdun with a fair young bride for my companion.

Ah, how sweet a change there was in my life and in my home! The village children no longer shrank appalled as the dark horseman rode by, the village crones no longer crossed themselves; for a woman rode by his side – a woman whose charities had won the love of all those ignorant creatures, and whose companionship had transformed the gloomy lord of the château into a loving husband and a gentle master. The old retainers forgot the untimely fate of my cousin, and served me with cordial willingness, for love of their young mistress.

There are no words which can tell the pure and perfect happiness of that time. I felt like a traveller who had traversed the frozen seas of an arctic region, remote from human love or human companionship, to find himself on a sudden in the bosom of a verdant valley, in the sweet atmosphere of home. The change seemed too bright to be real; and I strove in vain to put away from my mind the vague suspicion that my new life was but some fantastic dream.

So brief were those halcyon hours, that, looking back on them now, it is scarcely strange if I am still half inclined to fancy the first days of my married life could have been no more than a dream.

Neither in my days of gloom nor in my days of happiness had I been troubled by the recollection of André's blasphemous oath.

The words which with his last breath he had whispered in my ear were vain and meaningless to me. He had vented his rage in those idle threats, as he might have vented it in idle execrations.

That he will haunt the footsteps of his enemy after death is the one revenge which a dying man can promise himself; and if men had power thus to avenge themselves, the earth would be peopled with phantoms.

I had lived for three years at Puy Verdun; sitting alone in the solemn midnight by the hearth where he had sat, pacing the corridors that had echoed his footfall; and in all that time my fancy had never so played me false as to shape the shadow of the dead. Is it strange, then, if I had forgotten Andre's horrible promise? There was no portrait of my cousin at Puy Verdun. It was the age of boudoir art, and a miniature set in the lid of a gold bonbonnière, or hidden artfully in a massive bracelet, was more fashionable than a clumsy life-size image, fit only to hang on the gloomy walls of a provincial château rarely visited by its owner. My cousin's fair face had adorned more than one bonbonnière, and had been concealed in more than one bracelet; but it was not among the faces that looked down from the panelled walls of Puy Verdun.

In the library I found a picture which awoke painful associations. It was the portrait of a De Brissac, who had flourished in the time of Francis the First; and it was from this picture that my cousin André had copied the quaint hunting-dress he wore at the Regent's ball. The library was a room in which I spent a good deal of my life; and I ordered a curtain to be hung before this picture.

We had been married three months, when Eveline one day asked, 'Who is the lord of the château nearest to this?'

I looked with her in astonishment.

'My dearest,' I answered, 'do you not know that there is no other château within forty miles of Puy Verdun?'

'Indeed!' she said; 'that is strange.'

I asked her why the fact seemed strange to her; and after much entreaty I obtained from her the reason of her surprise.

In her walks about the park and woods during the last month, she had met a man who, by his dress and bearing, was obviously of noble rank. She had imagined that he occupied some château near at hand, and that his estate adjoined ours. I was at a loss to imagine who this stranger could be; for my estate of Puy Verdun lay in the heart of a desolate region, and unless when some traveller's coach went lumbering and jingling through the village, one had little more chance of encountering a gentleman than of meeting a demigod.

'Have you seen this man often, Eveline?' I asked.

She answered, in a tone which had a touch of sadness, 'I see him every day.'

'Where, dearest?'

'Sometimes in the park, sometimes in the wood. You know the little cascade, Hector, where there is some old neglected rock-work that forms a kind of cavern. I have taken a fancy to that spot, and have spent many mornings there reading. Of late I have seen the stranger there every morning.'

'He has never dared to address you?'

'Never. I have looked up from my book, and have seen him standing at a little distance, watching me silently. I have continued reading; and when I have raised my eyes again I have found him gone. He must approach and depart with a stealthy tread, for I never hear his footfall. Sometimes I have almost wished that he would speak to me. It is so terrible to see him standing silently there.'

'He is some insolent peasant who seeks to frighten you.'

My wife shook her head.

'He is no peasant,' she answered. 'It is not by his dress alone I judge, for that is strange to me. He has an air of nobility which it is impossible to mistake.'

'Is he young or old?'

'He is young and handsome.'

I was much disturbed by the idea of this stranger's intrusion on my wife's solitude; and I went straight to the village to inquire if any stranger had been seen there. I could hear of no one. I questioned the servants closely, but without result. Then I determined to accompany my wife in her walks, and to judge for myself of the rank of the stranger.

For a week I devoted all my mornings to rustic rambles with Eveline in the park and woods; and in all that week we saw no one but an occasional peasant in sabots, or one of our own house-hold returning from a neighbouring farm.

I was a man of studious habits, and those summer rambles disturbed the even current of my life. My wife perceived this, and entreated me to trouble myself no further.

'I will spend my mornings in the pleasaunce, Hector,' she said; 'the stranger cannot intrude upon me there.'

'I begin to think the stranger is only a phantasm of your own romantic brain,' I replied, smiling at the earnest face lifted to mine. 'A châtelaine who is always reading romances may well meet handsome cavaliers in the woodlands. I daresay I have Mdlle. Scuderi to thank for this noble stranger, and that he is only the great Cyrus in modern costume.'

'Ah, that is the point which mystifies me, Hector,' she said. 'The stranger's costume is not modern. He looks as an old picture might look if it could descend from its frame.'

Her words pained me, for they reminded me of that hidden picture in the library, and the quaint hunting costume of orange and purple, which André de Brissac wore at the Regent's ball.

After this my wife confined her walks to the pleasaunce; and for many weeks I heard no more of the nameless stranger. I dismissed all thought of him from my mind, for a graver and heavier care had come upon me. My wife's health began to droop. The change in her was so gradual as to be almost imperceptible to those who watched her day by day. It was only when she put on a rich gala dress which she had not worn for months that I saw how wasted the form must be on which the embroidered bodice hung so loosely, and how wan and dim were the eyes which had once been brilliant as the jewels she wore in her hair.

I sent a messenger to Paris to summon one of the court physicians; but I knew that many days must needs elapse before he could arrive at Puy Verdun.

In the interval I watched my wife with unutterable fear.

It was not her health only that had declined. The change was more painful to behold than any physical alteration. The bright and sunny spirit had vanished, and in the place of my joyous young bride I beheld a woman weighed down by rooted melancholy. In vain I sought to fathom the cause of my darling's sadness. She assured me that she had no reason for sorrow or discontent, and that if she seemed sad without a motive, I must forgive her sadness, and consider it as a misfortune rather than a fault.

I told her that the court physician would speedily find some cure for her despondency, which must needs arise from physical causes, since she had no real ground for sorrow. But although she said nothing, I could see she had no hope or belief in the healing powers of medicine.

One day, when I wished to beguile her from that pensive silence in which she was wont to sit an hour at a time, I told her, laughing, that she appeared to have forgotten her mysterious cavalier of the wood, and it seemed also as if he had forgotten her.

To my wonderment, her pale face became of a sudden crimson; and from crimson changed to pale again in a breath.

'You have never seen him since you deserted your woodland grotto?' I said.

She turned to me with a heart-rending look.

'Hector,' she cried, 'I see him every day; and it is that which is killing me.'

She burst into a passion of tears when she had said this. I took her in my arms as if she had been a frightened child, and tried to comfort her.

'My darling, this is madness,' I said. 'You know that no stranger can come to you in the pleasaunce. The moat is ten feet wide and always full of water, and the gates are kept locked day and night by old Massou. The châtelaine of a mediæval fortress need fear no intruder in her antique garden.'

My wife shook her head sadly.

'I see him every day,' she said.

On this I believed that my wife was mad. I shrank from questioning her more closely concerning her mysterious visitant. It would be ill, I thought, to give a form and substance to the shadow that tormented her by too close inquiry about its look and manner, its coming and going.

I took care to assure myself that no stranger to the household could by any possibility penetrate to the pleasaunce. Having done this, I was fain to await the coming of the physician.

He came at last. I revealed to him the conviction which was my misery. I told him that I believed my wife to be mad. He saw her – spent an hour alone with her, and then came to me. To my un-speakable relief he assured me of her sanity.

'It is just possible that she may be affected by one delusion,' he said; 'but she is so reasonable upon all other points, that I can scarcely bring myself to believe her the subject of a monomania. I am rather inclined to think that she really sees the person of whom she speaks. She described him to me with a perfect minuteness. The descriptions of scenes or individuals given by patients afflicted with monomania are always more or less disjointed; but your wife spoke to me as clearly and calmly as I am now speaking to you. Are you sure there is no one who can approach her in that garden where she walks?'

'I am quite sure.'

'Is there any kinsman of your steward, or hanger-on of your household, – a young man with a fair womanish face, very pale and rendered remarkable by a crimson scar, which looks like the mark of a blow?'

'My God!' I cried, as the light broke in upon me all at once. 'And the dress – the strange old-fashioned dress?'

'The man wears a hunting costume of purple and orange,' answered the doctor.

I knew then that André de Brissac had kept his word, and that in the hour when my life was brightest his shadow had come between me and happiness.

I showed my wife the picture in the library, for I would fain assure myself that there was some error in my fancy about my cousin. She shook like a leaf when she beheld it, and clung to me convulsively.

'This is witchcraft, Hector,' she said. 'The dress in that picture is the dress of the man I see in the pleasaunce; but the face is not his.'

Then she described to me the face of the stranger; and it was my cousin's face line for line – André de Brissac, whom she had never seen in the flesh. Most vividly of all did she describe the cruel mark upon his face, the trace of a fierce blow from an open hand.

After this I carried my wife away from Puy Verdun. We wandered far – through the southern provinces, and into the very heart of Switzerland. I thought to distance the ghastly phantom, and I fondly hoped that change of scene would bring peace to my wife.

It was not so. Go where we would, the ghost of André de Brissac followed us. To my eyes that fatal shadow never revealed itself. That would have been too poor a vengeance. It was my wife's innocent heart which André made the instrument of his revenge. The unholy presence destroyed her life. My constant companionship could not shield her from the horrible intruder. In vain did I watch her; in vain did I strive to comfort her.

'He will not let me be at peace,' she said; 'he comes between us, Hector. He is standing between us now. I can see his face with the red mark upon it plainer that I see yours.'

One fair moonlight night, when we were together in a mountain village in the Tyrol, my wife cast herself at my feet, and told me she was the worst and vilest of women. 'I have confessed all to my director,' she said; 'from the first I have not hidden my sin from Heaven. But I feel that death is near me; and before I die I would fain reveal my sin to you.'

'What sin, my sweet one?'

'When first the stranger came to me in the forest, his presence bewildered and distressed me, and I shrank from him as from something strange and terrible. He came again and again; by and by I found myself thinking of him, and watching for his coming. His image haunted me perpetually; I strove in vain to shut his face out of my mind. Then followed an interval in which I did not see him; and, to my shame and anguish, I found that life seemed dreary and desolate without him. After that came the time in which he haunted the pleasaunce; and – O, Hector, kill me if you will, for I deserve no mercy at your hands! – I grew in those days to count the hours that must elapse before his coming, to take no pleasure save in the sight of that pale face with the red brand upon it. He plucked all old familiar joys out of my heart, and left in it but one weird unholy pleasure – the delight of his presence. For a year I have lived but to see him. And now curse me, Hector; for this is my sin. Whether it comes of the baseness of my own heart, or is the work of witchcraft, I know not; but I know that I have striven against this wickedness in vain.'

I took my wife to my breast, and forgave her. In sooth, what had I to forgive? Was the fatality that overshadowed us any work of hers? On the next night she died, with her hand in mine; and at the very last she told me, sobbing and affrighted, that he was by her side.

The Fall of the House of Usher

Edgar Allan Poe

Son cœur est un luth suspendu;
Sitôt qu'on le touche il résonne.
De Béranger

During the whole of a dull, dark, and soundless day in the autumn of the year, when the clouds hung oppressively low in the heavens, I had been passing alone, on horseback, through a singularly dreary tract of country; and at length found myself, as the shades of the evening drew on, within view of the melancholy House of Usher. I know not how it was—but, with the first glimpse of the building, a sense of insufferable gloom pervaded my spirit. I say insufferable; for the feeling was unrelieved by any of that half-pleasurable, because poetic, sentiment, with which the mind usually receives even the sternest natural images of the desolate or terrible. I looked upon the scene before me—upon the mere house, and the simple landscape features of the domain—upon the bleak walls—upon the vacant eye-like windows—upon a few rank sedges—and upon a few white trunks of decayed trees—with an utter depression of soul which I can compare to no earthly sensation more properly than to the after-dream of the reveler upon opium—the bitter lapse into everyday life—the hideous dropping off of the veil. There was an iciness, a sinking, a sickening of the heart—an unredeemed dreariness of thought which no goading of the imagination could torture into aught of the sublime. What was it—I paused to think—what was it that so unnerved me in the contemplation of the House of Usher? It was a mystery all insoluble; nor could I grapple with the shadowy fancies that crowded upon me as I pondered. I was forced to fall back upon the unsatisfactory conclusion, that while, beyond doubt, there are combinations of very simple natural objects which have the power of thus affecting us, still the analysis of this power lies among considerations beyond our depth. It was possible, I reflected, that a mere different arrangement of the particulars of the scene, of the details of the picture, would be sufficient to modify, or perhaps to annihilate its capacity for sorrowful impression; and, acting upon this idea, I reined my horse to the precipitous brink of a black and lurid tarn that lay in unruffled luster by the dwelling, and gazed down—but with a shudder even more thrilling than before—upon the remodeled and inverted images of the gray sedge, and the ghastly tree-stems, and the vacant and eye-like windows.

Nevertheless, in this mansion of gloom I now proposed to myself a sojourn of some weeks. Its proprietor, Roderick Usher, had been one of my boon companions in boyhood; but many years had elapsed since our last meeting. A letter, however, had lately reached me in a distant part of the country—a letter from him—which, in its wildly importunate nature, had admitted of no other than a personal reply. The MS. gave evidence of nervous agitation. The writer spoke of acute bodily illness—of a mental disorder which oppressed him—and of an earnest desire to see me, as his best, and indeed his only personal friend, with a view of attempting, by the cheerfulness of my society, some alleviation of his malady. It was the manner in which all this, and much more, was said—it was the apparent heart that went with his request—which allowed me no room for hesitation; and I accordingly obeyed forthwith what I still considered a very singular summons.

Although, as boys, we had been even intimate associates, yet I really knew little of my friend. His reserve had been always excessive and habitual. I was aware, however, that his very ancient family had been noted, time out of mind, for a peculiar sensibility of temperament, displaying itself, through long ages, in many works of exalted art, and manifested, of late, in repeated deeds of munificent yet unobtrusive charity, as well as in a passionate devotion to the intricacies, perhaps even more than to the orthodox and easily recognizable beauties, of musical science. I had learned, too, the very remarkable fact, that the stem of the Usher race, all time-honored as it was, had put forth, at no period, any enduring branch; in other words, that the entire family lay in the direct line of descent, and had always, with very trifling and very temporary variation, so lain. It was this deficiency, I considered, while running over in thought the perfect keeping of the character of the premises with the accredited character of the people, and while speculating upon the possible influence which the one, in the long lapse of centuries, might have exercised upon the other—it was this deficiency, perhaps, of collateral issue, and the consequent undeviating transmission, from sire to son, of the patrimony with the name, which had, at length, so identified the two as to merge the original title of the estate in the quaint and equivocal appellation of the "House of Usher"—an appellation which seemed to include, in the minds of the peasantry who used it, both the family and the family mansion.

I have said that the sole effect of my somewhat childish experiment—that of looking down within the tarn—had been to deepen the first singular impression. There can be no doubt that the consciousness of the rapid increase of my superstition—for why should I not so term it?—served mainly to accelerate the increase itself. Such, I have long known, is the paradoxical law of all sentiments having terror as a basis. And it might have been for this reason only, that, when I again uplifted my eyes to the house itself, from its image in the pool, there grew in my mind a strange fancy—a fancy so ridiculous, indeed, that I but mention it to show the vivid force of the sensations which oppressed me. I had so worked upon my imagination as really to believe that about the whole mansion and domain there hung an atmosphere peculiar to themselves and their immediate vicinity—an atmosphere which had no affinity with the air of heaven, but which had reeked up from the decayed trees, and the gray wall, and the silent tarn—a pestilent and mystic vapor, dull, sluggish, faintly discernible, and leaden-hued.

Shaking off from my spirit what must have been a dream, I scanned more narrowly the real aspect of the building. Its principal feature seemed to be that of an excessive antiquity. The discoloration of ages had been great. Minute fungi overspread the whole exterior, hanging in a fine tangled web-work from the eaves. Yet all this was apart from any extraordinary dilapidation. No portion of the masonry had fallen; and there appeared to be a wild inconsistency between its still perfect adaptation of parts, and the crumbling condition of the individual stones. In this there was much that reminded me of the specious totality of old woodwork which has rotted for long years in some neglected vault, with no disturbance from the breath of the external air. Beyond this indication of extensive decay, however, the fabric gave little token of instability. Perhaps the eye of a scrutinizing observer might have discovered a barely perceptible fissure, which, extending from the roof of the building in front, made its way down the wall in a zigzag direction, until it became lost in the sullen waters of the tarn.

Noticing these things, I rode over a short causeway to the house. A servant in waiting took my horse, and I entered the Gothic archway of the hall. A valet, of stealthy step, thence conducted me, in silence, through many dark and intricate passages in my progress to the studio of his master. Much that I encountered on the way contributed, I know not how, to heighten the vague sentiments of which I have already spoken. While the objects around me—while the carvings of the ceilings, the somber tapestries of the walls, the ebon blackness of the floors, and the phantasmagoric armorial trophies which rattled as I strode, were but matters to which, or to such as which, I had been accustomed from my infancy—while I hesitated not to acknowledge how familiar was all this—I still wondered to find how unfamiliar were the fancies which ordinary images were stirring up. On one of the staircases, I met the physician of the family. His countenance, I thought, wore a mingled expression of low cunning and perplexity. He accosted me with trepidation and passed on. The valet now threw open a door and ushered me into the presence of his master.

The room in which I found myself was very large and lofty. The windows were long, narrow, and pointed, and at so vast a distance from the black oaken floor as to be altogether inaccessible from within. Feeble gleams of encrimsoned light made their way through the trellised panes, and served to render sufficiently distinct the more prominent objects around; the eye, however, struggled in vain to reach the remoter angles of the chamber, or the recesses of the vaulted and fretted ceiling. Dark draperies hung upon the walls. The general furniture was profuse, comfortless, antique, and tattered. Many books and musical instruments lay scattered about, but failed to give any vitality to the scene. I felt that I breathed an atmosphere of sorrow. An air of stern, deep, and irredeemable gloom hung over and pervaded all.

Upon my entrance, Usher arose from a sofa on which he had been lying at full length, and greeted me with a vivacious warmth which had much in it, I at first thought, of an overdone cordiality—of the constrained effort of the ennuyé man of the world. A glance, however, at his countenance, convinced me of his perfect sincerity. We sat down; and for some moments, while he spoke not, I gazed upon him with a feeling half of pity, half of awe. Surely, man had never before so terribly altered, in so brief a period, as had Roderick Usher! It was with difficulty that I could bring myself to admit the identity of the wan being before me with the companion of my early boyhood. Yet the character of his face had been at all times remarkable. A cadaverousness of complexion; an eye large, liquid, and luminous beyond comparison; lips somewhat thin and very pallid, but of a surpassingly beautiful curve; a nose of a delicate Hebrew model, but with a breadth of nostril unusual in similar formations; a finely-molded chin, speaking, in its want of prominence, of a want of moral energy; hair of a more than web-like softness and tenuity; these features, with an inordinate expansion above the regions of the temple, made up altogether a countenance not easily to be forgotten. And now in the mere exaggeration of the prevailing character of these features, and of the expression they were wont to convey, lay so much of change that I doubted to whom I spoke. The now ghastly pallor of the skin, and the now miraculous luster of the eye, above all things startled and even awed me. The silken hair, too, had been suffered to grow all unheeded, and as, in its wild gossamer texture, it floated rather than fell about the face, I could not, even with effort, connect its arabesque expression with any idea of simple humanity.

In the manner of my friend I was at once struck with an incoherence—an inconsistency; and I soon found this to arise from a series of feeble and futile struggles to overcome an habitual trepidancy—an excessive nervous agitation. For something of this nature I had indeed been prepared, no less by his letter, than by reminiscences of certain boyish traits, and by conclusions deduced from his peculiar physical conformation and temperament. His action was alternately vivacious and sullen. His voice varied rapidly from a tremulous indecision (when the animal spirits seemed utterly in abeyance) to that species of energetic concision—that abrupt, weighty, unhurried, and hollow-sounding enunciation—that leaden, self-balanced and perfectly modulated guttural utterance, which may be observed in the lost drunkard, or the irreclaimable eater of opium, during the periods of his most intense excitement.

It was thus that he spoke of the object of my visit, of his earnest desire to see me, and of the solace he expected me to afford him. He entered, at some length, into what he conceived to be the nature of his malady. It was, he said, a constitutional and a family evil, and one for which he despaired to find a remedy—a mere nervous affection, he immediately added, which would undoubtedly soon pass off. It displayed itself in a host of unnatural sensations. Some of these, as he detailed them, interested and bewildered me; although, perhaps, the terms, and the general manner of the narration had their weight. He suffered much from a morbid acuteness of the senses; the most insipid food was alone endurable; he could wear only garments of certain texture; the odors of all flowers were oppressive; his eyes were tortured by even a faint light; and there were but peculiar sounds, and these from stringed instruments, which did not inspire him with horror.

To an anomalous species of terror I found him a bounden slave. "I shall perish," said he, "I must perish in this deplorable folly. Thus, thus, and not otherwise, shall I be lost. I dread the events of the future, not in themselves, but in their results. I shudder at the thought of any, even the most trivial, incident, which may operate upon this intolerable agitation of soul. I have, indeed, no abhorrence of danger, except in its absolute effect—in terror. In this unnerved—in this pitiable condition—I feel that the period will sooner or later arrive when I must abandon life and reason together, in some struggle with the grim phantasm, Fear."

I learned, moreover, at intervals, and through broken and equivocal hints, another singular feature of his mental condition. He was enchained by certain superstitious impressions in regard to the dwelling which he tenanted, and whence, for many years, he had never ventured forth—in regard to an influence whose supposititious force was conveyed in terms too shadowy here to be restated—an influence which some peculiarities in the mere form and substance of his family mansion, had, by dint of long sufferance, he said, obtained over his spirit—an effect which the physique of the gray walls and turrets, and of the dim tarn into which they all looked down, had, at length, brought about upon the morale of his existence.

He admitted, however, although with hesitation, that much of the peculiar gloom which thus afflicted him could be traced to a more natural and far more palpable origin—to the severe and long-continued illness—indeed to the evidently approaching dissolution—of a tenderly beloved sister—his sole companion for long years—his last and only relative on earth. "Her decease," he said, with a bitterness which I can never forget, "would leave him (him the hopeless and the frail) the last of the ancient race of the Ushers." While he spoke, the Lady Madeline (for so was she called) passed slowly through a remote portion of the apartment, and, without having noticed my presence, disappeared. I regarded her with an utter astonishment not unmingled with dread—and yet I found it impossible to account for such feelings. A sensation of stupor oppressed me, as my eyes followed her retreating steps. When a door, at length, closed upon her, my glance sought instinctively and eagerly the countenance of the brother—but he had buried his face in his hands, and I could only perceive that a far more than ordinary wanness had overspread the emaciated fingers through which trickled many passionate tears.

The disease of the Lady Madeline had long baffled the skill of her physicians. A settled apathy, a gradual wasting away of the person, and frequent although transient affections of a partially cataleptical character, were the unusual diagnosis. Hitherto she had steadily borne up against the pressure of her malady, and had not betaken herself finally to bed; but, on the closing in of the evening of my arrival at the house, she succumbed (as her brother told me at night with inexpressible agitation) to the prostrating power of the destroyer; and I learned that the glimpse I had obtained of her person would thus probably be the last I should obtain—that the lady, at least while living, would be seen by me no more.

For several days ensuing, her name was unmentioned by either Usher or myself: and during this period I was busied in earnest endeavors to alleviate the melancholy of my friend. We painted and read together; or I listened, as if in a dream, to the wild improvisations of his speaking guitar. And thus, as a closer and still closer intimacy admitted me more unreservedly into the recesses of his spirit, the more bitterly did I perceive the futility of all attempt at cheering a mind from which darkness, as if an inherent positive quality, poured forth upon all objects of the moral and physical universe, in one unceasing radiation of gloom.

I shall ever bear about me a memory of the many solemn hours I thus spent alone with the master of the House of Usher. Yet I should fail in any attempt to convey an idea of the exact character of the studies, or of the occupations, in which he involved me, or led me the way. An excited and highly distempered ideality threw a sulfureous luster over all. His long improvised dirges will ring for ever in my ears. Among other things, I hold painfully in mind a certain singular perversion and amplification of the wild air of the last waltz of Von Weber. From the paintings over which his elaborate fancy brooded, and which grew, touch by touch, into vagueness at which I shuddered the more thrillingly, because I shuddered knowing not why;—from these paintings (vivid as their images now are before me) I would in vain endeavor to educe more than a small portion which should lie within the compass of merely written words. By the utter simplicity, by the nakedness of his designs, he arrested and overawed attention. If ever mortal painted an idea, that mortal was Roderick Usher. For me at least—in the circumstances then surrounding me—there arose out of the pure abstractions which the hypochondriac contrived to throw upon his canvas, an intensity of intolerable awe, no shadow of which felt I ever yet in the contemplation of the certainly glowing yet too concrete reveries of Fuseli.

One of the phantasmagoric conceptions of my friend, partaking not so rigidly of the spirit of abstraction, may be shadowed forth, although feebly, in words. A small picture presented the interior of an immensely long and rectangular vault or tunnel, with low walls, smooth, white, and without interruption or device. Certain accessory points of the design served well to convey the idea that this excavation lay at an exceeding depth below the surface of the earth. No outlet was observed in any portion of its vast extent, and no torch, or other artificial source of light was discernible; yet a flood of intense rays rolled throughout, and bathed the whole in a ghastly and inappropriate splendor.

I have just spoken of that morbid condition of the auditory nerve which rendered all music intolerable to the sufferer, with the exception of certain effects of stringed instruments. It was, perhaps, the narrow limits to which he thus confined himself upon the guitar, which gave birth in great measure, to the fantastic character of his performances. But the fervid facility of his impromptus could not be so accounted for. They must have been, and were, in the notes, as well as in the words of his wild fantasias (for he not unfrequently accompanied himself with rhymed verbal improvisations), the result of that intense mental collectedness and concentration to which I have previously alluded as observable only in particular moments of the highest artificial excitement. The words of one of these rhapsodies I have easily remembered. I was, perhaps, the more forcibly impressed with it, as he gave it, because, in the under or mystic current of its meaning, I fancied that I perceived, and for the first time, a full consciousness on the part of Usher, of the tottering of his lofty reason upon her throne. The verses, which were entitled "The Haunted Palace," ran very nearly, if not accurately, thus:

I

In the greenest of our valleys,
By good angels tenanted,
Once a fair and stately palace—
Radiant palace—reared its head.
In the monarch Thought's dominion—
It stood there!
Never seraph spread a pinion
Over fabric half so fair.

II

Banners yellow, glorious, golden,
On its roof did float and flow;
(This—all this—was in the olden
Time long ago)
And every gentle air that dallied,

In that sweet day,
  Along the ramparts plumed and pallid,
A wingèd odor went away.

III

  Wanderers in that happy valley
Through two luminous windows saw
  Spirits moving musically
To a lute's well tunèd law,
  Round about a throne, where sitting
(Porphyrogene!)
  In state his glory well befitting,
The ruler of the realm was seen.

IV

  And all with pearl and ruby glowing
Was the fair palace door,
  Through which came flowing, flowing, flowing
And sparkling evermore,
  A troop of echoes whose sweet duty
Was but to sing,
  In voices of surpassing beauty,
The wit and wisdom of their king.

V

  But evil things, in robes of sorrow,
Assailed the monarch's high estate;
  (Ah, let us mourn, for never morrow
Shall dawn upon him, desolate!)
  And, round about his home, the glory
That blushed and bloomed
  Is but a dim-remembered story
Of the old time entombed.

VI

  And travelers now within that valley,
Through the red-litten windows, see

Vast forms that move fantastically
To a discordant melody;
While, like a rapid ghastly river,
Through the pale door,
A hideous throng rush out forever,
And laugh—but smile no more.

I well remember that suggestions arising from this ballad, led us into a train of thought wherein there became manifest an opinion of Usher's which I mention not so much on account of its novelty (for other men have thought thus), as on account of the pertinacity with which he maintained it. This opinion, in its general form, was that of the sentience of all vegetable things. But, in his disordered fancy, the idea had assumed a more daring character, and trespassed, under certain conditions, upon the kingdom of inorganization. I lack words to express the full extent, or the earnest abandon of his persuasion. The belief, however, was connected (as I have previously hinted) with the gray stones of the home of his forefathers. The conditions of the sentience had been here, he imagined, fulfilled in the method of collocation of these stones—in the order of their arrangement, as well as in that of the many fungi which overspread them, and of the decayed trees which stood around—above all, in the long undisturbed endurance of this arrangement, and in its reduplication in the still waters of the tarn. Its evidence—the evidence of the sentience—was to be seen, he said (and I here started as he spoke) in the gradual yet certain condensation of an atmosphere of their own about the waters and the walls. The result was discoverable, he added, in that silent, yet importunate and terrible influence which for centuries had molded the destinies of his family, and which made him what I now saw him—what he was. Such opinions need no comment, and I will make none.

Our books—the books which, for years, had formed no small portion of the mental existence of the invalid—were, as might be supposed, in strict keeping with this character of phantasm. We pored together over such works as the *Ververt et Chartreuse* of Gresset; the *Belphegor* of Machiavelli; the *Heaven and Hell* of Swedenborg; the *Subterranean Voyage of Nicholas Klimm* by Holberg; the *Chiromancy* of Robert Flud, of Jean D'Indaginé, and of De la Chambre; the *Journey into the Blue Distance* of Tieck; and the *City of the Sun* of Campanella. One favorite volume was a small octavo edition of the *Directorium Inquisitorum*, by the Dominican Eymeric de Gironne; and there were passages in *Pomponius Mela*, about the old African Satyrs and Ægipans, over which Usher would sit dreaming for hours. His chief delight, however, was found in the perusal of an exceedingly rare and curious book in quarto Gothic—the manual of a forgotten church—the *Vigiliae Mortuorum Secundum Chorum Ecclesiae Maguntinae*.

I could not help thinking of the wild ritual of this work, and of its probable influence upon the hypochondriac, when, one evening, having informed me abruptly that the Lady Madeline was no more, he stated his intention of preserving her corpse for a fortnight (previously to its final interment), in one of the numerous vaults within the main walls of the building. The worldly reason, however, assigned for this singular proceeding, was one which I did not feel at liberty to dispute. The brother had been led to his resolution (so he told me) by consideration of the unusual character of the malady of the deceased, of certain obtrusive and eager inquiries on the part of her medical men, and of the remote and exposed situation of the burial ground of the family. I will not deny that when I called to mind the sinister countenance of the person whom I met upon the staircase, on the day of my arrival at the house, I had no desire to oppose what I regarded as at best but a harmless, and by no means an unnatural, precaution.

At the request of Usher, I personally aided him in the arrangements for the temporary entombment. The body having been encoffined, we two alone bore it to its rest. The vault in which we placed it (and which had been so long unopened that our torches, half smothered in its oppressive atmosphere, gave us little opportunity for investigation) was small, damp, and entirely without means of admission for light; lying, at great depth, immediately beneath that portion of the building in which was my own sleeping apartment. It had been used, apparently, in remote feudal times, for the worst purpose of a donjon-keep, and, in later days, as a place of deposit for powder, or some other highly combustible substance, as a portion of its floor, and the whole interior of a long archway through which we reached it, were carefully sheathed with copper. The door, of massive iron, had been, also, similarly protected. Its immense weight caused an unusually sharp grating sound, as it moved upon its hinges.

Having deposited our mournful burden upon trestles within this region of horror, we partially turned aside the yet unscrewed lid of the coffin, and looked upon the face of the tenant. A striking similitude between the brother and sister now first arrested my attention; and Usher, divining, perhaps, my thoughts, murmured out some few words from which I learned that the deceased and himself had been twins, and that sympathies of a scarcely intelligible nature had always existed between them. Our glances, however, rested not long upon the dead—for we could not regard her unawed. The disease which had thus entombed the lady in the maturity of youth, had left, as usual in all maladies of a strictly cataleptical character, the mockery of a faint blush upon the bosom and the face, and that suspiciously lingering smile upon the lip which is so terrible in death. We replaced and screwed down the lid, and, having secured the door of iron, made our way, with toil, into the scarcely less gloomy apartments of the upper portion of the house.

And now, some days of bitter grief having elapsed, an observable change came over the features of the mental disorder of my friend. His ordinary manner had vanished. His ordinary occupations were neglected or forgotten. He roamed from chamber to chamber with hurried, unequal, and objectless step. The pallor of his countenance had assumed, if possible, a more ghastly hue—but the luminousness of his eye had utterly gone out. The once occasional huskiness of his tone was heard no more; and a tremulous quaver, as if of extreme terror, habitually characterized his utterance. There were times, indeed, when I thought his unceasingly agitated mind was laboring with some oppressive secret, to divulge which he struggled for the necessary courage. At times, again, I was obliged to resolve all into the mere inexplicable vagaries of madness, for I beheld him gazing upon vacancy for long hours, in an attitude of the profoundest attention, as if listening to some imaginary sound. It was no wonder that his condition terrified—that it infected me. I felt creeping upon me, by slow yet certain degrees, the wild influences of his own fantastic yet impressive superstitions.

It was, especially, upon retiring to bed late in the night of the seventh or eighth day after the placing of the Lady Madeline within the donjon, that I experienced the full power of such feelings. Sleep came not near my couch—while the hours waned and waned away. I struggled to reason off the nervousness which had dominion over me. I endeavored to believe that much, if not all of what I felt, was due to the bewildering influence of the gloomy furniture of the room—of the dark and tattered draperies, which, tortured into motion by the breath of a rising tempest, swayed fitfully to and fro upon the walls, and rustled uneasily about the decorations of the bed. But my efforts were fruitless. An irrepressible tremor gradually pervaded my frame; and, at length, there sat upon my very heart an incubus of utterly causeless alarm. Shaking this off with a gasp and a struggle, I uplifted myself upon the pillows, and, peering earnestly within the intense darkness of the chamber, hearkened—I know not why, except that an instinctive spirit prompted me—to certain low and indefinite sounds which came, through the pauses of the storm, at long intervals, I knew not whence. Overpowered by an intense sentiment of horror, unaccountable yet unendurable, I threw on my clothes with haste (for I felt that I should sleep no more during the night), and endeavored to arouse myself from the pitiable condition into which I had fallen, by pacing rapidly to and fro through the apartment.

I had taken but few turns in this manner, when a light step on an adjoining staircase arrested my attention. I presently recognized it as that of Usher. In an instant afterward he rapped, with a gentle touch, at my door, and entered, bearing a lamp. His countenance was, as usual cadaverously wan—but, moreover, there was a species of mad hilarity in his eyes—an evident restrained hysteria in his whole demeanor. His air appalled me—but anything was preferable to the solitude which I had so long endured, and I even welcomed his presence as a relief.

"And you have not seen it?" he said abruptly, after having stared about him for some moments in silence—"you have not then seen it?—but, stay! you shall." Thus speaking, and having carefully shaded his lamp, he hurried to one of the casements, and threw it freely open to the storm.

The impetuous fury of the entering gust nearly lifted us from our feet. It was, indeed, a tempestuous yet sternly beautiful night, and one wildly singular in its terror and its beauty. A whirlwind had apparently collected its force in our vicinity; for there were frequent and violent alterations in the direction of the wind; and the exceeding density of the clouds (which hung so low as to press upon the turrets of the house) did not prevent our perceiving the lifelike velocity with which they flew careering from all points against each other, without passing away into the distance. I say that even their exceeding density did not prevent our perceiving this—yet we had no glimpse of the moon or stars—nor was there any flashing forth of the lighting. But the under surfaces of the huge masses of agitated vapor, as well as all terrestrial objects immediately around us, were glowing in the unnatural light of a faintly luminous and distinctly visible gaseous exhalation which hung about and enshrouded the mansion.

"You must not—you shall not behold this!" said I, shudderingly, to Usher, as I led him, with a gentle violence, from the window to a seat. "These appearances, which bewilder you, are merely electrical phenomena not uncommon—or it may be that they have their ghastly origin in the rank miasma of the tarn. Let us close this casement;—the air is chilling and dangerous to your frame. Here is one of your favorite romances. I will read, and you shall listen;—and so we will pass away this terrible night together."

The antique volume which I had taken up was the *Mad Trist* of Sir Launcelot Canning; but I had called it a favorite of Usher's more in sad jest than in earnest; for, in truth, there is little in its uncouth and unimaginative prolixity which could have had interest for the lofty and spiritual ideality of my friend. It was, however, the only book immediately at hand; and I indulged a vague hope that the excitement which now agitated the hypochondriac, might find relief (for the history of mental disorder is full of similar anomalies) even in the extremeness of the folly which I should read. Could I have judged, indeed, by the wild overstrained air of vivacity with which he hearkened, or apparently hearkened, to the words of the tale, I might well have congratulated myself upon the success of my design.

I had arrived at that well-known portion of the story where Ethelred, the hero of the *Trist*, having sought in vain for peaceable admission into the dwelling of the hermit, proceeds to make good an entrance by force. Here, it will be remembered, the words of the narrative run thus:

"And Ethelred, who was by nature of a doughty heart, and who was now mighty withal, on account of the powerfulness of the wine which he had drunken, waited no longer to hold parley with the hermit, who in sooth, was of an obstinate and maliceful turn, but, feeling the rain upon his shoulders, and fearing the rising of the tempest, uplifted his mace outright, and, with blows, made quickly room in the plankings of the door for his gauntleted hand; and now pulling therewith sturdily, he so cracked, and ripped, and tore all asunder, that the noise of the dry and hollow-sounding wood alarmed and reverberated throughout the forest."

At the termination of this sentence I started, and for a moment, paused; for it appeared to me (although I at once concluded that my excited fancy had deceived me)—it appeared to me that, from some very remote portion of the mansion, there came, indistinctly, to my ears, what might have been, in its exact similarity of character, the echo (but a stifled and dull one certainly) of the very cracking and ripping sound which Sir Launcelot had so particularly described. It was, beyond doubt, the coincidence alone which had arrested my attention; for, amid the rattling of the sashes of the casements, and the ordinary commingled noises of the still increasing storm, the sound, in itself, had nothing, surely, which should have interested or disturbed me. I continued the story:

"But the good champion Ethelred, now entering within the door, was sore enraged and amazed to perceive no signal of the maliceful hermit; but, in the stead thereof, a dragon of a scaly and prodigious demeanor, and of a fiery tongue, which sate in guard before a palace of gold, with a floor of silver; and upon the wall there hung a shield of shining brass with this legend enwritten—

Who entereth herein, a conqueror hath bin;
Who slayeth the dragon, the shield he shall win;

and Ethelred uplifted his mace, and struck upon the head of the dragon, which fell before him, and gave up his pesty breath, with a shriek so horrid and harsh, and withal so piercing, that Ethelred had fain to close his ears with his hands against the dreadful noise of it, the like whereof was never before heard."

Here again I paused abruptly, and now a feeling of wild amazement—for there could be no doubt whatever that, in this instance, I did actually hear (although from what direction it proceeded I found it impossible to say) a low and apparently distant, but harsh, protracted, and most unusual screaming or grating sound—the exact counterpart of what my fancy had already conjured up for the dragon's unnatural shriek as described by the romancer.

Oppressed, as I certainly was, upon the occurrence of the second and most extraordinary coincidence, by a thousand conflicting sensations, in which wonder and extreme terror were predominant, I still retained sufficient presence of mind to avoid exciting, by any observation, the sensitive nervousness of my companion. I was by no means certain that he had noticed the sounds in question; although, assuredly, a strange alteration had, during the last few minutes, taken place in his demeanor. From a position fronting my own, he had gradually brought round his chair, so as to sit with his face to the door of the chamber; and thus I could but partially perceive his features, although I saw that his lips trembled as if he were murmuring inaudibly. His head had dropped upon his breast—yet I knew that he was not asleep, from the wide and rigid opening of the eye as I caught a glance of it in profile. The motion of his body, too, was at variance with this idea—for he rocked from side to side with a gentle yet constant and uniform sway. Having rapidly taken notice of all this, I resumed the narrative of Sir Launcelot, which thus proceeded:

"And now, the champion, having escaped from the terrible fury of the dragon, bethinking himself of the brazen shield, and of the breaking up of the enchantment which was upon it, removed the carcass from out of the way before him, and approached valorously over the silver pavement of the castle to where the shield was upon the wall; which in sooth tarried not for his full coming, but fell down at his feet upon the silver floor, with a mighty great and terrible ringing sound."

No sooner had these syllables passed my lips, than—as if a shield of brass had indeed, at the moment, fallen heavily upon a floor of silver—I became aware of a distinct, hollow, metallic, and clangorous, yet apparently muffled reverberation. Completely unnerved, I leaped to my feet; but the measured rocking movement of Usher was undisturbed. I rushed to the chair in which he sat. His eyes were bent fixedly before him, and throughout his whole countenance there reigned a stony rigidity. But, as I placed my hand upon his shoulder, there came a strong shudder over his whole person; a sickly smile quivered about his lips; and I saw that he spoke in a low, hurried, and gibbering murmur, as if unconscious of my presence. Bending closely over him, I at length drank in the hideous import of his words.

"Not hear it?—yes, I hear it, and have heard it. Long—long—long—

many minutes, many hours, many days, have I heard it—yet I dared not—oh, pity me, miserable wretch that I am!—I dared not—I dared not speak! We have put her living in the tomb! Said I not that my senses were acute? I now tell you that I heard her first feeble movements in the hollow coffin. I heard them—many, many days ago—yet I dared not—I dared not speak! And now—to-night—Ethelred—ha! ha!—the breaking of the hermit's door, and the death-cry of the dragon, and the clangor of the shield!—say, rather, the rending of her coffin, and the grating of the iron hinges of her prison, and her struggles within the coppered archway of the vault! Oh whither shall I fly? Will she not be here anon? Is she not hurrying to upbraid me for my haste? Have I not heard her footstep on the stair? Do I not distinguish that heavy and horrible beating of her heart? Madman!" here he sprang furiously to his feet, and shrieked out his syllables, as if in the effort he were giving up his soul—"Madman! I tell you that she now stands without the door!"

As if in the superhuman energy of his utterance there had been found the potency of a spell—the huge antique panels to which the speaker pointed, threw slowly back, upon the instant, their ponderous and ebony jaws. It was the work of the rushing gust—but then without those doors there did stand the lofty and enshrouded figure of the Lady Madeline of Usher. There was blood upon her white robes, and the evidence of some bitter struggle upon every portion of her emaciated frame. For a moment she remained trembling and reeling to and fro upon the threshold, then, with a low moaning cry, fell heavily inward upon the person of her brother, and in her violent and now final death-agonies, bore him to the floor a corpse, and a victim to the terrors he had anticipated.

From that chamber, and from that mansion, I fled aghast. The storm was still abroad in all its wrath as I found myself crossing the old causeway. Suddenly there shot along the path a wild light, and I turned to see whence a gleam so unusual could have issued; for the vast house and its shadows were alone behind me. The radiance was that of the full, setting, and blood-red moon which now shone vividly through that once barely discernible fissure of which I have before spoken as extending from the roof of the building, in a zigzag direction, to the base. While I gazed, this fissure rapidly widened—there came a fierce breath of the whirlwind—the entire orb of the satellite burst at once upon my sight—my brain reeled as I saw the mighty walls rushing asunder—there was a long tumultuous shouting sound like the voice of a thousand waters—and the deep and dank tarn at my feet closed sullenly and silently over the fragments of the "House of Usher."

The Iron Shroud

William Mudford

The castle of the Prince of Tolfi was built on the summit of the towering and precipitous rock of Scylla, and commanded a magnificent view of Sicily in all its grandeur. Here, during the wars of the middle ages, when the fertile plains of Italy were devastated by hostile factions, those prisoners were confined, for whose ransom a costly price was demanded. Here, too, in a dungeon, excavated deep in the solid rock, the miserable victim was immured, whom revenge pursued, – the dark, fierce, and unpitying revenge of an Italian heart.

VIVENZIO – the noble and the generous, the fearless in battle, and the pride of Naples in her sunny hours of peace – the young, the brave, the proud Vivenzio, fell beneath this subtle and remorseless spirit. He was the prisoner of Tolfi, and he languished in that rock-encircled dungeon, which stood alone, and whose portals never opened twice upon a living captive.

It had the semblance of a vast cage, for the roof, and floor, and sides, were of iron, solidly wrought, and spaciously constructed. High above there ran a range of seven grated windows, guarded with massy bars of the same metal, which admitted light and air. Save these, and the tall folding-doors beneath them which occupied the centre, no chink, or chasm, or projection, broke the smooth black surface of the walls. An iron bedstead, littered with straw, stood in one corner: and beside it, a vessel with water, and a coarse dish filled with coarser food.

Even the intrepid soul of Vivenzio shrunk with dismay as he entered this abode, and heard the ponderous doors triple-locked by the silent ruffians who conducted him to it. Their silence seemed prophetic of his fate, of the living grave that had been prepared for him. His menaces and his entreaties, his indignant appeals for justice, and his impatient questioning of their intentions, were alike vain. They listened, but spoke not. Fit ministers of a crime that should have no tongue!

How dismal was the sound of their retiring steps! And, as their faint echoes died along the winding passages, a fearful presage grew within him, that never more the face, or voice, or tread, of man, would greet his senses. He had seen human beings for the last time! And he had looked his last upon the bright sky, and upon the smiling earth, and upon a beautiful world he loved, and whose minion he had been! Here he was to end his life – a life he had just begun to revel in! And by what means? By secret poison? or by murderous assault? No – for then it had been needless to bring him thither. Famine perhaps – a thousand deaths in one! It was terrible to think of it; but it was yet more terrible to picture long, long years of captivity, in a solitude so appalling, a loneliness so dreary, that thought, for want of fellowship, would lose itself in madness, or stagnate into idiocy.

He could not hope to escape, unless he had the power, with his bare hands, of rending asunder the solid iron walls of his prison. He could not hope for liberty from the relenting mercies of his enemy. His instant death, under any form of refined cruelty, was not the object of Tolfi, for he might have inflicted it, and he had not. It was too evident, therefore, he was reserved for some premeditated scheme of subtle vengeance; and what vengeance could transcend in fiendish malice, either the slow death of famine, or the still slower one of solitary incarceration, till the last lingering spark of life expired, or till reason fled, and nothing should remain to perish but the brute functions of the body?

It was evening when Vivenzio entered his dungeon, and the approaching shades of night wrapped it in total darkness, as he paced up and down, revolving in his mind these horrible forebodings. No tolling bell from the castle, or from any neighbouring church or convent, struck upon his ear to tell how the hours passed. Frequently he would stop and listen for some sound that might betoken the vicinity of man; but the solitude of the desert, the silence of the tomb, are not so still and deep as the oppressive desolation by which he was encompassed. His heart sank within him, and he threw himself dejectedly down upon his couch of straw. Here sleep gradually obliterated the consciousness of misery, and bland dreams wafted his delighted spirit to scenes which were once glowing realities for him, in whose ravishing illusions he soon lost the remembrance that he was Tolfi's prisoner.

When he awoke, it was daylight; but how long he had slept he knew not. It might be early morning, or it might be sultry noon, for he could measure time by no other note of its progress than light and darkness. He had been so happy in his sleep, amid friends who loved him, and the sweeter endearments of those who loved him as friends could not, that in the first moments of waking, his startled mind seemed to admit the knowledge of his situation, as if it had burst upon it for the first time, fresh in all its appalling horrors. He gazed round with an air of doubt and amazement, and took up a handful of the straw upon which he lay, as though he would ask himself what it meant. But memory, too faithful to her office, soon unveiled the melancholy past, while reason, shuddering at the task, flashed before his eyes the tremendous future. The contrast overpowered him. He remained for some time lamenting, like a truth, the bright visions that had vanished; and recoiling from the present, which clung to him as a poisoned garment.

When he grew more calm, he surveyed his gloomy dungeon. Alas! the stronger light of day only served to confirm what the gloomy indistinctness of the preceding evening had partially disclosed, the utter impossibility of escape. As, however, his eyes wandered round and round, and from place to place, he noticed two circumstances which excited his surprise and curiosity. The one, he thought, might be fancy; but the other was positive. His pitcher of water, and the dish which contained his food, had been removed from his side while he slept, and now stood near the door. Were he even inclined to doubt this, by supposing he had mistaken the spot where he saw them over-night, he could not, for the pitcher now in his dungeon was neither of the same form nor colour as the other, while the food was changed for some other of better quality. He had been visited, therefore, during the night. But how had the person obtained entrance? Could he have slept so soundly, that the unlocking and opening of those ponderous portals were effected without waking him? He would have said this was not possible, but that in doing so, he must admit a greater difficulty, an entrance by other means, of which he was convinced there existed none. It was not intended, then, that he should be left to perish from hunger. But the secret and mysterious mode of supplying him with food, seemed to indicate he was to have no opportunity of communicating with a human being.

The other circumstance which had attracted his notice, was the disappearance, as he believed, of one of the seven grated windows that ran along the top of his prison. He felt confident that he had observed and counted them; for he was rather surprised at their number, and there was something peculiar in their form, as well as in the manner of their arrangement, at unequal distances. It was so much easier, however, to suppose he was mistaken, than that a portion of the solid iron, which formed the walls, could have escaped from its position, that he soon dismissed the thought from his mind.

Vivenzio partook of the food that was before him, without apprehension. It might be poisoned; but if it were he knew he could not escape death, should such be the design of Tolfi, and the quickest death would be the speediest release.

The day passed wearily and gloomily; though not without a faint hope that, by keeping watch at night, he might observe when the person came again to bring him food, which he supposed he would do in the same way as before. The mere thought of being approached by a living creature, and the opportunity it might present of learning the doom prepared, or preparing, for him, imparted some comfort. Besides, if he came alone, might he not in a furious onset overpower him? Or he might be accessible to pity, or the influence of such munificent rewards as he could bestow, if once more at liberty and master of himself. Say he were armed. The worst that could befall, if nor bribe, nor prayers, nor force prevailed, was a friendly blow, which, though dealt in a damned cause, might work a desired end. There was no chance so desperate, but it looked lovely in Vivenzio's eyes, compared with the idea of being totally abandoned.

The night came, and Vivenzio watched. Morning came, and Vivenzio was confounded! He must have slumbered without knowing it. Sleep must have stolen over him when exhausted by fatigue, and in that interval of feverish repose, he had been baffled: for there stood his replenished pitcher of water, and there his day's meal! Nor was this all. Casting his looks towards the windows of his dungeon, he counted but FIVE! *Here* was no deception; and he was now convinced there had been none the day before. But what did all this portend? Into what strange and mysterious den had he been cast? He gazed till his eyes ached; he could discover nothing to explain the mystery. That it was so, he knew. Why it was so, he racked his imagination in vain to conjecture. He examined the doors. A simple circumstance convinced him they had not been opened.

A wisp of straw, which he had carelessly thrown against them the preceding day, as he paced to and fro, remained where he had cast it, though it must have been displaced by the slightest motion of either of the doors. This was evidence that could not be disputed; and it followed there must be some secret machinery in the walls by which a person could enter. He inspected them closely. They appeared to him one solid and compact mass of iron; or joined, if joined they were, with such nice art, that no mark of division was perceptible. Again and again he surveyed them – and the floor – and the roof – and that range of visionary windows, as he was now almost tempted to consider them: he could discover nothing, absolutely nothing, to relieve his doubts or satisfy his curiosity. Sometimes he fancied that altogether the dungeon had a more contracted appearance – that it looked smaller; but this he ascribed to fancy, and the impression naturally produced upon his mind by the undeniable disappearance of two of the windows.

With intense anxiety, Vivenzio looked forward to the return of night; and as it approached, he resolved that no treacherous sleep should again betray him. Instead of seeking his bed of straw, he continued to walk up and down his dungeon till daylight, straining his eyes in every direction through the darkness, to watch for any appearances that might explain these mysteries. While thus engaged, and as nearly as he could judge (by the time that afterwards elapsed before the morning came in), about two o'clock, there was a slight tremulous motion of the floors. He stooped. The motion lasted nearly a minute; but it was so extremely gentle, that he almost doubted whether it was real, or only imaginary. He listened. Not a sound could be heard. Presently, however, he felt a rush of cold air blow upon him; and dashing towards the quarter whence it seemed to proceed, he stumbled over something which he judged to be the water ewer. The rush of cold air was no longer perceptible; and as Vivenzio stretched out his hands, he found himself close to the walls. He remained motionless for a considerable time; but nothing occurred during the remainder of the night to excite his attention, though he continued to watch with unabated vigilance.

The first approaches of the morning were visible through the grated windows, breaking, with faint divisions of light, the darkness that still pervaded every other part, long before Vivenzio was enabled to distinguish any object in his dungeon. Instinctively and fearfully he turned his eyes, hot and inflamed with watching, towards them. There were FOUR! He could *see* only four: but it might be that some intervening object prevented the fifth from becoming perceptible; and he waited impatiently to ascertain if it were so. As the light strengthened, however, and penetrated every corner of the cell, other objects of amazement struck his sight. On the ground lay the broken fragments of the pitcher he had used the day before, and at a small distance from them, nearer to the wall, stood the one he had noticed the first night. It was filled with water, and beside it was his food. He was now certain that, by some mechanical contrivance, an opening was obtained through the iron wall, and that through this opening the current of air had found entrance. But how noiseless! For had a feather almost waved at the time, he must have heard it. Again he examined that part of the wall; but both to sight and touch it appeared one even and uniform surface, while to repeated and violent blows there was no reverberating sound indicative of hollowness.

This perplexing mystery had for a time withdrawn his thoughts from the windows; but now, directing his eyes again towards them, he saw that the fifth had disappeared in the same manner as the preceding two, without the least distinguishable alteration of external appearances. The remaining four looked as the seven had originally looked; that is, occupying, at irregular distances, the top of the wall on that side of the dungeon. The tall folding-door, too, still seemed to stand beneath, in the centre of these four, as it had at first stood in the centre of the seven. But he could no longer doubt, what, on the preceding day, he fancied might be the effect of visual deception. The dungeon *was* smaller. The roof had lowered – and the opposite ends had contracted the intermediate distance by a space equal, he thought, to that over which the three windows had extended. He was bewildered in vain imaginings to account for these things. Some frightful purpose – some devilish torture of mind or body – some unheard-of device for producing exquisite misery, lurked, he was sure, in what had taken place.

Oppressed with this belief, and distracted more by the dreadful uncertainty of whatever fate impended, than he could be dismayed, he thought, by the knowledge of the worst, he sat ruminating, hour after hour, yielding his fears in succession to every haggard fancy. At last a horrible suspicion flashed suddenly across his mind, and he started up with a frantic air. 'Yes!' he exclaimed, looking wildly round his dungeon, and shuddering as he spoke – 'Yes! it must be so! I see it! – I feel the maddening truth like scorching flames upon my brain! Eternal God! – support me! it must be so! – Yes, yes, *that* is to be my fate! Yon roof will descend! – these walls will hem me round – and slowly, slowly, crush me in their iron arms! Lord God! look down upon me, and in mercy strike me with instant death! Oh, fiend – oh, devil – is this your revenge?'

He dashed himself upon the ground in agony; – tears burst from him, and the sweat stood in large drops upon his face – he sobbed aloud – he tore his hair – he rolled about like one suffering intolerable anguish of body, and would have bitten the iron floor beneath him; he breathed fearful curses upon Tolfi, and the next moment passionate prayers to heaven for immediate death. Then the violence of his grief became exhausted, and he lay still, weeping as a child would weep. The twilight of departing day shed its gloom around him ere he arose from that posture of utter and hopeless sorrow. He had taken no food. Not one drop of water had cooled the fever of his parched lips. Sleep had not visited his eyes for six-and-thirty hours. He was faint with hunger; weary with watching, and with the excess of his emotions. He tasted of his food; he drank with avidity of the water; and reeling like a drunken man to his straw, cast himself upon it to brood again over the appalling image that had fastened itself upon his almost frenzied thoughts.

He slept. But his slumbers were not tranquil. He resisted, as long as he could, their approach; and when, at last, enfeebled nature yielded to their influence, he found no oblivion from his cares. Terrible dreams haunted him – ghastly visions harrowed up his imagination – he shouted and screamed, as if he already felt the dungeon's ponderous roof descending on him – he breathed hard and thick, as though writhing between its iron walls. Then would he spring up – stare wildly about him – stretch forth his hands, to be sure he yet had space enough to live – and, muttering some incoherent words, sink down again, to pass through the same fierce vicissitudes of delirious sleep.

The morning of the fourth day dawned upon Vivenzio. But it was high noon before his mind shook off its stupor, or he awoke to a full consciousness of his situation. And what a fixed energy of despair sat upon his pale features, as he cast his eyes upwards, and gazed upon the THREE windows that now alone remained! The three! – there were no more! – and they seemed to number his own allotted days. Slowly and calmly he next surveyed the top and sides, and comprehended all the meaning of the diminished height of the former, as well as of the gradual approximation of the latter. The contracted dimensions of his mysterious prison were now too gross and palpable to be the juggle of his heated imagination. Still lost in wonder at the means, Vivenzio could put no cheat upon his reason, as to the end. By what horrible ingenuity it was contrived, that walls, and roof, and windows, should thus silently and imperceptibly, without noise, and without motion almost, fold, as it were, within each other, he knew not. He only knew they did so; and he vainly strove to persuade himself it was the intention of the contriver, to rack the miserable wretch who might be immured there with anticipation, merely, of a fate, from which, in the very crisis of his agony, he was to be reprieved.

Gladly would he have clung even to this possibility, if his heart would have let him; but he felt a dreadful assurance of its fallacy. And what matchless inhumanity it was to doom the sufferer to such lingering torments – to lead him day by day to so appalling a death, unsupported by the consolations of religion, unvisited by any human being, abandoned to himself, deserted of all, and denied even the sad privilege of knowing that his cruel destiny would awaken pity! Alone he was to perish! – alone he was to wait a slow coming torture, whose most exquisite pangs would be inflicted by that very solitude and that tardy coming!

'It is not death I fear,' he exclaimed, 'but the death I must prepare for! Methinks, too, I could meet even that – all horrible and revolting as it is – if it might overtake me now. But where shall I find fortitude to tarry till it come? How can I outlive the three long days and nights I have to live? There is no power within me to bid the hideous spectre hence – none to make it familiar to my thoughts; or myself, patient of its errand. My thoughts, rather, will flee from me, and I grow mad in looking at it. Oh! for a deep sleep to fall upon me! That so, in death's likeness, I might embrace death itself, and drink no more of the cup that is presented to me, than my fainting spirit has already tasted!'

In the midst of these lamentations, Vivenzio noticed that his accustomed meal, with the pitcher of water, had been conveyed, as before, into his dungeon. But this circumstance no longer excited his surprise. His mind was overwhelmed with others of a far greater magnitude. It suggested, however, a feeble hope of deliverance; and there is no hope so feeble as not to yield some support to a heart bending under despair. He resolved to watch, during the ensuing night, for the signs he had before observed; and should he again feel the gentle, tremulous motion of the floor, or the current of air, to seize that moment for giving audible expression to his misery. Some person must be near him, and within reach of his voice, at the instant when his food was supplied; someone, perhaps, susceptible of pity. Or if not, to be told even that his apprehensions were just, and that his fate *was* to be what he foreboded, would be preferable to a suspense which hung upon the possibility of his worst fears being visionary.

The night came; and as the hour approached when Vivenzio imagined he might expect the signs, he stood fixed and silent as a statue. He feared to breathe, almost, lest he might lose any sound which would warn him of their coming. While thus listening, with every faculty of mind and body strained to an agony of attention, it occurred to him he should be more sensible of the motion, probably, if he stretched himself along the iron floor. He accordingly laid himself softly down, and had not been long in that position when – yes – he was certain of it – the floor moved under him! He sprang up, and in a voice suffocated nearly with emotion, called aloud. He paused – the motion ceased – he felt no stream of air – all was hushed – no voice answered to his – he burst into tears, and as he sank to the ground, in renewed anguish, exclaimed – 'Oh, my God! my God! You alone have power to save me now, or strengthen me for the trial you permit.'

Another morning dawned upon the wretched captive, and the fatal index of his doom met his eyes. Two windows! – and *two* days – and all would be over! Fresh food – fresh water! The mysterious visit had been paid, though he had implored it in vain. But how awfully was his prayer answered in what he now saw! The roof of the dungeon was within a foot of his head. The two ends were so near, that in six paces he trod the space between them. Vivenzio shuddered as he gazed, and as his steps traversed the narrowed area. But his feelings no longer vented themselves in frantic wailings. With folded arms, and clenched teeth, with eyes that were bloodshot from much watching, and fixed with a vacant glare upon the ground, with a hard quick breathing, and a hurried walk, he strode backwards and forwards in silent musing for several hours. What mind shall conceive, what tongue utter, or what pen describe the dark and terrible character of his thoughts? Like the fate that moulded them, they had no similitude in the wide range of this world's agony for man. Suddenly he stopped, and his eyes were riveted upon that part of the wall which was over his bed of straw. Words are inscribed there! A human language, traced by a human hand! He rushes towards them; but his blood freezes as he reads: –

'I, Ludovico Sforza, tempted by the gold of the Prince of Tolfi, spent three years in contriving and executing this accursed triumph of my art. When it was completed, the perfidious Tolfi, more devil than man, who conducted me hither one morning, to be witness, as he said, of its perfection, doomed me to be the first victim of my own pernicious skill; lest, as he declared, I should divulge the secret, or repeat the effort of my ingenuity. May God pardon him, as I hope he will me, that ministered to his unhallowed purpose! Miserable wretch, whoe'er thou art, that readest these lines, fall on thy knees, and invoke, as I have done, His sustaining mercy, who alone can nerve thee to meet the vengeance of Tolfi, armed with this tremendous engine which, in a few hours, must crush *you*, as it will the needy wretch who made it.'

A deep groan burst from Vivenzio. He stood, like one transfixed, with dilated eyes, expanded nostrils, and quivering lips, gazing at this fatal inscription. It was as if a voice from the sepulchre had sounded in his ears, 'Prepare!' Hope forsook him. There was his sentence, recorded in those dismal words. The future stood unveiled before him, ghastly and appalling. His brain already feels the descending horror – his bones seem to crack and crumble in the mighty grasp of the iron walls!

Unknowing what it is he does, he fumbles in his garment for some weapon of self-destruction. He clenches his throat in his convulsive gripe, as though he would strangle himself at once. He stares upon the walls, and his warring spirit demands, 'Will they not anticipate their office if I dash my head against them?' An hysterical laugh chokes him as he exclaims, 'Why should I? He was but a man who died first in their fierce embrace; and I should be less than man not to do as much!'

The evening sun was descending, and Vivenzio beheld its golden beams streaming through one of the windows. What a thrill of joy shot through his soul at the sight! It was a precious link, that united him, for the moment, with the world beyond. There was ecstasy in the thought. As he gazed, long and earnestly, it seemed as if the windows had lowered sufficiently for him to reach them. With one bound he was beneath them – with one wild spring he clung to the bars. Whether it was so contrived, purposely to madden with delight the wretch who looked, he knew not; but, at the extremity of a long vista, cut through the solid rocks, the ocean, the sky, the setting sun, olive groves, shady walks, and, in the farthest distance, delicious glimpses of magnificent Sicily, burst upon his sight. How exquisite was the cool breeze as it swept across his cheek, loaded with fragrance! He inhaled it as though it were the breath of continued life. And there was a freshness in the landscape, and in the rippling of the calm green sea, that fell upon his withering heart like dew upon the parched earth. How he gazed, and panted, and still clung to his hold! sometimes hanging by one hand, sometimes by the other, and then grasping the bars with both, as loth to quit the smiling paradise outstretched before him; till exhausted, and his hands swollen and benumbed, he dropped helpless down, and lay stunned for a considerable time by the fall.

When he recovered, the glorious vision had vanished. He was in darkness. He doubted whether it was not a dream that had passed before his sleeping fancy; but gradually his scattered thoughts returned, and with them came remembrance. Yes! he had looked once again upon the gorgeous splendour of nature! Once again his eyes had trembled beneath their veiled lids, at the sun's radiance, and sought repose in the soft verdure of the olive-tree, or the gentle swell of undulating waves. Oh, that he were a mariner, exposed upon those waves to the worst fury of storm and tempest; or a very wretch, loathsome with disease, plague-stricken, and his body one leprous contagion from crown to sole, hunted forth to gasp out the remnant of infectious life beneath those verdant trees, so he might shun the destiny upon whose edge he tottered!

Vain thoughts like these would steal over his mind from time to time, in spite of himself; but they scarcely moved it from that stupor into which it had sunk, and which kept him, during the whole night, like one who had been drugged with opium. He was equally insensible to the calls of hunger and of thirst, though the third day was now commencing since even a drop of water had passed his lips. He remained on the ground, sometimes sitting, sometimes lying; at intervals, sleeping heavily; and when not sleeping, silently brooding over what was to come, or talking aloud, in disordered speech, of his wrongs, of his friends, of his home, and of those he loved, with a confused mingling of all.

In this pitiable condition, the sixth and last morning dawned upon Vivenzio, if dawn it might be called – the dim, obscure light which faintly struggled through the ONE SOLITARY window of his dungeon. He could hardly be said to notice the melancholy token. And yet he did notice it; for as he raised his eyes and saw the portentous sign, there was a slight convulsive distortion of his countenance. But what did attract his notice, and at the sight of which his agitation was excessive, was the change his iron bed had undergone. It was a bed no longer. It stood before him, the visible semblance of a funeral couch or bier! When he beheld this, he started from the ground; and, in raising himself, suddenly struck his head against the roof, which was now so low that he could no longer stand upright. 'God's will be done!' was all he said, as he crouched his body, and placed his hand upon the bier; for such it was. The iron bedstead had been so contrived, by the mechanical art of Ludovico Sforza, that as the advancing walls came in contact with its head and feet, a pressure was produced upon concealed springs, which, when made to play, set in motion a very simple though ingeniously-contrived machinery, that effected the transformation. The object was, of course, to heighten, in the closing scene of this horrible drama, all the feelings of despair and anguish, which the preceding ones had aroused. For the same reason, the last window was so made as to admit only a shadowy kind of gloom rather than light, that the wretched captive might be surrounded, as it were, with every seeming preparation for approaching death.

Vivenzio seated himself on his bier. Then he knelt and prayed fervently; and sometimes tears would gush from him. The air seemed thick, and he breathed with difficulty; or it might be that he fancied it was so, from the hot and narrow limits of his dungeon, which were now so diminished that he could neither stand up nor lie down at his full length. But his wasted spirits and oppressed mind no longer struggled within him. He was past hope, and fear shook him no more. Happy if thus revenge had struck its final blow; for he would have fallen beneath it almost unconscious of a pang. But such a lethargy of the soul, after such an excitement of its fiercest passions, had entered into the diabolical calculations of Tolfi; and the fell artificer of his designs had imagined a counteracting device.

The tolling of an enormous bell struck upon the ears of Vivenzio! He started. It beat but once. The sound was so close and stunning, that it seemed to shatter his very brain, while it echoed through the rocky passages like reverberating peals of thunder. This was followed by a sudden crash of the roof and walls, as if they were about to fall upon and close around him at once. Vivenzio screamed, and instinctively spread forth his arms, as though he had a giant's strength to hold them back. They had moved nearer to him, and were now motionless. Vivenzio looked up, and saw the roof almost touching his head, even as he sat cowering beneath it; and he felt that a farther contraction of but a few inches only must commence the frightful operation. Roused as he had been, he now gasped for breath. His body shook violently – he was bent nearly double. His hands rested upon either wall, and his feet were drawn under him to avoid the pressure in front. Thus he remained for more than an hour, when that deafening bell beat again, and again there came the crash of horrid death. But the concussion was now so great that it struck Vivenzio down. As he lay gathered up in lessened bulk, the bell beat loud and frequent – crash succeeded crash – and on, and on, and on came the mysterious engine of death, till Vivenzio's smothered groans were heard no more! He was horribly crushed by the ponderous roof and collapsing sides – and the flattened bier was his *Iron Shroud*.

A Chapter in the History of a Tyrone Family

Sheridan Le Fanu

INTRODUCTION

In the following narrative, I have endeavoured to give as nearly as possible the *ipsissima verba* of the valued friend from whom I received it, conscious that any aberration from *her* mode of telling the tale of her own life would at once impair its accuracy and its effect. Would that, with her words, I could also bring before you her animated gesture, her expressive countenance, the solemn and thrilling air and accent with which she related the dark passages in her strange story; and, above all, that I could communicate the impressive consciousness that the narrator had seen with her own eyes, and personally acted in the scenes which she described; these accompaniments, taken with the additional circumstance that she who told the tale was one far too deeply and sadly impressed with religious principle to misrepresent or fabricate what she repeated as fact, gave to the tale a depth of interest which the events recorded could hardly, themselves, have produced. I became acquainted with the lady from whose lips I heard this narrative nearly twenty years since, and the story struck my fancy so much that I committed it to paper while it was still fresh in my mind; and should its perusal afford you entertainment for a listless half hour, my labour shall not have been bestowed in vain. I find that I have taken the story down as she told it, in the first person, and perhaps this is as it should be.

She began as follows:

My maiden name was Richardson,[1] the designation of a family of some distinction in the county of Tyrone. I was the younger of two daughters, and we were the only children. There was a difference in our ages of nearly six years, so that I did not, in my childhood, enjoy that close companionship which sisterhood, in other circumstances, necessarily involves; and while I was still a child, my sister was married. The person upon whom she bestowed her hand was a Mr Carew, a gentleman of property and consideration in the north of England. I remember well the eventful day of the wedding; the thronging carriages, the noisy menials, the loud laughter, the merry faces, and the gay dresses. Such sights were then new to me, and harmonised ill with the sorrowful feelings with which I regarded the event which was to separate me, as it turned out, for ever from a sister whose tenderness alone had hitherto more than supplied all that I wanted in my mother's affection. The day soon arrived which was to remove the happy couple from Ashtown House. The carriage stood at the hall-door, and my poor sister kissed me again and again, telling me that I should see her soon. The carriage drove away, and I gazed after it until my eyes filled with tears, and, returning slowly to my chamber, I wept more bitterly and, so to speak, more desolately, than ever I had done before. My father had never seemed to love or to take an interest in me. He had desired a son, and I think he never thoroughly forgave me my unfortunate sex. My having come into the world at all as his child he regarded as a kind

1 I have carefully altered the names as they appear in the original MSS, for the reader will see that some of the circumstances recorded are not of a kind to reflect honour upon those involved in them; and as many are still living, in every way honoured and honourable, who stand in close relation to the principal actors in this drama, the reader will see the necessity of the course which we have adopted.

of fraudulent intrusion, and as his antipathy to me had its origin in an imperfection of mine, too radical for removal, I never even hoped to stand high in his good graces. My mother was, I dare say, as fond of me as she was of anyone; but she was a woman of a masculine and a worldly cast of mind. She had no tenderness or sympathy for the weaknesses, or even for the affections, of woman's nature and her demeanour towards me was peremptory, and often even harsh. It is not to be supposed, then, that I found in the society of my parents much to supply the loss of my sister. About a year after her marriage, we received letters from Mr Carew, containing accounts of my sister's health, which, though not actually alarming, were calculated to make us seriously uneasy. The symptoms most dwelt upon were loss of appetite and cough. The letters concluded by intimating that he would avail himself of my father and mother's repeated invitation to spend some time at Ashtown, particularly as the physician who had been consulted as to my sister's health had strongly advised a removal to her native air. There were added repeated assurances that nothing serious was apprehended, as it was supposed that a deranged state of the liver was the only source of the symptoms which at first had seemed to intimate consumption.

In accordance with this announcement, my sister and Mr Carew arrived in Dublin, where one of my father's carriages awaited them, in readiness to start upon whatever day or hour they might choose for their departure. It was arranged that Mr Carew was, as soon as the day upon which they were to leave Dublin was definitely fixed, to write to my father, who intended that the two last stages should be performed by his own horses, upon whose speed and safety far more reliance might be placed than upon those of the ordinary post-horses, which were at that time, almost without exception, of the very worst order. The journey, one of about ninety miles, was to be divided; the larger portion being reserved for the second day. On Sunday a letter reached us, stating that the party would leave Dublin on Monday, and, in due course, reach Ashtown upon Tuesday evening. Tuesday came, the evening closed in, and yet no carriage; darkness came on, and still no sign of our expected visitors. Hour after hour passed away, and it was now past twelve; the night was remarkably calm, scarce a breath stirring, so that any sound, such as that produced by the rapid movement of a vehicle, would have been audible at a considerable distance. For some such sound I was feverishly listening.

It was, however, my father's rule to close the house at nightfall, and the window-shutters being fastened, I was unable to reconnoitre the avenue as I would have wished. It was nearly one o'clock, and we began almost to despair of seeing them upon that night, when I thought I distinguished the sound of wheels, but so remote and faint as to make me at first very uncertain. The noise approached; it became louder and clearer; it stopped for a moment. I now heard the shrill screaming of the rusty iron, as the avenue-gate revolved on its hinges; again came the sound of wheels in rapid motion.

'It is they,' said I, starting up; 'the carriage is in the avenue.' We all stood for a few moments breathlessly listening. On thundered the vehicle with the speed of a whirlwind; crack went the whip, and clatter went the wheels, as it rattled over the uneven pavement of the court. A general and furious barking from all the dogs about the house, hailed its arrival. We hurried to the hall in time to hear the steps let down with the sharp clanging noise peculiar to the operation, and the hum of voices exerted in the bustle of arrival. The hall-door was now thrown open, and we all stepped forth to greet our visitors. The court was perfectly empty; the moon was shining broadly and brightly upon all around; nothing was to be seen but the tall trees with their long spectral shadows, now wet with the dews of midnight. We stood gazing from right to left, as if suddenly awakened from a dream; the dogs walked suspiciously, growling and snuffing about the court, and by totally and suddenly ceasing their former loud barking, expressing the predominance of fear. We stared one upon another in perplexity and dismay, and I think I never beheld more pale faces assembled. By my father's direction, we looked about to find anything which might indicate or account for the noise which we had heard; but no such thing was to be seen – even the mire which lay upon the avenue was undisturbed. We returned to the house, more panic-struck than I can describe. On the next day, we learned by a messenger, who had ridden hard the greater part of the night, that my sister was dead. On Sunday evening, she had retired to bed rather unwell, and, on Monday, her indisposition declared itself unequivocally to be malignant fever. She became hourly worse and, on Tuesday night, a little after midnight, she expired.[2] I mention this circumstance, because it was one upon which a thousand wild and fantastical reports were founded, though one would have thought that the truth scarcely required to be improved upon; and again, because it produced a strong and lasting effect upon my spirits, and indeed, I am inclined to think, upon my character. I was, for several years after this occurrence, long after the violence of my grief subsided, so wretchedly low-spirited and nervous, that I could scarcely be said to live; and during this time, habits of indecision, arising out of a listless acquiescence in the will of others, a fear of encountering even the slightest opposition, and a disposition to shrink from what are commonly called amusements,

2 The residuary legatee of the late Frances Purcell, who has the honour of selecting such of his lamented old friend's manuscripts as may appear fit for publication, in order that the lore which they contain may reach the world before scepticism and utility have robbed our species of the precious gift of credulity, and scornfully kicked before them, or trampled into annihilation those harmless fragments of picturesque superstition which it is our object to preserve, has been subjected to the charge of dealing too largely in the marvellous; and it has been half insinuated that such is his love for diablerie, that he is content to wander a mile out of his way, in order to meet a fiend or a goblin, and thus to sacrifice all regard for truth and accuracy to the idle hope of affrighting the imagination, and thus pandering to the bad taste of his reader. He begs leave, then, to take this opportunity of asserting his perfect innocence of all the crimes laid to his charge, and to assure his reader that he never *pandered to his bad taste*, nor went one inch out of his way to introduce witch, fairy, devil, ghost, or any other of the grim fraternity of the redoubted Raw-head-and-bloody-bones. His province, touching these tales, has been attended with no difficulty and little responsibility; indeed, he is accountable for nothing more than an alteration in the names of persons mentioned therein, when such a step seemed necessary, and for an occasional note, whenever he conceived it possible, innocently, to edge in a word. These tales have been *written down*, as the heading of each announces, by the Rev. Francis Purcell, P.P., of Drumcoolagh; and in all the instances, which are many, in which the present writer has had an opportunity of comparing the manuscript of his departed friend with the actual traditions which are current amongst the families whose fortunes they pretend to illustrate, he has uniformly found that whatever of supernatural occurred in the story, so far from having been exaggerated by him, had been rather softened down, and, wherever it could be attempted, accounted for.

grew upon me so strongly, that I have scarcely even yet altogether overcome them.

We saw nothing more of Mr Carew. He returned to England as soon as the melancholy rites attendant upon the event which I have just mentioned were performed; and not being altogether inconsolable, he married again within two years; after which, owing to the remoteness of our relative situations, and other circumstances, we gradually lost sight of him.

I was now an only child; and, as my elder sister had died without issue, it was evident that, in the ordinary course of things, my father's property, which was altogether in his power, would go to me; and the consequence was, that before I was fourteen, Ashtown House was besieged by a host of suitors. However, whether it was that I was too young, or that none of the aspirants to my hand stood sufficiently high in rank or wealth, I was suffered by both parents to do exactly as I pleased; and well was it for me, as I afterwards found, that fortune, or rather Providence, had so ordained it, that I had not suffered my affections to become in any degree engaged, for my mother would never have suffered any *silly fancy* of mine, as she was in the habit of styling an attachment, to stand in the way of her ambitious views – views which she was determined to carry into effect, in defiance of every obstacle, and in order to accomplish which she would not have hesitated to sacrifice anything so unreasonable and contemptible as a girlish passion.

When I reached the age of sixteen, my mother's plans began to develop themselves; and, at her suggestion, we moved to Dublin to sojourn for the winter, in order that no time might be lost in disposing of me to the best advantage. I had been too long accustomed to consider myself as of no importance whatever, to believe for a moment that I was in reality the cause of all the bustle and preparation which surrounded me, and being thus relieved from the pain which a consciousness of my real situation would have inflicted, I journeyed towards the capital with a feeling of total indifference.

My father's wealth and connection had established him in the best society, and, consequently, upon our arrival in the metropolis we commanded whatever enjoyment or advantages its gaieties afforded. The tumult and novelty of the scenes in which I was involved did not fail considerably to amuse me, and my mind gradually recovered its tone, which was naturally cheerful. It was almost immediately known and reported that I was an heiress, and of course my attractions were pretty generally acknowledged. Among the many gentlemen whom it was my fortune to please, one, ere long, established himself in my mother's good graces, to the exclusion of all less important aspirants. However, I had not understood or even remarked his attentions, nor in the slightest degree suspected his or my mother's plans respecting me, when I was made aware of them rather abruptly by my mother herself.

We had attended a splendid ball, given by Lord M—, at his residence in Stephen's Green, and I was, with the assistance of my waiting-maid, employed in rapidly divesting myself of the rich ornaments which, in profuseness and value, could scarcely have found their equals in any private family in Ireland. I had thrown myself into a lounging-chair beside the fire, listless and exhausted, after the fatigues of the evening, when I was aroused from the reverie into which I had fallen by the sound of footsteps approaching my chamber, and my mother entered.

'Fanny, my dear,' said she, in her softest tone, 'I wish to say a word or two with you before I go to rest. You are not fatigued, love, I hope?'

'No, no, madam, I thank you,' said I, rising at the same time from my seat, with the formal respect so little practised now.

'Sit down, my dear,' said she, placing herself upon a chair beside me; 'I must chat with you for a quarter of an hour or so. Saunders' (to the maid) 'you may leave the room; do not close the room-door, but shut that of the lobby.'

This precaution against curious ears having been taken as directed, my mother proceeded.

'You have observed, I should suppose, my dearest Fanny – indeed, you MUST have observed Lord Glenfallen's marked attentions to you?'

'I assure you, madam—' I began.

'Well, well, that is all right,' interrupted my mother; 'of course you must be modest upon the matter; but listen to me for a few moments, my love, and I will prove to your satisfaction that your modesty is quite unnecessary in this case. You have done better than we could have hoped, at least so very soon. Lord Glenfallen is in love with you. I give you joy of your conquest;' and saying this, my mother kissed my forehead.

'In love with me!' I exclaimed, in unfeigned astonishment.

'Yes, in love with you,' repeated my mother; 'devotedly, distractedly in love with you. Why, my dear, what is there wonderful in it? Look in the glass, and look at these,' she continued, pointing with a smile to the jewels which I had just removed from my person, and which now lay a glittering heap upon the table.

'May there not,' said I, hesitating between confusion and real alarm – 'is it not possible that some mistake may be at the bottom of all this?'

'Mistake, dearest! none,' said my mother. 'None; none in the world. Judge for yourself; read this, my love.' And she placed in my hand a letter, addressed to herself, the seal of which was broken. I read it through with no small surprise. After some very fine complimentary flourishes upon my beauty and perfections, as also upon the antiquity and high reputation of our family, it went on to make a formal proposal of marriage, to be communicated or not to me at present, as my mother should deem expedient; and the letter wound up by a request that the writer might be permitted, upon our return to Ashtown House, which was soon to take place, as the spring was now tolerably advanced, to visit us for a few days, in case his suit was approved.

'Well, well, my dear,' said my mother, impatiently; 'do you know who Lord Glenfallen is?'

'I do, madam,' said I rather timidly, for I dreaded an altercation with my mother.

'Well, dear, and what frightens you?' continued she. 'Are you afraid of a title? What has he done to alarm you? he is neither old nor ugly.'

I was silent, though I might have said, 'He is neither young nor handsome.'

'My dear Fanny,' continued my mother, 'in sober seriousness you have been most fortunate in engaging the affections of a nobleman such as Lord Glenfallen, young and wealthy, with first-rate – yes, acknowledged *first-rate* abilities, and of a family whose influence is not exceeded by that of any in Ireland. Of course you see the offer in the same light that I do – indeed I think you *must*.'

This was uttered in no very dubious tone. I was so much astonished by the suddenness of the whole communication that I literally did not know what to say.

'You are not in love?' said my mother, turning sharply, and fixing her dark eyes upon me with severe scrutiny.

'No, madam,' said I, promptly; horrified, as what young lady would not have been, at such a query.

'I'm glad to hear it,' said my mother, *drily*. 'Once, nearly twenty years ago, a friend of mine consulted me as to how he should deal with a daughter who had made what they call a love-match – beggared herself, and disgraced her family; and I said, without hesitation, take no care for her, but cast her off. Such punishment I awarded for an offence committed against the reputation of a family not my own; and what I advised respecting the child of another, with full as small compunction I would DO with mine. I cannot conceive anything more unreasonable or intolerable than that the fortune and the character of a family should be marred by the idle caprices of a girl.'

She spoke this with great severity, and paused as if she expected some observation from me.

I, however, said nothing.

'But I need not explain to you, my dear Fanny,' she continued, 'my views upon this subject; you have always known them well, and I have never yet had reason to believe you likely, voluntarily, to offend me, or to abuse or neglect any of those advantages which reason and duty tell you should be improved. Come hither, my dear; kiss me, and do not look so frightened. Well, now, about this letter, you need not answer it yet; of course you must be allowed time to make up your mind. In the meantime I will write to his lordship to give him my permission to visit us at Ashtown. Good-night, my love.'

And thus ended one of the most disagreeable, not to say astounding, conversations I had ever had. It would not be easy to describe exactly what were my feelings towards Lord Glenfallen; – whatever might have been my mother's suspicions, my heart was perfectly disengaged – and hitherto, although I had not been made in the slightest degree acquainted with his real views, I had liked him very much, as an agreeable, well-informed man, whom I was always glad to meet in society. He had served in the navy in early life, and the polish which his manners received in his after intercourse with courts and cities had not served to obliterate that frankness of manner which belongs proverbially to the sailor. Whether this apparent candour went deeper than the outward bearing, I was yet to learn. However, there was no doubt that, as far as I had seen of Lord Glenfallen, he was, though perhaps not so young as might have been desired in a lover, a singularly pleasing man; and whatever feeling unfavourable to him had found its way into my mind, arose altogether from the dread, not an unreasonable one, that constraint might be practised upon my inclinations. I reflected, however, that Lord Glenfallen was a wealthy man, and one highly thought of; and although I could never expect to love him in the romantic sense of the term, yet I had no doubt but that, all things considered, I might be more happy with him than I could hope to be at home. When next I met him it was with no small embarrassment, his tact and good breeding, however, soon reassured me, and effectually prevented my awkwardness being remarked upon. And I had the satisfaction of leaving Dublin for the country with the full conviction that nobody, not even those most intimate with me, even suspected the fact of Lord Glenfallen's having made me a formal proposal. This was to me a very serious subject of self-gratulation, for, besides my instinctive dread of becoming the topic of the speculations of gossip, I felt that if the situation which I occupied in relation to him were made publicly known, I should stand committed in a manner which would scarcely leave me the power of retraction.

The period at which Lord Glenfallen had arranged to visit Ashtown House was now fast approaching, and it became my mother's wish to form me thoroughly to her will, and to obtain my consent to the proposed marriage before his arrival, so that all things might proceed smoothly, without apparent opposition or objection upon my part. Whatever objections, therefore, I had entertained were to be subdued; whatever disposition to resistance I had exhibited or had been supposed to feel, were to be completely eradicated before he made his appearance; and my mother addressed herself to the task with a decision and energy against which even the barriers, which her imagination had created, could hardly have stood. If she had, however, expected any determined opposition from me, she was agreeably disappointed. My heart was perfectly free, and all my feelings of liking and preference were in favour of Lord Glenfallen; and I well knew that in case I refused to dispose of myself as I was desired, my mother had alike the power and the will to render my existence as utterly miserable as even the most ill-assorted marriage could possibly have done. You will remember, my good friend, that I was very young and very completely under the control of my parents, both of whom, my mother particularly, were unscrupulously determined in matters of this kind, and willing, when voluntary obedience on the part of those within their power was withheld, to compel a forced acquiescence by an unsparing use of all the engines of the most stern and rigorous domestic discipline. All these combined, not unnaturally, induced me to resolve upon yielding at once, and without useless opposition, to what appeared almost to be my fate. The appointed time was come, and my now accepted suitor arrived; he was in high spirits, and, if possible, more entertaining than ever. I was not, however, quite in the mood to enjoy his sprightliness; but whatever I wanted in gaiety was amply made up in the triumphant and gracious good-humour of my mother, whose smiles of benevolence and exultation were showered around as bountifully as the summer sunshine. I will not weary you with unnecessary prolixity. Let it suffice to say, that I was married to Lord Glenfallen with all the attendant pomp and circumstance of wealth, rank, and grandeur. According to the usage of the times, now humanely reformed, the ceremony was made, until long past midnight, the season of wild, uproarious, and promiscuous feasting and revelry. Of all this I have a painfully vivid recollection, and particularly of the little annoyances inflicted upon me by the dull and coarse jokes of the wits and wags who abound in all such places, and upon all such occasions. I was not sorry when, after a few days, Lord Glenfallen's carriage appeared at the door to convey us both from Ashtown; for any change would have been a relief from the irksomeness of ceremonial and formality which the visits received in honour of my newly-acquired titles hourly entailed upon me.

It was arranged that we were to proceed to Cahergillagh, one of the Glenfallen estates, lying, however, in a southern county, so that, owing to the difficulty of the roads at the time, a tedious journey of three days intervened. I set forth with my noble companion, followed by the regrets of some, and by the envy of many; though God knows I little deserved the latter. The three days of travel were now almost spent, when, passing the brow of a wild heathy hill, the domain of Cahergillagh opened suddenly upon our view. It formed a striking and a beautiful scene. A lake of considerable extent stretching away towards the west, and reflecting from its broad, smooth waters, the rich glow of the setting sun, was overhung by steep hills, covered by a rich mantle of velvet sward, broken here and there by the gray front of some old rock, and exhibiting on their shelving sides, their slopes and hollows, every variety of light and shade; a thick wood of dwarf oak, birch, and hazel skirted these hills, and clothed the shores of the lake, running out in rich luxuriance upon every promontory, and spreading upward considerably upon the side of the hills.

'There lies the enchanted castle,' said Lord Glenfallen, pointing towards a considerable level space intervening between two of the picturesque hills, which rose dimly around the lake. This little plain was chiefly occupied by the same low, wild wood which covered the other parts of the domain; but towards the centre a mass of taller and statelier forest trees stood darkly grouped together, and among them stood an ancient square tower, with many buildings of a humbler character, forming together the manorhouse, or, as it was more usually called, the Court of Cahergillagh. As we approached the level upon which the mansion stood, the winding road gave us many glimpses of the time-worn castle and its surrounding buildings; and seen as it was through the long vistas of the fine old trees, and with the rich glow of evening upon it, I have seldom beheld an object more picturesquely striking. I was glad to perceive, too, that here and there the blue curling smoke ascended from stacks of chimneys now hidden by the rich, dark ivy which, in a great measure, covered the building. Other indications of comfort made themselves manifest as we approached; and indeed, though the place was evidently one of considerable antiquity, it had nothing whatever of the gloom of decay about it.

'You must not, my love,' said Lord Glenfallen, 'imagine this place worse than it is. I have no taste for antiquity – at least I should not choose a house to reside in because it is old. Indeed I do not recollect that I was even so romantic as to overcome my aversion to rats and rheumatism, those faithful attendants upon your noble relics of feudalism; and I much prefer a snug, modern, unmysterious bedroom, with well-aired sheets, to the waving tapestry, mildewed cushions, and all the other interesting appliances of romance. However, though I cannot promise you all the discomfort generally belonging to an old castle, you will find legends and ghostly lore enough to claim your respect; and if old Martha be still to the fore, as I trust she is, you will soon have a supernatural and appropriate anecdote for every closet and corner of the mansion; but here we are – so, without more ado, welcome to Cahergillagh!'

We now entered the hall of the castle, and while the domestics were employed in conveying our trunks and other luggage which we had brought with us for immediate use to the apartments which Lord Glenfallen had selected for himself and me, I went with him into a spacious sitting-room, wainscoted with finely polished black oak, and hung round with the portraits of various worthies of the Glenfallen family. This room looked out upon an extensive level covered with the softest green sward, and irregularly bounded by the wild wood I have before mentioned, through the leafy arcade formed by whose boughs and trunks the level beams of the setting sun were pouring. In the distance a group of dairymaids were plying their task, which they accompanied throughout with snatches of Irish songs which, mellowed by the distance, floated not unpleasingly to the ear; and beside them sat or lay, with all the grave importance of conscious protection, six or seven large dogs of various kinds. Farther in the distance, and through the cloisters of the arching wood, two or three ragged urchins were employed in driving such stray kine as had wandered farther than the rest to join their fellows. As I looked upon this scene which I have described, a feeling of tranquillity and happiness came upon me, which I have never experienced in so strong a degree; and so strange to me was the sensation that my eyes filled with tears. Lord Glenfallen mistook the cause of my emotion, and taking me kindly and tenderly by the hand, he said: 'Do not suppose, my love, that it is my intention to *settle* here. Whenever you desire to leave this, you have only to let me know your wish, and it shall be complied with; so I must entreat of you not to suffer any circumstances which I can control to give you one moment's uneasiness. But here is old Martha; you must be introduced to her, one of the heirlooms of our family.' A hale, good-humoured, erect old woman was Martha, and an agreeable contrast to the grim, decrepit hag which my fancy had conjured up, as the depository of all the horrible tales in which I doubted not this old place was most fruitful. She welcomed me and her master with a profusion of gratulations, alternately kissing our hands and apologising for the liberty, until at length Lord Glenfallen put an end to this somewhat fatiguing ceremonial by requesting her to conduct me to my chamber if it were prepared for my reception. I followed Martha up an old-fashioned oak staircase into a long, dim passage, at the end of which lay the door which communicated with the apartments which had been selected for our use; here the old woman stopped, and respectfully requested me to proceed.

I accordingly opened the door, and was about to enter, when something like a mass of black tapestry, as it appeared, disturbed by my sudden approach, fell from above the door, so as completely to screen the aperture; the startling unexpectedness of the occurrence, and the rustling noise which the drapery made in its descent, caused me involuntarily to step two or three paces backwards. I turned, smiling and half-ashamed, to the old servant, and said: 'You see what a coward I am.' The woman looked puzzled, and, without saying any more, I was about to draw aside the curtain and enter the room, when, upon turning to do so, I was surprised to find that nothing whatever interposed to obstruct the passage. I went into the room, followed by the servant-woman, and was amazed to find that it, like the one below, was wainscoted, and that nothing like drapery was to be found near the door.

'Where is it?' said I; 'what has become of it?'

'What does your ladyship wish to know?' said the old woman.

'Where is the black curtain that fell across the door, when I attempted first to come to my chamber?' answered I.

'The cross of Christ about us!' said the old woman, turning suddenly pale.

'What is the matter, my good friend?' said I; 'you seem frightened.'

'Oh no, no, your ladyship,' said the old woman, endeavouring to conceal her agitation; but in vain, for tottering towards a chair, she sank into it, looking so deadly pale and horror-struck that I thought every moment she would faint.

'Merciful God, keep us from harm and danger!' muttered she at length.

'What can have terrified you so?' said I, beginning to fear that she had seen something more than had met my eye. 'You appear ill, my poor woman!'

'Nothing, nothing, my lady,' said she, rising. 'I beg your ladyship's pardon for making so bold. May the great God defend us from misfortune!'

'Martha,' said I, 'something *has* frightened you very much, and I insist on knowing what it is; your keeping me in the dark upon the subject will make me much more uneasy than *anything* you could tell me. I desire you, therefore, to let me know what agitates you; I command you to tell me.'

'Your ladyship said you saw a black curtain falling across the door when you were coming into the room,' said the old woman.

'I did,' said I; 'but though the whole thing appears somewhat strange, I cannot see anything in the matter to agitate you so excessively.'

'It's for no good you saw that, my lady,' said the crone; 'something terrible is coming. It's a sign, my lady – a sign that never fails.'

'Explain, explain what you mean, my good woman,' said I, in spite of myself, catching more than I could account for, of her superstitious terror.

'Whenever something – something *bad* is going to happen to the Glenfallen family, someone that belongs to them sees a black handkerchief or curtain just waved or falling before their faces. I saw it myself,' continued she, lowering her voice, 'when I was only a little girl, and I'll never forget it. I often heard of it before, though I never saw it till then, nor since, praised be God. But I was going into Lady Jane's room to waken her in the morning; and sure enough when I got first to the bed and began to draw the curtain, something dark was waved across the division, but only for a moment; and when I saw rightly into the bed, there was she lying cold and dead, God be merciful to me! So, my lady, there is small blame to me to be daunted when anyone of the family sees it; for it's many's the story I heard of it, though I saw it but once.'

I was not of a superstitious turn of mind, yet I could not resist a feeling of awe very nearly allied to the fear which my companion had so unreservedly expressed; and when you consider my situation, the loneliness, antiquity, and gloom of the place, you will allow that the weakness was not without excuse. In spite of old Martha's boding predictions, however, time flowed on in an unruffled course. One little incident however, though trifling in itself, I must relate, as it serves to make what follows more intelligible. Upon the day after my arrival, Lord Glenfallen of course desired to make me acquainted with the house and domain; and accordingly we set forth upon our ramble. When returning, he became for some time silent and moody, a state so unusual with him as considerably to excite my surprise. I endeavoured by observations and questions to arouse him – but in vain. At length, as we approached the house, he said, as if speaking to himself: ''Twere madness – madness

– madness,' repeating the words bitterly – 'sure and speedy ruin.' There was here a long pause; and at length, turning sharply towards me, in a tone very unlike that in which he had hitherto addressed me, he said: 'Do you think it possible that a woman can keep a secret?'

'I am sure,' said I, 'that women are very much belied upon the score of talkativeness, and that I may answer your question with the same directness with which you put it – I reply that I *do* think a woman can keep a secret.'

'But I do not,' said he, drily.

We walked on in silence for a time. I was much astonished at his unwonted abruptness – I had almost said rudeness. After a considerable pause he seemed to recollect himself, and with an effort resuming his sprightly manner, he said: 'Well, well, the next thing to keeping a secret well is, not to desire to possess one – talkativeness and curiosity generally go together. Now I shall make test of you, in the first place, respecting the latter of these qualities. I shall be your *Bluebeard* – tush, why do I trifle thus? Listen to me, my dear Fanny; I speak now in solemn earnest. What I desire is intimately, inseparably, connected with your happiness and honour as well as my own; and your compliance with my request will not be difficult. It will impose upon you a very trifling restraint during your sojourn here, which certain events which have occurred since our arrival have determined me shall not be a long one. You must promise me, upon your sacred honour, that you will visit *only* that part of the castle which can be reached from the front entrance, leaving the back entrance and the part of the building commanded immediately by it to the menials, as also the small garden whose high wall you see yonder; and never at any time seek to pry or peep into them, nor to open the door which communicates from the front part of the house through the corridor with the back. I do not urge this in jest or in caprice, but from a solemn conviction that danger and misery will be the certain consequences of your not observing what I prescribe. I cannot explain myself further at present. Promise me, then, these things, as you hope for peace here, and for mercy hereafter.'

I did make the promise as desired, and he appeared relieved; his manner recovered all its gaiety and elasticity: but the recollection of the strange scene which I have just described dwelt painfully upon my mind. More than a month passed away without any occurrence worth recording; but I was not destined to leave Cahergillagh without further adventure. One day, intending to enjoy the pleasant sunshine in a ramble through the woods, I ran up to my room to procure my bonnet and shawl. Upon entering the chamber, I was surprised and somewhat startled to find it occupied. Beside the fireplace, and nearly opposite the door, seated in a large, old-fashioned elbow-chair, was placed the figure of a lady. She appeared to be nearer fifty than forty, and was dressed suitably to her age, in a handsome suit of flowered silk; she had a profusion of trinkets and jewellery about her person, and many rings upon her fingers. But although very rich, her dress was not gaudy or in ill taste. But what was remarkable in the lady was, that although her features were handsome, and upon the whole pleasing, the pupil of each eye was dimmed with the whiteness of cataract, and she was evidently stone-blind. I was for some seconds so surprised at this unaccountable apparition, that I could not find words to address her.

'Madam,' said I, 'there must be some mistake here – this is my bed-chamber.'

'Marry come up,' said the lady, sharply; '*your* chamber! Where is Lord Glenfallen?'

'He is below, madam,' replied I; 'and I am convinced he will be not a little surprised to find you here.'

'I do not think he will,' said she; 'with your good leave, talk of what you know something about. Tell him I want him. Why does the minx dilly-dally so?'

In spite of the awe which this grim lady inspired, there was something in her air of confident superiority which, when I considered our relative situations, was not a little irritating.

'Do you know, madam, to whom you speak?' said I.

'I neither know nor care,' said she; 'but I presume that you are someone about the house, so again I desire you, if you wish to continue here, to bring your master hither forthwith.'

'I must tell you, madam,' said I, 'that I am Lady Glenfallen.'

'What's that?' said the stranger, rapidly.

'I say, madam,' I repeated, approaching her that I might be more distinctly heard, 'that I am Lady Glenfallen.'

'It's a lie, you trull!' cried she, in an accent which made me start, and at the same time, springing forward, she seized me in her grasp, and shook me violently, repeating, 'It's a lie – it's a lie!' with a rapidity and vehemence which swelled every vein of her face. The violence of her action, and the fury which convulsed her face, effectually terrified me, and disengaging myself from her grasp, I screamed as loud as I could for help. The blind woman continued to pour out a torrent of abuse upon me, foaming at the mouth with rage, and impotently shaking her clenched fists towards me.

I heard Lord Glenfallen's step upon the stairs, and I instantly ran out; as I passed him I perceived that he was deadly pale, and just caught the words: 'I hope that demon has not hurt you?'

I made some answer, I forget what, and he entered the chamber, the door of which he locked upon the inside. What passed within I know not; but I heard the voices of the two speakers raised in loud and angry altercation.

I thought I heard the shrill accents of the woman repeat the words, 'Let her look to herself;' but I could not be quite sure. This short sentence, however, was, to my alarmed imagination, pregnant with fearful meaning. The storm at length subsided, though not until after a conference of more than two long hours. Lord Glenfallen then returned, pale and agitated. 'That unfortunate woman,' said he, 'is out of her mind. I daresay she treated you to some of her ravings; but you need not dread any further interruption from her: I have brought her so far to reason. She did not hurt you, I trust.'

'No, no,' said I; 'but she terrified me beyond measure.'

'Well,' said he, 'she is likely to behave better for the future; and I dare swear that neither you nor she would desire, after what has passed, to meet again.'

This occurrence, so startling and unpleasant, so involved in mystery, and giving rise to so many painful surmises, afforded me no very agreeable food for rumination. All attempts on my part to arrive at the truth were baffled; Lord Glenfallen evaded all my inquiries, and at length peremptorily forbid any further allusion to the matter. I was thus obliged to rest satisfied with what I had actually seen, and to trust to time to resolve the perplexities in which the whole transaction had involved me. Lord Glenfallen's temper and spirits gradually underwent a complete and most painful change; he became silent and abstracted, his manner to me was abrupt and often harsh, some grievous anxiety seemed ever present to his mind; and under its influence his spirits sunk and his temper became soured. I soon perceived that his gaiety was rather that which the stir and excitement of society produce, than the result of a healthy habit of mind; every day confirmed me in the opinion, that the considerate good-nature which I had so much admired in him was little more than a mere manner; and to my infinite grief and surprise, the gay, kind, open-hearted nobleman who had for months followed and flattered me, was rapidly assuming the form of a gloomy, morose, and singularly selfish man. This was a bitter discovery, and I strove to conceal it from myself as long as I could; but the truth was not to be denied, and I was forced to believe that Lord Glenfallen no longer loved me, and that he was at little pains to conceal the alteration in his sentiments. One morning after breakfast, Lord Glenfallen had been for some time walking silently up and down the room, buried in his moody reflections, when pausing suddenly, and turning towards me, he exclaimed: 'I have it – I have it! We must go abroad, and stay there too; and if that does not answer, why – why, we must try some more effectual expedient. Lady Glenfallen, I have become involved in heavy embarrassments. A wife, you know, must share the fortunes of her husband, for better for worse; but I will waive my right if you prefer remaining here – here at Cahergillagh. For I would not have you seen elsewhere without the state to which your rank entitles you; besides, it would break your poor mother's heart,' he added, with sneering gravity. 'So make up your mind – Cahergillagh or France. I will start if possible in a week, so determine between this and then.'

He left the room, and in a few moments I saw him ride past the window, followed by a mounted servant. He had directed a domestic to inform me that he should not be back until the next day. I was in very great doubt as to what course of conduct I should pursue, as to accompanying him in the continental tour so suddenly determined upon. I felt that it would be a hazard too great to encounter; for at Cahergillagh I had always the consciousness to sustain me, that if his temper at any time led him into violent or unwarrantable treatment of me, I had a remedy within reach, in the protection and support of my own family, from all useful and effective communication with whom, if once in France, I should be entirely debarred. As to remaining at Cahergillagh in solitude, and, for aught I knew, exposed to hidden dangers, it appeared to me scarcely less objectionable than the former proposition; and yet I feared that with one or other I must comply, unless I was prepared to come to an actual breach with Lord Glenfallen. Full of these unpleasing doubts and perplexities, I retired to rest. I was wakened, after having slept uneasily for some hours, by some person shaking me rudely by the shoulder; a small lamp burned in my room, and by its light, to my horror and amazement, I discovered that my visitant was the self-same blind old lady who had so terrified me a few weeks before. I started up in the bed, with a view to ring the bell, and alarm the domestics; but she instantly anticipated me by saying: 'Do not be frightened, silly girl! If I had wished to harm you I could have done it while you were sleeping; I need not have wakened you. Listen to me, now, attentively and fearlessly, for what I have to say interests you to the full as much as it does me. Tell me here, in the presence of God, did Lord Glenfallen marry you – *actually marry* you? Speak the truth, woman.'

'As surely as I live and speak,' I replied, 'did Lord Glenfallen marry me, in presence of more than a hundred witnesses.'

'Well,' continued she, 'he should have told you *then,* before you married him, that he had a wife living, which wife I am. I feel you tremble – tush! do not be frightened. I do not mean to harm you. Mark me now – you are *not* his wife. When I make my story known you will be so neither in the eye of God nor of man. You must leave this house upon to-morrow. Let the world know that your husband has another wife living; go you into retirement, and leave him to justice, which will surely overtake him. If you remain in this house after to-morrow you will reap the bitter fruits of your sin.' So saying, she quitted the room, leaving me very little disposed to sleep.

Here was food for my very worst and most terrible suspicions; still there was not enough to remove all doubt. I had no proof of the truth of this woman's statement. Taken by itself, there was nothing to induce me to attach weight to it; but when I viewed it in connection with the extraordinary mystery of some of Lord Glenfallen's proceedings, his strange anxiety to exclude me from certain portions of the mansion, doubtless lest I should encounter this person – the strong influence, nay, command which she possessed over him, a circumstance clearly established by the very fact of her residing in the very place where, of all others, he should least have desired to find her – her thus acting, and continuing to act in direct contradiction to his wishes; when, I say, I viewed her disclosure in connection with all these circumstances, I could not help feeling that there was at least a fearful verisimilitude in the allegations which she had made. Still I was not satisfied, nor nearly so. Young minds have a reluctance almost insurmountable to believing, upon anything short of unquestionable proof, the existence of premeditated guilt in anyone whom they have ever trusted; and in support of this feeling I was assured that if the assertion of Lord Glenfallen, which nothing in this woman's manner had led me to disbelieve, were true, namely that her mind was unsound, the whole fabric of my doubts and fears must fall to the ground. I determined to state to Lord Glenfallen freely and accurately the substance of the communication which I had just heard, and in his words and looks to seek for its proof or refutation. Full of these thoughts, I remained wakeful and excited all night, every moment fancying that I heard the step or saw the figure of my recent visitor, towards whom I felt a species of horror and dread which I can hardly describe. There was something in her face, though her features had evidently been handsome, and were not, at first sight, unpleasing, which, upon a nearer inspection, seemed to indicate the habitual prevalence and indulgence of evil passions, and a power of expressing mere animal anger, with an intenseness that I have seldom seen equalled, and to which an almost unearthly effect was given by the convulsive quivering of the sightless eyes. You may easily suppose that it was no very pleasing reflection to me to consider that, whenever caprice might induce her to return, I was within the reach of this violent and, for aught I knew, insane woman, who had, upon that very night, spoken to me in a tone of menace, of which her mere words, divested of the manner and look with which she uttered them, can convey but a faint idea. Will you believe me when I tell you that I was actually afraid to leave my bed in order to secure the door, lest I should again encounter the dreadful object lurking in some corner or peeping from behind the window-curtains, so very a child was I in my fears.

The morning came, and with it Lord Glenfallen. I knew not, and indeed I cared not, where he might have been; my thoughts were wholly engrossed by the terrible fears and suspicions which my last night's conference had suggested to me. He was, as usual, gloomy and abstracted, and I feared in no very fitting mood to hear what I had to say with patience, whether the charges were true or false. I was, however, determined not to suffer the opportunity to pass, or Lord Glenfallen to leave the room, until, at all hazards, I had unburdened my mind.

'My lord,' said I, after a long silence, summoning up all my firmness – 'my lord, I wish to say a few words to you upon a matter of very great importance, of very deep concernment to you and to me.' I fixed my eyes upon him to discern, if possible, whether the announcement caused him any uneasiness; but no symptom of any such feeling was perceptible.

'Well, my dear,' said he, 'this is no doubt a very grave preface, and portends, I have no doubt, something extraordinary. Pray let us have it without more ado.'

He took a chair, and seated himself nearly opposite to me.

'My lord,' said I, 'I have seen the person who alarmed me so much a short time since, the blind lady, again, upon last night.' His face, upon which my eyes were fixed, turned pale; he hesitated for a moment, and then said:

'And did you, pray, madam, so totally forget or spurn my express command, as to enter that portion of the house from which your promise, I might say your oath, excluded you? – answer me that!' he added fiercely.

'My lord,' said I, 'I have neither forgotten your *commands*, since such they were, nor disobeyed them. I was, last night, wakened from my sleep, as I lay in my own chamber, and accosted by the person whom I have mentioned. How she found access to the room I cannot pretend to say.'

'Ha! this must be looked to,' said he, half reflectively; 'and pray,' added he, quickly, while in turn he fixed his eyes upon me, 'what did this person say? since some comment upon her communication forms, no doubt, the sequel to your preface.'

'Your lordship is not mistaken,' said I; 'her statement was so extraordinary that I could not think of withholding it from you. She told me, my lord, that you had a wife living at the time you married me, and that she was that wife.'

Lord Glenfallen became ashy pale, almost livid; he made two or three efforts to clear his voice to speak, but in vain, and turning suddenly from me, he walked to the window. The horror and dismay which, in the olden time, overwhelmed the woman of Endor when her spells unexpectedly conjured the dead into her presence, were but types of what I felt when thus presented with what appeared to be almost unequivocal evidence of the guilt whose existence I had before so strongly doubted. There was a silence of some moments, during which it were hard to conjecture whether I or my companion suffered most. Lord Glenfallen soon recovered his self-command; he returned to the table, again sat down and said:

'What you have told me has so astonished me, has unfolded such a tissue of motiveless guilt, and in a quarter from which I had so little reason to look for ingratitude or treachery, that your announcement almost deprived me of speech; the person in question, however, has one excuse, her mind is, as I told you before, unsettled. You should have remembered that, and hesitated to receive as unexceptionable evidence against the honour of your husband, the ravings of a lunatic. I now tell you that this is the last time I shall speak to you upon this subject, and, in the presence of the God who is to judge me, and as I hope for mercy in the day of judgment, I swear that the charge thus brought against me is utterly false, unfounded, and ridiculous; I defy the world in any point to taint my honour; and, as I have never taken the opinion of madmen touching your character or morals, I think it but fair to require that you will evince a like tenderness for me; and now, once for all, never again dare to repeat to me your insulting suspicions, or the clumsy and infamous calumnies of fools. I shall instantly let the worthy lady who contrived this somewhat original device, understand fully my opinion upon the matter. Good morning;' and with these words he left me again in doubt, and involved in all horrors of the most agonising suspense. I had reason to think that Lord Glenfallen wreaked his vengeance upon the author of the strange story which I had heard, with a violence which was not satisfied with mere words, for old Martha, with whom I was a great favourite, while attending me in my room, told me that she feared her master had ill-used the poor blind Dutch woman, for that she had heard her scream as if the very life were leaving her, but added a request that I should not speak of what she had told me to anyone, particularly to the master.

'How do you know that she is a Dutch woman?' inquired I, anxious to learn anything whatever that might throw a light upon the history of this person, who seemed to have resolved to mix herself up in my fortunes.

'Why, my lady,' answered Martha, 'the master often calls her the Dutch hag, and other names you would not like to hear, and I am sure she is neither English nor Irish; for, whenever they talk together, they speak some queer foreign lingo, and fast enough, I'll be bound. But I ought not to talk about her at all; it might be as much as my place is worth to mention her – only you saw her first yourself, so there can be no great harm in speaking of her now.'

'How long has this lady been here?' continued I.

'She came early on the morning after your ladyship's arrival,' answered she; 'but do not ask me any more, for the master would think nothing of turning me out of doors for daring to speak of her at all, much less to you, my lady.'

I did not like to press the poor woman further, for her reluctance to speak on this topic was evident and strong. You will readily believe that upon the very slight grounds which my information afforded, contradicted as it was by the solemn oath of my husband, and derived from what was, at best, a very questionable source, I could not take any very decisive measure whatever; and as to the menace of the strange woman who had thus unaccountably twice intruded herself into my chamber, although, at the moment, it occasioned me some uneasiness, it was not, even in my eyes, sufficiently formidable to induce my departure from Cahergillagh.

A few nights after the scene which I have just mentioned, Lord Glenfallen having, as usual, early retired to his study, I was left alone in the parlour to amuse myself as best I might. It was not strange that my thoughts should often recur to the agitating scenes in which I had recently taken a part. The subject of my reflections, the solitude, the silence, and the lateness of the hour, as also the depression of spirits to which I had of late been a constant prey, tended to produce that nervous excitement which places us wholly at the mercy of the imagination. In order to calm my spirits I was endeavouring to direct my thoughts into some more pleasing channel, when I heard, or thought I heard, uttered, within a few yards of me, in an odd, half-sneering tone, the words, 'There is blood upon your ladyship's throat.' So vivid was the impression that I started to my feet, and involuntarily placed my hand upon my neck. I looked around the room for the speaker, but in vain. I went then to the room-door, which I opened, and peered into the passage, nearly faint with horror lest some leering, shapeless thing should greet me upon the threshold. When I had gazed long enough to assure myself that no strange object was within sight, 'I have been too much of a rake lately; I am racking out my nerves,' said I, speaking aloud, with a view to reassure myself. I rang the bell, and, attended by old Martha, I retired to settle for the night. While the servant was – as was her custom – arranging the lamp which I have already stated always burned during the night in my chamber, I was employed in undressing, and, in doing so, I had recourse to a large looking-glass which occupied a considerable portion of the wall in which it was fixed, rising from the ground to a height of about six feet – this mirror filled the space of a large panel in the wainscoting opposite the foot of the bed. I had hardly been before it for the lapse of a minute when something like a black pall was slowly waved between me and it.

'Oh, God! there it is,' I exclaimed, wildly. 'I have seen it again, Martha – the black cloth.'

'God be merciful to us, then!' answered she, tremulously crossing herself. 'Some misfortune is over us.'

'No, no, Martha,' said I, almost instantly recovering my collectedness; for, although of a nervous temperament, I had never been superstitious. 'I do not believe in omens. You know I saw, or fancied I saw, this thing before, and nothing followed.'

'The Dutch lady came the next morning,' replied she.

'But surely her coming scarcely deserved such a dreadful warning,' I replied.

'She is a strange woman, my lady,' said Martha; 'and she is not *gone* yet – mark my words.'

'Well, well, Martha,' said I, 'I have not wit enough to change your opinions, nor inclination to alter mine; so I will talk no more of the matter. Good-night,' and so I was left to my reflections. After lying for about an hour awake, I at length fell into a kind of doze; but my imagination was still busy, for I was startled from this unrefreshing sleep by fancying that I heard a voice close to my face exclaim as before: 'There is blood upon your ladyship's throat.' The words were instantly followed by a loud burst of laughter. Quaking with horror, I awakened, and heard my husband enter the room. Even this was a relief. Scared as I was, however, by the tricks which my imagination had played me, I preferred remaining silent, and pretending to sleep, to attempting to engage my husband in conversation, for I well knew that his mood was such, that his words would not, in all probability, convey anything that had not better be unsaid and unheard.

Lord Glenfallen went into his dressing-room, which lay upon the right-hand side of the bed. The door lying open, I could see him by himself, at full length upon a sofa, and, in about half an hour, I became aware, by his deep and regularly drawn respiration, that he was fast asleep. When slumber refuses to visit one, there is something peculiarly irritating, not to the temper, but to the nerves, in the consciousness that someone is in your immediate presence, actually enjoying the boon which you are seeking in vain; at least, I have always found it so, and never more than upon the present occasion. A thousand annoying imaginations harassed and excited me; every object which I looked upon, though ever so familiar, seemed to have acquired a strange phantom-like character, the varying shadows thrown by the flickering of the lamplight, seemed shaping themselves into grotesque and unearthly forms, and whenever my eyes wandered to the sleeping figure of my husband, his features appeared to undergo the strangest and most demoniacal contortions. Hour after hour was told by the old clock, and each succeeding one found me, if possible, less inclined to sleep than its predecessor. It was now considerably past three; my eyes, in their involuntary wanderings, happened to alight upon the large mirror which was, as I have said, fixed in the wall opposite the foot of the bed. A view of it was commanded from where I lay, through the curtains. As I gazed fixedly upon it, I thought I perceived the broad sheet of glass shifting its position in relation to the bed; I riveted my eyes upon it with intense scrutiny; it was no deception, the mirror, as if acting of its own impulse, moved slowly aside, and disclosed a dark aperture in the wall, nearly as large as an ordinary door; a figure evidently stood in this, but the light was too dim to define it accurately. It stepped cautiously into the chamber, and with so little noise, that had I not actually seen it, I do not think I should have been aware of its presence. It was arrayed in a kind of woollen night-dress, and a white handkerchief or cloth was bound tightly about the head; I had no difficulty, in spite of the strangeness of the attire, in recognising the blind woman whom I so much dreaded. She stooped down, bringing her head nearly to the ground, and in that attitude she remained motionless for some moments, no doubt in order to ascertain if any suspicious sound were stirring. She was apparently satisfied by her observations, for she immediately recommenced her silent progress towards a ponderous mahogany dressing-table of my husband's. When she had reached it, she paused again, and appeared to listen attentively for some minutes; she then noiselessly opened one of the drawers, from which, having groped for some time, she took something, which I soon perceived to be a case of razors. She opened it, and tried the edge of each of the two instruments upon the skin of her hand; she quickly selected one, which she fixed firmly in her grasp. She now stooped down as before, and having listened for a time, she, with the hand that was disengaged, groped her way into the dressing-room where Lord Glenfallen lay fast asleep. I was fixed as if in the tremendous spell of a nightmare. I could not stir even a finger; I could not lift my voice; I could not even breathe; and though I expected every moment to see the sleeping man murdered, I could not even close my eyes to shut out the horrible spectacle, which I had not the power to avert. I saw the woman approach the sleeping figure, she laid the unoccupied hand lightly along his clothes, and having thus ascertained his identity, she, after a brief interval, turned back and again entered my chamber; here she bent down again to listen.

I had now not a doubt but that the razor was intended for my throat; yet the terrific fascination which had locked all my powers so long, still continued to bind me fast. I felt that my life depended upon the slightest ordinary exertion, and yet I could not stir one joint from the position in which I lay, nor even make noise enough to waken Lord Glenfallen. The murderous woman now, with long, silent steps, approached the bed; my very heart seemed turning to ice; her left hand, that which was disengaged, was upon the pillow; she gradually slid it forward towards my head, and in an instant, with the speed of lightning, it was clutched in my hair, while, with the other hand, she dashed the razor at my throat. A slight inaccuracy saved me from instant death; the blow fell short, the point of the razor grazing my throat. In a moment, I know not how, I found myself at the other side of the bed, uttering shriek after shriek; the wretch was, however, determined if possible to murder me. Scrambling along by the curtains, she rushed round the bed towards me; I seized the handle of the door to make my escape. It was, however, fastened. At all events, I could not open it. From the mere instinct of recoiling terror, I shrunk back into a corner. She was now within a yard of me. Her hand was upon my face. I closed my eyes fast, expecting never to open them again, when a blow, inflicted from behind by a strong arm, stretched the monster senseless at my feet. At the same moment the door opened, and several domestics, alarmed by my cries, entered the apartment.

I do not recollect what followed, for I fainted. One swoon succeeded another, so long and death-like, that my life was considered very doubtful. At about ten o'clock, however, I sunk into a deep and refreshing sleep, from which I was awakened at about two, that I might swear my deposition before a magistrate, who attended for that purpose. I accordingly did so, as did also Lord Glenfallen, and the woman was fully committed to stand her trial at the ensuing assizes. I shall never forget the scene which the examination of the blind woman and of the other parties afforded.

She was brought into the room in the custody of two servants. She wore a kind of flannel wrapper which had not been changed since the night before. It was torn and soiled, and here and there smeared with blood, which had flowed in large quantities from a wound in her head. The white handkerchief had fallen off in the scuffle, and her grizzled hair fell in masses about her wild and deadly pale countenance.

She appeared perfectly composed, however, and the only regret she expressed throughout, was at not having succeeded in her attempt, the object of which she did not pretend to conceal. On being asked her name, she called herself the Countess Glenfallen, and refused to give any other title.

'The woman's name is Flora Van-Kemp,' said Lord Glenfallen.

'It *was*, it *was*, you perjured traitor and cheat!' screamed the woman; and then there followed a volley of words in some foreign language. 'Is there a magistrate here?' she resumed; 'I am Lord Glenfallen's wife – I'll prove it – write down my words. I am willing to be hanged or burned, so *he* meets his deserts. I did try to kill that doll of his; but it was he who put it into my head to do it – two wives were too many; I was to murder her, or she was to hang me; listen to all I have to say.'

Here Lord Glenfallen interrupted.

'I think, sir,' said he, addressing the magistrate, 'that we had better proceed to business; this unhappy woman's furious recriminations but waste our time. If she refuses to answer your questions, you had better, I presume, take my depositions.'

'And are you going to swear away my life, you black-perjured murderer?' shrieked the woman. 'Sir, sir, sir, you must hear me,' she continued, addressing the magistrate; 'I can convict him – he bid me murder that girl, and then, when I failed, he came behind me, and struck me down, and now he wants to swear away my life. Take down all I say.'

'If it is your intention,' said the magistrate, 'to confess the crime with which you stand charged, you may, upon producing sufficient evidence, criminate whom you please.'

'Evidence! – I have no evidence but myself,' said the woman. 'I will swear it all – write down my testimony – write it down, I say – we shall hang side by side, my brave lord – all your own handy-work, my gentle husband.' This was followed by a low, insolent, and sneering laugh, which, from one in her situation, was sufficiently horrible.

'I will not at present hear anything,' replied he, 'but distinct answers to the questions which I shall put to you upon this matter.'

'Then you shall hear nothing,' replied she sullenly, and no inducement or intimidation could bring her to speak again.

Lord Glenfallen's deposition and mine were then given, as also those of the servants who had entered the room at the moment of my rescue. The magistrate then intimated that she was committed, and must proceed directly to gaol, whither she was brought in a carriage; of Lord Glenfallen's, for his lordship was naturally by no means indifferent to the effect which her vehement accusations against himself might produce, if uttered before every chance hearer whom she might meet with between Cahergillagh and the place of confinement whither she was despatched.

During the time which intervened between the committal and the trial of the prisoner, Lord Glenfallen seemed to suffer agonies of mind which baffle all description; he hardly ever slept, and when he did, his slumbers seemed but the instruments of new tortures, and his waking hours were, if possible, exceeded in intensity of terrors by the dreams which disturbed his sleep. Lord Glenfallen rested, if to lie in the mere attitude of repose were to do so, in his dressing-room, and thus I had an opportunity of witnessing, far oftener than I wished it, the fearful workings of his mind. His agony often broke out into such fearful paroxysms that delirium and total loss of reason appeared to be impending. He frequently spoke of flying from the country, and bringing with him all the witnesses of the appalling scene upon which the prosecution was founded; then, again, he would fiercely lament that the blow which he had inflicted had not ended all.

The assizes arrived, however, and upon the day appointed Lord Glenfallen and I attended in order to give our evidence. The cause was called on, and the prisoner appeared at the bar. Great curiosity and interest were felt respecting the trial, so that the court was crowded to excess.

The prisoner, however, without appearing to take the trouble of listening to the indictment, pleaded guilty, and no representations on the part of the court availed to induce her to retract her plea. After much time had been wasted in a fruitless attempt to prevail upon her to reconsider her words, the court proceeded, according to the usual form, to pass sentence. This having been done, the prisoner was about to be removed, when she said, in a low, distinct voice:

'A word – a word, my lord! – Is Lord Glenfallen here in the court?' On being told that he was, she raised her voice to a tone of loud menace, and continued:

'Hardress, Earl of Glenfallen, I accuse you here in this court of justice of two crimes, – first, that you married a second wife, while the first was living; and again, that you prompted me to the murder, for attempting which I am to die. Secure him – chain him – bring him here.'

There was a laugh through the court at these words, which were naturally treated by the judge as a violent extemporary recrimination, and the woman was desired to be silent.

'You won't take him, then?' she said; 'you won't try him? You'll let him go free?'

It was intimated by the court that he would certainly be allowed 'to go free,' and she was ordered again to be removed. Before, however, the mandate was executed, she threw her arms wildly into the air, and uttered one piercing shriek so full of preternatural rage and despair, that it might fitly have ushered a soul into those realms where hope can come no more. The sound still rang in my ears, months after the voice that had uttered it was for ever silent. The wretched woman was executed in accordance with the sentence which had been pronounced.

For some time after this event, Lord Glenfallen appeared, if possible, to suffer more than he had done before, and altogether his language, which often amounted to half confessions of the guilt imputed to him, and all the circumstances connected with the late occurrences, formed a mass of evidence so convincing that I wrote to my father, detailing the grounds of my fears, and imploring him to come to Cahergillagh without delay, in order to remove me from my husband's control, previously to taking legal steps for a final separation. Circumstanced as I was, my existence was little short of intolerable, for, besides the fearful suspicions which attached to my husband, I plainly perceived that if Lord Glenfallen were not relieved, and that speedily, insanity must supervene. I therefore expected my father's arrival, or at least a letter to announce it, with indescribable impatience.

About a week after the execution had taken place, Lord Glenfallen one morning met me with an unusually sprightly air.

'Fanny,' said he, 'I have it now for the first time in my power to explain to your satisfaction everything which has hitherto appeared suspicious or mysterious in my conduct. After breakfast come with me to my study, and I shall, I hope, make all things clear.'

This invitation afforded me more real pleasure than I had experienced for months. Something had certainly occurred to tranquillize my husband's mind in no ordinary degree, and I thought it by no means impossible that he would, in the proposed interview, prove himself the most injured and innocent of men. Full of this hope, I repaired to his study at the appointed hour. He was writing busily when I entered the room, and just raising his eyes, he requested me to be seated. I took a chair as he desired, and remained silently awaiting his leisure, while he finished, folded, directed, and sealed his letter. Laying it then upon the table with the address downward, he said,

'My dearest Fanny, I know I must have appeared very strange to you and very unkind – often even cruel. Before the end of this week I will show you the necessity of my conduct – how impossible it was that I should have seemed otherwise. I am conscious that many acts of mine must have inevitably given rise to painful suspicions – suspicions which, indeed, upon one occasion, you very properly communicated to me. I have got two letters from a quarter which commands respect, containing information as to the course by which I may be enabled to prove the negative of all the crimes which even the most credulous suspicion could lay to my charge. I expected a third by this morning's post, containing documents which will set the matter for ever at rest, but owing, no doubt, to some neglect, or, perhaps, to some difficulty in collecting the papers, some inevitable delay, it has not come to hand this morning, according to my expectation. I was finishing one to the very same quarter when you came in, and if a sound rousing be worth anything, I think I shall have a special messenger before two days have passed. I have been anxiously considering with myself, as to whether I had better imperfectly clear up your doubts by submitting to your inspection the two letters which I have already received, or wait till I can triumphantly vindicate myself by the production of the documents which I have already mentioned, and I have, I think, not unnaturally decided upon the latter course. However, there is a person in the next room whose testimony is not without its value excuse me for one moment.'

So saying, he arose and went to the door of a closet which opened from the study; this he unlocked, and half opening the door, he said, 'It is only I,' and then slipped into the room and carefully closed and locked the door behind him.

I immediately heard his voice in animated conversation. My curiosity upon the subject of the letter was naturally great, so, smothering any little scruples which I might have felt, I resolved to look at the address of the letter which lay, as my husband had left it, with its face upon the table. I accordingly drew it over to me and turned up the direction. For two or three moments I could scarce believe my eyes, but there could be no mistake – in large characters were traced the words, 'To the Archangel Gabriel in Heaven.'

I had scarcely returned the letter to its original position, and in some degree recovered the shock which this unequivocal proof of insanity produced, when the closet door was unlocked, and Lord Glenfallen re-entered the study, carefully closing and locking the door again upon the outside.

'Whom have you there?' inquired I, making a strong effort to appear calm.

'Perhaps,' said he, musingly, 'you might have some objection to seeing her, at least for a time.'

'Who is it?' repeated I.

'Why,' said he, 'I see no use in hiding it – the blind Dutchwoman. I have been with her the whole morning. She is very anxious to get out of that closet; but you know she is odd, she is scarcely to be trusted.'

A heavy gust of wind shook the door at this moment with a sound as if something more substantial were pushing against it.

'Ha, ha, ha! – do you hear her?' said he, with an obstreperous burst of laughter. The wind died away in a long howl, and Lord Glenfallen, suddenly checking his merriment, shrugged his shoulders, and muttered:

'Poor devil, she has been hardly used.'

'We had better not tease her at present with questions,' said I, in as unconcerned a tone as I could assume, although I felt every moment as if I should faint.

'Humph! may be so,' said he. 'Well, come back in an hour or two, or when you please, and you will find us here.'

He again unlocked the door, and entered with the same precautions which he had adopted before, locking the door upon the inside; and as I hurried from the room, I heard his voice again exerted as if in eager parley. I can hardly describe my emotions; my hopes had been raised to the highest, and now, in an instant, all was gone – the dreadful consummation was accomplished – the fearful retribution had fallen upon the guilty man – the mind was destroyed – the power to repent was gone. The agony of the hours which followed what I would still call my *awful* interview with Lord Glenfallen, I cannot describe; my solitude was, however, broken in upon by Martha, who came to inform me of the arrival of a gentleman, who expected me in the parlour. I accordingly descended, and, to my great joy, found my father seated by the fire. This expedition upon his part was easily accounted for: my communications had touched the honour of the family. I speedily informed him of the dreadful malady which had fallen upon the wretched man.

My father suggested the necessity of placing some person to watch him, to prevent his injuring himself or others. I rang the bell, and desired that one Edward Cooke, an attached servant of the family, should be sent to me. I told him distinctly and briefly the nature of the service required of him, and, attended by him, my father and I proceeded at once to the study. The door of the inner room was still closed, and everything in the outer chamber remained in the same order in which I had left it. We then advanced to the closet-door, at which we knocked, but without receiving any answer. We next tried to open the door, but in vain – it was locked upon the inside. We knocked more loudly, but in vain. Seriously alarmed, I desired the servant to force the door, which was, after several violent efforts, accomplished, and we entered the closet. Lord Glenfallen was lying on his face upon a sofa.

'Hush!' said I, 'he is asleep.' We paused for a moment.

'He is too still for that,' said my father.

We all of us felt a strong reluctance to approach the figure.

'Edward,' said I, 'try whether your master sleeps.'

The servant approached the sofa where Lord Glenfallen lay. He leant his ear towards the head of the recumbent figure, to ascertain whether the sound of breathing was audible. He turned towards us, and said:

'My lady, you had better not wait here; I am sure he is dead!'

'Let me see the face,' said I, terribly agitated; 'you *may* be mistaken.'

The man then, in obedience to my command, turned the body round, and, gracious God! what a sight met my view. He was, indeed, perfectly dead. The whole breast of the shirt, with its lace frill, was drenched with gore, as was the couch underneath the spot where he lay. The head hung back, as it seemed, almost severed from the body by a frightful gash, which yawned across the throat. The instrument which had inflicted it was found under his body. All, then, was over; I was never to learn the history in whose termination I had been so deeply and so tragically involved.

The severe discipline which my mind had undergone was not bestowed in vain. I directed my thoughts and my hopes to that place where there is no more sin, nor danger, nor sorrow.

Thus ends a brief tale whose prominent incidents many will recognise as having marked the history of a distinguished family; and though it refers to a somewhat distant date, we shall be found not to have taken, upon that account, any liberties with the facts, but in our statement of all the incidents to have rigorously and faithfully adhered to the truth.

The Death of Halpin Frayser

Ambrose Bierce

I

For by death is wrought greater change than hath been shown. Whereas in general the spirit that removed cometh back upon occasion, and is sometimes seen of those in flesh (appearing in the form of the body it bore) yet it hath happened that the veritable body without the spirit hath walked. And it is attested of those encountering who have lived to speak thereon that a lich so raised up hath no natural affection, nor remembrance thereof, but only hate. Also, it is known that some spirits which in life were benign become by death evil altogether.

–Hali.

One dark night in midsummer a man waking from a dreamless sleep in a forest lifted his head from the earth, and staring a few moments into the blackness, said: "Catherine Larue." He said nothing more; no reason was known to him why he should have said so much.

The man was Halpin Frayser. He lived in St. Helena, but where he lives now is uncertain, for he is dead. One who practices sleeping in the woods with nothing under him but the dry leaves and the damp earth, and nothing over him but the branches from which the leaves have fallen and the sky from which the earth has fallen, cannot hope for great longevity, and Frayser had already attained the age of thirty-two. There are persons in this world, millions of persons, and far and away the best persons, who regard that as a very advanced age. They are the children. To those who view the voyage of life from the port of departure the bark that has accomplished any considerable distance appears already in close approach to the farther shore. However, it is not certain that Halpin Frayser came to his death by exposure.

He had been all day in the hills west of the Napa Valley, looking for doves and such small game as was in season. Late in the afternoon it had come on to be cloudy, and he had lost his bearings; and although he had only to go always downhill—everywhere the way to safety when one is lost—the absence of trails had so impeded him that he was overtaken by night while still in the forest. Unable in the darkness to penetrate the thickets of manzanita and other undergrowth, utterly bewildered and overcome with fatigue, he had lain down near the root of a large madroño and fallen into a dreamless sleep. It was hours later, in the very middle of the night, that one of God's mysterious messengers, gliding ahead of the incalculable host of his companions sweeping westward with the dawn line, pronounced the awakening word in the ear of the sleeper, who sat upright and spoke, he knew not why, a name, he knew not whose.

Halpin Frayser was not much of a philosopher, nor a scientist. The circumstance that, waking from a deep sleep at night in the midst of a forest, he had spoken aloud a name that he had not in memory and hardly had in mind did not arouse an enlightened curiosity to investigate the phenomenon. He thought it odd, and with a little perfunctory shiver, as if in deference to a seasonal presumption that the night was chill, he lay down again and went to sleep. But his sleep was no longer dreamless.

He thought he was walking along a dusty road that showed white in the gathering darkness of a summer night. Whence and whither it led, and why he traveled it, he did not know, though all seemed simple and natural, as is the way in dreams; for in the Land Beyond the Bed surprises cease from troubling and the judgment is at rest. Soon he came to a parting of the ways; leading from the highway was a road less traveled, having the appearance, indeed, of having been long abandoned, because, he thought, it led to something evil; yet he turned into it without hesitation, impelled by some imperious necessity.

As he pressed forward he became conscious that his way was haunted by invisible existences whom he could not definitely figure to his mind. From among the trees on either side he caught broken and incoherent whispers in a strange tongue which yet he partly understood. They seemed to him fragmentary utterances of a monstrous conspiracy against his body and soul.

It was now long after nightfall, yet the interminable forest through which he journeyed was lit with a wan glimmer having no point of diffusion, for in its mysterious lumination nothing cast a shadow. A shallow pool in the guttered depression of an old wheel rut, as from a recent rain, met his eye with a crimson gleam. He stooped and plunged his hand into it. It stained his fingers; it was blood! Blood, he then observed, was about him everywhere. The weeds growing rankly by the roadside showed it in blots and splashes on their big, broad leaves. Patches of dry dust between the wheelways were pitted and spattered as with a red rain. Defiling the trunks of the trees were broad maculations of crimson, and blood dripped like dew from their foliage.

All this he observed with a terror which seemed not incompatible with the fulfillment of a natural expectation. It seemed to him that it was all in expiation of some crime which, though conscious of his guilt, he could not rightly remember. To the menaces and mysteries of his surroundings the consciousness was an added horror. Vainly he sought by tracing life backward in memory, to reproduce the moment of his sin; scenes and incidents came crowding tumultuously into his mind, one picture effacing another, or commingling with it in confusion and obscurity, but nowhere could he catch a glimpse of what he sought. The failure augmented his terror; he felt as one who has murdered in the dark, not knowing whom nor why. So frightful was the situation—the mysterious light burned with so silent and awful a menace; the noxious plants, the trees that by common consent are invested with a melancholy or baleful character, so openly in his sight conspired against his peace; from overhead and all about came so audible and startling whispers and the sighs of creatures so obviously not of earth—that he could endure it no longer, and with a great effort to break some malign spell that bound his faculties to silence and inaction, he shouted with the full strength of his lungs! His voice broken, it seemed, into an infinite multitude of unfamiliar sounds, went babbling and stammering away into the distant reaches of the forest, died into silence, and all was as before. But he had made a beginning at resistance and was encouraged. He said:

"I will not submit unheard. There may be powers that are not malignant traveling this accursed road. I shall leave them a record and an appeal. I shall relate my wrongs, the persecutions that I endure—I, a helpless mortal, a penitent, an unoffending poet!" Halpin Frayser was a poet only as he was a penitent: in his dream.

Taking from his clothing a small red-leather pocketbook, one-half of which was leaved for memoranda, he discovered that he was without a pencil. He broke a twig from a bush, dipped it into a pool of blood and wrote rapidly. He had hardly touched the paper with the point of his twig when a low, wild peal of laughter broke out at a measureless distance away, and growing ever louder, seemed approaching ever nearer; a soulless, heartless, and unjoyous laugh, like that of the loon, solitary by the lakeside at midnight; a laugh which culminated in an unearthly shout close at hand, then died away by slow gradations, as if the accursed being that uttered it had withdrawn over the verge of the world whence it had come. But the man felt that this was not so—that it was near by and had not moved.

A strange sensation began slowly to take possession of his body and his mind. He could not have said which, if any, of his senses was affected; he felt it rather as a consciousness—a mysterious mental assurance of some overpowering presence—some supernatural malevolence different in kind from the invisible existences that swarmed about him, and superior to them in power. He knew that it had uttered that hideous laugh. And now it seemed to be approaching him; from what direction he did not know—dared not conjecture. All his former fears were forgotten or merged in the gigantic terror that now held him in thrall. Apart from that, he had but one thought: to complete his written appeal to the benign powers who, traversing the haunted wood, might some time rescue him if he should be denied the blessing of annihilation. He wrote with terrible rapidity, the twig in his fingers rilling blood without renewal; but in the middle of a sentence his hands denied their service to his will, his arms fell to his sides, the book to the earth; and powerless to move or cry out, he found himself staring into the sharply drawn face and blank, dead eyes of his own mother, standing white and silent in the garments of the grave!

II

In his youth Halpin Frayser had lived with his parents in Nashville, Tennesee. The Fraysers were well-to-do, having a good position in such society as had survived the wreck wrought by civil war. Their children had the social and educational opportunities of their time and place, and had responded to good associations and instruction with agreeable manners and cultivated minds. Halpin being the youngest and not over robust was perhaps a trifle "spoiled." He had the double disadvantage of a mother's assiduity and a father's neglect. Frayser *père* was what no Southern man of means is not—a politician. His country, or rather his section and State, made demands upon his time and attention so exacting that to those of his family he was compelled to turn an ear partly deafened by the thunder of the political captains and the shouting, his own included.

Young Halpin was of a dreamy, indolent and rather romantic turn, somewhat more addicted to literature than law, the profession to which he was bred. Among those of his relations who professed the modern faith of heredity it was well understood that in him the character of the late Myron Bayne, a maternal great-grandfather, had revisited the glimpses of the moon—by which orb Bayne had in his lifetime been sufficiently affected to be a poet of no small Colonial distinction. If not specially observed, it was observable that while a Frayser who was not the proud possessor of a sumptuous copy of the ancestral "poetical works" (printed at the family expense, and long ago withdrawn from an inhospitable market) was a rare Frayser indeed, there was an illogical indisposition to honor the great deceased in the person of his spiritual successor. Halpin was pretty generally deprecated as an intellectual black sheep who was likely at any moment to disgrace the flock by bleating in meter. The Tennessee Fraysers were a practical folk—not practical in the popular sense of devotion to sordid pursuits, but having a robust contempt for any qualities unfitting a man for the wholesome vocation of politics.

In justice to young Halpin it should be said that while in him were pretty faithfully reproduced most of the mental and moral characteristics ascribed by history and family tradition to the famous Colonial bard, his succession to the gift and faculty divine was purely inferential. Not only had he never been known to court the muse, but in truth he could not have written correctly a line of verse to save himself from the Killer of the Wise. Still, there was no knowing when the dormant faculty might wake and smite the lyre.

In the meantime the young man was rather a loose fish, anyhow. Between him and his mother was the most perfect sympathy, for secretly the lady was herself a devout disciple of the late and great Myron Bayne, though with the tact so generally and justly admired in her sex (despite the hardy calumniators who insist that it is essentially the same thing as cunning) she had always taken care to conceal her weakness from all eyes but those of him who shared it. Their common guilt in respect of that was an added tie between them. If in Halpin's youth his mother had "spoiled" him, he had assuredly done his part toward being spoiled. As he grew to such manhood as is attainable by a Southerner who does not care which way elections go the attachment between him and his beautiful mother—whom from early childhood he had called Katy—became yearly stronger and more tender. In these two romantic natures was manifest in a signal way that neglected phenomenon, the dominance of the sexual element in all the relations of life, strengthening, softening, and beautifying even those of consanguinity. The two were nearly inseparable, and by strangers observing their manner were not infrequently mistaken for lovers.

Entering his mother's boudoir one day Halpin Frayser kissed her upon the forehead, toyed for a moment with a lock of her dark hair which had escaped from its confining pins, and said, with an obvious effort at calmness:

"Would you greatly mind, Katy, if I were called away to California for a few weeks?"

It was hardly needful for Katy to answer with her lips a question to which her telltale cheeks had made instant reply. Evidently she would greatly mind; and the tears, too, sprang into her large brown eyes as corroborative testimony.

"Ah, my son," she said, looking up into his face with infinite tenderness, "I should have known that this was coming. Did I not lie awake a half of the night weeping because, during the other half, Grandfather Bayne had come to me in a dream, and standing by his portrait—young, too, and handsome as that—pointed to yours on the same wall? And when I looked it seemed that I could not see the features; you had been painted with a face cloth, such as we put upon the dead. Your father has laughed at me, but you and I, dear, know that such things are not for nothing. And I saw below the edge of the cloth the marks of hands on your throat—forgive me, but we have not been used to keep such things from each other. Perhaps you have another interpretation. Perhaps it does not mean that you will go to California. Or maybe you will take me with you?"

It must be confessed that this ingenious interpretation of the dream in the light of newly discovered evidence did not wholly commend itself to the son's more logical mind; he had, for the moment at least, a conviction that it foreshadowed a more simple and immediate, if less tragic, disaster than a visit to the Pacific Coast. It was Halpin Frayser's impression that he was to be garroted on his native heath.

"Are there not medicinal springs in California?" Mrs. Frayser resumed before he had time to give her the true reading of the dream—" places where one recovers from rheumatism and neuralgia? Look—my fingers feel so stiff; and I am almost sure they have been giving me great pain while I slept."

She held out her hands for his inspection. What diagnosis of her case the young man may have thought it best to conceal with a smile the historian is unable to state, but for himself he feels bound to say that fingers looking less stiff, and showing fewer evidences of even insensible pain, have seldom been submitted for medical inspection by even the fairest patient desiring a prescription of unfamiliar scenes.

The outcome of it was that of these two odd persons having equally odd notions of duty, the one went to California, as the interest of his client required, and the other remained at home in compliance with a wish that her husband was scarcely conscious of entertaining.

While in San Francisco Halpin Frayser was walking one dark night along the water front of the city, when, with a suddenness that surprised and disconcerted him, he became a sailor. He was in fact "shanghaied" aboard a gallant, gallant ship, and sailed for a far countree. Nor did his misfortunes end with the voyage; for the ship was cast ashore on an island of the South Pacific, and it was six years afterward when the survivors were taken off by a venturesome trading schooner and brought back to San Francisco.

Though poor in purse, Frayser was no less proud in spirit than he had been in the years that seemed ages and ages ago. He would accept no assistance from strangers, and it was while living with a fellow survivor near the town of St. Helena, awaiting news and remittances from home, that he had gone gunning and dreaming.

III

The apparition confronting the dreamer in the haunted wood—the thing so like, yet so unlike his mother—was horrible! It stirred no love nor longing in his heart; it came unattended with pleasant memories of a golden past—inspired no sentiment of any kind; all the finer emotions were swallowed up in fear. He tried to turn and run from before it, but his legs were as lead; he was unable to lift his feet from the ground. His arms hung helpless at his sides; of his eyes only he retained control, and these he dared not remove from the lusterless orbs of the apparition, which he knew was not a soul without a body, but that most dreadful of all existences infesting that haunted wood—a body without a soul! In its blank stare was neither love, nor pity, nor intelligence—nothing to which to address an appeal for mercy. "An appeal will not lie," he thought, with an absurd reversion to professional slang, making the situation more horrible, as the fire of a cigar might light up a tomb.

For a time, which seemed so long that the world grew gray with age and sin, and the haunted forest, having fulfilled its purpose in this monstrous culmination of its terrors, vanished out of his consciousness with all its sights and sounds, the apparition stood within a pace, regarding him with the mindless malevolence of a wild brute; then thrust its hands forward and sprang upon him with appalling ferocity! The act released his physical energies without unfettering his will; his mind was still spellbound, but his powerful body and agile limbs, endowed with a blind, insensate life of their own, resisted stoutly and well. For an instant he seemed to see this unnatural contest between a dead intelligence and a breathing mechanism only as a spectator—such fancies are in dreams; then he regained his identity almost as if by a leap forward into his body, and the straining automaton had a directing will as alert and fierce as that of its hideous antagonist.

But what mortal can cope with a creature of his dream? The imagination creating the enemy is already vanquished; the combat's result is the combat's cause. Despite his struggles—despite his strength and activity, which seemed wasted in a void, he felt the cold fingers close upon his throat. Borne backward to the earth, he saw above him the dead and drawn face within a hand's breadth of his own, and then all was black. A sound as of the beating of distant drums—a murmur of swarming voices, a sharp, far cry signing all to silence, and Halpin Frayser dreamed that he was dead.

IV

A warm, clear night had been followed by a morning of drenching fog. At about the middle of the afternoon of the preceding day a little whiff of light vapor—a mere thickening of the atmosphere, the ghost of a cloud—had been observed clinging to the western side of Mount St. Helena, away up along the barren altitudes near the summit. It was so thin, so diaphanous, so like a fancy made visible, that one would have said: "Look quickly! in a moment it will be gone."

In a moment it was visibly larger and denser. While with one edge it clung to the mountain, with the other it reached farther and farther out into the air above the lower slopes. At the same time it extended itself to north and south, joining small patches of mist that appeared to come out of the mountain-side on exactly the same level, with an intelligent design to be absorbed. And so it grew and grew until the summit was shut out of view from the valley, and over the valley itself was an ever-extending canopy, opaque and gray. At Calistoga, which lies near the head of the valley and the foot of the mountain, there were a starless night and a sunless morning. The fog, sinking into the valley, had reached southward, swallowing up ranch after ranch, until it had blotted out the town of St. Helena, nine miles away. The dust in the road was laid; trees were adrip with moisture; birds sat silent in their coverts; the morning light was wan and ghastly, with neither color nor fire.

Two men left the town of St. Helena at the first glimmer of dawn, and walked along the road northward up the valley toward Calistoga. They carried guns on their shoulders, yet no one having knowledge of such matters could have mistaken them for hunters of bird or beast. They were a deputy sheriff from Napa and a detective from San Francisco—Holker and Jaralson, respectively. Their business was man-hunting.

"How far is it?" inquired Holker, as they strode along, their feet stirring white the dust beneath the damp surface of the road.

"The White Church? Only a half mile farther," the other answered. "By the way," he added, "it is neither white nor a church; it is an abandoned schoolhouse, gray with age and neglect. Religious services were once held in it when it—was white, and there is a graveyard that would delight a poet. Can you guess why I sent for you, and told you to come heeled?"

"Oh, I never have bothered you about things of that kind. I've always found you communicative when the time came. But if I may hazard a guess, you want me to help you arrest one of the corpses in the graveyard."

"You remember Branscom?" said Jaralson, treating his companion's wit with the inattention that it deserved.

"The chap who cut his wife's throat? I ought; I wasted a week's work on him and had my expenses for my trouble. There is a reward of five hundred dollars, but none of us ever got a sight of him. You don't mean to say——"

"Yes, I do. He has been under the noses of you fellows all the time. He comes by night to the old graveyard at the White Church."

"The devil! That's where they buried his wife."

"Well, you fellows might have had sense enough to suspect that he would return to her grave some time."

"The very last place that anyone would have expected him to return to."

"But you had exhausted all the other places. Learning your failure at them, I 'laid for him' there."

"And you found him?"

"Damn it! he found *me*. The rascal got the drop on me—regularly held me up and made me travel. It's God's mercy that he didn't go through me. Oh, he's a good one, and I fancy the half of that reward is enough for me if you're needy."

Holker laughed good humoredly, and explained that his creditors were never more importunate.

"I wanted merely to show you the ground, and arrange a plan with you," the detective explained. "I thought it as well for us to be heeled, even in daylight."

"The man must be insane," said the deputy sheriff. "The reward is for his capture and conviction. If he's mad he won't be convicted."

Mr. Holker was so profoundly affected by that possible failure of justice that he involuntarily stopped in the middle of the road, then resumed his walk with abated zeal.

"Well, he looks it," assented Jaralson. "I'm bound to admit that a more unshaven, unshorn, unkempt, and uneverything wretch I never saw outside the ancient and honorable order of tramps. But I've gone in for him, and can't make up my mind to let go. There's glory in it for us, anyhow. Not another soul knows that he is this side of the Mountains of the Moon."

"All right," Holker said; "we will go and view the ground," and he added, in the words of a once favorite inscription for tombstones: "'where you must shortly lie'—I mean, if old Branscom ever gets tired of you and your impertinent intrusion. By the way, I heard the other day that 'Branscom' was not his real name."

"What is?"

"I can't recall it. I had lost all interest in the wretch, and it did not fix itself in my memory—something like Pardee. The woman whose throat he had the bad taste to cut was a widow when he met her. She had come to California to look up some relatives—there are persons who will do that sometimes. But you know all that."

"Naturally."

"But not knowing the right name, by what happy inspiration did you find the right grave? The man who told me what the name was said it had been cut on the headboard."

"I don't know the right grave." Jaralson was apparently a trifle reluctant to admit his ignorance of so important a point of his plan. "I have been watching about the place generally. A part of our work this morning will be to identify that grave. Here is the White Church."

For a long distance the road had been bordered by fields on both sides, but now on the left there was a forest of oaks, madroños, and gigantic spruces whose lower parts only could be seen, dim and ghostly in the fog. The undergrowth was, in places, thick, but nowhere impenetrable. For some moments Holker saw nothing of the building, but as they turned into the woods it revealed itself in faint gray outline through the fog, looking huge and far away. A few steps more, and it was within an arm's length, distinct, dark with moisture, and insignificant in size. It had the usual country-schoolhouse form—belonged to the packing-box order of architecture; had an underpinning of stones, a moss-grown roof, and blank window spaces, whence both glass and sash had long departed. It was ruined, but not a ruin—a typical Californian substitute for what are known to guide-bookers abroad as "monuments of the past." With scarcely a glance at this uninteresting structure Jaralson moved on into the dripping undergrowth beyond.

"I will show you where he held me up," he said. "This is the graveyard."

Here and there among the bushes were small inclosures containing graves, sometimes no more than one. They were recognized as graves by the discolored stones or rotting boards at head and foot, leaning at all angles, some prostrate; by the ruined picket fences surrounding them; or, infrequently, by the mound itself showing its gravel through the fallen leaves. In many instances nothing marked the spot where lay the vestiges of some poor mortal—who, leaving "a large circle of sorrowing friends," had been left by them in turn—except a depression in the earth, more lasting than that in the spirits of the mourners. The paths, if any paths had been, were long obliterated; trees of a considerable size had been permitted to grow up from the graves and thrust aside with root or branch the enclosing fences. Over all was that air of abandonment and decay which seems nowhere so fit and significant as in a village of the forgotten dead.

As the two men, Jaralson leading, pushed their way through the growth of young trees, that enterprising man suddenly stopped and brought up his shotgun to the height of his breast, uttered a low note of warning, and stood motionless, his eyes fixed upon something ahead.

As well as he could, obstructed by brush, his companion, though seeing nothing, imitated the posture and so stood, prepared for what might ensue. A moment later Jaralson moved cautiously forward, the other following.

Under the branches of an enormous spruce lay the dead body of a man. Standing silent above it they noted such particulars as first strike the attention—the face, the attitude, the clothing; whatever most promptly and plainly answers the unspoken question of a sympathetic curiosity.

The body lay upon its back, the legs wide apart. One arm was thrust upward, the other outward; but the latter was bent acutely, and the hand was near the throat. Both hands were tightly clenched. The whole attitude was that of desperate but ineffectual resistance to—what?

Near by lay a shotgun and a game bag through the meshes of which was seen the plumage of shot birds. All about were evidences of a furious struggle; small sprouts of poison-oak were bent and denuded of leaf and bark; dead and rotting leaves had been pushed into heaps and ridges on both sides of the legs by the action of other feet than theirs; alongside the hips were unmistakable impressions of human knees.

The nature of the struggle was made clear by a glance at the dead man's throat and face. While breast and hands were white, those were purple—almost black. The shoulders lay upon a low mound, and the head was turned back at an angle otherwise impossible, the expanded eyes staring blankly backward in a direction opposite to that of the feet. From the froth filling the open mouth the tongue protruded, black and swollen. The throat showed horrible contusions; not mere finger-marks, but bruises and lacerations wrought by two strong hands that must have buried themselves in the yielding flesh, maintaining their terrible grasp until long after death. Breast, throat, face, were wet; the clothing was saturated; drops of water, condensed from the fog, studded the hair and mustache.

All this the two men observed without speaking—almost at a glance. Then Holker said:

"Poor devil! he had a rough deal."

Jaralson was making a vigilant circumspection of the forest, his shotgun held in both hands and at full cock, his finger upon the trigger.

"The work of a maniac," he said, without withdrawing his eyes from the enclosing wood. "It was done by Branscom—Pardee."

Something half hidden by the disturbed leaves on the earth caught

Holker's attention. It was a red-leather pocketbook. He picked it up and opened it. It contained leaves of white paper for memoranda, and upon the first leaf was the name "Halpin Frayser." Written in red on several succeeding leaves—scrawled as if in haste and barely legible—were the following lines, which Holker read aloud, while his companion continued scanning the dim gray confines of their narrow world and hearing matter of apprehension in the drip of water from every burdened branch:

"Enthralled by some mysterious spell, I stood
In the lit gloom of an enchanted wood.
The cypress there and myrtle twined their boughs,
Significant, in baleful brotherhood.

"The brooding willow whispered to the yew;
Beneath, the deadly nightshade and the rue,
With immortelles self-woven into strange
Funereal shapes, and horrid nettles grew.

"No song of bird nor any drone of bees,
Nor light leaf lifted by the wholesome breeze:
The air was stagnant all, and Silence was
A living thing that breathed among the trees.

"Conspiring spirits whispered in the gloom,
Half-heard, the stilly secrets of the tomb.
With blood the trees were all adrip; the leaves
Shone in the witch-light with a ruddy bloom.

"I cried aloud!—the spell, unbroken still,
Rested upon my spirit and my will.
Unsouled, unhearted, hopeless and forlorn,
I strove with monstrous presages of ill!

"At last the viewless——"

Holker ceased reading; there was no more to read. The manuscript broke off in the middle of a line.

"That sounds like Bayne," said Jaralson, who was something of a scholar in his way. He had abated his vigilance and stood looking down at the body.

"Who's Bayne?" Holker asked rather incuriously.

"Myron Bayne, a chap who flourished in the early years of the nation—more than a century ago. Wrote mighty dismal stuff; I have his collected works. That poem is not among them, but it must have been omitted by mistake."

"It is cold," said Holker; "let us leave here; we must have up the coroner from Napa."

Jaralson said nothing, but made a movement in compliance. Passing the end of the slight elevation of earth upon which the dead man's head and shoulders lay, his foot struck some hard substance under the rotting forest leaves, and he took the trouble to kick it into view. It was a fallen headboard, and painted on it were the hardly decipherable words, "Catharine Larue."

"Larue, Larue!" exclaimed Holker, with sudden animation. "Why, that is the real name of Branscom—not Pardee. And—bless my soul! how it all comes to me—the murdered woman's name had been Frayser!"

"There is some rascally mystery here," said Detective Jaralson. "I hate anything of that kind."

There came to them out of the fog—seemingly from a great distance—the sound of a laugh, a low, deliberate, soulless laugh, which had no more of joy than that of a hyena night-prowling in the desert; a laugh that rose by slow gradation, louder and louder, clearer, more distinct and terrible, until it seemed barely outside the narrow circle of their vision; a laugh so unnatural, so unhuman, so devilish, that it filled those hardy man-hunters with a sense of dread unspeakable! They did not move their weapons nor think of them; the menace of that horrible sound was not of the kind to be met with arms. As it had grown out of silence, so now it died away; from a culminating shout which had seemed almost in their ears, it drew itself away into the distance, until its failing notes, joyless and mechanical to the last, sank to silence at a measureless remove.

Luella Miller

Mary Wilkins Freeman

Close to the village street stood the one-story house in which Luella Miller, who had an evil name in the village, had dwelt. She had been dead for years, yet there were those in the village who, in spite of the clearer light which comes on a vantage-point from a long-past danger, half believed in the tale which they had heard from their childhood. In their hearts, although they scarcely would have owned it, was a survival of the wild horror and frenzied fear of their ancestors who had dwelt in the same age with Luella Miller. Young people even would stare with a shudder at the old house as they passed, and children never played around it as was their wont around an untenanted building. Not a window in the old Miller house was broken: the panes reflected the morning sunlight in patches of emerald and blue, and the latch of the sagging front door was never lifted, although no bolt secured it. Since Luella Miller had been carried out of it, the house had had no tenant except one friendless old soul who had no choice between that and the far-off shelter of the open sky. This old woman, who had survived her kindred and friends, lived in the house one week, then one morning no smoke came out of the chimney, and a body of neighbors, a score strong, entered and found her dead in her bed. There were dark whispers as to the cause of her death, and there were those who testified to an expression of fear so exalted that it showed forth the state of the departing soul upon the dead face. The old woman had been hale and hearty when she entered the house, and in seven days she was dead; it seemed that she had fallen a victim to some uncanny power. The minister talked in the pulpit with covert severity against the sin of superstition; still the belief prevailed. Not a soul in the village but would have chosen the almshouse rather than that dwelling. No vagrant, if he heard the tale, would seek shelter beneath that old roof, unhallowed by nearly half a century of superstitious fear.

There was only one person in the village who had actually known Luella Miller. That person was a woman well over eighty, but a marvel of vitality and unextinct youth. Straight as an arrow, with the spring of one recently let loose from the bow of life, she moved about the streets, and she always went to church, rain or shine. She had never married, and had lived alone for years in a house across the road from Luella Miller's.

This woman had none of the garrulousness of age, but never in all her life had she ever held her tongue for any will save her own, and she never spared the truth when she essayed to present it. She it was who bore testimony to the life, evil, though possibly wittingly or designedly so, of Luella Miller, and to her personal appearance. When this old woman spoke—and she had the gift of description, although her thoughts were clothed in the rude vernacular of her native village—one could seem to see Luella Miller as she had really looked. According to this woman, Lydia Anderson by name, Luella Miller had been a beauty of a type rather unusual in New England. She had been a slight, pliant sort of creature, as ready with a strong yielding to fate and as unbreakable as a willow. She had glimmering lengths of straight, fair hair, which she wore softly looped round a long, lovely face. She had blue eyes full of soft pleading, little slender, clinging hands, and a wonderful grace of motion and attitude.

"Luella Miller used to sit in a way nobody else could if they sat up and studied a week of Sundays," said Lydia Anderson, "and it was a sight to see her walk. If one of them willows over there on the edge of the brook could start up and get its roots free of the ground, and move off, it would go just the way Luella Miller used to. She had a green shot silk she used to wear, too, and a hat with green ribbon streamers, and a lace veil blowing across her face and out sideways, and a green ribbon flyin' from her waist. That was what she came out bride in when she married

Erastus Miller. Her name before she was married was Hill. There was always a sight of "l's" in her name, married or single. Erastus Miller was good lookin', too, better lookin' than Luella. Sometimes I used to think that Luella wa'n't so handsome after all. Erastus just about worshiped her. I used to know him pretty well. He lived next door to me, and we went to school together. Folks used to say he was waitin' on me, but he wa'n't. I never thought he was except once or twice when he said things that some girls might have suspected meant somethin'. That was before Luella came here to teach the district school. It was funny how she came to get it, for folks said she hadn't any education, and that one of the big girls, Lottie Henderson, used to do all the teachin' for her, while she sat back and did embroidery work on a cambric pocket-handkerchief. Lottie Henderson was a real smart girl, a splendid scholar, and she just set her eyes by Luella, as all the girls did. Lottie would have made a real smart woman, but she died when Luella had been here about a year—just faded away and died: nobody knew what ailed her. She dragged herself to that schoolhouse and helped Luella teach till the very last minute. The committee all knew how Luella didn't do much of the work herself, but they winked at it. It wa'n't long after Lottie died that Erastus married her. I always thought he hurried it up because she wa'n't fit to teach. One of the big boys used to help her after Lottie died, but he hadn't much government, and the school didn't do very well, and Luella might have had to give it up, for the committee couldn't have shut their eyes to things much longer. The boy that helped her was a real honest, innocent sort of fellow, and he was a good scholar, too. Folks said he overstudied, and that was the reason he was took crazy the year after Luella married, but I don't know. And I don't know what made Erastus Miller go into consumption of the blood the year after he was married: consumption wa'n't in his family. He just grew weaker and weaker, and went almost bent double when he tried to wait on Luella, and he spoke feeble, like an old man. He worked terrible hard till the last trying to save up a little to leave Luella. I've seen him out in the worst storms on a wood-sled—he used to cut and sell wood—and he was hunched up on top lookin' more dead than alive. Once I couldn't stand it: I went over and helped him pitch some wood on the cart—I was always strong in my arms. I wouldn't stop for all he told me to, and I guess he was glad enough for the help. That was only a week before he died. He fell on the kitchen floor while he was gettin' breakfast. He always got the breakfast and let Luella lay abed. He did all the sweepin' and the washin' and the ironin' and most of the cookin'. He couldn't bear to have Luella lift her finger, and she let him do for her. She lived like a queen for all the work she did. She didn't even do her sewin'. She said it made her shoulder ache to sew, and poor Erastus's sister Lily used to do all her sewin'. She wa'n't able to, either; she was never strong in her back, but she did it beautifully. She had to, to suit Luella, she was so dreadful particular. I never saw anythin' like the fagottin' and hemstitchin' that Lily Miller did for Luella. She made all Luella's weddin' outfit, and that green silk dress, after Maria Babbit cut it. Maria she cut it for nothin', and she did a lot more cuttin' and fittin' for nothin' for Luella, too. Lily Miller went to live with Luella after Erastus died. She gave up her home, though she was real attached to it and wa'n't a mite afraid to stay alone. She rented it and she went to live with Luella right away after the funeral."

Then this old woman, Lydia Anderson, who remembered Luella Miller, would go on to relate the story of Lily Miller. It seemed that on the removal of Lily Miller to the house of her dead brother, to live with his widow, the village people first began to talk. This Lily Miller had been hardly past her first youth, and a most robust and blooming woman, rosy-cheeked, with curls of strong, black hair overshadowing round, candid temples and bright dark eyes. It was not six months after she had taken up her residence with her sister-in-law that her rosy color faded and her pretty curves became wan hollows. White shadows began to show in the black rings of her hair, and the light died out of her eyes, her features sharpened, and there were pathetic lines at her mouth, which yet wore always an expression of utter sweetness and even happiness. She was devoted to her sister; there was no doubt that she loved her with her whole heart, and was perfectly content in her service. It was her sole anxiety lest she should die and leave her alone.

"The way Lily Miller used to talk about Luella was enough to make you mad and enough to make you cry," said Lydia Anderson. "I've been in there sometimes toward the last when she was too feeble to cook and carried her some blanc-mange or custard—somethin' I thought she might relish, and she'd thank me, and when I asked her how she was, say she felt better than she did yesterday, and asked me if I didn't think she looked better, dreadful pitiful, and say poor Luella had an awful time takin' care of her and doin' the work—she wa'n't strong enough to do anythin'—when all the time Luella wa'n't liftin' her finger and poor Lily didn't get any care except what the neighbors gave her, and Luella eat up everythin' that was carried in for Lily. I had it real straight that she did. Luella used to just sit and cry and do nothin'. She did act real fond of Lily, and she pined away considerable, too. There was those that thought she'd go into a decline herself. But after Lily died, her Aunt Abby Mixter came, and then Luella picked up and grew as fat and rosy as ever. But poor Aunt Abby begun to droop just the way Lily had, and I guess somebody wrote to her married daughter, Mrs. Sam Abbot, who lived in Barre, for she wrote her mother that she must leave right away and come and make her a visit, but Aunt Abby wouldn't go. I can see her now. She was a real good-lookin' woman, tall and large, with a big, square face and a high forehead that looked of itself kind of benevolent and good. She just tended out on Luella as if she had been a baby, and when her married daughter sent for her she wouldn't stir one inch. She'd always thought a lot of her daughter, too, but she said Luella needed her and her married daughter didn't. Her daughter kept writin' and writin', but it didn't do any good. Finally she came, and when she saw how bad her mother looked, she broke down and cried and all but went on her knees to have her come away. She spoke her mind out to Luella, too. She told her that she'd killed her husband and everybody that had anythin' to do with her, and she'd thank her to leave her mother alone. Luella went into hysterics, and Aunt Abby was so frightened that she called me after her daughter went. Mrs. Sam Abbot she went away fairly cryin' out loud in the buggy, the neighbors heard her, and well she might, for she never saw her mother again alive. I went in that night when Aunt Abby called for me, standin' in the door with her little green-checked shawl over her head. I can see her now. 'Do come over here, Miss Anderson,' she sung out, kind of gasping for breath. I didn't stop for anythin'. I put over as fast as I could, and when I got there, there was Luella laughin' and cryin' all together, and Aunt Abby trying to hush her, and all the time she herself was white as a sheet and shakin' so she could hardly stand. 'For the land sakes, Mrs. Mixter,' says I, 'you look worse than she does. You ain't fit to be up out of your bed.'

"'Oh, there ain't anythin' the matter with me,' says she. Then she went on talkin' to Luella. 'There, there, don't, don't, poor little lamb,' says she. 'Aunt Abby is here. She ain't goin' away and leave you. Don't, poor little lamb.'

"'Do leave her with me, Mrs. Mixter, and you get back to bed,' says I, for Aunt Abby had been layin' down considerable lately, though somehow she contrived to do the work.

"'I'm well enough,' says she. 'Don't you think she had better have the doctor, Miss Anderson?'

"'The doctor,' says I, 'I think YOU had better have the doctor. I think you need him much worse than some folks I could mention.' And I looked right straight at Luella Miller laughin' and cryin' and goin' on as if she was the centre of all creation. All the time she was actin' so—seemed as if she was too sick to sense anythin'—she was keepin' a sharp lookout as to how we took it out of the corner of one eye. I see her. You could never cheat me about Luella Miller. Finally I got real mad and I run home and I got a bottle of valerian I had, and I poured some boilin' hot water on a handful of catnip, and I mixed up that catnip tea with most half a wineglass of valerian, and I went with it over to Luella's. I marched right up to Luella, a-holdin' out of that cup, all smokin'. 'Now,' says I, 'Luella Miller, 'YOU SWALLER THIS!'

"'What is—what is it, oh, what is it?' she sort of screeches out. Then she goes off a-laughin' enough to kill.

"'Poor lamb, poor little lamb,' says Aunt Abby, standin' over her, all kind of tottery, and tryin' to bathe her head with camphor.

"'YOU SWALLER THIS RIGHT DOWN,' says I. And I didn't waste any ceremony. I just took hold of Luella Miller's chin and I tipped her head back, and I caught her mouth open with laughin', and I clapped that cup to her lips, and I fairly hollered at her: 'Swaller, swaller, swaller!' and she gulped it right down. She had to, and I guess it did her good. Anyhow, she stopped cryin' and laughin' and let me put her to bed, and she went to sleep like a baby inside of half an hour. That was more than poor Aunt Abby did. She lay awake all that night and I stayed with her, though she tried not to have me; said she wa'n't sick enough for watchers. But I stayed, and I made some good cornmeal gruel and I fed her a teaspoon every little while all night long. It seemed to me as if she was jest dyin' from bein' all wore out. In the mornin' as soon as it was light I run over to the Bisbees and sent Johnny Bisbee for the doctor. I told him to tell the doctor to hurry, and he come pretty quick. Poor Aunt

Abby didn't seem to know much of anythin' when he got there. You couldn't hardly tell she breathed, she was so used up. When the doctor had gone, Luella came into the room lookin' like a baby in her ruffled nightgown. I can see her now. Her eyes were as blue and her face all pink and white like a blossom, and she looked at Aunt Abby in the bed sort of innocent and surprised. 'Why,' says she, 'Aunt Abby ain't got up yet?'

"'No, she ain't,' says I, pretty short.

"'I thought I didn't smell the coffee,' says Luella.

"'Coffee,' says I. 'I guess if you have coffee this mornin' you'll make it yourself.'

"'I never made the coffee in all my life,' says she, dreadful astonished. 'Erastus always made the coffee as long as he lived, and then Lily she made it, and then Aunt Abby made it. I don't believe I CAN make the coffee, Miss Anderson.'

"'You can make it or go without, jest as you please,' says I.

"'Ain't Aunt Abby goin' to get up?' says she.

"'I guess she won't get up,' says I, 'sick as she is.' I was gettin' madder and madder. There was somethin' about that little pink-and-white thing standin' there and talkin' about coffee, when she had killed so many better folks than she was, and had jest killed another, that made me feel 'most as if I wished somebody would up and kill her before she had a chance to do any more harm.

"'Is Aunt Abby sick?' says Luella, as if she was sort of aggrieved and injured.

"'Yes,' says I, 'she's sick, and she's goin' to die, and then you'll be left alone, and you'll have to do for yourself and wait on yourself, or do without things.' I don't know but I was sort of hard, but it was the truth, and if I was any harder than Luella Miller had been I'll give up. I ain't never been sorry that I said it. Well, Luella, she up and had hysterics again at that, and I jest let her have 'em. All I did was to bundle her into the room on the other side of the entry where Aunt Abby couldn't hear her, if she wa'n't past it—I don't know but she was—and set her down hard in a chair and told her not to come back into the other room, and she minded. She had her hysterics in there till she got tired. When she found out that nobody was comin' to coddle her and do for her she stopped. At least I suppose she did. I had all I could do with poor

Aunt Abby tryin' to keep the breath of life in her. The doctor had told me that she was dreadful low, and give me some very strong medicine to give to her in drops real often, and told me real particular about the nourishment. Well, I did as he told me real faithful till she wa'n't able to swaller any longer. Then I had her daughter sent for. I had begun to realize that she wouldn't last any time at all. I hadn't realized it before, though I spoke to Luella the way I did. The doctor he came, and Mrs. Sam Abbot, but when she got there it was too late; her mother was dead. Aunt Abby's daughter just give one look at her mother layin' there, then she turned sort of sharp and sudden and looked at me.

"'Where is she?' says she, and I knew she meant Luella.

"'She's out in the kitchen,' says I. 'She's too nervous to see folks die. She's afraid it will make her sick.'

"The Doctor he speaks up then. He was a young man. Old Doctor Park had died the year before, and this was a young fellow just out of college. 'Mrs. Miller is not strong,' says he, kind of severe, 'and she is quite right in not agitating herself.'

"'You are another, young man; she's got her pretty claw on you,' thinks I, but I didn't say anythin' to him. I just said over to Mrs. Sam Abbot that Luella was in the kitchen, and Mrs. Sam Abbot she went out there, and I went, too, and I never heard anythin' like the way she talked to Luella Miller. I felt pretty hard to Luella myself, but this was more than I ever would have dared to say. Luella she was too scared to go into hysterics. She jest flopped. She seemed to jest shrink away to nothin' in that kitchen chair, with Mrs. Sam Abbot standin' over her and talkin' and tellin' her the truth. I guess the truth was most too much for her and no mistake, because Luella presently actually did faint away, and there wa'n't any sham about it, the way I always suspected there was about them hysterics. She fainted dead away and we had to lay her flat on the floor, and the Doctor he came runnin' out and he said somethin' about a weak heart dreadful fierce to Mrs. Sam Abbot, but she wa'n't a mite scared. She faced him jest as white as even Luella was layin' there lookin' like death and the Doctor feelin' of her pulse.

"'Weak heart,' says she, 'weak heart; weak fiddlesticks! There ain't nothin' weak about that woman. She's got strength enough to hang onto other folks till she kills 'em. Weak? It was my poor mother that was weak: this woman killed her as sure as if she had taken a knife to her.'

"But the Doctor he didn't pay much attention. He was bendin' over Luella layin' there with her yellow hair all streamin' and her pretty pink-and-white face all pale, and her blue eyes like stars gone out, and he was holdin' onto her hand and smoothin' her forehead, and tellin' me to get the brandy in Aunt Abby's room, and I was sure as I wanted to be that Luella had got somebody else to hang onto, now Aunt Abby was gone, and I thought of poor Erastus Miller, and I sort of pitied the poor young Doctor, led away by a pretty face, and I made up my mind I'd see what I could do.

"I waited till Aunt Abby had been dead and buried about a month, and the Doctor was goin' to see Luella steady and folks were beginnin' to talk; then one evenin', when I knew the Doctor had been called out of town and wouldn't be round, I went over to Luella's. I found her all dressed up in a blue muslin with white polka dots on it, and her hair curled jest as pretty, and there wa'n't a young girl in the place could compare with her. There was somethin' about Luella Miller seemed to draw the heart right out of you, but she didn't draw it out of ME. She was settin' rocking in the chair by her sittin'-room window, and Maria Brown had gone home. Maria Brown had been in to help her, or rather to do the work, for Luella wa'n't helped when she didn't do anythin'. Maria Brown was real capable and she didn't have any ties; she wa'n't married, and lived alone, so she'd offered. I couldn't see why she should do the work any more than Luella; she wa'n't any too strong; but she seemed to think she could and Luella seemed to think so, too, so she went over and did all the work—washed, and ironed, and baked, while Luella sat and rocked. Maria didn't live long afterward. She began to fade away just the same fashion the others had. Well, she was warned, but she acted real mad when folks said anythin': said Luella was a poor, abused woman, too delicate to help herself, and they'd ought to be ashamed, and if she died helpin' them that couldn't help themselves she would—and she did.

"'I s'pose Maria has gone home,' says I to Luella, when I had gone in and sat down opposite her.

"'Yes, Maria went half an hour ago, after she had got supper and washed the dishes,' says Luella, in her pretty way.

"'I suppose she has got a lot of work to do in her own house to-night,' says I, kind of bitter, but that was all thrown away on Luella

Miller. It seemed to her right that other folks that wa'n't any better able than she was herself should wait on her, and she couldn't get it through her head that anybody should think it WA'N'T right.

"'Yes,' says Luella, real sweet and pretty, 'yes, she said she had to do her washin' to-night. She has let it go for a fortnight along of comin' over here.'

"'Why don't she stay home and do her washin' instead of comin' over here and doin' YOUR work, when you are just as well able, and enough sight more so, than she is to do it?' says I.

"Then Luella she looked at me like a baby who has a rattle shook at it. She sort of laughed as innocent as you please. 'Oh, I can't do the work myself, Miss Anderson,' says she. 'I never did. Maria HAS to do it.'

"Then I spoke out: 'Has to do it!' says I. 'Has to do it!' She don't have to do it, either. Maria Brown has her own home and enough to live on. She ain't beholden to you to come over here and slave for you and kill herself.'

"Luella she jest set and stared at me for all the world like a doll-baby that was so abused that it was comin' to life.

"'Yes,' says I, 'she's killin' herself. She's goin' to die just the way Erastus did, and Lily, and your Aunt Abby. You're killin' her jest as you did them. I don't know what there is about you, but you seem to bring a curse,' says I. 'You kill everybody that is fool enough to care anythin' about you and do for you.'

"She stared at me and she was pretty pale.

"'And Maria ain't the only one you're goin' to kill,' says I. 'You're goin' to kill Doctor Malcom before you're done with him.'

"Then a red color came flamin' all over her face. 'I ain't goin' to kill him, either,' says she, and she begun to cry.

"'Yes, you BE!' says I. Then I spoke as I had never spoke before. You see, I felt it on account of Erastus. I told her that she hadn't any business to think of another man after she'd been married to one that had died for her: that she was a dreadful woman; and she was, that's true enough, but sometimes I have wondered lately if she knew it—if she wa'n't like a baby with scissors in its hand cuttin' everybody without knowin' what it was doin'.

"Luella she kept gettin' paler and paler, and she never took her eyes off my face. There was somethin' awful about the way she looked at me and never spoke one word. After awhile I quit talkin' and I went home. I watched that night, but her lamp went out before nine o'clock, and when Doctor Malcom came drivin' past and sort of slowed up he see there wa'n't any light and he drove along. I saw her sort of shy out of meetin' the next Sunday, too, so he shouldn't go home with her, and I begun to think mebbe she did have some conscience after all. It was only a week after that that Maria Brown died—sort of sudden at the last, though everybody had seen it was comin'. Well, then there was a good deal of feelin' and pretty dark whispers. Folks said the days of witchcraft had come again, and they were pretty shy of Luella. She acted sort of offish to the Doctor and he didn't go there, and there wa'n't anybody to do anythin' for her. I don't know how she DID get along. I wouldn't go in there and offer to help her—not because I was afraid of dyin' like the rest, but I thought she was just as well able to do her own work as I was to do it for her, and I thought it was about time that she did it and stopped killin' other folks. But it wa'n't very long before folks began to say that Luella herself was goin' into a decline jest the way her husband, and Lily, and Aunt Abby and the others had, and I saw myself that she looked pretty bad. I used to see her goin' past from the store with a bundle as if she could hardly crawl, but I remembered how Erastus used to wait and 'tend when he couldn't hardly put one foot before the other, and I didn't go out to help her.

"But at last one afternoon I saw the Doctor come drivin' up like mad with his medicine chest, and Mrs. Babbit came in after supper and said that Luella was real sick.

"'I'd offer to go in and nurse her,' says she, 'but I've got my children to consider, and mebbe it ain't true what they say, but it's queer how many folks that have done for her have died.'

"I didn't say anythin', but I considered how she had been Erastus's wife and how he had set his eyes by her, and I made up my mind to go in the next mornin', unless she was better, and see what I could do; but the next mornin' I see her at the window, and pretty soon she came steppin' out as spry as you please, and a little while afterward Mrs. Babbit came in and told me that the Doctor had got a girl from out of town, a Sarah Jones, to come there, and she said she was pretty sure that the Doctor was goin' to marry Luella.

"I saw him kiss her in the door that night myself, and I knew it was true. The woman came that afternoon, and the way she flew around was a caution. I don't believe Luella had swept since Maria died. She swept and dusted, and washed and ironed; wet clothes and dusters and carpets were flyin' over there all day, and every time Luella set her foot out when the Doctor wa'n't there there was that Sarah Jones helpin' of her up and down the steps, as if she hadn't learned to walk.

"Well, everybody knew that Luella and the Doctor were goin' to be married, but it wa'n't long before they began to talk about his lookin' so poorly, jest as they had about the others; and they talked about Sarah Jones, too.

"Well, the Doctor did die, and he wanted to be married first, so as to leave what little he had to Luella, but he died before the minister could get there, and Sarah Jones died a week afterward.

"Well, that wound up everything for Luella Miller. Not another soul in the whole town would lift a finger for her. There got to be a sort of panic. Then she began to droop in good earnest. She used to have to go to the store herself, for Mrs. Babbit was afraid to let Tommy go for her, and I've seen her goin' past and stoppin' every two or three steps to rest. Well, I stood it as long as I could, but one day I see her comin' with her arms full and stoppin' to lean against the Babbit fence, and I run out and took her bundles and carried them to her house. Then I went home and never spoke one word to her though she called after me dreadful kind of pitiful. Well, that night I was taken sick with a chill, and I was sick as I wanted to be for two weeks. Mrs. Babbit had seen me run out to help Luella and she came in and told me I was goin' to die on account of it. I didn't know whether I was or not, but I considered I had done right by Erastus's wife.

"That last two weeks Luella she had a dreadful hard time, I guess. She was pretty sick, and as near as I could make out nobody dared go near her. I don't know as she was really needin' anythin' very much, for there was enough to eat in her house and it was warm weather, and she made out to cook a little flour gruel every day, I know, but I guess she had a hard time, she that had been so petted and done for all her life.

"When I got so I could go out, I went over there one morning. Mrs. Babbit had just come in to say she hadn't seen any smoke and she didn't know but it was somebody's duty to go in, but she couldn't help thinkin' of her children, and I got right up, though I hadn't been out of the house for two weeks, and I went in there, and Luella she was layin' on the bed, and she was dyin'.

"She lasted all that day and into the night. But I sat there after the new doctor had gone away. Nobody else dared to go there. It was about midnight that I left her for a minute to run home and get some medicine I had been takin', for I begun to feel rather bad.

"It was a full moon that night, and just as I started out of my door to cross the street back to Luella's, I stopped short, for I saw something."

Lydia Anderson at this juncture always said with a certain defiance that she did not expect to be believed, and then proceeded in a hushed voice:

"I saw what I saw, and I know I saw it, and I will swear on my death bed that I saw it. I saw Luella Miller and Erastus Miller, and Lily, and Aunt Abby, and Maria, and the Doctor, and Sarah, all goin' out of her door, and all but Luella shone white in the moonlight, and they were all helpin' her along till she seemed to fairly fly in the midst of them. Then it all disappeared. I stood a minute with my heart poundin', then I went over there. I thought of goin' for Mrs. Babbit, but I thought she'd be afraid. So I went alone, though I knew what had happened. Luella was layin' real peaceful, dead on her bed."

This was the story that the old woman, Lydia Anderson, told, but the sequel was told by the people who survived her, and this is the tale which has become folklore in the village.

Lydia Anderson died when she was eighty-seven. She had continued wonderfully hale and hearty for one of her years until about two weeks before her death.

One bright moonlight evening she was sitting beside a window in her parlor when she made a sudden exclamation, and was out of the house and across the street before the neighbor who was taking care of her could stop her. She followed as fast as possible and found Lydia Anderson stretched on the ground before the door of Luella Miller's deserted house, and she was quite dead.

The next night there was a red gleam of fire athwart the moonlight and the old house of Luella Miller was burned to the ground. Nothing is now left of it except a few old cellar stones and a lilac bush, and in summer a helpless trail of morning glories among the weeds, which might be considered emblematic of Luella herself.

The Invisible Girl

Mary Shelley

This slender narrative has no pretensions to the regularity of a story, or the development of situations and feelings; it is but a slight sketch, delivered nearly as it was narrated to me by one of the humblest of the actors concerned: nor will I spin out a circumstance interesting principally from its singularity and truth, but narrate, as concisely as I can, how I was surprised on visiting what seemed a ruined tower, crowning a bleak promontory overhanging the sea, that flows between Wales and Ireland, to find that though the exterior preserved all the savage rudeness that betokened many a war with the elements, the interior was fitted up somewhat in the guise of a summer-house, for it was too small to deserve any other name. It consisted but of the ground-floor, which served as an entrance, and one room above, which was reached by a staircase made out of the thickness of the wall. This chamber was floored and carpeted, decorated with elegant furniture; and, above all, to attract the attention and excite curiosity, there hung over the chimney-piece – for to preserve the apartment from damp a fireplace had been built evidently since it had assumed a guise so dissimilar to the object of its construction – a picture simply painted in water-colours, which deemed more than any part of the adornments of the room to be at war with the rudeness of the building, the solitude in which it was placed, and the desolation of the surrounding scenery. This drawing represented a lovely girl in the very pride and bloom of youth; her dress was simple, in the fashion of the beginning of the eighteenth century; her countenance was embellished by a look of mingled innocence and intelligence, to which was added the imprint of serenity of soul and natural cheerfulness. She was reading one of those folio romances which have so long been the delight of the enthusiastic and young; her mandolin was at her feet – her parakeet perched on a huge mirror near her; the arrangement of furniture and hangings gave token of a luxurious dwelling, and her attire also evidently that of home and privacy, yet bore with it an appearance of ease and girlish ornament, as if she wished to please. Beneath this picture was inscribed in golden letters, 'The Invisible Girl.'

Rambling about a country nearly uninhabited, having lost my way, and being overtaken by a shower, I had lighted on this dreary-looking tenement, which seemed to rock in the blast, and to be hung up there as the very symbol of desolation. I was gazing wistfully and cursing inwardly my stars which led me to a ruin that could afford no shelter, though the storm began to pelt more seriously than before, when I saw an old woman's head popped out from a kind of loophole, and as suddenly withdrawn; – a minute after a feminine voice called to me from within, and penetrating a little brambly maze that screened a door, which I had not before observed, so skilfully had the planter succeeded in concealing art with nature, I found the good dame standing on the threshold and inviting me to take refuge within. 'I had just come up from our cot hard by,' she said, 'to look after the things, as I do every day, when the rain came on – will ye walk up till it is over?' I was about to observe that the cot hard by, at the venture of a few rain drops, was better than a ruined tower, and to ask my kind hostess whether 'the things' were pigeons or crows that she was come to look after, when the matting of the floor and the carpeting of the staircase struck my eye. I was still more surprised when I saw the room above; and beyond all, the picture and its singular inscription, naming her invisible, whom the painter had coloured forth into very agreeable visibility, awakened my most lively curiosity; the result of this, of my exceeding politeness towards the old woman, and her own natural garrulity, was a kind of garbled narrative which my imagination eked out, and future inquiries rectified, till it assumed the following form.

Some years before, in the afternoon of a September day, which, though tolerably fair, gave many tokens of a tempestuous night, a gentleman arrived at a little coast town about ten miles from this place; he expressed his desire to hire a boat to carry him to the town of — about fifteen miles farther on the coast. The menaces which the sky held forth made the fishermen loathe to venture, till at length two, one the father of a numerous family, bribed by the bountiful reward the stranger promised, the other, the son of my hostess, induced by youthful daring, agreed to undertake the voyage. The wind was fair, and they hoped to make good way before nightfall, and to get into port ere the rising of the storm. They pushed off with good cheer, at least the fishermen did; as for the stranger, the deep mourning which he wore was not half so black as the melancholy that wrapt his mind. He looked as if he had never smiled – as if some unutterable thought, dark as night and bitter as death, had built its nest within his bosom, and brooded therein eternally; he did not mention his name; but one of the villagers recognised him as Henry Vernon, the son of a baronet who possessed a mansion about three miles distant from the town for which he was bound. This mansion was almost abandoned by the family; but Henry had, in a romantic fit, visited it about three years before, and Sir Peter had been down there during the previous spring for about a couple of months.

The boat did not make so much way as was expected; the breeze failed them as they got out to sea, and they were fain with oar as well as sail to try to weather the promontory that jutted out between them and the spot they desired to reach. They were yet far distant when the shifting wind began to exert its strength, and to blow with violent though unequal blasts. Night came on pitchy dark, and the howling waves rose and broke with frightful violence, menacing to overwhelm the tiny bark that dared resist their fury. They were forced to lower every sail, and take to their oars; one man was obliged to bale out the water, and Vernon himself took an oar, and rowing with desperate energy, equalled the force of the more practised boatmen. There had been much talk between the sailors before the tempest came on; now, except a brief command, all were silent. One thought of his wife and children, and silently cursed the caprice of the stranger that endangered in its effects, not only his life, but their welfare; the other feared less, for he was a daring lad, but he worked hard, and had no time for speech; while Vernon bitterly regretting the thoughtlessness which had made him cause others to share a peril, unimportant as far as he himself was concerned, now tried to cheer them with a voice full of animation and courage, and now pulled yet more strongly at the oar he held. The only person who did not seem wholly intent on the work he was about, was the man who baled; every now and then he gazed intently round, as if the sea held afar off, on its tumultuous waste, some object that he strained his eyes to discern. But all was blank, except as the crests of the high waves showed themselves, or far out on the verge of the horizon, a kind of lifting of the clouds betokened greater violence for the blast. At length he exclaimed, 'Yes, I see it! – the larboard oar! – now! if we can make yonder light, we are saved!' Both the rowers instinctively turned their heads, – but cheerless darkness answered their gaze.

'You cannot see it,' cried their companion, 'but we are nearing it; and, please God, we shall outlive this night.' Soon he took the oar from Vernon's hand, who, quite exhausted, was failing in his strokes. He rose and looked for the beacon which promised them safety; – it glimmered with so faint a ray, that now he said, 'I see it;' and again, 'it is nothing:' still, as they made way, it dawned upon his sight, growing more steady and distinct as it beamed across the lurid waters, which themselves became smoother, so that safety seemed to arise from the bosom of the ocean under the influence of that flickering gleam.

'What beacon is it that helps us at our need?' asked Vernon, as the men, now able to manage their oars with greater ease, found breath to answer his question.

'A fairy one, I believe,' replied the elder sailor, 'yet no less a true: it burns in an old tumble-down tower, built on the top of a rock which looks over the sea. We never saw it before this summer; and now each night it is to be seen, – at least when it is looked for, for we cannot see it from our village; – and it is such an out-of-the-way place that no one has need to go near it, except through a chance like this. Some say it is burnt by witches, some say by smugglers; but this I know, two parties have been to search, and found nothing but the bare walls of the tower. All is deserted by day, and dark by night; for no light was to be seen while we were there, though it burned sprightly enough when we were out at sea.'

'I have heard say,' observed the younger sailor, 'it is burnt by the ghost of a maiden who lost her sweetheart in these parts; he being wrecked, and his body found at the foot of the tower: she goes by the name among us of the "Invisible Girl".'

The voyagers had now reached the landing-place at the foot of the tower. Vernon cast a glance upward, – the light was still burning. With some difficulty, struggling with the breakers, and blinded by night, they contrived to get their little bark to shore, and to draw her up on the beach. They then scrambled up the precipitous pathway, overgrown by weeds and underwood, and, guided by the more experienced fisherman, they found the entrance to the tower; door or gate there was none, and all was dark as the tomb, and silent and almost as cold as death.

'This will never do,' said Vernon; 'surely our hostess will show her light, if not herself, and guide our darkling steps by some sign of life and comfort.'

'We will get to the upper chamber,' said the sailor, 'if I can but hit upon the broken-down steps; but you will find no trace of the Invisible Girl nor her light either, I warrant.'

'Truly a romantic adventure of the most disagreeable kind,' muttered Vernon, as he stumbled over the unequal ground; 'she of the beacon-light must be both ugly and old, or she would not be so peevish and inhospitable.'

With considerable difficulty, and after divers knocks and bruises, the adventurers at length succeeded in reaching the upper storey; but all was blank and bare, and they were fain to stretch themselves on the hard floor, when weariness, both of mind and body, conduced to steep their senses in sleep.

Long and sound were the slumbers of the mariners. Vernon but forgot himself for an hour; then throwing off drowsiness, and finding his rough couch uncongenial to repose, he got up and placed himself at the hole that served for a window – for glass there was none, and there being not even a rough bench, he leant his back against the embrasure, as the only rest he could find. He had forgotten his danger, the mysterious beacon, and its invisible guardian: his thoughts were occupied on the horrors of his own fate, and the unspeakable wretchedness that sat like a nightmare on his heart.

It would require a good-sized volume to relate the causes which had changed the once happy Vernon into the most woeful mourner that ever clung to the outer trappings of grief, as slight though cherished symbols of the wretchedness within. Henry was the only child of Sir Peter Vernon, and as much spoiled by his father's idolatry as the old baronet's violent and tyrannical temper would permit. A young orphan was educated in his father's house, who in the same way was treated with generosity and kindness, and yet who lived in deep awe of Sir Peter's authority, who was a widower; and these two children were all he had to exert his power over, or to whom to extend his affection. Rosina was a cheerful-tempered girl, a little timid, and careful to avoid displeasing her protector; but so docile, so kind-hearted, and so affectionate, that she felt even less than Henry the discordant spirit of his parent. It is a tale often told; they were playmates and companions in childhood, and lovers in after days. Rosina was frightened to imagine that this secret affection, and the vows they pledged, might be disapproved of by Sir Peter. But sometimes she consoled herself by thinking that perhaps she was in reality her Henry's destined bride, brought up with him under the design of their future union; and Henry, while he felt that this was not the case, resolved to wait only until he was of age to declare and accomplish his wishes in making the sweet Rosina his wife. Meanwhile he was careful to avoid premature discovery of his intentions, so to secure his beloved girl from persecution and insult. The old gentleman was very conveniently blind; he lived always in the country, and the lovers spent their lives together, unrebuked and uncontrolled. It was enough that Rosina played on her mandolin, and sang Sir Peter to sleep every day after dinner; she was the sole female in the house above the rank of a servant, and had her own way in the disposal of her time. Even when Sir Peter frowned, her innocent caresses and sweet voice were powerful to smooth the rough current of his temper. If ever human spirit lived in an earthly paradise, Rosina did at this time: her pure love was made happy by Henry's constant presence; and the confidence they felt in each other, and the security with which they looked forward to the future, rendered their path one of roses under a cloudless sky. Sir Peter was the slight drawback that only rendered their *tête-à-tête* more delightful, and gave value to the sympathy they each bestowed on the other. All at once an ominous personage made its appearance in Vernon

Place, in the shape of a widow sister of Sir Peter, who, having succeeded in killing her husband and children with the effects of her vile temper, came, like a harpy, greedy for new prey, under her brother's roof. She too soon detected the attachment of the unsuspicious pair. She made all speed to impart her discovery to her brother, and at once to restrain and inflame his rage. Through her contrivance Henry was suddenly despatched on his travels abroad, that the coast might be clear for the persecution of Rosina; and then the richest of the lovely girl's many admirers, whom, under Sir Peter's single reign, she was allowed, nay, almost commanded, to dismiss, so desirous was he of keeping her for his own comfort, was selected, and she was ordered to marry him. The scenes of violence to which she was now exposed, the bitter taunts of the odious Mrs Bainbridge, and the reckless fury of Sir Peter, were the more frightful and overwhelming from their novelty. To all she could only oppose a silent, tearful, but immutable steadiness of purpose: no threats, no rage could extort from her more than a touching prayer that they would not hate her, because she could not obey.

'There must be something we don't see under all this,' said Mrs Bainbridge; 'take my word for it, brother, she corresponds secretly with Henry. Let us take her down to your seat in Wales, where she will have no pensioned beggars to assist her; and we shall see if her spirit be not bent to our purpose.'

Sir Peter consented, and they all three took up their abode in the solitary and dreary-looking house before alluded to as belonging to the family. Here poor Rosina's sufferings grew intolerable. Before, surrounded by well-known scenes, and in perpetual intercourse with kind and familiar faces, she had not despaired in the end of conquering by her patience the cruelty of her persecutors; – nor had she written to Henry, for his name had not been mentioned by his relatives, nor their attachment alluded to, and she felt an instinctive wish to escape the dangers about her without his being annoyed, or the sacred secret of her love being laid bare, and wronged by the vulgar abuse of his aunt or the bitter curses of his father. But when she was taken to Wales, and made a prisoner in her apartment, when the flinty mountains about her seemed feebly to imitate the stony hearts she had to deal with, her courage began to fail. The only attendant permitted to approach her was Mrs Bainbridge's maid; and under the tutelage of her fiend-like mistress, this woman was used as a decoy to entice the poor prisoner into confidence, and then to be betrayed. The simple, kind-hearted Rosina was a facile dupe, and at last, in the excess of her despair, wrote to Henry, and gave the letter to this woman to be forwarded. The letter in itself would have softened marble; it did not speak of their mutual vows, it but asked him to intercede with his father, that he would restore her to the place she had formerly held in his affections, and cease from a cruelty that would destroy her. 'For I may die,' wrote the hapless girl, 'but marry another – never!' That single word, indeed, had sufficed to betray her secret, had it not been already discovered; as it was, it gave increased fury to Sir Peter, as his sister triumphantly pointed it out to him, for it need hardly be said that while the ink of the address was yet wet, and the seal still warm, Rosina's letter was carried to this lady. The culprit was summoned before them. What ensued none could tell; for their own sakes the cruel pair tried to palliate their part. Voices were high, and the soft murmur of Rosina's tone was lost in the howling of Sir Peter and the snarling of his sister. 'Out of doors you shall go,' roared the old man; 'under my roof you shall not spend another night.' And the words infamous seductress, and worse, such as had never met the poor girl's ear before, were caught by listening servants; and to each angry speech of the baronet, Mrs Bainbridge added an envenomed point worse than all.

More dead then alive, Rosina was at last dismissed. Whether guided by despair, whether she took Sir Peter's threats literally, or whether his sister's orders were more decisive, none knew, but Rosina left the house; a servant saw her cross the park, weeping, and wringing her hands as she went. What became of her none could tell; her disappearance was not disclosed to Sir Peter till the following day, and then he showed by his anxiety to trace her steps and to find her, that his words had been but idle threats. The truth was, that though Sir Peter went to frightful lengths to prevent the marriage of the heir of his house with the portionless orphan, the object of his charity, yet in his heart he loved Rosina, and half his violence to her rose from anger at himself for treating her so ill. Now remorse began to sting him, as messenger after messenger came back without tidings of his victim. He dared not confess his worst fears to himself; and when his inhuman sister, trying to harden her conscience by angry words, cried, 'The vile hussy has too surely made away with herself out of revenge to us,' an oath the most tremendous, and a look sufficient to make even her tremble, commanded her silence. Her conjecture, however, appeared too true: a dark and rushing stream that flowed at the extremity of the park had doubtless received the lovely form, and quenched the life of this unfortunate girl. Sir Peter, when his endeavours to find her proved fruitless, returned to town, haunted by the image of his victim, and forced to acknowledge in his own heart that he would willingly lay down his life, could he see her again, even though it were as the bride of his son – his son, before whose questioning he quailed like the veriest coward; for when Henry was told of the death of Rosina, he suddenly returned from abroad to ask the cause – to visit her grave, and mourn her loss in the groves and valleys which had been the scenes of their mutual happiness. He made a thousand inquiries, and an ominous silence alone replied. Growing more earnest and more anxious, at length he drew from servants and dependants, and his odious aunt herself, the whole dreadful truth. From that moment despair struck his heart, and misery named him her own. He fled from his father's presence; and the recollection that one whom he ought to revere was guilty of so dark a crime, haunted him, as of old the Eumenides tormented the souls of men given up to their torturings. His first, his only wish, was to visit Wales, and to learn if any new discovery had been made, and whether it were possible to recover the mortal remains of the lost Rosina, so to satisfy the unquiet longings of his miserable heart. On this expedition was he bound when he made his appearance at the village before named; and now, in the deserted tower, his thoughts were busy with images of despair and death, and what his beloved one had suffered before her gentle nature had been goaded to such a deed of woe.

While immersed in gloomy reverie, to which the monotonous roaring of the sea made fit accompaniment, hours flew on, and Vernon was at last aware that the light of morning was creeping from out its eastern retreat, and dawning over the wild ocean, which still broke in furious tumult on the rocky beach. His companions now roused themselves, and prepared to depart. The food they had brought with them was damaged by sea-water, and their hunger, after hard labour and many hours' fasting, had become ravenous. It was impossible to put to sea in their shattered boat; but there stood a fisher's cot about two miles off, in a recess in the bay, of which the promontory on which the tower stood formed one side; and to this they hastened to repair. They did not spend a second thought on the light which had saved them, nor its cause, but left the ruin in search of a more hospitable asylum. Vernon cast his eyes round as he quitted it, but no vestige of an inhabitant met his eye, and he began to persuade himself that the beacon had been a creation of fancy merely. Arriving at the cottage in question, which was inhabited by a fisherman and his family, they made a homely breakfast, and then prepared to return to the tower, to refit their boat, and, if possible, bring her round. Vernon accompanied them, together with their host and his son. Several questions were asked concerning the Invisible Girl and her light, each agreeing that the apparition was novel, and not one being able to give even an explanation of how the name had become affixed to the unknown cause of this singular appearance; though both of the men of the cottage affirmed that once or twice they had seen a female figure in the adjacent wood, and that now and then a stranger girl made her appearance at another cot a mile off, on the other side of the promontory, and bought bread; they suspected both these to be the same, but could not tell. The inhabitants of the cot, indeed, appeared too stupid even to feel curiosity, and had never made any attempt at discovery. The whole day was spent by the sailors in repairing the boat; and the sound of hammers, and the voices of the men at work, resounded along the coast, mingled with the dashing of the waves. This was no time to explore the ruin for one who, whether human or supernatural, so evidently withdrew herself from intercourse with every living being. Vernon, however, went over the tower, and searched every nook in vain. The dingy bare walls bore no token of serving as a shelter; and even a little recess in the wall of the staircase, which he had not before observed, was equally empty and desolate. Quitting the tower, he wandered in the pine wood that surrounded it, and, giving up all thought of solving the mystery, was soon engrossed by thoughts that touched his heart more nearly, when suddenly there appeared on the ground at his feet the vision of a slipper. Since Cinderella so tiny a slipper had never been seen; as plain as shoe could speak, it told a tale of elegance, loveliness, and youth. Vernon picked it up. He had often admired Rosina's singularly small foot, and his first thought was a question whether this little slipper would have fitted it. It was very strange! – it must belong to the Invisible Girl. Then there was a fairy form that kindled that light – a form of such material substance that its foot needed to be shod; and yet how shod? – with kid so fine, and of shape so exquisite, that it exactly resembled such as Rosina wore! Again the recurrence of the image of the beloved dead came forcibly across him; and a thousand home-felt associations, childish yet sweet, and lover-like though trifling, so filled Vernon's heart, that he threw himself his length on the ground, and wept more bitterly than ever the miserable fate of the sweet orphan.

In the evening the men quitted their work, and Vernon returned with them to the cot where they were to sleep, intending to pursue their voyage, weather permitting, the following morning. Vernon said nothing of his slipper, but returned with his rough associates. Often he looked back; but the tower rose darkly over the dim waves, and no light appeared. Preparations had been made in the cot for their accommodation, and the only bed in it was offered Vernon; but he refused to deprive his hostess, and, spreading his cloak on a heap of dry leaves, endeavoured to give himself up to repose. He slept for some hours; and when he awoke, all was still, save that the hard breathing of the sleepers in the same room with him interrupted the silence. He rose, and, going to the window, looked out over the now placid sea towards the mystic tower. The light was burning there, sending its slender rays across the waves. Congratulating himself on a circumstance he had not anticipated, Vernon softly left the cottage, and, wrapping his cloak round him, walked with a swift pace round the bay towards the tower. He reached it; still the light was burning. To enter and restore the maiden her shoe, would be but an act of courtesy; and Vernon intended to do this with such caution as to come unaware, before its wearer could, with her accustomed arts, withdraw herself from his eyes; but, unluckily, while yet making his way up the narrow pathway, his foot dislodged a loose fragment, that fell with crash and sound down the precipice. He sprung forward, on this, to retrieve by speed the advantage he had lost by this unlucky accident. He reached the door; he entered: all was silent, but also all was dark. He paused in the room below; he felt sure that a slight sound met his ear. He ascended the steps, and entered the upper chamber; but blank obscurity met his penetrating gaze, the starless night admitted not even a twilight glimmer through the only aperture. He closed his eyes, to try, on opening them again, to be able to catch some faint, wandering ray on the visual nerve; but it was in vain. He groped round the room; he stood still, and held his breath; and then, listening intently, he felt sure that another occupied the chamber with him, and that its atmosphere was slightly agitated by another's respiration. He remembered the recess in the staircase; but before he approached it he spoke; – he hesitated a moment what to say. 'I must believe,' he said, 'that misfortune alone can cause your seclusion; and if the assistance of a man – of a gentleman' –

An exclamation interrupted him; a voice from the grave spoke his name – the accents of Rosina syllabled, 'Henry! – is it indeed Henry whom I hear?'

He rushed forward, directed by the sound, and clasped in his arms the living form of his own lamented girl – his own Invisible Girl he called her; for even yet, as he felt her heart beat near his, and as he entwined her waist with his arm, supporting her as she almost sank to the ground with agitation, he could not see her; and, as her sobs prevented her speech, no sense but the instinctive one that filled his heart with tumultuous gladness, told him that the slender, wasted form he pressed so fondly was the living shadow of the Hebe beauty he had adored.

The morning saw this pair thus strangely restored to each other on the tranquil sea, sailing with a fair wind for L—, whence they were to proceed to Sir Peter's seat, which, three months before, Rosina had quitted in such agony and terror. The morning light dispelled the shadows that had veiled her, and disclosed the fair person of the Invisible Girl. Altered indeed she was by suffering and woe, but still the same sweet smile played on her lips, and the tender light of her soft blue eyes were all her own. Vernon drew out the slipper, and showed the cause that had occasioned him to resolve to discover the guardian of the mystic beacon; even now he dared not inquire how she had existed in that desolate spot, or wherefore she had so sedulously avoided observation, when the right thing to have been done was to have sought him immediately, under whose care, protected by whose love, no danger need be feared. But Rosina shrunk from him as he spoke, and a deathlike pallor came over her cheek, as she faintly whispered, 'Your father's curse – your father's dreadful threats!' It appeared, indeed, that Sir Peter's violence, and the cruelty of Mrs Bainbridge, had succeeded in impressing Rosina with wild and unvanquishable terror. She had fled from their house without plan or forethought – driven by frantic horror and overwhelming fear, she had left it with scarcely any money, and there seemed to her no possibility of either returning or proceeding onward. She had no friend except Henry in the wide world; whither could she go? – to have sought Henry would have sealed their fates to misery; for, with an oath, Sir Peter had declared he would rather see them both in their coffins than married. After wandering about, hiding by day, and only venturing forth at night, she had come to this deserted tower, which seemed a place of refuge. How she had lived since then she could hardly tell: she had lingered in the woods by day, or slept in the vault of the tower, an asylum none were acquainted with or had discovered: by night she burned the pinecones of the wood, and night was her dearest time; for it seemed to her as if security came with darkness. She was unaware that Sir Peter had left that part of the country, and was terrified lest her hiding-place should be revealed to him. Her only hope was that Henry would return – that Henry would never rest till he had found her. She confessed that the long interval and the approach of winter had visited her with dismay; she feared that, as her strength was failing, and her form wasting to a skeleton, that she might die, and never see her own Henry more.

An illness, indeed, in spite of all his care, followed her restoration to security and the comforts of civilised life; many months went by before the bloom revisiting her cheeks, and her limbs regaining their roundness, she resembled once more the picture drawn of her in her days of bliss before any visitation of sorrow. It was a copy of this portrait that decorated the tower, the scene of her suffering, in which I had found shelter. Sir Peter, overjoyed to be relieved from the pangs of remorse, and delighted again to see his orphan ward, whom he really loved, was now as eager as before he had been averse to bless her union with his son. Mrs Bainbridge they never saw again. But each year they spent a few months in their Welsh mansion, the scene of their early wedded happiness, and the spot where again poor Rosina had awoke to life and joy after her cruel persecutions. Henry's fond care had fitted up the tower, and decorated it as I saw; and often did he come over, with his 'Invisible Girl,' to renew, in the very scene of its occurrence, the remembrance of all the incidents which had led to their meeting again, during the shades of night, in that sequestered ruin.

No. 252 Rue M. le Prince

Ralph Adams Cram

When in May, 1886, I found myself at last in Paris, I naturally determined to throw myself on the charity of an old chum of mine, Eugene Marie d'Ardeche, who had forsaken Boston a year or more ago on receiving word of the death of an aunt who had left him such property as she possessed. I fancy this windfall surprised him not a little, for the relations between the aunt and nephew had never been cordial, judging from Eugene's remarks touching the lady, who was, it seems, a more or less wicked and witch-like old person, with a penchant for black magic, at least such was the common report.

Why she should leave all her property to d'Ardeche, no one could tell, unless it was that she felt his rather hobbledehoy tendencies towards Buddhism and occultism might some day lead him to her own unhallowed height of questionable illumination. To be sure d'Ardeche reviled her as a bad old woman, being himself in that state of enthusiastic exaltation which sometimes accompanies a boyish fancy for occultism; but in spite of his distant and repellent attitude, Mlle. Blaye de Tartas made him her sole heir, to the violent wrath of a questionable old party known to infamy as the Sar Torrevieja, the "King of the Sorcerers." This malevolent old portent, whose gray and crafty face was often seen in the Rue M. le Prince during the life of Mlle. de Tartas had, it seems, fully expected to enjoy her small wealth after her death; and when it appeared that she had left him only the contents of the gloomy old house in the Quartier Latin, giving the house itself and all else of which she died possessed to her nephew in America, the Sar proceeded to remove everything from the place, and then to curse it elaborately and comprehensively, together with all those who should ever dwell therein.

Whereupon he disappeared.

This final episode was the last word I received from Eugene, but I knew the number of the house, 252 Rue M. le Prince. So, after a day or two given to a first cursory survey of Paris, I started across the Seine to find Eugene and compel him to do the honors of the city.

Everyone who knows the Latin Quarter knows the Rue M. le Prince, running up the hill towards the Garden of the Luxembourg. It is full of queer houses and odd corners,—or was in '86,—and certainly No. 252 was, when I found it, quite as queer as any. It was nothing but a doorway, a black arch of old stone between and under two new houses painted yellow. The effect of this bit of seventeenth-century masonry, with its dirty old doors, and rusty broken lantern sticking gaunt and grim out over the narrow sidewalk, was, in its frame of fresh plaster, sinister in the extreme.

I wondered if I had made a mistake in the number; it was quite evident that no one lived behind those cobwebs. I went into the doorway of one of the new hôtels and interviewed the concierge.

No, M. d'Ardeche did not live there, though to be sure he owned the mansion; he himself resided in Meudon, in the country house of the late Mlle. de Tartas. Would Monsieur like the number and the street?

Monsieur would like them extremely, so I took the card that the concierge wrote for me, and forthwith started for the river, in order that I might take a steamboat for Meudon. By one of those coincidences which happen so often, being quite inexplicable, I had not gone twenty paces down the street before I ran directly into the arms of Eugene d'Ardeche. In three minutes we were sitting in the queer little garden of the Chien Bleu, drinking vermouth and absinthe, and talking it all over.

"You do not live in your aunt's house?" I said at last, interrogatively.

"No, but if this sort of thing keeps on I shall have to. I like Meudon much better, and the house is perfect, all furnished, and nothing in it newer than the last century. You must come out with me tonight and see it. I have got a jolly room fixed up for my Buddha. But there is something wrong with this house opposite. I can't keep a tenant in it,—not four days. I have had three, all within six months, but the stories have gone around and a man would as soon think of hiring the Cour des Comptes to live in as No. 252. It is notorious. The fact is, it is haunted the worst way."

I laughed and ordered more vermouth.

"That is all right. It is haunted all the same, or enough to keep it empty, and the funny part is that no one knows *how* it is haunted. Nothing is ever seen, nothing heard. As far as I can find out, people just have the horrors there, and have them so bad they have to go to the hospital afterwards. I have one ex-tenant in the Bicêtre now. So the house stands empty, and as it covers considerable ground and is taxed for a lot, I don't know what to do about it. I think I'll either give it to that child of sin, Torrevieja, or else go and live in it myself. I shouldn't mind the ghosts, I am sure."

"Did you ever stay there?"

"No, but I have always intended to, and in fact I came up here today to see a couple of rake-hell fellows I know, Fargeau and Duchesne, doctors in the Clinical Hospital beyond here, up by the Parc Mont Souris. They promised that they would spend the night with me some time in my aunt's house,—which is called around here, you must know, 'la Bouche d'Enfer,'—and I thought perhaps they would make it this week, if they can get off duty. Come up with me while I see them, and then we can go across the river to Véfour's and have some luncheon, you can get your things at the Chatham, and we will go out to Meudon, where of course you will spend the night with me."

The plan suited me perfectly, so we went up to the hospital, found Fargeau, who declared that he and Duchesne were ready for anything, the nearer the real "bouche d'enfer" the better; that the following Thursday they would both be off duty for the night, and that on that day they would join in an attempt to outwit the devil and clear up the mystery of No. 252.

"Does M. l'Américain go with us?" asked Fargeau.

"Why of course," I replied, "I intend to go, and you must not refuse me, d'Ardeche; I decline to be put off. Here is a chance for you to do the honors of your city in a manner which is faultless. Show me a real live ghost, and I will forgive Paris for having lost the Jardin Mabille."

So it was settled.

Later we went down to Meudon and ate dinner in the terrace room of the villa, which was all that d'Ardeche had said, and more, so utterly was its atmosphere that of the seventeenth century. At dinner Eugene told me more about his late aunt, and the queer goings on in the old house.

Mlle. Blaye lived, it seems, all alone, except for one female servant of her own age; a severe, taciturn creature, with massive Breton features and a Breton tongue, whenever she vouchsafed to use it. No one ever was seen to enter the door of No. 252 except Jeanne the servant and the Sar Torrevieja, the latter coming constantly from none knew whither, and always entering, *never leaving*. Indeed, the neighbors, who for eleven years had watched the old sorcerer sidle crab-wise up to the bell almost every day, declared vociferously that *never* had he been seen to leave the house. Once, when they decided to keep absolute guard, the watcher, none other than Maître Garceau of the Chien Bleu, after keeping his eyes fixed on the door from ten o'clock one morning when the Sar arrived until four in the afternoon, during which time the door was unopened (he knew this, for had he not gummed a ten-centime stamp over the joint and was not the stamp unbroken) nearly fell down when the sinister figure of Torrevieja slid wickedly by him with a dry "Pardon, Monsieur!" and disappeared again through the black doorway.

This was curious, for No. 252 was entirely surrounded by houses, its only windows opening on a courtyard into which no eye could look from the hôtels of the Rue M. le Prince and the Rue de l'Ecole, and the mystery was one of the choice possessions of the Latin Quarter.

Once a year the austerity of the place was broken, and the denizens of the whole quarter stood open-mouthed watching many carriages drive up to No. 252, many of them private, not a few with crests on the door panels, from all of them descending veiled female figures and men with coat collars turned up. Then followed curious sounds of music from within, and those whose houses joined the blank walls of No. 252 became for the moment popular, for by placing the ear against the wall strange music could distinctly be heard, and the sound of monotonous chanting voices now and then. By dawn the last guest would have departed, and for another year the hôtel of Mlle. de Tartas was ominously silent.

Eugene declared that he believed it was a celebration of "Walpurgisnacht," and certainly appearances favored such a fancy.

"A queer thing about the whole affair is," he said, "the fact that every one in the street swears that about a month ago, while I was out in Concarneau for a visit, the music and voices were heard again, just as when my revered aunt was in the flesh. The house was perfectly empty, as I tell you, so it is quite possible that the good people were enjoying an hallucination."

I must acknowledge that these stories did not reassure me; in fact, as Thursday came near, I began to regret a little my determination to spend the night in the house. I was too vain to back down, however, and the perfect coolness of the two doctors, who ran down Tuesday to Meudon to make a few arrangements, caused me to swear that I would die of fright before I would flinch. I suppose I believed more or less in ghosts, I am sure now that I am older I believe in them, there are in fact few things I can *not* believe. Two or three inexplicable things had happened to me, and, although this was before my adventure with Rendel in Pæstum, I had a strong predisposition to believe some things that I could not explain, wherein I was out of sympathy with the age.

Well, to come to the memorable night of the twelfth of June, we had made our preparations, and after depositing a big bag inside the doors of No. 252, went across to the Chien Bleu, where Fargeau and Duchesne turned up promptly, and we sat down to the best dinner Père Garceau could create.

I remember I hardly felt that the conversation was in good taste. It began with various stories of Indian fakirs and Oriental jugglery, matters in which Eugene was curiously well read, swerved to the horrors of the great Sepoy mutiny, and thus to reminiscences of the dissecting-room. By this time we had drunk more or less, and Duchesne launched into a photographic and Zolaesque account of the only time (as he said) when he was possessed of the panic of fear; namely, one night many years ago, when he was locked by accident into the dissecting-room of the Loucine, together with several cadavers of a rather unpleasant nature. I ventured to protest mildly against the choice of subjects, the result being a perfect carnival of horrors, so that when we finally drank our last *crème de cacao* and started for "la Bouche d'Enfer," my nerves were in a somewhat rocky condition.

It was just ten o'clock when we came into the street. A hot dead wind drifted in great puffs through the city, and ragged masses of vapor swept the purple sky; an unsavory night altogether, one of those nights of hopeless lassitude when one feels, if one is at home, like doing nothing but drink mint juleps and smoke cigarettes.

Eugene opened the creaking door, and tried to light one of the lanterns; but the gusty wind blew out every match, and we finally had to close the outer doors before we could get a light. At last we had all the lanterns going, and I began to look around curiously. We were in a long, vaulted passage, partly carriageway, partly footpath, perfectly bare but for the street refuse which had drifted in with eddying winds. Beyond lay the courtyard, a curious place rendered more curious still by the fitful moonlight and the flashing of four dark lanterns. The place had evidently been once a most noble palace. Opposite rose the oldest portion, a three-story wall of the time of Francis I, with a great wisteria vine covering half. The wings on either side were more modern, seventeenth century, and ugly, while towards the street was nothing but a flat unbroken wall.

The great bare court, littered with bits of paper blown in by the wind, fragments of packing cases, and straw, mysterious with flashing lights and flaunting shadows, while low masses of torn vapor drifted overhead, hiding, then revealing the stars, and all in absolute silence, not even the sounds of the streets entering this prison-like place, was weird and uncanny in the extreme. I must confess that already I began to feel a slight disposition towards the horrors, but with that curious inconsequence which so often happens in the case of those who are deliberately growing scared, I could think of nothing more reassuring than those delicious verses of Lewis Carroll's:—

> "Just the place for a Snark! I have said it twice,
> That alone should encourage the crew.
> Just the place for a Snark! I have said it thrice,
> What I tell you three times is true,"

—which kept repeating themselves over and over in my brain with feverish insistence.

Even the medical students had stopped their chaffing, and were studying the surroundings gravely.

"There is one thing certain," said Fargeau, "*anything* might have happened here without the slightest chance of discovery. Did ever you see such a perfect place for lawlessness?"

"And *anything* might happen here now, with the same certainty of impunity," continued Duchesne, lighting his pipe, the snap of the match making us all start. "D'Ardeche, your lamented relative was certainly well fixed; she had full scope here for her traditional experiments in demonology."

"Curse me if I don't believe that those same traditions were more or less founded on fact," said Eugene. "I never saw this court under these conditions before, but I could believe anything now. What's that!"

"Nothing but a door slamming," said Duchesne, loudly.

"Well, I wish doors wouldn't slam in houses that have been empty eleven months."

"It is irritating," and Duchesne slipped his arm through mine; "but we must take things as they come. Remember we have to deal not only with the spectral lumber left here by your scarlet aunt, but as well with the supererogatory curse of that hell-cat Torrevieja. Come on! let's get inside before the hour arrives for the sheeted dead to squeak and gibber in these lonely halls. Light your pipes, your tobacco is a sure protection against 'your whoreson dead bodies'; light up and move on."

We opened the hall door and entered a vaulted stone vestibule, full of dust, and cobwebby.

"There is nothing on this floor," said Eugene, "except servants' rooms and offices, and I don't believe there is anything wrong with them. I never heard that there was, any way. Let's go up stairs."

So far as we could see, the house was apparently perfectly uninteresting inside, all eighteenth-century work, the façade of the main building being, with the vestibule, the only portion of the Francis I work.

"The place was burned during the Terror," said Eugene, "for my great-uncle, from whom Mlle. de Tartas inherited it, was a good and true Royalist; he went to Spain after the Revolution, and did not come back until the accession of Charles X, when he restored the house, and then died, enormously old. This explains why it is all so new."

The old Spanish sorcerer to whom Mlle. de Tartas had left her personal property had done his work thoroughly. The house was absolutely empty, even the wardrobes and bookcases built in had been carried away; we went through room after room, finding all absolutely dismantled, only the windows and doors with their casings, the parquet floors, and the florid Renaissance mantels remaining.

"I feel better," remarked Fargeau. "The house may be haunted, but it don't look it, certainly; it is the most respectable place imaginable."

"Just you wait," replied Eugene. "These are only the state apartments, which my aunt seldom used, except, perhaps, on her annual 'Walpurgisnacht.' Come up stairs and I will show you a better *mise en scène.*"

On this floor, the rooms fronting the court, the sleeping-rooms, were quite small,—("They are the bad rooms all the same," said Eugene,)—four of them, all just as ordinary in appearance as those below. A corridor ran behind them connecting with the wing corridor, and from this opened a door, unlike any of the other doors in that it was covered with green baize, somewhat moth-eaten. Eugene selected a key from the bunch he carried, unlocked the door, and with some difficulty forced it to swing inward; it was as heavy as the door of a safe.

"We are now," he said, "on the very threshold of hell itself; these rooms in here were my scarlet aunt's unholy of unholies. I never let them with the rest of the house, but keep them as a curiosity. I only wish Torrevieja had kept out; as it was, he looted them, as he did the rest of the house, and nothing is left but the walls and ceiling and floor. They are something, however, and may suggest what the former condition must have been. Tremble and enter."

The first apartment was a kind of anteroom, a cube of perhaps twenty feet each way, without windows, and with no doors except that by which we entered and another to the right. Walls, floor, and ceiling were covered with a black lacquer, brilliantly polished, that flashed the light of our lanterns in a thousand intricate reflections. It was like the inside of an enormous Japanese box, and about as empty. From this we passed to another room, and here we nearly dropped our lanterns. The room was circular, thirty feet or so in diameter, covered by a hemispherical dome; walls and ceiling were dark blue, spotted with gold stars; and reaching from floor to floor across the dome stretched a colossal figure in red lacquer of a nude woman kneeling, her legs reaching out along the floor on either side, her head touching the lintel of the door through which we had entered, her arms forming its sides, with the forearms extended and stretching along the walls until they met the long feet. The most astounding, misshapen, absolutely terrifying thing, I think, I ever saw. From the navel hung a great white object, like the traditional roe's egg of the Arabian Nights. The floor was of red lacquer, and in it was inlaid a pentagram the size of the room, made of wide strips of brass. In the centre of this pentagram was a circular disk of black stone, slightly saucer-shaped, with a small outlet in the middle.

The effect of the room was simply crushing, with this gigantic red figure crouched over it all, the staring eyes fixed on one, no matter what his position. None of us spoke, so oppressive was the whole thing.

The third room was like the first in dimensions, but instead of being black it was entirely sheathed with plates of brass, walls, ceiling, and floor,—tarnished now, and turning green, but still brilliant under the lantern light. In the middle stood an oblong altar of porphyry, its longer dimensions on the axis of the suite of rooms, and at one end, opposite the range of doors, a pedestal of black basalt.

This was all. Three rooms, stranger than these, even in their emptiness, it would be hard to imagine. In Egypt, in India, they would not be entirely out of place, but here in Paris, in a commonplace *hôtel*, in the Rue M. le Prince, they were incredible.

We retraced our steps, Eugene closed the iron door with its baize covering, and we went into one of the front chambers and sat down, looking at each other.

"Nice party, your aunt," said Fargeau. "Nice old party, with amiable tastes; I am glad we are not to spend the night in *those* rooms."

"What do you suppose she did there?" inquired Duchesne. "I know more or less about black art, but that series of rooms is too much for me."

"My impression is," said d'Ardeche, "that the brazen room was a kind of sanctuary containing some image or other on the basalt base, while the stone in front was really an altar,—what the nature of the sacrifice might be I don't even guess. The round room may have been used for invocations and incantations. The pentagram looks like it. Any way it is all just about as queer and *fin de siècle* as I can well imagine.

Look here, it is nearly twelve, let's dispose of ourselves, if we are going to hunt this thing down."

The four chambers on this floor of the old house were those said to be haunted, the wings being quite innocent, and, so far as we knew, the floors below. It was arranged that we should each occupy a room, leaving the doors open with the lights burning, and at the slightest cry or knock we were all to rush at once to the room from which the warning sound might come. There was no communication between the rooms to be sure, but, as the doors all opened into the corridor, every sound was plainly audible.

The last room fell to me, and I looked it over carefully.

It seemed innocent enough, a commonplace, square, rather lofty Parisian sleeping-room, finished in wood painted white, with a small marble mantel, a dusty floor of inlaid maple and cherry, walls hung with an ordinary French paper, apparently quite new, and two deeply embrasured windows looking out on the court.

I opened the swinging sash with some trouble, and sat down in the window seat with my lantern beside me trained on the only door, which gave on the corridor.

The wind had gone down, and it was very still without,—still and hot. The masses of luminous vapor were gathering thickly overhead, no longer urged by the gusty wind. The great masses of rank wisteria leaves, with here and there a second blossoming of purple flowers, hung dead over the window in the sluggish air. Across the roofs I could hear the sound of a belated *fiacre* in the streets below. I filled my pipe again and waited.

For a time the voices of the men in the other rooms were a companionship, and at first I shouted to them now and then, but my voice echoed rather unpleasantly through the long corridors, and had a suggestive way of reverberating around the left wing beside me, and coming out at a broken window at its extremity like the voice of another man. I soon gave up my attempts at conversation, and devoted myself to the task of keeping awake.

It was not easy; why did I eat that lettuce salad at Père Garceau's? I should have known better. It was making me irresistibly sleepy, and wakefulness was absolutely necessary. It was certainly gratifying to know that I could sleep, that my courage was by me to that extent, but in the interests of science I must keep awake. But almost never, it seemed, had sleep looked so desirable. Half a hundred times, nearly, I would doze for an instant, only to awake with a start, and find my pipe gone out. Nor did the exertion of relighting it pull me together. I struck my match mechanically, and with the first puff dropped off again. It was most vexing. I got up and walked around the room. It was most annoying. My cramped position had almost put both my legs to sleep. I could hardly stand. I felt numb, as though with cold. There was no longer any sound from the other rooms, nor from without. I sank down in my window seat. How dark it was growing! I turned up the lantern. That pipe again, how obstinately it kept going out! and my last match was gone. The lantern, too, was *that* going out? I lifted my hand to turn it up again. It felt like lead, and fell beside me.

Then I awoke,—absolutely. I remembered the story of "The Haunters and the Haunted." *This* was the Horror. I tried to rise, to cry out. My body was like lead, my tongue was paralyzed. I could hardly move my eyes. And the light was going out. There was no question about that. Darker and darker yet; little by little the pattern of the paper was swallowed up in the advancing night. A prickling numbness gathered in every nerve, my right arm slipped without feeling from my lap to my side, and I could not raise it,—it swung helpless. A thin, keen humming began in my head, like the cicadas on a hillside in September. The darkness was coming fast.

Yes, this was it. Something was subjecting me, body and mind, to slow paralysis. Physically I was already dead. If I could only hold my mind, my consciousness, I might still be safe, but could I? Could I resist the mad horror of this silence, the deepening dark, the creeping numbness? I knew that, like the man in the ghost story, my only safety lay here.

It had come at last. My body was dead, I could no longer move my eyes. They were fixed in that last look on the place where the door had been, now only a deepening of the dark.

Utter night: the last flicker of the lantern was gone. I sat and waited; my mind was still keen, but how long would it last? There was a limit even to the endurance of the utter panic of fear.

Then the end began. In the velvet blackness came two white eyes, milky, opalescent, small, far away,—awful eyes, like a dead dream. More beautiful than I can describe, the flakes of white flame moving from the perimeter inward, disappearing in the centre, like a never ending flow of opal water into a circular tunnel. I could not have moved my eyes had I possessed the power: they devoured the fearful, beautiful things that grew slowly, slowly larger, fixed on me, advancing, growing more beautiful, the white flakes of light sweeping more swiftly into the blazing vortices, the awful fascination deepening in its insane intensity as the white, vibrating eyes grew nearer, larger.

Like a hideous and implacable engine of death the eyes of the unknown Horror swelled and expanded until they were close before me, enormous, terrible, and I felt a slow, cold, wet breath propelled with mechanical regularity against my face, enveloping me in its fetid mist, in its charnel-house deadliness.

With ordinary fear goes always a physical terror, but with me in the presence of this unspeakable Thing was only the utter and awful terror of the mind, the mad fear of a prolonged and ghostly nightmare. Again and again I tried to shriek, to make some noise, but physically I was utterly dead. I could only feel myself go mad with the terror of hideous death. The eyes were close on me,—their movement so swift that they seemed to be but palpitating flames, the dead breath was around me like the depths of the deepest sea.

Suddenly a wet, icy mouth, like that of a dead cuttle-fish, shapeless, jelly-like, fell over mine. The horror began slowly to draw my life from me, but, as enormous and shuddering folds of palpitating jelly swept sinuously around me, my will came back, my body awoke with the reaction of final fear, and I closed with the nameless death that enfolded me.

What was it that I was fighting? My arms sunk through the unresisting mass that was turning me to ice. Moment by moment new folds of cold jelly swept round me, crushing me with the force of Titans. I fought to wrest my mouth from this awful Thing that sealed it, but, if ever I succeeded and caught a single breath, the wet, sucking mass closed over my face again before I could cry out. I think I fought for hours, desperately, insanely, in a silence that was more hideous than any sound,—fought until I felt final death at hand, until the memory of all my life rushed over me like a flood, until I no longer had strength to wrench my face from that hellish succubus, until with a last mechanical struggle I fell and yielded to death.

*

Then I heard a voice say, "If he is dead, I can never forgive myself; I was to blame."

Another replied, "He is not dead, I know we can save him if only we reach the hospital in time. Drive like hell, *cocher*! twenty francs for you, if you get there in three minutes."

Then there was night again, and nothingness, until I suddenly awoke and stared around. I lay in a hospital ward, very white and sunny, some yellow *fleurs-de-lis* stood beside the head of the pallet, and a tall sister of mercy sat by my side.

To tell the story in a few words, I was in the Hôtel Dieu, where the men had taken me that fearful night of the twelfth of June. I asked for Fargeau or Duchesne, and by and by the latter came, and sitting beside the bed told me all that I did not know.

It seems that they had sat, each in his room, hour after hour, hearing nothing, very much bored, and disappointed. Soon after two o'clock Fargeau, who was in the next room, called to me to ask if I was awake. I gave no reply, and, after shouting once or twice, he took his lantern and came to investigate. The door was locked on the inside! He instantly called d'Ardeche and Duchesne, and together they hurled themselves against the door. It resisted. Within they could hear irregular footsteps dashing here and there, with heavy breathing. Although frozen with terror, they fought to destroy the door and finally succeeded by using a great slab of marble that formed the shelf of the mantel in Fargeau's room. As the door crashed in, they were suddenly hurled back against the walls of the corridor, as though by an explosion, the lanterns were extinguished, and they found themselves in utter silence and darkness.

As soon as they recovered from the shock, they leaped into the room and fell over my body in the middle of the floor. They lighted one of the lanterns, and saw the strangest sight that can be imagined. The floor and walls to the height of about six feet were running with something that seemed like stagnant water, thick, glutinous, sickening. As for me, I was drenched with the same cursed liquid. The odor of musk was nauseating. They dragged me away, stripped off my clothing, wrapped me in their coats, and hurried to the hospital, thinking me perhaps dead. Soon after sunrise d'Ardeche left the hospital, being assured that I was in a fair way to recovery, with time, and with Fargeau went up to examine by daylight the traces of the adventure that was so nearly fatal. They were too late. Fire engines were coming down the street as they passed the Académie. A neighbor rushed up to d'Ardeche: "O Monsieur! what misfortune, yet what fortune! It is true *la Bouche d'Enfer*—I beg pardon, the residence of the lamented Mlle. de Tartas,—was burned, but not wholly, only the ancient building. The wings were saved, and for that great credit is due the brave firemen. Monsieur will remember them, no doubt."

It was quite true. Whether a forgotten lantern, overturned in the excitement, had done the work, or whether the origin of the fire was more supernatural, it was certain that "the Mouth of Hell" was no more. A last engine was pumping slowly as d'Ardeche came up; half a dozen limp, and one distended, hose stretched through the *porte cochère,* and within only the façade of Francis I remained, draped still with the black stems of the wisteria. Beyond lay a great vacancy, where thin smoke was rising slowly. Every floor was gone, and the strange halls of Mlle. Blaye de Tartas were only a memory.

With d'Ardeche I visited the place last year, but in the stead of the ancient walls was then only a new and ordinary building, fresh and respectable; yet the wonderful stories of the old *Bouche d'Enfer* still lingered in the quarter, and will hold there, I do not doubt, until the Day of Judgment.

The Tapestried Chamber

Sir Walter Scott

The following narrative is given from the pen, so far as memory permits, in the same character in which it was presented to the author's ear; nor has he claim to further praise, or to be more deeply censured, than in proportion to the good or bad judgment which he has employed in selecting his materials, as he has studiously avoided any attempt at ornament which might interfere with the simplicity of the tale.

At the same time, it must be admitted that the particular class of stories which turns on the marvellous possesses a stronger influence when told than when committed to print. The volume taken up at noonday, though rehearsing the same incidents, conveys a much more feeble impression than is achieved by the voice of the speaker on a circle of fireside auditors, who hang upon the narrative as the narrator details the minute incidents which serve to give it authenticity, and lowers his voice with an affectation of mystery while he approaches the fearful and wonderful part. It was with such advantages that the present writer heard the following events related, more than twenty years since, by the celebrated Miss Seward of Litchfield, who, to her numerous accomplishments, added, in a remarkable degree, the power of narrative in private conversation. In its present form the tale must necessarily lose all the interest which was attached to it by the flexible voice and intelligent features of the gifted narrator. Yet still, read aloud to an undoubting audience by the doubtful light of the closing evening, or in silence by a decaying taper, and amidst the solitude of a half-lighted apartment, it may redeem its character as a good ghost story. Miss Seward always affirmed that she had derived her information from an authentic source, although she suppressed the names of the two persons chiefly concerned. I will not avail myself of any particulars I may have since received concerning the localities of the detail, but suffer them to rest under the same general description in which they were first related to me; and for the same reason I will not add to or diminish the narrative by any circumstance, whether more or less material, but simply rehearse, as I heard it, a story of supernatural terror.

About the end of the American war, when the officers of Lord Cornwallis's army, which surrendered at Yorktown, and others, who had been made prisoners during the impolitic and ill-fated controversy, were returning to their own country, to relate their adventures, and repose themselves after their fatigues, there was amongst them a general officer, to whom Miss S. gave the name of Browne, but merely, as I understood, to save the inconvenience of introducing a nameless agent in the narrative. He was an officer of merit, as well as a gentleman of high consideration for family and attainments.

Some business had carried General Browne upon a tour through the western counties, when, in the conclusion of a morning stage, he found himself in the vicinity of a small country town, which presented a scene of uncommon beauty, and of a character peculiarly English.

The little town, with its stately old church, whose tower bore testimony to the devotion of ages long past, lay amidst pastures and cornfields of small extent, but bounded and divided with hedgerow timber of great age and size. There were few marks of modern improvement. The environs of the place intimated neither the solitude of decay nor the bustle of novelty; the houses were old, but in good repair; and the beautiful little river murmured freely on its way to the left of the town, neither restrained by a dam nor bordered by a towing-path.

Upon a gentle eminence, nearly a mile to the southward of the town, were seen, amongst many venerable oaks and tangled thickets, the turrets of a castle as old as the walls of York and Lancaster, but which seemed to have received important alterations during the age of Elizabeth and her successor. It had not been a place of great size; but whatever accommodation it formerly afforded was, it must be supposed, still to be obtained within its walls. At least, such was the inference which General Browne drew from observing the smoke arise merrily from several of the ancient wreathed and carved chimney-stalks. The wall of the park ran alongside of the highway for two or three hundred yards; and through the different points by which the eye found glimpses into the woodland scenery, it seemed to be well stocked. Other points of view opened in succession – now a full one of the front of the old castle, and now a side glimpse at its particular towers, the former rich in all the bizarrerie of the Elizabethan school, while the simple and solid strength of other parts of the building seemed to show that they had been raised more for defence than ostentation.

Delighted with the partial glimpses which he obtained of the castle through the woods and glades by which this ancient feudal fortress was surrounded, our military traveller was determined to inquire whether it might not deserve a nearer view, and whether it contained family pictures or other objects of curiosity worthy of a stranger's visit, when, leaving the vicinity of the park, he rolled through a clean and well-paved street, and stopped at the door of a well-frequented inn.

Before ordering horses, to proceed on his journey, General Browne made inquiries concerning the proprietor of the château which had so attracted his admiration, and was equally surprised and pleased at hearing in reply a nobleman named, whom we shall call Lord Woodville. How fortunate! Much of Browne's early recollections, both at school and at college, had been connected with young Woodville, whom, by a few questions, he now ascertained to be the same with the owner of this fair domain. He had been raised to the peerage by the decease of his father a few months before, and, as the General learned from the landlord, the term of mourning being ended, was now taking possession of his paternal estate in the jovial season of merry, autumn, accompanied by a select party of friends, to enjoy the sports of a country famous for game.

This was delightful news to our traveller. Frank Woodville had been Richard Browne's fag at Eton, and his chosen intimate at Christ Church; their pleasures and their tasks had been the same; and the honest soldier's heart warmed to find his early friend in possession of so delightful a residence, and of an estate, as the landlord assured him with a nod and a wink, fully adequate to maintain and add to his dignity. Nothing was more natural than that the traveller should suspend a journey, which there was nothing to render hurried, to pay a visit to an old friend under such agreeable circumstances.

The fresh horses, therefore, had only the brief task of conveying the General's travelling carriage to Woodville Castle. A porter admitted them at a modern Gothic lodge, built in that style to correspond with the castle itself, and at the same time rang a bell to give warning of the approach of visitors. Apparently the sound of the bell had suspended the separation of the company, bent on the various amusements of the morning; for, on entering the court of the château, several young men were lounging about in their sporting dresses, looking at and criticizing the dogs which the keepers held in readiness to attend their pastime. As General Browne alighted, the young lord came to the gate of the hall, and for an instant gazed, as at a stranger, upon the countenance of his friend, on which war, with its fatigues and its wounds, had made a great alteration. But the uncertainty lasted no longer than till the visitor had spoken, and the hearty greeting which followed was such as can only be exchanged betwixt those who have passed together the merry days of careless boyhood or early youth.

'If I could have formed a wish, my dear Browne,' said Lord Woodville, 'it would have been to have you here, of all men, upon this occasion, which my friends are good enough to hold as a sort of holiday. Do not think you have been unwatched during the years you have been absent from us. I have traced you through your dangers, your triumphs, your misfortunes, and was delighted to see that, whether in victory or defeat, the name of my old friend was always distinguished with applause.'

The General made a suitable reply, and congratulated his friend on his new dignities, and the possession of a place and domain so beautiful.

'Nay, you have seen nothing of it as yet,' said Lord Woodville, 'and I trust you do not mean to leave us till you are better acquainted with it. It is true, I confess, that my present party is pretty large, and the old house, like other places of the kind, does not possess so much accommodation as the extent of the outward walls appears to promise. But we can give you a comfortable old-fashioned room, and I venture to suppose that your campaigns have taught you to be glad of worse quarters.'

The General shrugged his shoulders, and laughed. 'I presume,' he said, 'the worst apartment in your château is considerably superior to the old tobacco-cask in which I was fain to take up my night's lodging when I was in the Bush, as the Virginians call it, with the light corps. There I lay, like Diogenes himself, so delighted with my covering from the elements, that I made a vain attempt to have it rolled on to my next quarters; but my commander for the time would give way to no such luxurious provision, and I took farewell of my beloved cask with tears in my eyes.'

'Well, then, since you do not fear your quarters,' said Lord Woodville, 'you will stay with me a week at least. Of guns, dogs, fishing-rods, flies, and means of sport by sea and land, we have enough and to spare – you cannot pitch on an amusement but we will find the means of pursuing it. But if you prefer the gun and pointers, I will go with you myself, and see whether you have mended your shooting since you have been amongst the Indians of the back settlements.'

The General gladly accepted his friendly host's proposal in all its points. After a morning of manly exercise, the company met at dinner, where it was the delight of Lord Woodville to conduce to the display of the high properties of his recovered friend, so as to recommend him to his guests, most of whom were persons of distinction. He led General Browne to speak of the scenes he had witnessed; and as every word marked alike the brave officer and the sensible man, who retained possession of his cool judgment under the most imminent dangers, the company looked upon the soldier with general respect, as on one who had proved himself possessed of an uncommon portion of personal courage – that attribute of all others of which everybody desires to be thought possessed.

The day at Woodville Castle ended as usual in such mansions. The hospitality stopped within the limits of good order. Music, in which the young lord was a proficient, succeeded to the circulation of the bottle; cards and billiards, for those who preferred such amusements, were in readiness; but the exercise of the morning required early hours, and not long after eleven o'clock the guests began to retire to their several apartments.

The young lord himself conducted his friend, General Browne, to the chamber destined for him, which answered the description he had given of it, being comfortable, but old-fashioned. The bed was of the massive form used in the end of the seventeenth century, and the curtains of faded silk, heavily trimmed with tarnished gold. But then the sheets, pillows, and blankets looked delightful to the campaigner, when he thought of his 'mansion, the cask.' There was an air of gloom in the tapestry hangings, which, with their worn-out graces, curtained the walls of the little chamber, and gently undulated as the autumnal breeze found its way through the ancient lattice window, which pattered and whistled as the air gained entrance. The toilet, too, with its mirror, turbaned after the manner of the beginning of the century, with a coiffure of murrey-coloured silk, and its hundred strange-shaped boxes, providing for arrangements which had been obsolete for more than fifty years, had an antique, and in so far a melancholy, aspect. But nothing could blaze more brightly and cheerfully than the two large wax candles; or if aught could rival them, it was the flaming, bickering fagots in the chimney, that sent at once their gleam and their warmth through the snug apartment, which, notwithstanding the general antiquity of its appearance, was not wanting in the least convenience that modern habits rendered either necessary or desirable.

'This is an old-fashioned sleeping apartment, General,' said the young lord; 'but I hope you find nothing that makes you envy your old tobacco-cask.'

'I am not particular respecting my lodgings,' replied the General; 'yet were I to make any choice, I would prefer this chamber by many degrees to the gayer and more modern rooms of your family mansion. Believe me that, when I unite its modern air of comfort with its venerable antiquity, and recollect that it is your lordship's property, I shall feel in better quarters here than if I were in the best hotel London could afford.'

'I trust – I have no doubt – that you will find yourself as comfortable as I wish you, my dear General,' said the young nobleman; and once more bidding his guest good-night, he shook him by the hand, and withdrew.

The General once more looked round him, and internally congratulating himself on his return to peaceful life, the comforts of which were endeared by the recollection of the hardships and dangers he had lately sustained, undressed himself, and prepared for a luxurious night's rest.

Here, contrary to the custom of this species of tale, we leave the General in possession of his apartment until the next morning.

The company assembled for breakfast at an early hour, but without the appearance of General Browne, who seemed the guest that Lord Woodville was desirous of honouring above all whom his hospitality had assembled around him. He more than once expressed surprise at the General's absence, and at length sent a servant to make inquiry after him. The man brought back information that General Browne had been walking abroad since an early hour of the morning, in defiance of the weather, which was misty and ungenial.

'The custom of a soldier,' said the young nobleman to his friends. 'Many of them acquire habitual vigilance, and cannot sleep after the early hour at which their duty usually commands them to be alert.'

Yet the explanation which Lord Woodville thus offered to the company seemed hardly satisfactory to his own mind, and it was in a fit of silence and abstraction that he waited the return of the General. It took place near an hour after the breakfast bell had rung. He looked fatigued and feverish. His hair, the powdering and arrangement of which was at this time one of the most important occupations of a man's whole day, and marked his fashion as much as in the present time the tying of a cravat, or the want of one, was dishevelled, uncurled, void of powder, and dank with dew. His clothes were huddled on with a careless negligence, remarkable in a military man, whose real or supposed duties are usually held to include some attention to the toilet; and his looks were haggard and ghastly in a peculiar degree.

'So you have stolen a march upon us this morning, my dear General,' said Lord Woodville; 'or you have not found your bed so much to your mind as I had hoped and you seemed to expect. How did you rest last night?'

'Oh, excellently well! remarkably well! never better in my life,' said General Browne rapidly, and yet with an air of embarrassment which was obvious to his friend. He then hastily swallowed a cup of tea, and neglecting or refusing whatever else was offered, seemed to fall into a fit of abstraction.

'You will take the gun to-day, General?' said his friend and host, but had to repeat the question twice ere he received the abrupt answer, 'No, my lord; I am sorry I cannot have the opportunity of spending another day with your lordship; my post horses are ordered, and will be here directly.'

All who were present showed surprise, and Lord Woodville immediately replied, 'Post horses, my good friend! What can you possibly want with them when you promised to stay with me quietly for at least a week?'

'I believe,' said the General, obviously much embarrassed, 'that I might, in the pleasure of my first meeting with your lordship, have said something about stopping here a few days; but I have since found it altogether impossible.'

'That is very extraordinary,' answered the young nobleman. 'You seemed quite disengaged yesterday, and you cannot have had a summons to-day, for our post has not come up from the town, and therefore you cannot have received any letters.'

General Browne, without giving any further explanation, muttered something about indispensable business, and insisted on the absolute necessity of his departure in a manner which silenced all opposition on the part of his host, who saw that his resolution was taken, and forbore all further importunity.

'At least, however,' he said, 'permit me, my dear Browne, since go you will or must, to show you the view from the terrace, which the mist, that is now rising, will soon display.'

He threw open a sash-window, and stepped down upon the terrace as he spoke. The General followed him mechanically, but seemed little to attend to what his host was saying, as, looking across an extended and rich prospect, he pointed out the different objects worthy of observation. Thus they moved on till Lord Woodville had attained his purpose of drawing his guest entirely apart from the rest of the company, when, turning round upon him with an air of great solemnity, he addressed him thus: –

'Richard Browne, my old and very dear friend, we are now alone. Let me conjure you to answer me upon the word of a friend, and the honour of a soldier. How did you in reality rest during last night?'

'Most wretchedly indeed, my lord,' answered the General, in the same tone of solemnity – 'so miserably, that I would not run the risk of such a second night, not only for all the lands belonging to this castle, but for all the country which I see from this elevated point of view.'

'This is most extraordinary,' said the young lord, as if speaking to himself; 'then there must be something in the reports concerning that apartment.' Again turning to the General, he said, 'For God's sake, my dear friend, be candid with me, and let me know the disagreeable particulars which have befallen you under a roof, where, with consent of the owner, you should have met nothing save comfort.'

The General seemed distressed by this appeal, and paused a moment before he replied. 'My dear lord,' he at length said, 'what happened to me last night is of a nature so peculiar and so unpleasant, that I could hardly bring myself to detail it even to your lordship, were it not that, independent of my wish to gratify any request of yours, I think that sincerity on my part may lead to some explanation about a circumstance equally painful and mysterious. To others, the communication I am about to make, might place me in the light of a weak-minded, superstitious fool, who suffered his own imagination to delude and bewilder him; but you have known me in childhood and youth, and will not suspect me of having adopted in manhood the feelings and frailties from which my early years were free.' Here he paused, and his friend replied, –

'Do not doubt my perfect confidence in the truth of your communication, however strange it may be,' replied Lord Woodville. 'I know your firmness of disposition too well, to suspect you could be made the object of imposition, and am aware that your honour and your friendship will equally deter you from exaggerating whatever you may have witnessed.'

'Well, then,' said the General, 'I will proceed with my story as well as I can, relying upon your candour, and yet distinctly feeling that I would rather face a battery than recall to my mind the odious recollections of last night.'

He paused a second time, and then perceiving that Lord Woodville remained silent and in an attitude of attention, he commenced, though not without obvious reluctance, the history of his night's adventures in the Tapestried Chamber.

'I undressed and went to bed so soon as your lordship left me yesterday evening; but the wood in the chimney, which nearly fronted my bed, blazed brightly and cheerfully, and, aided by a hundred exciting recollections of my childhood and youth, which had been recalled by the unexpected pleasure of meeting your lordship, prevented me from falling immediately asleep. I ought, however, to say that these reflections were all of a pleasant and agreeable kind, grounded on a sense of having for a time exchanged the labour, fatigues, and dangers of my profession for the enjoyments of a peaceful life, and the reunion of those friendly and affectionate ties which I had torn asunder at the rude summons of war.

'While such pleasing reflections were stealing over my mind, and gradually lulling me to slumber, I was suddenly aroused by a sound like that of the rustling of a silken gown, and the tapping of a pair of high-heeled shoes, as if a woman were walking in the apartment. Ere I could draw the curtain to see what the matter was, the figure of a little woman passed between the bed and the fire. The back of this form was turned to me, and I could observe, from the shoulders and neck, it was that of an old woman, whose dress was an old-fashioned gown, which I think ladies call a sacque – that is, a sort of robe completely loose in the body, but gathered into broad plaits upon the neck and shoulders, which fall down to the ground, and terminate in a species of train.

'I thought the intrusion singular enough, but never harboured for a moment the idea that what I saw was anything more than the mortal form of some old woman about the establishment, who had a fancy to dress like her grandmother, and who, having perhaps (as your lordship mentioned that you were rather straitened for room) been dislodged from her chamber for my accommodation, had forgotten the circumstance, and returned by twelve to her old haunt. Under this persuasion I moved myself in bed and coughed a little, to make the intruder sensible of my being in possession of the premises. She turned slowly round, but, gracious Heaven! my lord, what a countenance did she display to me! There was no longer any question what she was, or any thought of her being a living being. Upon a face which wore the fixed features of a corpse were imprinted the traces of the vilest and most hideous passions which had animated her while she lived. The body of some atrocious criminal seemed to have been given up from the grave, and the soul restored from the penal fire, in order to form for a space a union with the ancient accomplice of its guilt. I started up in bed, and sat upright, supporting myself on my palms, as I gazed on this horrible spectre. The hag made, as it seemed, a single and swift stride to the bed where I lay, and squatted herself down upon it, in precisely the same attitude which I had assumed in the extremity of horror, advancing her diabolical countenance within half a yard of mine, with a grin which seemed to intimate the malice and the derision of an incarnate fiend.'

Here General Browne stopped, and wiped from his brow the cold perspiration with which the recollection of his horrible vision had covered it.

'My lord,' he said, 'I am no coward, I have been in all the mortal dangers incidental to my profession, and I may truly boast that no man ever knew Richard Browne dishonour the sword he wears; but in these horrible circumstances, under the eyes, and, as it seemed, almost in the grasp of an incarnation of an evil spirit, all firmness forsook me, all manhood melted from me like wax in the furnace, and I felt my hair individually bristle. The current of my life-blood ceased to flow, and I sank back in a swoon, as very a victim to panic terror as ever was a village girl, or a child of ten years old. How long I lay in this condition I cannot pretend to guess.

'But I was roused by the castle clock striking one, so loud that it seemed as if it were in the very room. It was some time before I dared open my eyes, lest they should again encounter the horrible spectacle. When, however, I summoned courage to look up, she was no longer visible. My first idea was to pull my bell, wake the servants, and remove to a garret or a hay-loft, to be ensured against a second visitation. Nay, I will confess the truth that my resolution was altered, not by the shame of exposing myself, but by the fear that, as the bell-cord hung by the chimney, I might, in making my way to it, be again crossed by the fiendish hag, who, I figured to myself, might be still lurking about some corner of the apartment.

'I will not pretend to describe what hot and cold fever-fits tormented me for the rest of the night, through broken sleep, weary vigils, and that dubious state which forms the neutral ground between them. A hundred terrible objects appeared to haunt me; but there was the great difference betwixt the vision which I have described, and those which followed, that I knew the last to be deceptions of my own fancy and over-excited nerves.

'Day at last appeared, and I rose from my bed ill in health and humiliated in mind. I was ashamed of myself as a man and a soldier, and still more so at feeling my own extreme desire to escape from the haunted apartment, which, however, conquered all other considerations; so that, huddling on my clothes with the most careless haste, I made my escape from your lordship's mansion, to seek in the open air some relief to my nervous system, shaken as it was by this horrible re-encounter with a visitant, for such I must believe her, from the other world. Your lordship has now heard the cause of my discomposure, and of my sudden desire to leave your hospitable castle. In other places I trust we may often meet, but God protect me from ever spending a second night under that roof!'

Strange as the General's tale was, he spoke with such a deep air of conviction that it cut short all the usual commentaries which are made on such stories. Lord Woodville never once asked him if he was sure he did not dream of the apparition, or suggested any of the possibilities by which it is fashionable to explain supernatural appearances as wild vagaries of the fancy, or deceptions of the optic nerves. On the contrary, he seemed deeply impressed with the truth and reality of what he had heard; and, after a considerable pause regretted, with much appearance of sincerity, that his early friend should in his house have suffered so severely.

'I am the more sorry for your pain, my dear Browne,' he continued, 'that it is the unhappy, though most unexpected, result of an experiment of my own. You must know that, for my father and grandfather's time, at least, the apartment which was assigned to you last night had been shut on account of reports that it was disturbed by supernatural sights and noises. When I came, a few weeks since, into possession of the estate, I thought the accommodation which the castle afforded for my friends was not extensive enough to permit the inhabitants of the invisible world to retain possession of a comfortable sleeping apartment. I therefore caused the Tapestried Chamber, as we call it, to be opened, and, without destroying its air of antiquity, I had such new articles of furniture placed in it as became the modern times. Yet, as the opinion that the room was haunted very strongly prevailed among the domestics, and was also known in the neighbourhood and to many of my friends, I feared some prejudice might be entertained by the first occupant of the Tapestried Chamber, which might tend to revive the evil report which it had laboured under, and so disappoint my purpose of rendering it a useful part or the house. I must confess, my dear Browne, that your arrival yesterday, agreeable to me for a thousand reasons besides, seemed the most favourable opportunity of removing the unpleasant rumours which attached to the room, since your courage was indubitable, and your mind free of any preoccupation on the subject. I could not, therefore, have chosen a more fitting subject for my experiment.'

'Upon my life,' said General Browne, somewhat hastily, 'I am infinitely obliged to your lordship – very particularly indebted indeed. I am likely to remember for some time the consequences of the experiment, as your lordship is pleased to call it.'

'Nay, now you are unjust, my dear friend,' said Lord Woodville. 'You have only to reflect for a single moment, in order to be convinced that I could not augur the possibility of the pain to which you have been so unhappily exposed. I was yesterday morning a complete sceptic on the subject of supernatural appearances. Nay, I am sure that, had I told you what was said about that room, those very reports would have induced you, by your own choice, to select it for your accommodation. It was my misfortune, perhaps my error, but really cannot be termed my fault, that you have been afflicted so strangely.'

'Strangely indeed!' said the General, resuming his good temper; 'and I acknowledge that I have no right to be offended with your lordship for treating me like what I used to think myself – a man of some firmness and courage. But I see my post horses are arrived, and I must not detain your lordship from your amusement.'

'Nay, my old friend,' said Lord Woodville, 'since you cannot stay with us another day – which, indeed, I can no longer urge – give me at least half an hour more. You used to love pictures, and I have a gallery of portraits, some of them by Vandyke, representing ancestry to whom this property and castle formerly belonged. I think that several of them will strike you as possessing merit.'

General Browne accepted the invitation, though somewhat unwillingly. It was evident he was not to breathe freely or at ease till he left Woodville Castle far behind him. He could not refuse his friend's invitation, however; and the less so, that he was a little ashamed of the peevishness which he had displayed towards his well-meaning entertainer.

The General, therefore, followed Lord Woodville through several rooms into a long gallery hung with pictures, which the latter pointed out to his guest, telling the names, and giving some account of the personages whose portraits presented themselves in progression. General Browne was but little interested in the details which these accounts conveyed to him. They were, indeed, of the kind which are usually found in an old family gallery. Here was a Cavalier who had ruined the estate in the royal cause; there a fine lady who had reinstated it by contracting a match with a wealthy Roundhead. There hung a gallant who had been in danger for corresponding with the exiled Court at Saint Germain's; here one who had taken arms for William at the Revolution; and there a third that had thrown his weight alternately into the scale of Whig and Tory.

While Lord Woodville was cramming these words into his guest's ear, 'against the stomach of his sense,' they gained the middle of the gallery, when he beheld General Browne suddenly start, and assume an attitude of the utmost surprise, not unmixed with fear, as his eyes were suddenly caught and riveted by a portrait of an old lady in a sacque, the fashionable dress of the end of the seventeenth century.

'There she is!' he exclaimed – 'there she is, in form and features, though Inferior in demoniac expression to the accursed hag who visited me last night!'

'If that be the case,' said the young nobleman, 'there can remain no longer any doubt of the horrible reality of your apparition. That is the picture of a wretched ancestress of mine, of whose crimes a black and fearful catalogue is recorded in a family history in my charter-chest. The recital of them would be too horrible; it is enough to say, that in yon fatal apartment incest and unnatural murder were committed. I will restore it to the solitude to which the better judgment of those who preceded me had consigned it; and never shall anyone, so long as I can prevent it, be exposed to a repetition of the supernatural horrors which could shake such courage as yours.'

Thus the friends, who had met with such glee, parted in a very different mood – Lord Woodville to command the Tapestried Chamber to be unmantled, and the door built up; and General Browne to seek in some less beautiful country, and with some less dignified friend, forgetfulness of the painful night which he had passed in Woodville Castle.

Berenice

Edgar Allan Poe

Dicebant mihi sodales si sepulchrum amicae visitarem
curas meas aliquantulum fore levatas.
Ebn Zaiat

Misery is manifold. The wretchedness of earth is multiform. Overreaching the wide horizon as the rainbow, its hues are as various as the hues of that arch,—as distinct too, yet as intimately blended. Overreaching the wide horizon as the rainbow! How is it that from beauty I have derived a type of unloveliness?—from the covenant of peace a simile of sorrow? But as, in ethics, evil is a consequence of good, so, in fact, out of joy is sorrow born. Either the memory of past bliss is the anguish of to-day, or the agonies which are have their origin in the ecstasies which might have been.

My baptismal name is Egæus; that of my family I will not mention. Yet there are no towers in the land more time-honored than my gloomy, gray, hereditary halls. Our line has been called a race of visionaries; and in many striking particulars—in the character of the family mansion—in the frescoes of the chief saloon—in the tapestries of the dormitories—in the chiseling of some buttresses in the armoury—but more especially in the gallery of antique paintings—in the fashion of the library chamber—

and, lastly, in the very peculiar nature of the library's contents, there is more than sufficient evidence to warrant the belief.

The recollections of my earliest years are connected with that chamber, and with its volumes—of which latter I will say no more. Here died my mother. Herein was I born. But it is mere idleness to say that I had not lived before—that the soul has no previous existence. You deny it?—let us not argue the matter. Convinced myself, I seek not to convince. There is, however, a remembrance of aerial forms—of spiritual and meaning eyes—of sounds, musical yet sad—a remembrance which will not be excluded; a memory like a shadow, vague, variable, indefinite, unsteady; and like a shadow, too, in the impossibility of my getting rid of it while the sunlight of my reason shall exist.

In that chamber was I born. Thus awaking from the long night of what seemed, but was not, nonentity, at once into the very regions of fairy-land—into a palace of imagination—into the wild dominions of monastic thought and erudition—it is not singular that I gazed around me with a startled and ardent eye—that I loitered away my boyhood in books, and dissipated my youth in reverie; but it is singular that as years rolled away, and the noon of manhood found me still in the mansion of my fathers—it is wonderful what stagnation there fell upon the springs of my life—wonderful how total an inversion took place in the character of my commonest thought. The realities of the world affected me as visions, and as visions only, while the wild ideas of the land of dreams became, in turn,—not the material of my every-day existence—but in very deed that existence utterly and solely in itself.

Berenice and I were cousins, and we grew up together in my paternal halls. Yet differently we grew—I ill of health, and buried in gloom—she agile, graceful, and overflowing with energy; hers the ramble on the hill-side—mine the studies of the cloister—I living within my own heart, and addicted body and soul to the most intense and painful meditation—she roaming carelessly through life with no thought of the shadows in her path, or the silent flight of the raven-winged hours. Berenice!—I call upon her name—Berenice!—and from the gray ruins of memory a thousand tumultuous recollections are startled at the sound! Ah! vividly is her image before me now, as in the early days of her light-heartedness and joy! Oh! gorgeous yet fantastic beauty! Oh! sylph amid the shrubberies of Arnheim! Oh! Naiad among its fountains!—

and then—then all is mystery and terror, and a tale which should not be told. Disease—a fatal disease—fell like the simoom upon her frame, and, even while I gazed upon her, the spirit of change swept over her, pervading her mind, her habits, and her character, and, in a manner the most subtle and terrible, disturbing even the identity of her person! Alas! the destroyer came and went, and the victim—where was she? I knew her not—or knew her no longer as Berenice.

Among the numerous train of maladies superinduced by that fatal and primary one which effected a revolution of so horrible a kind in the moral and physical being of my cousin, may be mentioned as the most distressing and obstinate in its nature, a species of epilepsy not unfrequently terminating in *trance* itself—trance very nearly resembling positive dissolution, and from which her manner of recovery was, in most instances, startlingly abrupt. In the meantime my own disease—for I have been told that I should call it by no other appellation—my own disease, then, grew rapidly upon me, and assumed finally a monomaniac character of a novel and extraordinary form—hourly and momently gaining vigor—and at length obtaining over me the most incomprehensible ascendency. This monomania, if I must so term it, consisted in a morbid irritability of those properties of the mind in metaphysical science termed the *attentive*. It is more than probable that I am not understood; but I fear, indeed, that it is in no manner possible to convey to the mind of the merely general reader, an adequate idea of that nervous *intensity of interest* with which, in my case, the powers of meditation (not to speak technically) busied and buried themselves, in the contemplation of even the most ordinary objects of the universe.

To muse for long unwearied hours with my attention riveted to some frivolous device on the margin, or in the typography of a book; to become absorbed for the better part of a summer's day, in a quaint shadow falling aslant upon the tapestry, or upon the door; to lose myself for an entire night in watching the steady flame of a lamp, or the embers of a fire; to dream away whole days over the perfume of a flower; to repeat monotonously some common word, until the sound, by dint of frequent repetition, ceased to convey any idea whatever to the mind; to lose all sense of motion or physical existence, by means of absolute bodily quiescence long and obstinately persevered in;—such were a few of the most common and least pernicious vagaries induced by a condition of the mental faculties, not, indeed, altogether unparalleled, but certainly bidding defiance to anything like analysis or explanation.

Yet let me not be misapprehended.—The undue, earnest, and morbid attention thus excited by objects in their own nature frivolous, must not be confounded in character with that ruminating propensity common to all mankind, and more especially indulged in by persons of ardent imagination. It was not even, as might be at first supposed, an extreme condition, or exaggeration of such propensity, but primarily and essentially distinct and different. In the one instance, the dreamer, or enthusiast, being interested by an object usually *not* frivolous, imperceptibly loses sight of this object in a wilderness of deductions and suggestions issuing therefrom, until, at the conclusion of a day-dream *often replete with luxury*, he finds the *incitamentum* or first cause of his musings entirely vanished and forgotten. In my case the primary object was *invariably frivolous*, although assuming, through the medium of my distempered vision, a refracted and unreal importance. Few deductions, if any, were made; and those few pertinaciously returning in upon the original object as a center. The meditations were *never* pleasurable; and, at the termination of the reverie, the first cause, so far from being out of sight, had attained that supernaturally exaggerated interest which was the prevailing feature of the disease. In a word, the powers of mind more particularly exercised were, with me, as I have said before, the *attentive*, and are, with the day-dreamer, the *speculative*.

My books, at this epoch, if they did not exactly serve to irritate the disorder, partook, it will be perceived, largely, in their imaginative and inconsequential nature, of the characteristic qualities of the disorder itself. I well remember, among others, the treatise of the noble Italian Cœlius Secundus Curio, *De Amplitudine Beati Regni Dei*; St Austin's great work, *The City of God*; and Tertullian, *De Carne Christi*, in which the paradoxical sentence, "*Mortuus est Dei filius; credibile est quia ineptum est: et sepultus resurrexit; certum est quia impossibile est,*" occupied my undivided time, for many weeks of laborious and fruitless investigation.

Thus it will appear that, shaken from its balance only by trivial things, my reason bore resemblance to that ocean-crag spoken of by Ptolemy Hephestion, which, steadily resisting the attacks of human violence, and the fiercer fury of the waters and the winds, trembled only to the touch of the flower called Asphodel. And although, to a careless thinker, it might appear a matter beyond doubt, that the alteration produced by her unhappy malady, in the *moral* condition of Berenice, would afford me many objects for the exercise of that intense and abnormal meditation whose nature I have been at some trouble in explaining, yet such was not in any degree the case. In the lucid intervals of my infirmity, her calamity, indeed, gave me pain, and, taking deeply to heart that total wreck of her fair and gentle life, I did not fail to ponder frequently and bitterly upon the wonder-working means by which so strange a revolution had been so suddenly brought to pass. But these reflections partook not of the idiosyncrasy of my disease, and were such as would have occurred, under similar circumstances, to the ordinary mass of mankind. True to its own character, my disorder reveled in the less important but more startling changes wrought in the *physical* frame of Berenice—in the singular and most appalling distortion of her personal identity.

During the brightest days of her unparalleled beauty, most surely I had never loved her. In the strange anomaly of my existence, feelings with me *had never been* of the heart, and my passions *always were* of the mind. Through the gray of the early morning—among the trellised shadows of the forest at noonday—and in the silence of my library at night, she had flitted by my eyes, and I had seen her—not as the living and breathing Berenice, but as the Berenice of a dream—not as a being of the earth, earthy, but as the abstraction of such a being—not as a thing to admire, but to analyze—not as an object of love, but as the theme of the most abstruse although desultory speculation. And *now*—now I shuddered in her presence, and grew pale at her approach; yet bitterly lamenting her fallen and desolate condition, I called to mind that she had loved me long, and, in an evil moment, I spoke to her of marriage.

And at length the period of our nuptials was approaching, when, upon an afternoon in the winter of the year,—one of those unseasonably warm, calm, and misty days which are the nurse of the beautiful Halcyon—I sat (and sat, as I thought, alone) in the inner apartment of the library. But uplifting my eyes I saw that Berenice stood before me.

Was it my own excited imagination—or the misty influence of the atmosphere—or the uncertain twilight of the chamber—or the gray draperies which fell around her figure—that caused in it so vacillating and indistinct an outline? I could not tell. She spoke no word, and I—

not for worlds could I have uttered a syllable. An icy chill ran through my frame; a sense of insufferable anxiety oppressed me; a consuming curiosity pervaded my soul; and sinking back upon the chair, I remained for some time breathless and motionless, with my eyes riveted upon her person. Alas! its emaciation was excessive, and not one vestige of the former being lurked in any single line of the contour. My burning glances at length fell upon the face.

The forehead was high, and very pale, and singularly placid; and the once jetty hair fell partially over it, and overshadowed the hollow temples with innumerable ringlets now of a vivid yellow, and jarring discordantly, in their fantastic character, with the reigning melancholy of the countenance. The eyes were lifeless, and lusterless, and seemingly pupilless, and I shrank involuntarily from their glassy stare to the contemplation of the thin and shrunken lips. They parted; and in a smile of peculiar meaning, *the teeth* of the changed Berenice disclosed themselves slowly to my view. Would to God that I had never beheld them, or that, having done so, I had died!

*

The shutting of a door disturbed me, and, looking up, I found that my cousin had departed from the chamber. But from the disordered chamber of my brain, had not, alas! departed, and would not be driven away, the white and ghastly *spectrum* of the teeth. Not a speck on their surface—not a shade on their enamel—not an indenture in their edges—but what that period of her smile had sufficed to brand in upon my memory. I saw them now even more unequivocally than I beheld them *then*. The teeth!—the teeth!—they were here, and there, and everywhere, and visibly and palpably before me; long, narrow, and excessively white, with the pale lips writhing about them, as in the very moment of their first terrible development. Then came the full fury of my monomania, and I struggled in vain against its strange and irresistible influence. In the multiplied objects of the external world I had no thoughts but for the teeth. For these I longed with a frenzied desire. All other matters and all different interests became absorbed in their single contemplation. They—they alone were present to the mental eye, and they, in their sole individuality, became the essence of my mental life. I held them in every light. I turned them in every attitude. I surveyed their characteristics. I dwelt upon their peculiarities. I pondered upon their conformation. I mused upon the alteration in their nature. I shuddered as I assigned to them in imagination a sensitive and sentient power, and even when unassisted by the lips, a capability of moral expression. Of Mad'selle Sallé it has been well said, "*que tous ses pas étaient des sentiments,*" and of Berenice I more seriously believed *que toutes ses dents étaient des idées. Des idées!*—ah here was the idiotic thought that destroyed me! *Des idées!*—ah therefore it was that I coveted them so madly! I felt that their possession could alone ever restore me to peace, in giving me back to reason.

And the evening closed in upon me thus—and then the darkness came, and tarried, and went—and the day again dawned—and the mists of a second night were now gathering around—and still I sat motionless in that solitary room; and still I sat buried in meditation, and still the *phantasma* of the teeth maintained its terrible ascendency as, with the most vivid and hideous distinctness, it floated about amid the changing lights and shadows of the chamber. At length there broke in upon my dreams a cry as of horror and dismay; and thereunto, after a pause, succeeded the sound of troubled voices, intermingled with many low moanings of sorrow, or of pain. I arose from my seat and, throwing open one of the doors of the library, saw standing out in the ante-chamber a servant maiden, all in tears, who told me that Berenice was—no more. She had been seized with epilepsy in the early morning, and now, at the closing in of the night, the grave was ready for its tenant, and all the preparations for the burial were completed.

*

I found myself sitting in the library, and again sitting there alone. It seemed that I had newly awakened from a confused and exciting dream. I knew that it was now midnight, and I was well aware that since the setting of the sun Berenice had been interred. But of that dreary period which intervened I had no positive—at least no definite comprehension. Yet its memory was replete with horror—horror more horrible from being vague, and terror more terrible from ambiguity. It was a fearful page in the record of my existence, written all over with dim, and hideous, and unintelligible recollections. I strived to decipher them, but in vain; while ever and anon, like the spirit of a departed sound, the shrill and piercing shriek of a female voice seemed to be ringing in my ears. I had done a deed—what was it? I asked myself the question aloud, and the whispering echoes of the chamber answered me, "What was it?"

On the table beside me burned a lamp, and near it lay a little box. It was of no remarkable character, and I had seen it frequently before, for it was the property of the family physician; but how came it there, upon my table, and why did I shudder in regarding it? These things were in no manner to be accounted for, and my eyes at length dropped to the open pages of a book, and to a sentence underscored therein. The words were the singular but simple ones of the poet Ebn Zaiat, *"Dicebant mihi sodales si sepulchrum amicae visitarem curas meas aliquantulum fore levatas."* Why then, as I perused them, did the hairs of my head erect themselves on end, and the blood of my body become congealed within my veins?

There came a light tap at the library door, and pale as the tenant of a tomb, a menial entered upon tiptoe. His looks were wild with terror, and he spoke to me in a voice tremulous, husky, and very low. What said he?—some broken sentences I heard. He told me of a wild cry disturbing the silence of the night—of the gathering together of the household—of a search in the direction of the sound;—and then his tones grew thrillingly distinct as he whispered me of a violated grave—of a disfigured body enshrouded, yet still breathing, still palpitating, *still alive*!

He pointed to my garments;—they were muddy and clotted with gore. I spoke not, and he took me gently by the hand;—it was indented with the impress of human nails. He directed my attention to some object against the wall;—I looked at it for some minutes;—it was a spade. With a shriek I bounded to the table, and grasped the box that lay upon it. But I could not force it open; and in my tremor it slipped from my hands, and fell heavily, and burst into pieces; and from it, with a rattling sound, there rolled out some instruments of dental surgery, intermingled with thirty-two small, white and ivory-looking substances that were scattered to and fro about the floor.

Olalla

Robert Louis Stevenson

'Now,' said the doctor, 'my part is done, and, I may say, with some vanity, well done. It remains only to get you out of this cold and poisonous city, and to give you two months of a pure air and an easy conscience. The last is your affair. To the first I think I can help you. It falls indeed rather oddly; it was but the other day the Padre came in from the country; and as he and I are old friends, although of contrary professions, he applied to me in a matter of distress among some of his parishioners. This was a family – but you are ignorant of Spain, and even the names of our grandees are hardly known to you; suffice it, then, that they were once great people, and are now fallen to the brink of destitution. Nothing now belongs to them but the residencia, and certain leagues of desert mountain, in the greater part of which not even a goat could support life. But the house is a fine old place, and stands at a great height among the hills, and most salubriously; and I had no sooner heard my friend's tale, than I remembered you. I told him I had a wounded officer, wounded in the good cause, who was now able to make a change; and I proposed that his friends should take you for a lodger. Instantly the Padre's face grew dark, as I had maliciously foreseen it would. It was out of the question, he said. Then let them starve, said I, for I have no sympathy with tatterdemalion pride. Thereupon we separated, not very content with one another; but yesterday, to my wonder, the Padre returned and made a submission: the difficulty, he said, he had found upon enquiry to be less than he had feared; or, in other words, these proud people had put their pride in their pocket. I closed with the offer; and, subject to your approval, I have taken rooms for you in the residencia. The air of these mountains will renew your blood; and the quiet in which you will there live is worth all the medicines in the world.'

'Doctor,' said I, 'you have been throughout my good angel, and your advice is a command. But tell me, if you please, something of the family with which I am to reside.'

'I am coming to that,' replied my friend; 'and, indeed, there is a difficulty in the way. These beggars are, as I have said, of very high descent and swollen with the most baseless vanity; they have lived for some generations in a growing isolation, drawing away, on either hand, from the rich who had now become too high for them, and from the poor, whom they still regarded as too low; and even to-day, when poverty forces them to unfasten their door to a guest, they cannot do so without a most ungracious stipulation. You are to remain, they say, a stranger; they will give you attendance, but they refuse from the first the idea of the smallest intimacy.'

I will not deny that I was piqued, and perhaps the feeling strengthened my desire to go, for I was confident that I could break down that barrier if I desired. 'There is nothing offensive in such a stipulation,' said I; 'and I even sympathise with the feeling that inspired it.'

'It is true they have never seen you,' returned the doctor politely; 'and if they knew you were the handsomest and the most pleasant man that ever came from England (where I am told that handsome men are common, but pleasant ones not so much so), they would doubtless make you welcome with a better grace. But since you take the thing so well, it matters not. To me, indeed, it seems discourteous. But you will find yourself the gainer. The family will not much tempt you. A mother, a son, and a daughter; an old woman said to be half-witted, a country lout, and a country girl, who stands very high with her confessor, and is, therefore,' chuckled the physician, 'most likely plain; there is not much in that to attract the fancy of a dashing officer.'

'And yet you say they are high-born,' I objected.

'Well, as to that, I should distinguish,' returned the doctor. 'The mother is; not so the children. The mother was the last representative of a princely stock, degenerate both in parts and fortune. Her father was not only poor, he was mad: and the girl ran wild about the residencia till his death. Then, much of the fortune having died with him, and the family being quite extinct, the girl ran wilder than ever, until at last she married, Heaven knows whom, a muleteer some say, others a smuggler; while there are some who uphold there was no marriage at all, and that Felipe and Olalla are bastards. The union, such as it was, was tragically dissolved some years ago; but they live in such seclusion, and the country at that time was in so much disorder, that the precise manner of the man's end is known only to the priest – if even to him.'

'I begin to think I shall have strange experiences,' said I.

'I would not romance, if I were you,' replied the doctor; 'you will find, I fear, a very grovelling and commonplace reality. Felipe, for instance, I have seen. And what am I to say? He is very rustic, very cunning, very loutish, and, I should say, an innocent; the others are probably to match. No, no, señor commandante, you must seek congenial society among the great sights of our mountains; and in these at least, if you are at all a lover of the works of nature, I promise you will not be disappointed.'

The next day Felipe came for me in a rough country cart, drawn by a mule; and a little before the stroke of noon, after I had said farewell to the doctor, the innkeeper, and different good souls who had befriended me during my sickness, we set forth out of the city by the Eastern gate, and began to ascend into the Sierra. I had been so long a prisoner, since I was left behind for dying after the loss of the convoy, that the mere smell of the earth set me smiling. The country through which we went was wild and rocky, partially covered with rough woods, now of the cork-tree, and now of the great Spanish chestnut, and frequently intersected by the beds of mountain torrents. The sun shone, the wind rustled joyously; and we had advanced some miles, and the city had already shrunk into an inconsiderable knoll upon the plain behind us, before my attention began to be diverted to the companion of my drive. To the eye, he seemed but a diminutive, loutish, well-made country lad, such as the doctor had described, mighty quick and active, but devoid of any culture; and this first impression was with most observers final. What began to strike me was his familiar, chattering talk; so strangely inconsistent with the terms on which I was to be received; and partly from his imperfect enunciation, partly from the sprightly incoherence of the matter, so very difficult to follow clearly without an effort of the mind. It is true I had before talked with persons of a similar mental constitution; persons who seemed to live (as he did) by the senses, taken and possessed by the visual object of the moment and unable to discharge their minds of that impression. His seemed to me (as I sat, distantly giving ear) a kind of conversation proper to drivers, who pass much of their time in a great vacancy of the intellect and threading the sights of a familiar country. But this was not the case of Felipe; by his own account, he was a home-keeper; 'I wish I was there now,' he said; and then, spying a tree by the wayside, he broke off to tell me that he had once seen a crow among its branches.

'A crow?' I repeated, struck by the ineptitude of the remark, and thinking I had heard imperfectly.

But by this time he was already filled with a new idea; hearkening with a rapt intentness, his head on one side, his face puckered; and he struck me rudely, to make me hold my peace. Then he smiled and shook his head.

'What did you hear?' I asked.

'O, it is all right,' he said; and began encouraging his mule with cries that echoed unhumanly up the mountain walls.

I looked at him more closely. He was superlatively well-built, light, and lithe and strong; he was well-featured; his yellow eyes were very large, though, perhaps, not very expressive; take him altogether, he was a pleasant-looking lad, and I had no fault to find with him, beyond that he was of a dusky hue, and inclined to hairiness; two characteristics that I disliked. It was his mind that puzzled, and yet attracted me. The doctor's phrase – an innocent – came back to me; and I was wondering if that were, after all, the true description, when the road began to go down into the narrow and naked chasm of a torrent. The waters thundered tumultuously in the bottom; and the ravine was filled full of the sound, the thin spray, and the claps of wind, that accompanied their descent. The scene was certainly impressive; but the road was in that part very securely walled in; the mule went steadily forward; and I was astonished to perceive the paleness of terror in the face of my companion. The voice of that wild river was inconstant, now sinking lower as if in weariness, now doubling its hoarse tones; momentary freshets seemed to swell its volume, sweeping down the gorge, raving and booming against the barrier walls; and I observed it was at each of these accessions to the clamour, that my driver more particularly winced and blanched. Some thoughts of Scottish superstition and the river Kelpie, passed across my mind; I wondered if perchance the like were prevalent in that part of Spain; and turning to Felipe, sought to draw him out.

'What is the matter?' I asked.

'O, I am afraid,' he replied.

'Of what are you afraid?' I returned. 'This seems one of the safest places on this very dangerous road.'

'It makes a noise,' he said, with a simplicity of awe that set my doubts at rest.

The lad was but a child in intellect; his mind was like his body, active and swift, but stunted in development; and I began from that time forth to regard him with a measure of pity, and to listen at first with indulgence, and at last even with pleasure, to his disjointed babble.

By about four in the afternoon we had crossed the summit of the mountain line, said farewell to the western sunshine, and began to go down upon the other side, skirting the edge of many ravines and moving through the shadow of dusky woods. There rose upon all sides the voice of falling water, not condensed and formidable as in the gorge of the river, but scattered and sounding gaily and musically from glen to glen. Here, too, the spirits of my driver mended, and he began to sing aloud in a falsetto voice, and with a singular bluntness of musical perception, never true either to melody or key, but wandering at will, and yet somehow with an effect that was natural and pleasing, like that of the of birds. As the dusk increased, I fell more and more under the spell of this artless warbling, listening and waiting for some articulate air, and still disappointed; and when at last I asked him what it was he sang – 'O,' cried he, 'I am just singing!' Above all, I was taken with a trick he had of unweariedly repeating the same note at little intervals; it was not so monotonous as you would think, or, at least, not disagreeable; and it seemed to breathe a wonderful contentment with what is, such as we love to fancy in the attitude of trees, or the quiescence of a pool.

Night had fallen dark before we came out upon a plateau, and drew up a little after, before a certain lump of superior blackness which I could only conjecture to be the residencia. Here, my guide, getting down from the cart, hooted and whistled for a long time in vain; until at last an old peasant man came towards us from somewhere in the surrounding dark, carrying a candle in his hand. By the light of this I was able to perceive a great arched doorway of a Moorish character: it was closed by iron-studded gates, in one of the leaves of which Felipe opened a wicket. The peasant carried off the cart to some out-building; but my guide and I passed through the wicket, which was closed again behind us; and by the glimmer of the candle, passed through a court, up a stone stair, along a section of an open gallery, and up more stairs again, until we came at last to the door of a great and somewhat bare apartment. This room, which I understood was to be mine, was pierced by three windows, lined with some lustrous wood disposed in panels, and carpeted with the skins of many savage animals. A bright fire burned in the chimney, and shed abroad a changeful flicker; close up to the blaze there was drawn a table, laid for supper; and in the far end a bed stood ready. I was pleased by these preparations, and said so to Felipe; and he, with the same simplicity of disposition that I held already remarked in him, warmly re-echoed my praises. 'A fine room,' he said; 'a very fine room. And fire, too; fire is good; it melts out the pleasure in your bones. And the bed,' he continued, carrying over the candle in that direction – 'see what fine sheets – how soft, how smooth, smooth;' and he passed his hand again and again over their texture, and then laid down his head and rubbed his cheeks among them with a grossness of content that somehow offended me. I took the candle from his hand (for I feared he would set the bed on fire) and walked back to the supper-table, where, perceiving a measure of wine, I poured out a cup and called to him to come and drink of it. He started to his feet at once and ran to me with a strong expression of hope; but when he saw the wine, he visibly shuddered.

'Oh, no,' he said, 'not that; that is for you. I hate it.'

'Very well, Señor,' said I; 'then I will drink to your good health, and to the prosperity of your house and family. Speaking of which,' I added, after I had drunk, 'shall I not have the pleasure of laying my salutations in person at the feet of the Señora, your mother?'

But at these words all the childishness passed out of his face, and was succeeded by a look of indescribable cunning and secrecy. He backed away from me at the same time, as though I were an animal about to leap or some dangerous fellow with a weapon, and when he had got near the door, glowered at me sullenly with contracted pupils. 'No,' he said at last, and the next moment was gone noiselessly out of the room; and I heard his footing die away downstairs as light as rainfall, and silence closed over the house.

After I had supped I drew up the table nearer to the bed and began to prepare for rest; but in the new position of the light, I was struck by a picture on the wall. It represented a woman, still young. To judge by her costume and the mellow unity which reigned over the canvas, she had long been dead; to judge by the vivacity of the attitude, the eyes and the features, I might have been beholding in a mirror the image of life. Her figure was very slim and strong, and of a just proportion; red tresses lay like a crown over her brow; her eyes, of a very golden brown, held mine with a look; and her face, which was perfectly shaped, was yet marred by a cruel, sullen, and sensual expression. Something in both face and figure, something exquisitely intangible, like the echo of an echo, suggested the features and bearing of my guide; and I stood awhile, unpleasantly attracted and wondering at the oddity of the resemblance. The common, carnal stock of that race, which had been originally designed for such high dames as the one now looking on me from the canvas, had fallen to baser uses, wearing country clothes, sitting on the shaft and holding the reins of a mule cart, to bring home a lodger. Perhaps an actual link subsisted; perhaps some scruple of the delicate flesh that was once clothed upon with the satin and brocade of the dead lady, now winced at the rude contact of Felipe's frieze.

The first light of the morning shone full upon the portrait, and, as I lay awake, my eyes continued to dwell upon it with growing complacency; its beauty crept about my heart insidiously, silencing my scruples one after another; and while I knew that to love such a woman were to sign and seal one's own sentence of degeneration, I still knew that, if she were alive, I should love her. Day after day the double knowledge of her wickedness and of my weakness grew clearer. She came to be the heroine of many day-dreams, in which her eyes led on to, and sufficiently rewarded, crimes. She cast a dark shadow on my fancy; and when I was out in the free air of heaven, taking vigorous exercise and healthily renewing the current of my blood, it was often a glad thought to me that my enchantress was safe in the grave, her wand of beauty broken, her lips closed in silence, her philtre spilt. And yet I had a half-lingering terror that she might not be dead after all, but re-arisen in the body of some descendant.

Felipe served my meals in my own apartment; and his resemblance to the portrait haunted me. At times it was not; at times, upon some change of attitude or flash of expression, it would leap out upon me like a ghost. It was above all in his ill tempers that the likeness triumphed. He certainly liked me; he was proud of my notice, which he sought to engage by many simple and childlike devices; he loved to sit close before my fire, talking his broken talk or singing his odd, endless, wordless songs, and sometimes drawing his hand over my clothes with an affectionate manner of caressing that never failed to cause in me an embarrassment of which I was ashamed. But for all that, he was capable of flashes of causeless anger and fits of sturdy sullenness. At a word of reproof, I have seen him upset the dish of which I was about to eat, and this not surreptitiously, but with defiance; and similarly at a hint of inquisition. I was not unnaturally curious, being in a strange place and surrounded by staring people; but at the shadow of a question, he shrank back, lowering and dangerous. Then it was that, for a fraction of a second, this rough lad might have been the brother of the lady in the frame. But these humours were swift to pass; and the resemblance died along with them.

In these first days I saw nothing of anyone but Felipe, unless the portrait is to be counted; and since the lad was plainly of weak mind, and had moments of passion, it may be wondered that I bore his dangerous neighbourhood with equanimity. As a matter of fact, it was for some time irksome; but it happened before long that I obtained over him so complete a mastery as set my disquietude at rest.

It fell in this way. He was by nature slothful, and much of a vagabond, and yet he kept by the house, and not only waited upon my wants, but laboured every day in the garden or small farm to the south of the residencia. Here he would be joined by the peasant whom I had seen on the night of my arrival, and who dwelt at the far end of the enclosure, about half a mile away, in a rude out-house; but it was plain to me that, of these two, it was Felipe who did most; and though I would sometimes see him throw down his spade and go to sleep among the very plants he had been digging, his constancy and energy were admirable in themselves, and still more so since I was well assured they were foreign to his disposition and the fruit of an ungrateful effort. But while I admired, I wondered what had called forth in a lad so shuttle-witted this enduring sense of duty. How was it sustained? I asked myself, and to what length did it prevail over his instincts? The priest was possibly his inspirer; but the priest came one day to the residencia. I saw him both come and go after an interval of close upon an hour, from a knoll where I was sketching, and all that time Felipe continued to labour undisturbed in the garden.

At last, in a very unworthy spirit, I determined to debauch the lad from his good resolutions, and, way-laying him at the gate, easily persuaded him to join me in a ramble. It was a fine day, and the woods to which I led him were green and pleasant and sweet-smelling and alive with the hum of insects. Here he discovered himself in a fresh character, mounting up to heights of gaiety that abashed me, and displaying an energy and grace of movement that delighted the eye. He leaped, he ran round me in mere glee; he would stop, and look and listen, and seem to drink in the world like a cordial; and then he would suddenly spring into a tree with one bound, and hang and gambol there like one at home. Little as he said to me, and that of not much import, I have rarely enjoyed more stirring company; the sight of his delight was a continual feast; the speed and accuracy of his movements pleased me to the heart; and I might have been so thoughtlessly unkind as to make a habit of these wants, had not chance prepared a very rude conclusion to my pleasure. By some swiftness or dexterity the lad captured a squirrel in a tree top. He was then some way ahead of me, but I saw him drop to the ground and crouch there, crying aloud for pleasure like a child. The sound stirred my sympathies, it was so fresh and innocent; but as I bettered my pace to draw near, the cry of the squirrel knocked upon my heart. I have heard and seen much of the cruelty of lads, and above all of peasants; but what I now beheld struck me into a passion of anger. I thrust the fellow aside, plucked the poor brute out of his hands, and with swift mercy killed it. Then I turned upon the torturer, spoke to him long out of the heat of my indignation, calling him names at which he seemed to wither; and at length, pointing toward the residencia, bade him begone and leave me, for I chose to walk with men, not with vermin. He fell upon his knees, and, the words coming to him with more cleanness than usual, poured out a stream of the most touching supplications, begging me in mercy to forgive him, to forget what he had done, to look to the future. 'O, I try so hard,' he said. 'O, commandante, bear with Felipe this once; he will never be a brute again!' Thereupon, much more affected than I cared to show, I suffered myself to be persuaded, and at last shook hands with him and made it up. But the squirrel, by way of penance, I made him bury; speaking of the poor thing's beauty, telling him what pains it had suffered, and how base a thing was the abuse of strength. 'See, Felipe,' said I, 'you are strong indeed; but in my hands you are as helpless as that poor thing of the trees. Give me your hand in mine. You cannot remove it. Now suppose that I were cruel like you, and took a pleasure in pain. I only tighten my hold, and see how you suffer.' He screamed aloud, his face stricken ashy and dotted with needle points of sweat; and when I set him free, he fell to the earth and nursed his hand and moaned over it like a baby. But he took the lesson in good part; and whether from that, or from what I had said to him, or the higher notion he now had of my bodily strength, his original affection was changed into a dog-like, adoring fidelity.

Meanwhile I gained rapidly in health. The residencia stood on the crown of a stony plateau; on every side the mountains hemmed it about; only from the roof, where was a bartizan, there might be seen between two peaks, a small segment of plain, blue with extreme distance. The air in these altitudes moved freely and largely; great clouds congregated there, and were broken up by the wind and left in tatters on the hilltops; a hoarse, and yet faint rumbling of torrents rose from all round; and one could there study all the ruder and more ancient characters of nature in something of their pristine force. I delighted from the first in the vigorous scenery and changeful weather; nor less in the antique and dilapidated mansion where I dwelt. This was a large oblong, flanked at two opposite corners by bastion-like projections, one of which commanded the door, while both were loopholed for musketry. The lower storey was, besides, naked of windows, so that the building, if garrisoned, could not be carried without artillery. It enclosed an open court planted with pomegranate trees. From this a broad flight of marble stairs ascended to an open gallery, running all round and resting, towards the court, on slender pillars. Thence again, several enclosed stairs led to the upper storeys of the house, which were thus broken up into distinct divisions.

The windows, both within and without, were closely shuttered; some of the stone-work in the upper parts had fallen; the roof, in one place, had been wrecked in one of the flurries of wind which were common in these mountains; and the whole house, in the strong, beating sunlight, and standing out above a grove of stunted cork-trees, thickly laden and discoloured with dust, looked like the sleeping palace of the legend. The court, in particular, seemed the very home of slumber. A hoarse cooing of doves haunted about the eaves; the winds were excluded, but when they blew outside, the mountain dust fell here as thick as rain, and veiled the red bloom of the pomegranates; shuttered windows and the closed doors of numerous cellars, and the vacant, arches of the gallery, enclosed it; and all day long the sun made broken profiles on the four sides, and paraded the shadow of the pillars on the gallery floor. At the ground level there was, however, a certain pillared recess, which bore the marks of human habitation. Though it was open in front upon the court, it was yet provided with a chimney, where a wood fire would be always prettily blazing; and the tile floor was littered with the skins of animals.

It was in this place that I first saw my hostess. She had drawn one of the skins forward and sat in the sun, leaning against a pillar. It was her dress that struck me first of all, for it was rich and brightly coloured, and shone out in that dusty courtyard with something of the same relief as the flowers of the pomegranates. At a second look it was her beauty of person that took hold of me. As she sat back – watching me, I thought, though with invisible eyes – and wearing at the same time an expression of almost imbecile good-humour and contentment, she showed a perfectness of feature and a quiet nobility of attitude that were beyond a statue's. I took off my hat to her in passing, and her face puckered with suspicion as swiftly and lightly as a pool ruffles in the breeze; but she paid no heed to my courtesy. I went forth on my customary walk a trifle daunted, her idol-like impassivity haunting me; and when I returned, although she was still in much the same posture, I was half surprised to see that she had moved as far as the next pillar, following the sunshine. This time, however, she addressed me with some trivial salutation, civilly enough conceived, and uttered in the same deep-chested, and yet indistinct and lisping tones, that had already baffled the utmost niceness of my hearing from her son. I answered rather at a venture; for not only did I fail to take her meaning with precision, but the sudden disclosure of her eyes disturbed me. They were unusually large, the iris golden like Felipe's, but the pupil at that moment so distended that they seemed almost black; and what affected me was not so much their size as (what was perhaps its consequence) the singular insignificance of their regard. A look more blankly stupid I have never met. My eyes dropped before it even as I spoke, and I went on my way upstairs to my own room, at once baffled and embarrassed. Yet, when I came there and saw the face of the portrait, I was again reminded of the miracle of family descent. My hostess was, indeed, both older and fuller in person; her eyes were of a different colour; her face, besides, was not only free from the ill-significance that offended and attracted me in the painting; it was devoid of either good or bad – a moral blank expressing literally naught. And yet there was a likeness, not so much speaking as immanent, not so much in any particular feature as upon the whole. It should seem, I thought, as if when the master set his signature to that grave canvas, he had not only caught the image of one smiling and false-eyed woman, but stamped the essential quality of a race.

From that day forth, whether I came or went, I was sure to find the Señora seated in the sun against a pillar, or stretched on a rug before the fire; only at times she would shift her station to the top round of the stone staircase, where she lay with the same nonchalance right across my path. In all these days, I never knew her to display the least spark of energy beyond what she expended in brushing and re-brushing her copious copper-coloured hair, or in lisping out, in the rich and broken hoarseness of her voice, her customary idle salutations to myself. These, I think, were her two chief pleasures, beyond that of mere quiescence. She seemed always proud of her remarks, as though they had been witticisms: and, indeed, though they were empty enough, like the conversation of many respectable persons, and turned on a very narrow range of subjects, they were never meaningless or incoherent; nay, they had a certain beauty of their own, breathing, as they did, of her entire contentment. Now she would speak of the warmth, in which (like her son) she greatly delighted; now of the flowers of the pomegranate trees, and now of the white doves and long-winged swallows that fanned the air of the court. The birds excited her. As they raked the eaves in their swift flight, or skimmed sidelong past her with a rush of wind, she would sometimes stir, and sit a little up, and seem to awaken from her doze of satisfaction. But for the rest of her days she lay luxuriously folded on herself and sunk in sloth and pleasure. Her invincible content at first annoyed me, but I came gradually to find repose in the spectacle, until at last it grew to be my habit to sit down beside her four times in the day, both coming and going, and to talk with her sleepily, I scarce knew of what. I had come to like her dull, almost animal neighbourhood; her beauty and her stupidity soothed and amused me. I began to find a kind of transcendental good sense in her remarks, and her unfathomable good nature moved me to admiration and envy. The liking was returned; she enjoyed my presence half-unconsciously, as a man in deep meditation may enjoy the babbling of a brook. I can scarce say she brightened when I came, for satisfaction was written on her face eternally, as on some foolish statue's; but I was made conscious of her pleasure by some more intimate communication than the sight. And one day, as I set within reach of her on the marble step, she suddenly shot forth one of her hands and patted mine. The thing was done, and she was back in her accustomed attitude, before my mind had received intelligence of the caress; and when I turned to look her in the face I could perceive no answerable sentiment. It was plain she attached no moment to the act, and I blamed myself for my own more uneasy consciousness.

The sight and (if I may so call it) the acquaintance of the mother confirmed the view I had already taken of the son. The family blood had been impoverished, perhaps by long inbreeding, which I knew to be a common error among the proud and the exclusive. No decline, indeed, was to be traced in the body, which had been handed down unimpaired in shapeliness and strength; and the faces of to-day were struck as sharply from the mint, as the face of two centuries ago that smiled upon me from the portrait. But the intelligence (that more precious heirloom) was degenerate; the treasure of ancestral memory ran low; and it had required the potent, plebeian crossing of a muleteer or mountain contrabandista to raise, what approached hebetude in the mother, into the active oddity of the son. Yet of the two, it was the mother I preferred. Of Felipe, vengeful and placable, full of starts and shyings, inconstant as a hare, I could even conceive as a creature possibly noxious. Of the mother I had no thoughts but those of kindness. And indeed, as spectators are apt ignorantly to take sides, I grew something of a partisan in the enmity which I perceived to smoulder between them. True, it seemed mostly on the mother's part. She would sometimes draw in her breath as he came near, and the pupils of her vacant eyes would contract as if with horror or fear. Her emotions, such as they were, were much upon the surface and readily shared; and this latent repulsion occupied my mind, and kept me wondering on what grounds it rested, and whether the son was certainly in fault.

I had been about ten days in the residencia, when there sprang up a high and harsh wind, carrying clouds of dust. It came out of malarious lowlands, and over several snowy sierras. The nerves of those on whom it blew were strung and jangled; their eyes smarted with the dust; their legs ached under the burthen of their body; and the touch of one hand upon another grew to be odious. The wind, besides, came down the gullies of the hills and stormed about the house with a great, hollow buzzing and whistling that was wearisome to the ear and dismally depressing to the mind. It did not so much blow in gusts as with the steady sweep of a waterfall, so that there was no remission of discomfort while it blew. But higher upon the mountain, it was probably of a more variable strength, with accesses of fury; for there came down at times a far-off wailing, infinitely grievous to hear; and at times, on one of the high shelves or terraces, there would start up, and then disperse, a tower of dust, like the smoke of an explosion.

I no sooner awoke in bed than I was conscious of the nervous tension and depression of the weather, and the effect grew stronger as the day proceeded. It was in vain that I resisted; in vain that I set forth upon my customary morning's walk; the irrational, unchanging fury of the storm had soon beat down my strength and wrecked my temper; and I returned to the residencia, glowing with dry heat, and foul and gritty with dust. The court had a forlorn appearance; now and then a glimmer of sun fled over it; now and then the wind swooped down upon the pomegranates, and scattered the blossoms, and set the window shutters clapping on the wall. In the recess the Señora was pacing to and fro with a flushed countenance and bright eyes; I thought, too, she was speaking to herself, like one in anger. But when I addressed her with my customary salutation, she only replied by a sharp gesture and continued her walk. The weather had distempered even this impassive creature; and as I went on upstairs I was the less ashamed of my own discomposure.

All day the wind continued; and I sat in my room and made a feint of reading, or walked up and down, and listened to the riot overhead. Night fell, and I had not so much as a candle. I began to long for some society, and stole down to the court. It was now plunged in the blue of the first darkness; but the recess was redly lighted by the fire. The wood had been piled high, and was crowned by a shock of flames, which the draught of the chimney brandished to and fro. In this strong and shaken brightness the Señora continued pacing from wall to wall with disconnected gestures, clasping her hands, stretching forth her arms, throwing back her head as in appeal to heaven. In these disordered movements the beauty and grace of the woman showed more clearly; but there was a light in her eye that struck on me unpleasantly; and when I had looked on awhile in silence, and seemingly unobserved, I turned tail as I had come, and groped my way back again to my own chamber.

By the time Felipe brought my supper and lights, my nerve was utterly gone; and, had the lad been such as I was used to seeing him, I should have kept him (even by force had that been necessary) to take off the edge from my distasteful solitude. But on Felipe, also, the wind had exercised its influence. He had been feverish all day; now that the night had come he was fallen into a low and tremulous humour that reacted on my own. The sight of his scared face, his starts and pallors and sudden harkenings, unstrung me; and when he dropped and broke a dish, I fairly leaped out of my seat.

'I think we are all mad to-day,' said I, affecting to laugh.

'It is the black wind,' he replied dolefully. 'You feel as if you must do something, and you don't know what it is.'

I noted the aptness of the description; but, indeed, Felipe had sometimes a strange felicity in rendering into words the sensations of the body. 'And your mother, too,' said I; 'she seems to feel this weather much. Do you not fear she may be unwell?'

He stared at me a little, and then said, 'No,' almost defiantly; and the next moment, carrying his hand to his brow, cried out lamentably on the wind and the noise that made his head go round like a millwheel. 'Who can be well?' he cried; and, indeed, I could only echo his question, for I was disturbed enough myself.

I went to bed early, wearied with day-long restlessness, but the poisonous nature of the wind, and its ungodly and unintermittent uproar, would not suffer me to sleep. I lay there and tossed, my nerves and senses on the stretch. At times I would doze, dream horribly, and wake again; and these snatches of oblivion confused me as to time. But it must have been late on in the night, when I was suddenly startled by an outbreak of pitiable and hateful cries. I leaped from my bed, supposing I had dreamed; but the cries still continued to fill the house, cries of pain, I thought, but certainly of rage also, and so savage and discordant that they shocked the heart. It was no illusion; some living thing, some lunatic or some wild animal, was being foully tortured. The thought of Felipe and the squirrel flashed into my mind, and I ran to the door, but it had been locked from the outside; and I might shake it as I pleased, I was a fast prisoner. Still the cries continued. Now they would dwindle down into a moaning that seemed to be articulate, and at these times I made sure they must be human; and again they would break forth and fill the house with ravings worthy of hell. I stood at the door and gave ear to them, till at last they died away. Long after that, I still lingered and still continued to hear them mingle in fancy with the storming of the wind; and when at last I crept to my bed, it was with a deadly sickness and a blackness of horror on my heart.

It was little wonder if I slept no more. Why had I been locked in? What had passed? Who was the author of these indescribable and shocking cries? A human being? It was inconceivable. A beast? The cries were scarce quite bestial; and what animal, short of a lion or a tiger, could thus shake the solid walls of the residencia? And while I was thus turning over the elements of the mystery, it came into my mind that I had not yet set eyes upon the daughter of the house. What was more probable than that the daughter of the Senora, and the sister of Felipe, should be herself insane? Or, what more likely than that these ignorant and half-witted people should seek to manage an afflicted kinswoman by violence? Here was a solution; and yet when I called to mind the cries (which I never did without a shuddering chill) it seemed altogether insufficient: not even cruelty could wring such cries from madness. But of one thing I was sure: I could not live in a house where such a thing was half conceivable, and not probe the matter home and, if necessary, interfere.

The next day came, the wind had blown itself out, and there was nothing to remind me of the business of the night. Felipe came to my bedside with obvious cheerfulness; as I passed through the court, the Señora was sunning herself with her accustomed immobility; and when I issued from the gateway, I found the whole face of nature austerely smiling, the heavens of a cold blue, and sown with great cloud islands, and the mountain-sides mapped forth into provinces of light and shadow. A short walk restored me to myself, and renewed within me the resolve to plumb this mystery; and when, from the vantage of my knoll, I had seen Felipe pass forth to his labours in the garden, I returned at once to the residencia to put my design in practice. The Señora appeared plunged in slumber; I stood awhile and marked her, but she did not stir; even if my design were indiscreet, I had little to fear from such a guardian; and turning away, I mounted to the gallery and began my exploration of the house.

All morning I went from one door to another, and entered spacious and faded chambers, some rudely shuttered, some receiving their full charge of daylight, all empty and unhomely. It was a rich house, on which Time had breathed his tarnish and dust had scattered disillusion. The spider swung there; the bloated tarantula scampered on the cornices; ants had their crowded highways on the floor of halls of audience; the big and foul fly, that lives on carrion and is often the messenger of death, had set up his nest in the rotten woodwork, and buzzed heavily about the rooms. Here and there a stool or two, a couch, a bed, or a great carved chair remained behind, like islets on the bare floors, to testify of man's bygone habitation; and everywhere the walls were set with the portraits of the dead. I could judge, by these decaying effigies, in the house of what a great and what a handsome race I was then wandering. Many of the men wore orders on their breasts and had the port of noble offices; the women were all richly attired; the canvases most of them by famous hands. But it was not so much these evidences of greatness that took hold upon my mind, even contrasted, as they were, with the present depopulation and decay of that great house. It was rather the parable of family life that I read in this succession of fair faces and shapely bodies. Never before had I so realised the miracle of the continued race, the creation and recreation, the weaving and changing and handing down of fleshly elements. That a child should be born of its mother, that it should grow and clothe itself (we know not how) with humanity, and put on inherited looks, and turn its head with the manner of one ascendant, and offer its hand with the gesture of another, are wonders dulled for us by repetition. But in the singular unity of look, in the common features and common bearing, of all these painted generations on the walls of the residencia, the miracle started out and looked me in the face. And an ancient mirror falling opportunely in my way, I stood and read my own features a long while, tracing out on either hand the filaments of descent and the bonds that knit me with my family.

At last, in the course of these investigations, I opened the door of a chamber that bore the marks of habitation. It was of large proportions and faced to the north, where the mountains were most wildly figured. The embers of a fire smouldered and smoked upon the hearth, to which a chair had been drawn close. And yet the aspect of the chamber was ascetic to the degree of sternness; the chair was uncushioned; the floor and walls were naked; and beyond the books which lay here and there in some confusion, there was no instrument of either work or pleasure. The sight of books in the house of such a family exceedingly amazed me; and I began with a great hurry, and in momentary fear of interruption, to go from one to another and hastily inspect their character. They were of all sorts, devotional, historical, and scientific, but mostly of a great age and in the Latin tongue. Some I could see to bear the marks of constant study; others had been torn across and tossed aside as if in petulance or disapproval. Lastly, as I cruised about that empty chamber, I espied some papers written upon with pencil on a table near the window. An unthinking curiosity led me to take one up. It bore a copy of verses, very roughly metred in the original Spanish, and which I may render somewhat thus –

Pleasure approached with pain and shame,
Grief with a wreath of lilies came.
Pleasure showed the lovely sun;
Jesu dear, how sweet it shone!
Grief with her worn hand pointed on,
  Jesu dear, to thee!

Shame and confusion at once fell on me; and, laying down the paper, I beat an immediate retreat from the apartment. Neither Felipe nor his mother could have read the books nor written these rough but feeling verses. It was plain I had stumbled with sacrilegious feet into the room of the daughter of the house. God knows, my own heart most sharply punished me for my indiscretion. The thought that I had thus secretly pushed my way into the confidence of a girl so strangely situated, and the fear that she might somehow come to hear of it, oppressed me like guilt. I blamed myself besides for my suspicions of the night before; wondered that I should ever have attributed those shocking cries to one of whom I now conceived as of a saint, spectral of mien, wasted with maceration, bound up in the practices of a mechanical devotion, and dwelling in a great isolation of soul with her incongruous relatives; and as I leaned on the balustrade of the gallery and looked down into the bright close of pomegranates and at the gaily dressed and somnolent woman, who just then stretched herself and delicately licked her lips as in the very sensuality of sloth, my mind swiftly compared the scene with the cold chamber looking northward on the mountains, where the daughter dwelt.

That same afternoon, as I sat upon my knoll, I saw the Padre enter the gates of the residencia. The revelation of the daughter's character had struck home to my fancy, and almost blotted out the horrors of the night before; but at sight of this worthy man the memory revived. I descended, then, from the knoll, and making a circuit among the woods, posted myself by the wayside to await his passage. As soon as he appeared I stepped forth and introduced myself as the lodger of the residencia. He had a very strong, honest countenance, on which it was easy to read the mingled emotions with which he regarded me, as a foreigner, a heretic, and yet one who had been wounded for the good cause. Of the family at the residencia he spoke with reserve, and yet with respect. I mentioned that I had not yet seen the daughter, whereupon he remarked that that was as it should be, and looked at me a little askance. Lastly, I plucked up courage to refer to the cries that had disturbed me in the night. He heard me out in silence, and then stopped and partly turned about, as though to mark beyond doubt that he was dismissing me.

'Do you take tobacco powder?' said he, offering his snuff-box; and then, when I had refused, 'I am an old man,' he added, 'and I may be allowed to remind you that you are a guest.'

'I have, then, your authority,' I returned, firmly enough, although I flushed at the implied reproof, 'to let things take their course, and not to interfere?'

He said 'yes,' and with a somewhat uneasy salute turned and left me where I was. But he had done two things: he had set my conscience at rest, and he had awakened my delicacy. I made a great effort, once more dismissed the recollections of the night, and fell once more to brooding on my saintly poetess. At the same time, I could not quite forget that I had been locked in, and that night when Felipe brought me my supper I attacked him warily on both points of interest.

'I never see your sister,' said I casually.

'Oh, no,' said he; 'she is a good, good girl,' and his mind instantly veered to something else.

'Your sister is pious, I suppose?' I asked in the next pause.

'Oh!' he cried, joining his hands with extreme fervour, 'a saint; it is she that keeps me up.'

'You are very fortunate,' said I, 'for the most of us, I am afraid, and myself among the number, are better at going down.'

'Senor,' said Felipe earnestly, 'I would not say that. You should not tempt your angel. If one goes down, where is he to stop?'

'Why, Felipe,' said I, 'I had no guess you were a preacher, and I may say a good one; but I suppose that is your sister's doing?'

He nodded at me with round eyes.

'Well, then,' I continued, 'she has doubtless reproved you for your sin of cruelty?'

'Twelve times!' he cried; for this was the phrase by which the odd creature expressed the sense of frequency. 'And I told her you had done so – I remembered that,' he added proudly – 'and she was pleased.'

'Then, Felipe,' said I, 'what were those cries that I heard last night? for surely they were cries of some creature in suffering.'

'The wind,' returned Felipe, looking in the fire.

I took his hand in mine, at which, thinking it to be a caress, he smiled with a brightness of pleasure that came near disarming my resolve. But I trod the weakness down. 'The wind,' I repeated; 'and yet I think it was this hand,' holding it up, 'that had first locked me in.' The lad shook visibly, but answered never a word. 'Well,' said I, 'I am a stranger and a guest. It is not my part either to meddle or to judge in your affairs; in these you shall take your sister's counsel, which I cannot doubt to be excellent. But in so far as concerns my own I will be no man's prisoner, and I demand that key.' Half an hour later my door was suddenly thrown open, and the key tossed ringing on the floor.

A day or two after I came in from a walk a little before the point of noon. The Señora was lying lapped in slumber on the threshold of the recess; the pigeons dozed below the eaves like snowdrifts; the house was under a deep spell of noontide quiet; and only a wandering and gentle wind from the mountain stole round the galleries, rustled among the pomegranates, and pleasantly stirred the shadows. Something in the stillness moved me to imitation, and I went very lightly across the court and up the marble staircase. My foot was on the topmost round, when a door opened, and I found myself face to face with Olalla. Surprise transfixed me; her loveliness struck to my heart; she glowed in the deep shadow of the gallery, a gem of colour; her eyes took hold upon mine and clung there, and bound us together like the joining of hands; and the moments we thus stood face to face, drinking each other in, were sacramental and the wedding of souls. I know not how long it was before I awoke out of a deep trance, and, hastily bowing, passed on into the upper stair. She did not move, but followed me with her great, thirsting eyes; and as I passed out of sight it seemed to me as if she paled and faded.

In my own room, I opened the window and looked out, and could not think what change had come upon that austere field of mountains that it should thus sing and shine under the lofty heaven. I had seen her – Olalla! And the stone crags answered, Olalla! and the dumb, unfathomable azure answered, Olalla! The pale saint of my dreams had vanished for ever; and in her place I beheld this maiden on whom God had lavished the richest colours and the most exuberant energies of life, whom he had made active as a deer, slender as a reed, and in whose great eyes he had lighted the torches of the soul. The thrill of her young life, strung like a wild animal's, had entered into me; the force of soul that had looked out from her eyes and conquered mine, mantled about my heart and sprang to my lips in singing. She passed through my veins: she was one with me.

I will not say that this enthusiasm declined; rather my soul held out in its ecstasy as in a strong castle, and was there besieged by cold and sorrowful considerations. I could not doubt but that I loved her at first sight, and already with a quivering ardour that was strange to my experience. What then was to follow? She was the child of an afflicted house, the Senora's daughter, the sister of Felipe; she bore it even in her beauty. She had the lightness and swiftness of the one, swift as an arrow, light as dew; like the other, she shone on the pale background of the world with the brilliancy of flowers. I could not call by the name of brother that half-witted lad, nor by the name of mother that immovable and lovely thing of flesh, whose silly eyes and perpetual simper now recurred to my mind like something hateful. And if I could not marry, what then? She was helplessly unprotected; her eyes, in that single and long glance which had been all our intercourse, had confessed a weakness equal to my own; but in my heart I knew her for the student of the cold northern chamber, and the writer of the sorrowful lines; and this was a knowledge to disarm a brute. To flee was more than I could find courage for; but I registered a vow of unsleeping circumspection.

As I turned from the window, my eyes alighted on the portrait. It had fallen dead, like a candle after sunrise; it followed me with eyes of paint. I knew it to be like, and marvelled at the tenacity of type in that declining race; but the likeness was swallowed up in difference. I remembered how it had seemed to me a thing unapproachable in the life, a creature rather of the painter's craft than of the modesty of nature, and I marvelled at the thought, and exulted in the image of Olalla. Beauty I had seen before, and not been charmed, and I had been often drawn to women, who were not beautiful except to me; but in Olalla all that I desired and had not dared to imagine was united.

I did not see her the next day, and my heart ached and my eyes longed for her, as men long for morning. But the day after, when I returned, about my usual hour, she was once more on the gallery, and our looks once more met and embraced. I would have spoken, I would have drawn near to her; but strongly as she plucked at my heart, drawing me like a magnet, something yet more imperious withheld me; and I could only bow and pass by; and she, leaving my salutation unanswered, only followed me with her noble eyes.

I had now her image by rote, and as I conned the traits in memory it seemed as if I read her very heart. She was dressed with something of her mother's coquetry, and love of positive colour. Her robe, which I know she must have made with her own hands, clung about her with a cunning grace. After the fashion of that country, besides, her bodice stood open in the middle, in a long slit, and here, in spite of the poverty of the house, a gold coin, hanging by a ribbon, lay on her brown bosom. These were proofs, had any been needed, of her inborn delight in life and her own loveliness. On the other hand, in her eyes that hung upon mine, I could read depth beyond depth of passion and sadness, lights of poetry and hope, blacknesses of despair, and thoughts that were above the earth. It was a lovely body, but the inmate, the soul, was more than worthy of that lodging. Should I leave this incomparable flower to wither unseen on these rough mountains? Should I despise the great gift offered me in the eloquent silence of her eyes? Here was a soul immured; should I not burst its prison? All side considerations fell off from me; were she the child of Herod I swore I should make her mine; and that very evening I set myself, with a mingled sense of treachery and disgrace, to captivate the brother. Perhaps I read him with more favourable eyes, perhaps the thought of his sister always summoned up the better qualities of that imperfect soul; but he had never seemed to me so amiable, and his very likeness to Olalla, while it annoyed, yet softened me.

A third day passed in vain – an empty desert of hours. I would not lose a chance, and loitered all afternoon in the court where (to give myself a countenance) I spoke more than usual with the Senora. God knows it was with a most tender and sincere interest that I now studied her; and even as for Felipe, so now for the mother, I was conscious of a growing warmth of toleration. And yet I wondered. Even while I spoke with her, she would doze off into a little sleep, and presently awake again without embarrassment; and this composure staggered me. And again, as I marked her make infinitesimal changes in her posture, savouring and lingering on the bodily pleasure of the movement, I was driven to wonder at this depth of passive sensuality. She lived in her body; and her consciousness was all sunk into and disseminated through her members, where it luxuriously dwelt. Lastly, I could not grow accustomed to her eyes. Each time she turned on me these great beautiful and meaningless orbs, wide open to the day, but closed against human inquiry – each time I had occasion to observe the lively changes of her pupils which expanded and contracted in a breath – I know not what it was came over me, I can find no name for the mingled feeling of disappointment, annoyance, and distaste that jarred along my nerves. I tried her on a variety of subjects, equally in vain; and at last led the talk to her daughter. But even there she proved indifferent; said she was pretty, which (as with children) was her highest word of commendation, but was plainly incapable of any higher thought; and when I remarked that Olalla seemed silent, merely yawned in my face and replied that speech was of no great use when you had nothing to say. 'People speak much, very much,' she added, looking at me with expanded pupils; and then again yawned and again showed me a mouth that was as dainty as a toy. This time I took the hint, and, leaving her to her repose, went up into my own chamber to sit by the open window, looking on the hills and not beholding them, sunk in lustrous and deep dreams, and hearkening in fancy to the note of a voice that I had never heard.

I awoke on the fifth morning with a brightness of anticipation that seemed to challenge fate. I was sure of myself, light of heart and foot, and resolved to put my love incontinently to the touch of knowledge. It should lie no longer under the bonds of silence, a dumb thing, living by the eye only, like the love of beasts; but should now put on the spirit, and enter upon the joys of the complete human intimacy. I thought of it with wild hopes, like a voyager to El Dorado; into that unknown and lovely country of her soul, I no longer trembled to adventure. Yet when I did indeed encounter her, the same force of passion descended on me and at once submerged my mind; speech seemed to drop away from me like a childish habit; and I but drew near to her as the giddy man draws near to the margin of a gulf. She drew back from me a little as I came; but her eyes did not waver from mine, and these lured me forward. At last, when I was already within reach of her, I stopped. Words were denied me; if I advanced I could but clasp her to my heart in silence; and all that was sane in me, all that was still unconquered, revolted against the thought of such an accost. So we stood for a second, all our life in our eyes, exchanging salvos of attraction and yet each resisting; and then, with a great effort of the will, and conscious at the same time of a sudden bitterness of disappointment, I turned and went away in the same silence.

What power lay upon me that I could not speak? And she, why was she also silent? Why did she draw away before me dumbly, with fascinated eyes? Was this love? or was it a mere brute attraction, mindless and inevitable, like that of the magnet for the steel? We had never spoken, we were wholly strangers: and yet an influence, strong as the grasp of a giant, swept us silently together. On my side, it filled me with impatience; and yet I was sure that she was worthy; I had seen her books, read her verses, and thus, in a sense, divined the soul of my mistress. But on her side, it struck me almost cold. Of me, she knew nothing but my bodily favour; she was drawn to me as stones fall to the earth; the laws that rule the earth conducted her, unconsenting, to my arms; and I drew back at the thought of such a bridal, and began to be jealous for myself. It was not thus that I desired to be loved. And then I began to fall into a great pity for the girl herself. I thought how sharp must be her mortification, that she, the student, the recluse, Felipe's saintly monitress, should have thus confessed an overweening weakness for a man with whom she had never exchanged a word. And at the coming of pity, all other thoughts were swallowed up; and I longed only to find and console and reassure her; to tell her how wholly her love was returned on my side, and how her choice, even if blindly made, was not unworthy.

The next day it was glorious weather; depth upon depth of blue over-canopied the mountains; the sun shone wide; and the wind in the trees and the many falling torrents in the mountains filled the air with delicate and haunting music. Yet I was prostrated with sadness. My heart wept for the sight of Olalla, as a child weeps for its mother. I sat down on a boulder on the verge of the low cliffs that bound the plateau to the north. Thence I looked down into the wooded valley of a stream, where no foot came. In the mood I was in, it was even touching to behold the place untenanted; it lacked Olalla; and I thought of the delight and glory of a life passed wholly with her in that strong air, and among these rugged and lovely surroundings, at first with a whimpering sentiment, and then again with such a fiery joy that I seemed to grow in strength and stature, like a Samson.

And then suddenly I was aware of Olalla drawing near. She appeared out of a grove of cork-trees, and came straight towards me; and I stood up and waited. She seemed in her walking a creature of such life and fire and lightness as amazed me; yet she came quietly and slowly. Her energy was in the slowness; but for inimitable strength, I felt she would have run, she would have flown to me. Still, as she approached, she kept her eyes lowered to the ground; and when she had drawn quite near, it was without one glance that she addressed me. At the first note of her voice I started. It was for this I had been waiting; this was the last test of my love. And lo, her enunciation was precise and clear, not lisping and incomplete like that of her family; and the voice, though deeper than usual with women, was still both youthful and womanly. She spoke in a rich chord; golden contralto strains mingled with hoarseness, as the red threads were mingled with the brown among her tresses. It was not only a voice that spoke to my heart directly; but it spoke to me of her. And yet her words immediately plunged me back upon despair.

'You will go away,' she said, 'to-day.'

Her example broke the bonds of my speech; I felt as lightened of a weight, or as if a spell had been dissolved. I know not in what words I answered; but, standing before her on the cliffs, I poured out the whole ardour of my love, telling her that I lived upon the thought of her, slept only to dream of her loveliness, and would gladly forswear my country, my language, and my friends, to live for ever by her side. And then, strongly commanding myself, I changed the note; I reassured, I comforted her; I told her I had divined in her a pious and heroic spirit, with which I was worthy to sympathise, and which I longed to share and lighten. 'Nature,' I told her, 'was the voice of God, which men disobey at peril; and if we were thus humbly drawn together, ay, even as by a miracle of love, it must imply a divine fitness in our souls; we must be made,' I said – 'made for one another. We should be mad rebels,' I cried out – 'mad rebels against God, not to obey this instinct.'

She shook her head. 'You will go to-day,' she repeated, and then with a gesture, and in a sudden, sharp note – 'no, not to-day,' she cried, 'to-morrow!'

But at this sign of relenting, power came in upon me in a tide. I stretched out my arms and called upon her name; and she leaped to me and clung to me. The hills rocked about us, the earth quailed; a shock as of a blow went through me and left me blind and dizzy. And the next moment she had thrust me back, broken rudely from my arms, and fled with the speed of a deer among the cork-trees.

I stood and shouted to the mountains; I turned and went back towards the residencia, waltzing upon air. She sent me away, and yet I had but to call upon her name and she came to me. These were but the weaknesses of girls, from which even she, the strangest of her sex, was not exempted. Go? Not I, Olalla – O, not I, Olalla, my Olalla! A bird sang near by; and in that season, birds were rare. It bade me be of good cheer. And once more the whole countenance of nature, from the ponderous and stable mountains down to the lightest leaf and the smallest darting fly in the shadow of the groves, began to stir before me and to put on the lineaments of life and wear a face of awful joy. The sunshine struck upon the hills, strong as a hammer on the anvil, and the hills shook; the earth, under that vigorous insulation, yielded up heady scents; the woods smouldered in the blaze. I felt the thrill of travail and delight run through the earth. Something elemental, something rude, violent, and savage, in the love that sang in my heart, was like a key to nature's secrets; and the very stones that rattled under my feet appeared alive and friendly. Olalla! Her touch had quickened, and renewed, and strung me up to the old pitch of concert with the rugged earth, to a swelling of the soul that men learn to forget in their polite assemblies. Love burned in me like rage; tenderness waxed fierce; I hated, I adored, I pitied, I revered her with ecstasy. She seemed the link that bound me in with dead things on the one hand, and with our pure and pitying God upon the other: a thing brutal and divine, and akin at once to the innocence and to the unbridled forces of the earth.

My head thus reeling, I came into the courtyard of the residencia, and the sight of the mother struck me like a revelation. She sat there, all sloth and contentment, blinking under the strong sunshine, branded with a passive enjoyment, a creature set quite apart, before whom my ardour fell away like a thing ashamed. I stopped a moment, and, commanding such shaken tones as I was able, said a word or two. She looked at me with her unfathomable kindness; her voice in reply sounded vaguely out of the realm of peace in which she slumbered, and there fell on my mind, for the first time, a sense of respect for one so uniformly innocent and happy, and I passed on in a kind of wonder at myself, that I should be so much disquieted.

On my table there lay a piece of the same yellow paper I had seen in the north room; it was written on with pencil in the same hand, Olalla's hand, and I picked it up with a sudden sinking of alarm, and read, 'If you have any kindness for Olalla, if you have any chivalry for a creature sorely wrought, go from here to-day; in pity, in honour, for the sake of

Him who died, I supplicate that you shall go.' I looked at this awhile in mere stupidity, then I began to awaken to a weariness and horror of life; the sunshine darkened outside on the bare hills, and I began to shake like a man in terror. The vacancy thus suddenly opened in my life unmanned me like a physical void. It was not my heart, it was not my happiness, it was life itself that was involved. I could not lose her. I said so, and stood repeating it. And then, like one in a dream, I moved to the window, put forth my hand to open the casement, and thrust it through the pane. The blood spurted from my wrist; and with an instantaneous quietude and command of myself, I pressed my thumb on the little leaping fountain, and reflected what to do. In that empty room there was nothing to my purpose; I felt, besides, that I required assistance. There shot into my mind a hope that Olalla herself might be my helper, and I turned and went downstairs, still keeping my thumb upon the wound.

There was no sign of either Olalla or Felipe, and I addressed myself to the recess, whither the Señora had now drawn quite back and sat dozing close before the fire, for no degree of heat appeared too much for her.

'Pardon me,' said I, 'if I disturb you, but I must apply to you for help.'

She looked up sleepily and asked me what it was, and with the very words I thought she drew in her breath with a widening of the nostrils and seemed to come suddenly and fully alive.

'I have cut myself,' I said, 'and rather badly. See!' And I held out my two hands from which the blood was oozing and dripping.

Her great eyes opened wide, the pupils shrank into points; a veil seemed to fall from her face, and leave it sharply expressive and yet inscrutable. And as I still stood, marvelling a little at her disturbance, she came swiftly up to me, and stooped and caught me by the hand; and the next moment my hand was at her mouth, and she had bitten me to the bone. The pang of the bite, the sudden spurting of blood, and the monstrous horror of the act, flashed through me all in one, and I beat her back; and she sprang at me again and again, with bestial cries, cries that I recognised, such cries as had awakened me on the night of the high wind. Her strength was like that of madness; mine was rapidly ebbing with the loss of blood; my mind besides was whirling with the abhorrent strangeness of the onslaught, and I was already forced against the wall, when Olalla ran betwixt us, and Felipe, following at a bound, pinned down his mother on the floor.

A trance-like weakness fell upon me; I saw, heard, and felt, but I was incapable of movement. I heard the struggle roll to and fro upon the floor, the yells of that catamount ringing up to Heaven as she strove to reach me. I felt Olalla clasp me in her arms, her hair falling on my face, and, with the strength of a man, raise and half drag, half carry me upstairs into my own room, where she cast me down upon the bed. Then I saw her hasten to the door and lock it, and stand an instant listening to the savage cries that shook the residencia. And then, swift and light as a thought, she was again beside me, binding up my hand, laying it in her bosom, moaning and mourning over it with dove-like sounds. They were not words that came to her, they were sounds more beautiful than speech, infinitely touching, infinitely tender; and yet as I lay there, a thought stung to my heart, a thought wounded me like a sword, a thought, like a worm in a flower, profaned the holiness of my love. Yes, they were beautiful sounds, and they were inspired by human tenderness; but was their beauty human?

All day I lay there. For a long time the cries of that nameless female thing, as she struggled with her half-witted whelp, resounded through the house, and pierced me with despairing sorrow and disgust. They were the death-cry of my love; my love was murdered; was not only dead, but an offence to me; and yet, think as I pleased, feel as I must, it still swelled within me like a storm of sweetness, and my heart melted at her looks and touch. This horror that had sprung out, this doubt upon Olalla, this savage and bestial strain that ran not only through the whole behaviour of her family, but found a place in the very foundations and story of our love – though it appalled, though it shocked and sickened me, was yet not of power to break the knot of my infatuation.

When the cries had ceased, there came a scraping at the door, by which I knew Felipe was without; and Olalla went and spoke to him – I know not what. With that exception, she stayed close beside me, now kneeling by my bed and fervently praying, now sitting with her eyes upon mine. So then, for these six hours I drank in her beauty, and silently perused the story in her face. I saw the golden coin hover on her breaths; I saw her eyes darken and brighten, and still speak no language but that of an unfathomable kindness; I saw the faultless face, and, through the robe, the lines of the faultless body. Night came at last, and in the growing darkness of the chamber, the sight of her slowly melted; but even then the touch of her smooth hand lingered in mine and talked with me. To lie thus in deadly weakness and drink in the traits of the beloved, is to reawake to love from whatever shock of disillusion. I reasoned with myself; and I shut my eyes on horrors, and again I was very bold to accept the worst. What mattered it, if that imperious sentiment survived; if her eyes still beckoned and attached me; if now, even as before, every fibre of my dull body yearned and turned to her? Late on in the night some strength revived in me, and I spoke: –

'Olalla,' I said, 'nothing matters; I ask nothing; I am content; I love you.'

She knelt down awhile and prayed, and I devoutly respected her devotions. The moon had begun to shine in upon one side of each of the three windows, and make a misty clearness in the room, by which I saw her indistinctly. When she rearose she made the sign of the cross.

'It is for me to speak,' she said, 'and for you to listen. I know; you can but guess. I prayed, how I prayed for you to leave this place. I begged it of you, and I know you would have granted me even this; or if not, O let me think so!'

'I love you,' I said.

'And yet you have lived in the world,' she said; after a pause, 'you are a man and wise; and I am but a child. Forgive me, if I seem to teach, who am as ignorant as the trees of the mountain; but those who learn much do but skim the face of knowledge; they seize the laws, they conceive the dignity of the design – the horror of the living fact fades from their memory. It is we who sit at home with evil who remember, I think, and are warned and pity. Go, rather, go now, and keep me in mind. So I shall have a life in the cherished places of your memory: a life as much my own, as that which I lead in this body.'

'I love you,' I said once more; and reaching out my weak hand, took hers, and carried it to my lips, and kissed it. Nor did she resist, but winced a little; and I could see her look upon me with a frown that was not unkindly, only sad and baffled. And then it seemed she made a call upon her resolution; plucked my hand towards her, herself at the same time leaning somewhat forward, and laid it on the beating of her heart.

'There,' she cried, 'you feel the very footfall of my life. It only moves for you; it is yours. But is it even mine? It is mine indeed to offer you, as I might take the coin from my neck, as I might break a live branch from a tree, and give it you. And yet not mine! I dwell, or I think I dwell (if I exist at all), somewhere apart, an impotent prisoner, and carried about and deafened by a mob that I disown. This capsule, such as throbs against the sides of animals, knows you at a touch for its master; ay, it loves you! But my soul, does my soul? I think not; I know not, fearing to ask. Yet when you spoke to me your words were of the soul; it is of the soul that you ask – it is only from the soul that you would take me.'

'Olalla,' I said, 'the soul and the body are one, and mostly so in love. What the body chooses, the soul loves; where the body clings, the soul cleaves; body for body, soul to soul, they come together at God's signal; and the lower part (if we can call aught low) is only the footstool and foundation of the highest.'

'Have you,' she said, 'seen the portraits in the house of my fathers? Have you looked at my mother or at Felipe? Have your eyes never rested on that picture that hangs by your bed? She who sat for it died ages ago; and she did evil in her life. But, look again: there is my hand to the least line, there are my eyes and my hair. What is mine, then, and what am I? If not a curve in this poor body of mine (which you love, and for the sake of which you dotingly dream that you love me) not a gesture that I can frame, not a tone of my voice, not any look from my eyes, no, not even now when I speak to him I love, but has belonged to others? Others, ages dead, have wooed other men with my eyes; other men have heard the pleading of the same voice that now sounds in your ears. The hands of the dead are in my bosom; they move me, they pluck me, they guide me; I am a puppet at their command; and I but reinform features and attributes that have long been laid aside from evil in the quiet of the grave. Is it me you love, friend? or the race that made me? The girl who does not know and cannot answer for the least portion of herself? or the stream of which she is a transitory eddy, the tree of which she is the passing fruit? The race exists; it is old, it is ever young, it carries its eternal destiny in its bosom; upon it, like waves upon the sea, individual succeeds to individual, mocked with a semblance of self-control, but they are nothing. We speak of the soul, but the soul is in the race.'

'You fret against the common law,' I said. 'You rebel against the voice of God, which he has made so winning to convince, so imperious to command. Hear it, and how it speaks between us! Your hand clings to mine, your heart leaps at my touch, the unknown elements of which we are compounded awake and run together at a look; the clay of the earth remembers its independent life and yearns to join us; we are drawn together as the stars are turned about in space, or as the tides ebb and flow, by things older and greater than we ourselves.'

'Alas!' she said, 'what can I say to you? My fathers, eight hundred years ago, ruled all this province: they were wise, great, cunning, and cruel; they were a picked race of the Spanish; their flags led in war; the king called them his cousin; the people, when the rope was slung for them or when they returned and found their hovels smoking, blasphemed their name. Presently a change began. Man has risen; if he has sprung from the brutes, he can descend again to the same level. The breath of weariness blew on their humanity and the cords relaxed; they began to go down; their minds fell on sleep, their passions awoke in gusts, heady and senseless like the wind in the gutters of the mountains; beauty was still handed down, but no longer the guiding wit nor the human heart; the seed passed on, it was wrapped in flesh, the flesh covered the bones, but they were the bones and the flesh of brutes, and their mind was as the mind of flies. I speak to you as I dare; but you have seen for yourself how the wheel has gone backward with my doomed race. I stand, as it were, upon a little rising ground in this desperate descent, and see both before and behind, both what we have lost and to what we are condemned to go farther downward. And shall I – I that dwell apart in the house of the dead, my body, loathing its ways – shall I repeat the spell? Shall I bind another spirit, reluctant as my own, into this bewitched and tempest-broken tenement that I now suffer in? Shall I hand down this cursed vessel of humanity, charge it with fresh life as with fresh poison, and dash it, like a fire, in the faces of posterity? But my vow has been given; the race shall cease from off the earth. At this hour my brother is making ready; his foot will soon be on the stair; and you will go with him and pass out of my sight for ever. Think of me sometimes as one to whom the lesson of life was very harshly told, but who heard it with courage; as one who loved you indeed, but who hated herself so deeply that her love was hateful to her; as one who sent you away and yet would have longed to keep you for ever; who had no dearer hope than to forget you, and no greater fear than to be forgotten.'

She had drawn towards the door as she spoke, her rich voice sounding softer and farther away; and with the last word she was gone, and I lay alone in the moonlit chamber. What I might have done had not I lain bound by my extreme weakness, I know not; but as it was there fell upon me a great and blank despair. It was not long before there shone in at the door the ruddy glimmer of a lantern, and Felipe coming, charged me without a word upon his shoulders, and carried me down to the great gate, where the cart was waiting. In the moonlight the hills stood out sharply, as if they were of cardboard; on the glimmering surface of the plateau, and from among the low trees which swung together and sparkled in the wind, the great black cube of the residencia stood out bulkily, its mass only broken by three dimly lighted windows in the northern front above the gate. They were Olalla's windows, and as the cart jolted onwards I kept my eyes fixed upon them till, where the road dipped into a valley, they were lost to my view forever. Felipe walked in silence beside the shafts, but from time to time he would cheek the mule and seem to look back upon me; and at length drew quite near and laid his hand upon my head. There was such kindness in the touch, and such a simplicity, as of the brutes, that tears broke from me like the bursting of an artery.

'Felipe,' I said, 'take me where they will ask no questions.'

He said never a word, but he turned his mule about, end for end, retraced some part of the way we had gone, and, striking into another path, led me to the mountain village, which was, as we say in Scotland, the kirkton of that thinly peopled district. Some broken memories dwell in my mind of the day breaking over the plain, of the cart stopping, of arms that helped me down, of a bare room into which I was carried, and of a swoon that fell upon me like sleep.

The next day and the days following the old priest was often at my side with his snuff-box and prayer book, and after a while, when I began to pick up strength, he told me that I was now on a fair way to recovery, and must as soon as possible hurry my departure; whereupon, without naming any reason, he took snuff and looked at me sideways. I did not affect ignorance; I knew he must have seen Olalla. 'Sir,' said I, 'you know that I do not ask in wantonness. What of that family?'

He said they were very unfortunate; that it seemed a declining race, and that they were very poor and had been much neglected.

'But she has not,' I said. 'Thanks, doubtless, to yourself, she is instructed and wise beyond the use of women.'

'Yes,' he said; 'the Señorita is well-informed. But the family has been neglected.'

'The mother?' I queried.

'Yes, the mother too,' said the Padre, taking snuff. 'But Felipe is a well-intentioned lad.'

'The mother is odd?' I asked.

'Very odd,' replied the priest.

'I think, sir, we beat about the bush,' said I. 'You must know more of my affairs than you allow. You must know my curiosity to be justified on many grounds. Will you not be frank with me?'

'My son,' said the old gentleman, 'I will be very frank with you on matters within my competence; on those of which I know nothing it does not require much discretion to be silent. I will not fence with you, I take your meaning perfectly; and what can I say, but that we are all in God's hands, and that His ways are not as our ways? I have even advised with my superiors in the church, but they, too, were dumb. It is a great mystery.'

'Is she mad?' I asked.

'I will answer you according to my belief. She is not,' returned the Padre, 'or she was not. When she was young – God help me, I fear I neglected that wild lamb – she was surely sane; and yet, although it did not run to such heights, the same strain was already notable; it had been so before her in her father, ay, and before him, and this inclined me, perhaps, to think too lightly of it. But these things go on growing, not only in the individual but in the race.'

'When she was young,' I began, and my voice failed me for a moment, and it was only with a great effort that I was able to add, 'was she like Olalla?'

'Now God forbid!' exclaimed the Padre. 'God forbid that any man should think so slightingly of my favourite penitent. No, no; the Señorita (but for her beauty, which I wish most honestly she had less of) has not a hair's resemblance to what her mother was at the same age. I could not bear to have you think so; though, Heaven knows, it were, perhaps, better that you should.'

At this, I raised myself in bed, and opened my heart to the old man; telling him of our love and of her decision, owning my own horrors, my own passing fancies, but telling him that these were at an end; and with something more than a purely formal submission, appealing to his judgment.

He heard me very patiently and without surprise; and when I had done, he sat for some time silent. Then he began: 'The church,' and instantly broke off again to apologise. 'I had forgotten, my child, that you were not a Christian,' said he. 'And indeed, upon a point so highly unusual, even the church can scarce be said to have decided. But would you have my opinion? The Señorita is, in a matter of this kind, the best judge; I would accept her judgment.'

On the back of that he went away, nor was he thenceforward so assiduous in his visits; indeed, even when I began to get about again, he plainly feared and deprecated my society, not as in distaste but much as a man might be disposed to flee from the riddling sphynx. The villagers, too, avoided me; they were unwilling to be my guides upon the mountain. I thought they looked at me askance, and I made sure that the more superstitious crossed themselves on my approach. At first I set this down to my heretical opinions; but it began at length to dawn upon me that if I was thus redoubted it was because I had stayed at the residencia. All men despise the savage notions of such peasantry; and yet I was conscious of a chill shadow that seemed to fall and dwell upon my love. It did not conquer, but I may not deny that it restrained my ardour.

Some miles westward of the village there was a gap in the sierra, from which the eye plunged direct upon the residencia; and thither it became my daily habit to repair. A wood crowned the summit; and just where the pathway issued from its fringes, it was overhung by a considerable shelf of rock, and that, in its turn, was surmounted by a crucifix of the size of life and more than usually painful in design. This was my perch; thence, day after day, I looked down upon the plateau, and the great old house, and could see Felipe, no bigger than a fly, going to and fro about the garden. Sometimes mists would draw across the view, and be broken up again by mountain winds; sometimes the plain slumbered below me in unbroken sunshine; it would sometimes be all blotted out by rain. This distant post, these interrupted sights of the place where my life had been so strangely changed, suited the indecision of my humour.

I passed whole days there, debating with myself the various elements of our position; now leaning to the suggestions of love, now giving an ear to prudence, and in the end halting irresolute between the two.

One day, as I was sitting on my rock, there came by that way a somewhat gaunt peasant wrapped in a mantle. He was a stranger, and plainly did not know me even by repute; for, instead of keeping the other side, he drew near and sat down beside me, and we had soon fallen in talk. Among other things he told me he had been a muleteer, and in former years had much frequented these mountains; later on, he had followed the army with his mules, had realised a competence, and was now living retired with his family.

'Do you know that house?' I inquired, at last, pointing to the residencia, for I readily wearied of any talk that kept me from the thought of Olalla.

He looked at me darkly and crossed himself.

'Too well,' he said, 'it was there that one of my comrades sold himself to Satan; the Virgin shield us from temptations! He has paid the price; he is now burning in the reddest place in Hell!'

A fear came upon me; I could answer nothing; and presently the man resumed, as if to himself: 'Yes,' he said, 'O yes, I know it. I have passed its doors. There was snow upon the pass, the wind was driving it; sure enough there was death that night upon the mountains, but there was worse beside the hearth. I took him by the arm, Senor, and dragged him to the gate; I conjured him, by all he loved and respected, to go forth with me; I went on my knees before him in the snow; and I could see he was moved by my entreaty. And just then she came out on the gallery, and called him by his name; and he turned, and there was she standing with a lamp in her hand and smiling on him to come back. I cried out aloud to God, and threw my arms about him, but he put me by, and left me alone. He had made his choice; God help us. I would pray for him, but to what end? there are sins that not even the Pope can loose.'

'And your friend,' I asked, 'what became of him?'

'Nay, God knows,' said the muleteer. 'If all be true that we hear, his end was like his sin, a thing to raise the hair.'

'Do you mean that he was killed?' I asked.

'Sure enough, he was killed,' returned the man. 'But how? Ay, how? But these are things that it is sin to speak of.'

'The people of that house . . . ' I began.

But he interrupted me with a savage outburst. 'The people?' he cried. 'What people? There are neither men nor women in that house of Satan's! What? have you lived here so long, and never heard?' And here he put his mouth to my ear and whispered, as if even the fowls of the mountain might have over-heard and been stricken with horror.

What he told me was not true, nor was it even original; being, indeed, but a new edition, vamped up again by village ignorance and superstition, of stories nearly as ancient as the race of man. It was rather the application that appalled me. In the old days, he said, the church would have burned out that nest of basilisks; but the arm of the church was now shortened; his friend Miguel had been unpunished by the hands of men, and left to the more awful judgment of an offended God. This was wrong; but it should be so no more. The Padre was sunk in age; he was even bewitched himself; but the eyes of his flock were now awake to their own danger; and some day – ay, and before long – the smoke of that house should go up to heaven.

He left me filled with horror and fear. Which way to turn I knew not; whether first to warn the Padre, or to carry my ill-news direct to the threatened inhabitants of the residencia. Fate was to decide for me; for, while I was still hesitating, I beheld the veiled figure of a woman drawing near to me up the pathway. No veil could deceive my penetration; by every line and every movement I recognised Olalla; and keeping hidden behind a corner of the rock, I suffered her to gain the summit. Then I came forward. She knew me and paused, but did not speak; I, too, remained silent; and we continued for some time to gaze upon each other with a passionate sadness.

'I thought you had gone,' she said at length. 'It is all that you can do for me – to go. It is all I ever asked of you. And you still stay. But do you know, that every day heaps up the peril of death, not only on your head, but on ours? A report has gone about the mountain; it is thought you love me, and the people will not suffer it.'

I saw she was already informed of her danger, and I rejoiced at it. 'Olalla,' I said, 'I am ready to go this day, this very hour, but not alone.'

She stepped aside and knelt down before the crucifix to pray, and I stood by and looked now at her and now at the object of her adoration, now at the living figure of the penitent, and now at the ghastly, daubed countenance, the painted wounds, and the projected ribs of the image. The silence was only broken by the wailing of some large birds that circled sidelong, as if in surprise or alarm, about the summit of the hills. Presently Olalla rose again, turned towards me, raised her veil, and, still leaning with one hand on the shaft of the crucifix, looked upon me with a pale and sorrowful countenance.

'I have laid my hand upon the cross,' she said. 'The Padre says you are no Christian; but look up for a moment with my eyes, and behold the face of the Man of Sorrows. We are all such as He was – the inheritors of sin; we must all bear and expiate a past which was not ours; there is in all of us – ay, even in me – a sparkle of the divine. Like Him, we must endure for a little while, until morning returns bringing peace. Suffer me to pass on upon my way alone; it is thus that I shall be least lonely, counting for my friend Him who is the friend of all the distressed; it is thus that I shall be the most happy, having taken my farewell of earthly happiness, and willingly accepted sorrow for my portion.'

I looked at the face of the crucifix, and, though I was no friend to images, and despised that imitative and grimacing art of which it was a rude example, some sense of what the thing implied was carried home to my intelligence. The face looked down upon me with a painful and deadly contraction; but the rays of a glory encircled it, and reminded me that the sacrifice was voluntary. It stood there, crowning the rock, as it still stands on so many highway sides, vainly preaching to passers-by, an emblem of sad and noble truths; that pleasure is not an end, but an accident; that pain is the choice of the magnanimous; that it is best to suffer all things and do well. I turned and went down the mountain in silence; and when I looked back for the last time before the wood closed about my path, I saw Olalla still leaning on the crucifix.

Ethan Brand

Nathaniel Hawthorne

Bartram the lime-burner, a rough, heavy-looking man, begrimed with charcoal, sat watching his kiln at nightfall, while his little son played at building houses with the scattered fragments of marble, when, on the hill-side below them, they heard a roar of laughter, not mirthful, but slow, and even solemn, like a wind shaking the boughs of the forest.

"Father, what is that?" asked the little boy, leaving his play, and pressing betwixt his father's knees.

"Oh, some drunken man, I suppose," answered the lime-burner; "some merry fellow from the bar-room in the village, who dared not laugh loud enough within doors lest he should blow the roof of the house off. So here he is, shaking his jolly sides at the foot of Graylock."

"But, father," said the child, more sensitive than the obtuse, middle-aged clown, "he does not laugh like a man that is glad. So the noise frightens me!"

"Don't be a fool, child!" cried his father, gruffly. "You will never make a man, I do believe; there is too much of your mother in you. I have known the rustling of a leaf startle you. Hark! Here comes the merry fellow now. You shall see that there is no harm in him."

Bartram and his little son, while they were talking thus, sat watching the same lime-kiln that had been the scene of Ethan Brand's solitary and meditative life, before he began his search for the Unpardonable Sin.

Many years, as we have seen, had now elapsed, since that portentous night when the *idea* was first developed. The kiln, however, on the mountain-side, stood unimpaired, and was in nothing changed since he had thrown his dark thoughts into the intense glow of its furnace, and melted them, as it were, into the one thought that took possession of his life. It was a rude, round, tower-like structure about twenty feet high, heavily built of rough stones, and with a hillock of earth heaped about the larger part of its circumference; so that the blocks and fragments of marble might be drawn by cart-loads, and thrown in at the top. There was an opening at the bottom of the tower, like an over-mouth, but large enough to admit a man in a stooping posture, and provided with a massive iron door. With the smoke and jets of flame issuing from the chinks and crevices of this door, which seemed to give admittance into the hill-side, it resembled nothing so much as the private entrance to the infernal regions, which the shepherds of the Delectable Mountains were accustomed to show to pilgrims.

There are many such lime-kilns in that tract of country, for the purpose of burning the white marble which composes a large part of the substance of the hills. Some of them, built years ago, and long deserted, with weeds growing in the vacant round of the interior, which is open to the sky, and grass and wild-flowers rooting themselves into the chinks of the stones, look already like relics of antiquity, and may yet be overspread with the lichens of centuries to come. Others, where the limeburner still feeds his daily and night-long fire, afford points of interest to the wanderer among the hills, who seats himself on a log of wood or a fragment of marble, to hold a chat with the solitary man. It is a lonesome, and, when the character is inclined to thought, may be an intensely thoughtful occupation; as it proved in the case of Ethan Brand, who had mused to such strange purpose, in days gone by, while the fire in this very kiln was burning.

The man who now watched the fire was of a different order, and troubled himself with no thoughts save the very few that were requisite to his business. At frequent intervals, he flung back the clashing weight of the iron door, and, turning his face from the insufferable glare, thrust in huge logs of oak, or stirred the immense brands with a long pole. Within the furnace were seen the curling and riotous flames, and the burning marble, almost molten with the intensity of heat; while without, the reflection of the fire quivered on the dark intricacy of the surrounding forest, and showed in the foreground a bright and ruddy little picture of the hut, the spring beside its door, the athletic and coal-begrimed figure of the lime-burner, and the half-frightened child, shrinking into the protection of his father's shadow. And when, again, the iron door was closed, then reappeared the tender light of the half-full moon, which vainly strove to trace out the indistinct shapes of the neighboring mountains; and, in the upper sky, there was a flitting congregation of clouds, still faintly tinged with the rosy sunset, though thus far down into the valley the sunshine had vanished long and long ago.

The little boy now crept still closer to his father, as footsteps were heard ascending the hill-side, and a human form thrust aside the bushes that clustered beneath the trees.

"Halloo! who is it?" cried the lime-burner, vexed at his son's timidity, yet half infected by it. "Come forward, and show yourself, like a man, or I'll fling this chunk of marble at your head!"

"You offer me a rough welcome," said a gloomy voice, as the unknown man drew nigh. "Yet I neither claim nor desire a kinder one, even at my own fireside."

To obtain a distincter view, Bartram threw open the iron door of the kiln, whence immediately issued a gush of fierce light, that smote full upon the stranger's face and figure. To a careless eye there appeared nothing very remarkable in his aspect, which was that of a man in a coarse brown, country-made suit of clothes, tall and thin, with the staff and heavy shoes of a wayfarer. As he advanced, he fixed his eyes – which were very bright – intently upon the brightness of the furnace, as if he beheld, or expected to behold, some object worthy of note within it.

"Good evening, stranger," said the lime-burner; "whence come you, so late in the day?"

"I come from my search," answered the wayfarer; "for, at last, it is finished."

"Drunk! – or crazy!" muttered Bartram to himself. "I shall have trouble with the fellow. The sooner I drive him away, the better."

The little boy, all in a tremble, whispered to his father, and begged him to shut the door of the kiln, so that there might not be so much light; for that there was something in the man's face which he was afraid to look at, yet could not look away from. And, indeed, even the lime-burner's dull and torpid sense began to be impressed by an indescribable something in that thin, rugged, thoughtful visage, with the grizzled hair hanging wildly about it, and those deeply sunken eyes, which gleamed like fires within the entrance of a mysterious cavern. But, as he closed the door, the stranger turned towards him, and spoke in a quiet, familiar way, that made Bartram feel as if he were a sane and sensible man, after all.

"Your task draws to an end, I see," said he. "This marble has already been burning three days. A few hours more will convert the stone to lime."

"Why, who are you?" exclaimed the lime-burner. "You seem as well acquainted with my business as I am myself."

"And well I may be," said the stranger; "for I followed the same craft many a long year, and here, too, on this very spot. But you are a newcomer in these parts. Did you never hear of Ethan Brand?"

"The man that went in search of the Unpardonable Sin?" asked Bartram, with a laugh.

"The same," answered the stranger. "He has found what he sought, and therefore he comes back again."

"What! then you are Ethan Brand himself?" cried the lime-burner, in amazement. "I am a new-comer here, as you say, and they call it eighteen years since you left the foot of Graylock. But, I can tell you, the good folks still talk about Ethan Brand, in the village yonder, and what a strange errand took him away from his lime-kiln. Well, and so you have found the Unpardonable Sin?"

"Even so!" said the stranger, calmly.

"If the question is a fair one," proceeded Bartram, "where might it be?"

Ethan Brand laid his finger on his own heart.

"Here!" replied he.

And then, without mirth in his countenance, but as if moved by an involuntary recognition of the infinite absurdity of seeking throughout the world for what was the closest of all things to himself, and looking into every heart, save his own, for what was hidden in no other breast, he broke into a laugh of scorn. It was the same slow, heavy laugh, that had almost appalled the lime-burner when it heralded the wayfarer's approach.

The solitary mountain-side was made dismal by it. Laughter, when out of place, mistimed, or bursting forth from a disordered state of feeling, may be the most terrible modulation of the human voice. The laughter of one asleep, even if it be a little child, – the madman's laugh, – the wild, screaming laugh of a born idiot, – are sounds that we sometimes tremble to hear, and would always willingly forget. Poets have imagined no utterance of fiends or hobgoblins so fearfully appropriate as a laugh. And even the obtuse lime-burner felt his nerves shaken, as this strange man looked inward at his own heart, and burst into laughter that rolled away into the night, and was indistinctly reverberated among the hills.

"Joe," said he to his little son, "scamper down to the tavern in the village, and tell the jolly fellows there that Ethan Brand has come back, and that he has found the Unpardonable Sin!"

The boy darted away on his errand, to which Ethan Brand made no objection, nor seemed hardly to notice it. He sat on a log of wood, looking steadfastly at the iron door of the kiln. When the child was out of sight, and his swift and light footsteps ceased to be heard treading first on the fallen leaves and then on the rocky mountain-path, the lime-burner began to regret his departure. He felt that the little fellow's presence had been a barrier between his guest and himself, and that he must now deal, heart to heart, with a man who, on his own confession, had committed the one only crime for which Heaven could afford no mercy. That crime, in its indistinct blackness, seemed to overshadow him, and made his memory riotous with a throng of evil shapes that asserted their kindred with the Master Sin, whatever it might be, which it was within the scope of man's corrupted nature to conceive and cherish. They were all of one family; they went to and fro between his breast and Ethan Brand's, and carried dark greetings from one to the other.

Then Bartram remembered the stories which had grown traditionary in reference to this strange man, who had come upon him like a shadow of the night, and was making himself at home in his old place, after so long absence, that the dead people, dead and buried for years, would have had more right to be at home, in any familiar spot, than he. Ethan Brand, it was said, had conversed with Satan himself in the lurid blaze of this very kiln. The legend had been matter of mirth heretofore, but looked grisly now. According to this tale, before Ethan Brand departed on his search, he had been accustomed to evoke a fiend from the hot furnace of the lime-kiln, night after night, in order to confer with him about the Unpardonable Sin; the man and the fiend each laboring to frame the image of some mode of guilt which could neither be atoned for nor forgiven. And, with the first gleam of light upon the mountain-top, the fiend crept in at the iron door, there to abide the intensest element of fire until again summoned forth to share in the dreadful task of extending man's possible guilt beyond the scope of Heaven's else infinite mercy.

While the lime-burner was struggling with the horror of these thoughts, Ethan Brand rose from the log, and flung open the door of the kiln. The action was in such accordance with the idea in Bartram's mind, that he almost expected to see the Evil One issue forth, red-hot, from the raging furnace.

"Hold! hold!" cried he, with a tremulous attempt to laugh; for he was ashamed of his fears, although they overmastered him. "Don't, for mercy's sake, bring out your Devil now!"

"Man!" sternly replied Ethan Brand, "what need have I of the Devil? I have left him behind me, on my track. It is with such half-way sinners as you that he busies himself. Fear not, because I open the door. I do but act by old custom, and am going to trim your fire, like a lime-burner, as I was once."

He stirred the vast coals, thrust in more wood, and bent forward to gaze into the hollow prison-house of the fire, regardless of the fierce glow that reddened upon his face. The lime-burner sat watching him, and half suspected this strange guest of a purpose, if not to evoke a fiend, at least to plunge into the flames, and thus vanish from the sight of man. Ethan Brand, however, drew quietly back, and closed the door of the kiln.

"I have looked," said he, "into many a human heart that was seven times hotter with sinful passions than yonder furnace is with fire. But I found not there what I sought. No, not the Unpardonable Sin!"

"What is the Unpardonable Sin?" asked the lime-burner; and then he shrank farther from his companion, trembling lest his question should be answered.

"It is a sin that grew within my own breast," replied Ethan Brand, standing erect with a pride that distinguishes all enthusiasts of his stamp. "A sin that grew nowhere else! The sin of an intellect that triumphed over the sense of brotherhood with man and reverence for God, and sacrificed everything to its own mighty claims! The only sin that deserves a recompense of immortal agony! Freely, were it to do again, would I incur the guilt. Unshrinkingly I accept the retribution!"

"The man's head is turned," muttered the lime-burner to himself. "He may be a sinner like the rest of us, – nothing more likely, – but, I'll be sworn, he is a madman too."

Nevertheless, he felt uncomfortable at his situation, alone with Ethan Brand on the wild mountain-side, and was right glad to hear the rough murmur of tongues, and the footsteps of what seemed a pretty numerous party, stumbling over the stones and rustling through the underbrush. Soon appeared the whole lazy regiment that was wont to infest the village tavern, comprehending three or four individuals who had drunk flip beside the bar-room fire through all the winters, and smoked their pipes beneath the stoop through all the summers, since Ethan Brand's departure. Laughing boisterously, and mingling all their voices together in unceremonious talk, they now burst into the moonshine and narrow streaks of firelight that illuminated the open space before the lime-kiln. Bartram set the door ajar again, flooding the spot with light, that the whole company might get a fair view of Ethan Brand, and he of them.

There, among other old acquaintances, was a once ubiquitous man, now almost extinct, but whom we were formerly sure to encounter at the hotel of every thriving village throughout the country. It was the stage-agent. The present specimen of the genus was a wilted and smoke-dried man, wrinkled and red-nosed, in a smartly cut, brown, bobtailed coat, with brass buttons, who, for a length of time unknown, had kept his desk and corner in the bar-room, and was still puffing what seemed to be the same cigar that he had lighted twenty years before. He had great fame as a dry joker, though, perhaps, less on account of any intrinsic humor than from a certain flavor of brandy-toddy and tobacco-smoke, which impregnated all his ideas and expressions, as well as his person. Another well-remembered, though strangely altered, face was that of Lawyer Giles, as people still called him in courtesy; an elderly ragamuffin, in his soiled shirtsleeves and tow-cloth trousers. This poor fellow had been an attorney, in what he called his better days, a sharp practitioner, and in great vogue among the village litigants; but flip, and sling, and toddy, and cocktails, imbibed at all hours, morning, noon, and night, had caused him to slide from intellectual to various kinds and degrees of bodily labor, till at last, to adopt his own phrase, he slid into a soap-vat. In other words, Giles was now a soap-boiler, in a small way. He had come to be but the fragment of a human being, a part of one foot having been chopped off by an axe, and an entire hand torn away by the devilish grip of a steam-engine. Yet, though the corporeal hand was gone, a spiritual member remained; for, stretching forth the stump, Giles steadfastly averred that he felt an invisible thumb and fingers with as vivid a sensation as before the real ones were amputated. A maimed and miserable wretch he was; but one, nevertheless, whom the world could not trample on, and had no right to scorn, either in this or any previous stage of his misfortunes, since he had still kept up the courage and spirit of a man, asked nothing in charity, and with his one hand – and that the left one – fought a stern battle against want and hostile circumstances.

Among the throng, too, came another personage, who, with certain points of similarity to Lawyer Giles, had many more of difference. It was the village doctor; a man of some fifty years, whom, at an earlier period of his life, we introduced as paying a professional visit to Ethan Brand during the latter's supposed insanity. He was now a purple-visaged, rude, and brutal, yet half-gentlemanly figure, with something wild, ruined, and desperate in his talk, and in all the details of his gesture and manners. Brandy possessed this man like an evil spirit, and made him as surly and savage as a wild beast, and as miserable as a lost soul; but there was supposed to be in him such wonderful skill, such native gifts of healing, beyond any which medical science could impart, that society caught hold of him, and would not let him sink out of its reach. So, swaying to and fro upon his horse, and grumbling thick accents at the bedside, he visited all the sick-chambers for miles about among the mountain towns, and sometimes raised a dying man, as it were, by miracle, or quite as often, no doubt, sent his patient to a grave that was dug many a year too soon. The doctor had an everlasting pipe in his mouth, and, as somebody said, in allusion to his habit of swearing, it was always alight with hell-fire.

These three worthies pressed forward, and greeted Ethan Brand each after his own fashion, earnestly inviting him to partake of the contents of a certain black bottle, in which, as they averred, he would find something far better worth seeking than the Unpardonable Sin. No mind, which has wrought itself by intense and solitary meditation into a high state of enthusiasm, can endure the kind of contact with low and vulgar modes of thought and feeling to which Ethan Brand was now subjected. It made him doubt – and, strange to say, it was a painful doubt – whether he had indeed found the Unpardonable Sin, and found it within himself. The whole question on which he had exhausted life, and more than life, looked like a delusion.

"Leave me," he said bitterly, "ye brute beasts, that have made yourselves so, shrivelling up your souls with fiery liquors! I have done with you. Years and years ago, I groped into your hearts and found nothing there for my purpose. Get ye gone!"

"Why, you uncivil scoundrel," cried the fierce doctor, "is that the way you respond to the kindness of your best friends? Then let me tell you the truth. You have no more found the Unpardonable Sin than yonder boy Joe has. You are but a crazy fellow, – I told you so twenty years ago, – neither better nor worse than a crazy fellow, and the fit companion of old Humphrey, here!"

He pointed to an old man, shabbily dressed, with long white hair, thin visage, and unsteady eyes. For some years past this aged person had been wandering about among the hills, inquiring of all travellers whom he met for his daughter. The girl, it seemed, had gone off with a company of circus-performers, and occasionally tidings of her came to the village, and fine stories were told of her glittering appearance as she rode on horseback in the ring, or performed marvellous feats on the tight-rope.

The white-haired father now approached Ethan Brand, and gazed unsteadily into his face.

"They tell me you have been all over the earth," said he, wringing his hands with earnestness. "You must have seen my daughter, for she makes a grand figure in the world, and everybody goes to see her. Did she send any word to her old father, or say when she was coming back?"

Ethan Brand's eye quailed beneath the old man's. That daughter, from whom he so earnestly desired a word of greeting, was the Esther of our tale, the very girl whom, with such cold and remorseless purpose, Ethan Brand had made the subject of a psychological experiment, and wasted, absorbed, and perhaps annihilated her soul, in the process.

"Yes," he murmured, turning away from the hoary wanderer, "it is no delusion. There is an Unpardonable Sin!"

While these things were passing, a merry scene was going forward in the area of cheerful light, beside the spring and before the door of the hut. A number of the youth of the village, young men and girls, had hurried up the hill-side, impelled by curiosity to see Ethan Brand, the hero of so many a legend familiar to their childhood. Finding nothing, however, very remarkable in his aspect, – nothing but a sunburnt wayfarer, in plain garb and dusty shoes, who sat looking into the fire as if he fancied pictures among the coals, – these young people speedily grew tired of observing him. As it happened, there was other amusement at hand. An old German Jew travelling with a diorama on his back, was passing down the mountain-road towards the village just as the party turned aside from it, and, in hopes of eking out the profits of the day, the showman had kept them company to the lime-kiln.

"Come, old Dutchman," cried one of the young men, "let us see your pictures, if you can swear they are worth looking at!"

"Oh yes, Captain," answered the Jew, – whether as a matter of courtesy or craft, he styled everybody Captain, – "I shall show you, indeed, some very superb pictures!"

So, placing his box in a proper position, he invited the young men and girls to look through the glass orifices of the machine, and proceeded to exhibit a series of the most outrageous scratchings and daubings, as specimens of the fine arts, that ever an itinerant showman had the face to impose upon his circle of spectators. The pictures were worn out, moreover, tattered, full of cracks and wrinkles, dingy with tobacco-smoke, and otherwise in a most pitiable condition. Some purported to be cities, public edifices, and ruined castles in Europe; others represented Napoleon's battles and Nelson's sea-fights; and in the midst of these would be seen a gigantic, brown, hairy hand, – which might have been mistaken for the Hand of Destiny, though, in truth, it was only the showman's, – pointing its forefinger to various scenes of the conflict, while its owner gave historical illustrations. When, with much merriment at its abominable deficiency of merit, the exhibition was concluded, the German bade little Joe put his head into the box. Viewed through the magnifying-glasses, the boy's round, rosy visage assumed the strangest imaginable aspect of an immense Titanic child, the mouth grinning broadly, and the eyes and every other feature overflowing with fun at the joke. Suddenly, however, that merry face turned pale, and its expression changed to horror, for this easily impressed and excitable child had become sensible that the eye of Ethan Brand was fixed upon him through the glass.

"You make the little man to be afraid, Captain," said the German Jew, turning up the dark and strong outline of his visage from his stooping posture. "But look again, and, by chance, I shall cause you to see somewhat that is very fine, upon my word!"

Ethan Brand gazed into the box for an instant, and then starting back, looked fixedly at the German. What had he seen? Nothing, apparently; for a curious youth, who had peeped in almost at the same moment, beheld only a vacant space of canvas.

"I remember you now," muttered Ethan Brand to the showman.

"Ah, Captain," whispered the Jew of Nuremberg, with a dark smile, "I find it to be a heavy matter in my show-box, – this Unpardonable Sin! By my faith, Captain, it has wearied my shoulders, this long day, to carry it over the mountain."

"Peace," answered Ethan Brand, sternly, "or get thee into the furnace yonder!"

The Jew's exhibition had scarcely concluded, when a great, elderly dog – who seemed to be his own master, as no person in the company laid claim to him – saw fit to render himself the object of public notice. Hitherto, he had shown himself a very quiet, well-disposed old dog, going round from one to another, and, by way of being sociable, offering his rough head to be patted by any kindly hand that would take so much trouble. But now, all of a sudden, this grave and venerable quadruped, of his own mere motion, and without the slightest suggestion from anybody else, began to run round after his tail, which, to heighten the absurdity of the proceeding, was a great deal shorter than it should have been. Never was seen such headlong eagerness in pursuit of an object that could not possibly be attained; never was heard such a tremendous outbreak of growling, snarling, barking, and snapping, – as if one end of the ridiculous brute's body were at deadly and most unforgivable enmity with the other. Faster and faster, round about went the cur; and faster and still faster fled the unapproachable brevity of his tail; and louder and fiercer grew his yells of rage and animosity; until, utterly exhausted, and as far from the goal as ever, the foolish old dog ceased his performance as suddenly as he had begun it. The next moment he was as mild, quiet, sensible, and respectable in his deportment, as when he first scraped acquaintance with the company.

As may be supposed, the exhibition was greeted with universal laughter, clapping of hands, and shouts of encore, to which the canine performer responded by wagging all that there was to wag of his tail, but appeared totally unable to repeat his very successful effort to amuse the spectators.

Meanwhile, Ethan Brand had resumed his seat upon the log, and moved, as it might be, by a perception of some remote analogy between his own case and that of this self-pursuing cur, he broke into the awful laugh, which, more than any other token, expressed the condition of his inward being. From that moment, the merriment of the party was at an end; they stood aghast, dreading lest the inauspicious sound should be reverberated around the horizon, and that mountain would thunder it to mountain, and so the horror be prolonged upon their ears. Then, whispering one to another that it was late, – that the moon was almost down, – that the August night was growing chill, – they hurried homewards, leaving the lime-burner and little Joe to deal as they might with their unwelcome guest. Save for these three human beings, the open space on the hill-side was a solitude, set in a vast gloom of forest. Beyond that darksome verge, the firelight glimmered on the stately trunks and almost black foliage of pines, intermixed with the lighter verdure of sapling oaks, maples, and poplars, while here and there lay the gigantic corpses of dead trees, decaying on the leaf-strewn soil. And it seemed to little Joe – a timorous and imaginative child – that the silent forest was holding its breath until some fearful thing should happen.

Ethan Brand thrust more wood into the fire, and closed the door of the kiln; then looking over his shoulder at the lime-burner and his son, he bade, rather than advised, them to retire to rest.

"For myself, I cannot sleep," said he. "I have matters that it concerns me to meditate upon. I will watch the fire, as I used to do in the old time."

"And call the Devil out of the furnace to keep you company, I suppose," muttered Bartram, who had been making intimate acquaintance with the black bottle above mentioned. "But watch, if you like, and call as many devils as you like! For my part, I shall be all the better for a snooze. Come, Joe!"

As the boy followed his father into the hut, he looked back at the wayfarer, and the tears came into his eyes, for his tender spirit had an intuition of the bleak and terrible loneliness in which this man had enveloped himself.

When they had gone, Ethan Brand sat listening to the crackling of the kindled wood, and looking at the little spirts of fire that issued through the chinks of the door. These trifles, however, once so familiar, had but the slightest hold of his attention, while deep within his mind he was reviewing the gradual but marvellous change that had been wrought upon him by the search to which he had devoted himself. He remembered how the night dew had fallen upon him, – how the dark forest had whispered to him, – how the stars had gleamed upon him, – a simple and loving man, watching his fire in the years gone by, and ever musing as it burned. He remembered with what tenderness, with what love and sympathy for mankind and what pity for human guilt and woe, he had first begun to contemplate those ideas which afterwards became the inspiration of his life; with what reverence he had then looked into the heart of man, viewing it as a temple originally divine, and, however desecrated, still to be held sacred by a brother; with what awful fear he had deprecated the success of his pursuit, and prayed that the Unpardonable Sin might never be revealed to him. Then ensued that vast intellectual development, which, in its progress, disturbed the counterpoise between his mind and heart. The Idea that possessed his life had operated as a means of education; it had gone on cultivating his powers to the highest point of which they were susceptible; it had raised him from the level of an unlettered laborer to stand on a star-lit eminence, whither the philosophers of the earth, laden with the lore of universities, might vainly strive to clamber after him. So much for the intellect! But where was the heart? That, indeed, had withered, – had contracted, – had hardened, – had perished! It had ceased to partake of the universal throb. He had lost his hold of the magnetic chain of humanity. He was no longer a brother-man, opening the chambers or the dungeons of our common nature by the key of holy sympathy, which gave him a right to share in all its secrets; he was now a cold observer, looking on mankind as the subject of his experiment, and, at length, converting man and woman to be his puppets, and pulling the wires that moved them to such degrees of crime as were demanded for his study.

Thus Ethan Brand became a fiend. He began to be so from the moment that his moral nature had ceased to keep the pace of improvement with his intellect. And now, as his highest effort and inevitable development, – as the bright and gorgeous flower, and rich, delicious fruit of his life's labor, – he had produced the Unpardonable Sin!

"What more have I to seek? what more to achieve?" said Ethan Brand to himself. "My task is done, and well done!"

Starting from the log with a certain alacrity in his gait and ascending the hillock of earth that was raised against the stone circumference of the lime-kiln, he thus reached the top of the structure. It was a space of perhaps ten feet across, from edge to edge, presenting a view of the upper surface of the immense mass of broken marble with which the kiln was heaped. All these innumerable blocks and fragments of marble were red-hot and vividly on fire, sending up great spouts of blue flame, which quivered aloft and danced madly, as within a magic circle, and sank and rose again, with continual and multitudinous activity. As the lonely man bent forward over this terrible body of fire, the blasting heat smote up against his person with a breath that, it might be supposed, would have scorched and shrivelled him up in a moment.

Ethan Brand stood erect, and raised his arms on high. The blue flames played upon his face, and imparted the wild and ghastly light which alone could have suited its expression; it was that of a fiend on the verge of plunging into his gulf of intensest torment.

"O Mother Earth," cried he, "who art no more my Mother, and into whose bosom this frame shall never be resolved! O mankind, whose brotherhood I have cast off, and trampled thy great heart beneath my feet! O stars of heaven, that shone on me of old, as if to light me onward and upward! – farewell all, and forever. Come, deadly element of Fire, – henceforth my familiar friend! Embrace me, as I do thee!"

That night the sound of a fearful peal of laughter rolled heavily through the sleep of the lime-burner and his little son; dim shapes of horror and anguish haunted their dreams, and seemed still present in the rude hovel, when they opened their eyes to the daylight.

"Up, boy, up!" cried the lime-burner, staring about him. "Thank Heaven, the night is gone, at last; and rather than pass such another, I would watch my lime-kiln, wide awake, for a twelvemonth. This Ethan Brand, with his humbug of an Unpardonable Sin, has done me no such mighty favor, in taking my place!"

He issued from the hut, followed by little Joe, who kept fast hold of his father's hand. The early sunshine was already pouring its gold upon the mountain-tops, and though the valleys were still in shadow, they smiled cheerfully in the promise of the bright day that was hastening onward. The village, completely shut in by hills, which swelled away gently about it, looked as if it had rested peacefully in the hollow of the great hand of Providence. Every dwelling was distinctly visible; the little spires of the two churches pointed upwards, and caught a fore-glimmering of brightness from the sun-gilt skies upon their gilded weather-cocks. The tavern was astir, and the figure of the old, smoke-dried stage-agent, cigar in mouth, was seen beneath the stoop. Old Graylock was glorified with a golden cloud upon his head. Scattered likewise over the breasts of the surrounding mountains, there were heaps of hoary mist, in fantastic shapes, some of them far down into the valley, others high up towards the summits, and still others, of the same family of mist or cloud, hovering in the gold radiance of the upper atmosphere. Stepping from one to another of the clouds that rested on the hills, and thence to the loftier brotherhood that sailed in air, it seemed almost as if a mortal man might thus ascend into the heavenly regions. Earth was so mingled with sky that it was a day-dream to look at it.

To supply that charm of the familiar and homely, which Nature so readily adopts into a scene like this, the stage-coach was rattling down the mountain-road, and the driver sounded his horn, while Echo caught up the notes, and intertwined them into a rich and varied and elaborate harmony, of which the original performer could lay claim to little share. The great hills played a concert among themselves, each contributing a strain of airy sweetness.

Little Joe's face brightened at once.

"Dear father," cried he, skipping cheerily to and fro, "that strange man is gone, and the sky and the mountains all seem glad of it!"

"Yes," growled the lime-burner, with an oath, "but he has let the fire go down, and no thanks to him if five hundred bushels of lime are not spoiled. If I catch the fellow hereabouts again, I shall feel like tossing him into the furnace!"

With his long pole in his hand, he ascended to the top of the kiln. After a moment's pause, he called to his son.

"Come up here, Joe!" said he.

So little Joe ran up the hillock, and stood by his father's side. The marble was all burnt into perfect, snow-white lime. But on its surface, in the midst of the circle, – snow-white too, and thoroughly converted into lime, – lay a human skeleton, in the attitude of a person who, after long toil, lies down to long repose. Within the ribs – strange to say – was the shape of a human heart.

"Was the fellow's heart made of marble?" cried Bartram, in some perplexity at this phenomenon. "At any rate, it is burnt into what looks like special good lime; and, taking all the bones together, my kiln is half a bushel the richer for him."

So saying, the rude lime-burner lifted his pole, and, letting it fall upon the skeleton, the relics of Ethan Brand were crumbled into fragments.

The Old Nurse's Story

Elizabeth Gaskell

You know, my dears, that your mother was an orphan, and an only child; and I dare say you have heard that your grandfather was a clergyman up in Westmoreland, where I come from. I was just a girl in the village school, when, one day, your grandmother came in to ask the mistress if there was any scholar there who would do for a nurse-maid; and mighty proud I was, I can tell ye, when the mistress called me up, and spoke to my being a good girl at my needle, and a steady, honest girl, and one whose parents were very respectable, though they might be poor. I thought I should like nothing better than to serve the pretty young lady, who was blushing as deep as I was, as she spoke of the coming baby, and what I should have to do with it. However, I see you don't care so much for this part of my story, as for what you think is to come, so I'll tell you at once. I was engaged and settled at the parsonage before Miss Rosamond (that was the baby, who is now your mother) was born. To be sure, I had little enough to do with her when she came, for she was never out of her mother's arms, and slept by her all night long; and proud enough was I sometimes when missis trusted her to me. There never was such a baby before or since, though you've all of you been fine enough in your turns; but for sweet, winning ways, you've none of you come up to your mother. She took after her mother, who was a real lady born; a Miss Furnivall, a grand-daughter of Lord Furnivall's, in Northumberland. I believe she had neither brother nor sister, and had been brought up in my lord's family till she had married your grandfather, who was just a curate, son to a shopkeeper in Carlisle – but a clever, fine gentleman as ever was – and one who was a right-down hard worker in his parish, which was very wide, and scattered all abroad over the Westmoreland Fells. When your mother, little Miss Rosamond, was about four or five years old, both her parents died in a fortnight – one after the other. Ah! that was a sad time. My pretty young mistress and me was looking for another baby, when my master came home from one of his long rides, wet and tired, and took the fever he died of; and then she never held up her head again, but just lived to see her dead baby, and have it laid on her breast, before she sighed away her life. My mistress had asked me, on her death-bed, never to leave Miss Rosamond; but if she had never spoken a word, I would have gone with the little child to the end of the world.

The next thing, and before we had well stilled our sobs, the executors and guardians came to settle the affairs. They were my poor young mistress's own cousin, Lord Furnivall, and Mr Esthwaite, my master's brother, a shopkeeper in Manchester; not so well-to-do then as he was afterwards, and with a large family rising about him. Well! I don't know if it were their settling, or because of a letter my mistress wrote on her death-bed to her cousin, my lord; but somehow it was settled that Miss Rosamond and me were to go to Furnivall Manor House, in Northumberland; and my lord spoke as if it had been her mother's wish that she should live with his family, and as if he had no objections, for that one or two more or less could make no difference in so grand a household. So, though that was not the way in which I should have wished the coming of my bright and pretty pet to have been looked at – who was like a sunbeam in any family, be it never so grand – I was well pleased that all the folks in the Dale should stare and admire, when they heard I was going to be young lady's maid at my Lord Furnivall's at Furnivall Manor.

But I made a mistake in thinking we were to go and live where my lord did. It turned out that the family had left Furnivall Manor House fifty years or more. I could not hear that my poor young mistress had ever been there, though she had been brought up in the family; and I was sorry for that, for I should have liked Miss Rosamond's youth to have passed where her mother's had been.

My lord's gentleman, from whom I asked as many questions as I durst, said that the Manor House was at the foot of the Cumberland Fells, and a very grand place; that an old Miss Furnivall, a great-aunt of my lord's, lived there, with only a few servants; but that it was a very healthy place, and my lord had thought that it would suit Miss Rosamond very well for a few years, and that her being there might perhaps amuse his old aunt.

I was bidden by my lord to have Miss Rosamond's things ready by a certain day. He was a stern, proud man, as they say all the Lords Furnivall were; and he never spoke a word more than was necessary. Folk did say he had loved my young mistress; but that, because she knew that his father would object, she would never listen to him, and married Mr Esthwaite; but I don't know. He never married, at any rate. But he never took much notice of Miss Rosamond; which I thought he might have done if he had cared for her dead mother. He sent his gentleman with us to the Manor House, telling him to join him at Newcastle that same evening; so there was no great length of time for him to make us known to all the strangers before he, too, shook us off; and we were left, two lonely young things (I was not eighteen) in the great old Manor House. It seems like yesterday that we drove there. We had left our own dear parsonage very early, and we had both cried as if our hearts would break, though we were travelling in my lord's carriage, which I thought so much of once. And now it was long past noon on a September day, and we stopped to change horses for the last time at a little smoky town, all full of colliers and miners. Miss Rosamond had fallen asleep, but Mr Henry told me to waken her, that she might see the park and the Manor House as we drove up. I thought it rather a pity; but I did what he bade me, for fear he should complain of me to my lord. We had left all signs of a town, or even a village, and were then inside the gates of a large wild park – not like the parks here in the south, but with rocks, and the noise of running water, and gnarled thorn-trees, and old oaks, all white and peeled with age.

The road went up about two miles, and then we saw a great and stately house, with many trees close around it, so close that in some places their branches dragged against the walls when the wind blew, and some hung broken down; for no one seemed to take much charge of the place; – to lop the wood, or to keep the moss-covered carriage-way in order. Only in front of the house all was clear. The great oval drive was without a weed; and neither tree nor creeper was allowed to grow over the long, many-windowed front; at both sides of which a wing projected, which were each the ends of other side fronts; for the house, although it was so desolate, was even grander than I expected. Behind it rose the Fells, which seemed unenclosed and bare enough; and on the left hand of the house, as you stood facing it, was a little, old-fashioned flower-garden, as I found out afterwards. A door opened out upon it from the west front; it had been scooped out of the thick, dark wood for some old Lady Furnivall; but the branches of the great forest-trees had grown and overshadowed it again, and there were very few flowers that would live there at that time.

When we drove up to the great front entrance, and went into the hall, I thought we should be lost – it was so large, and vast, and grand. There was a chandelier all of bronze, hung down from the middle of the ceiling; and I had never seen one before, and looked at it all in amaze. Then, at one end of the hall, was a great fireplace, as large as the sides of the houses in my country, with massy andirons and dogs to hold the wood; and by it were heavy, old-fashioned sofas. At the opposite end of the hall, to the left as you went in – on the western side – was an organ built into the wall, and so large that it filled up the best part of that end. Beyond it, on the same side, was a door; and opposite, on each side of the fireplace, were also doors leading to the east front; but those I never went through as long as I stayed in the house, so I can't tell you what lay beyond.

The afternoon was closing in, and the hall, which had no fire lighted in it, looked dark and gloomy; but we did not stay there a moment. The old servant, who had opened the door for us, bowed to Mr Henry, and took us in through the door at the further side of the great organ, and led us through several smaller halls and passages into the west drawing-room, where he said that Miss Furnivall was sitting. Poor little Miss Rosamond held very tight to me, as if she were scared and lost in that great place; and as for myself, I was not much better. The west drawing-room was very cheerful-looking, with a warm fire in it, and plenty of good, comfortable furniture about. Miss Furnivall was an old lady not far from eighty, I should think, but I do not know. She was thin and tall, and had a face as full of fine wrinkles as if they had been drawn all over it with a needle's point. Her eyes were very watchful, to make up, I suppose, for her being so deaf as to be obliged to use a trumpet. Sitting with her, working at the same great piece of tapestry, was Mrs Stark, her maid and companion, and almost as old as she was. She had lived with Miss Furnivall ever since they both were young, and now she seemed more like a friend than a servant; she looked so cold, and gray, and stony, as if she had never loved or cared for anyone; and I don't suppose she did care for anyone, except her mistress; and, owing to the great deafness of the latter, Mrs Stark treated her very much as if she were a child. Mr Henry gave some message from my lord, and then he bowed good-bye to us all – taking no notice of my sweet little Miss Rosamond's outstretched hand – and left us standing there, being looked at by the two old ladies through their spectacles.

I was right glad when they rung for the old footman who had shown us in at first, and told him to take us to our rooms. So we went out of that great drawing-room, and into another sitting-room, and out of that, and then up a great flight of stairs, and along a broad gallery – which was something like a library, having books all down one side, and windows and writing-tables all down the other – till we came to our rooms, which I was not sorry to hear were just over the kitchens; for I began to think I should be lost in that wilderness of a house. There was an old nursery, that had been used for all the little lords and ladies long ago, with a pleasant fire burning in the grate, and the kettle boiling on the hob, and tea-things spread out on the table; and out of that room was the night-nursery, with a little crib for Miss Rosamond close to my bed. And old James called up Dorothy, his wife, to bid us welcome; and both he and she were so hospitable and kind, that by-and-by Miss Rosamond and me felt quite at home; and by the time tea was over, she was sitting on Dorothy's knee, and chattering away as fast as her little tongue could go. I soon found out that Dorothy was from Westmoreland, and that bound her and me together, as it were; and I would never wish to meet with kinder people than were old James and his wife. James had lived pretty nearly all his life in my lord's family, and thought there was no one so grand as they. He even looked down a little on his wife; because, till he had married her, she had never lived in any but a farmer's household. But he was very fond of her, as well he might be. They had one servant under them, to do all the rough work. Agnes they called her; and she and me, and James and Dorothy, with Miss Furnivall and Mrs Stark, made up the family; always remembering my sweet little Miss Rosamond! I used to wonder what they had done before she came, they thought so much of her now. Kitchen and drawing-room, it was all the same. The hard, sad Miss Furnivall, and the cold Mrs Stark, looked pleased when she came fluttering in like a bird, playing and pranking hither and thither, with a continual murmur, and pretty prattle of gladness. I am sure, they were sorry many a time when she flitted away into the kitchen, though they were too proud to ask her to stay with them, and were a little surprised at her taste; though to be sure, as Mrs Stark said, it was not to be wondered at, remembering what stock her father had come of. The great, old rambling house was a famous place for little Miss Rosamond. She made expeditions all over it, with me at her heels: all, except the east wing, which was never opened, and whither we never thought of going. But in the western and northern part was many a pleasant room; full of things that were curiosities to us, though they might not have been to people who had seen more. The windows were darkened by the sweeping boughs of the trees, and the ivy which had overgrown them; but, in the green gloom, we could manage to see old china jars and carved ivory boxes, and great heavy books, and, above all, the old pictures!

Once, I remember, my darling would have Dorothy go with us to tell us who they all were; for they were all portraits of some of my lord's family, though Dorothy could not tell us the names of every one. We had gone through most of the rooms, when we came to the old state drawing-room over the hall, and there was a picture of Miss Furnivall; or, as she was called in those days, Miss Grace, for she was the younger sister. Such a beauty she must have been! but with such a set, proud look, and such scorn looking out of her handsome eyes, with her eyebrows just a little raised, as if she wondered how anyone could have the impertinence to look at her, and her lip curled at us, as we stood there gazing. She had a dress on, the like of which I had never seen before, but it was all the fashion when she was young: a hat of some soft white stuff like beaver, pulled a little over her brows, and a beautiful plume of feathers sweeping round it on one side; and her gown of blue satin was open in front to a quilted white stomacher.

'Well, to be sure!' said I, when I had gazed my fill. 'Flesh is grass, they do say; but who would have thought that Miss Furnivall had been such an out-and-out beauty, to see her now?'

'Yes,' said Dorothy. 'Folks change sadly. But if what my master's father used to say was true, Miss Furnivall, the elder sister, was handsomer than Miss Grace. Her picture is here somewhere; but, if I show it you, you must never let on, even to James, that you have seen it Can the little lady hold her tongue, think you?' asked she.

I was not so sure, for she was such a little sweet, bold, open-spoken child, so I set her to hide herself; and then I helped Dorothy to turn a great picture, that leaned with its face towards the wall, and was not hung up as the others were. To be sure, it beat Miss Grace for beauty; and I think, for scornful pride, too, though in that matter it might be hard to choose. I could have looked at it an hour but Dorothy seemed half frightened at having shown it to me, and hurried it back again, and bade me run and find Miss Rosamond, for that there were some ugly places about the house, where she should like ill for the child to go. I was a brave, high-spirited girl, and thought little of what the old woman said, for I liked hide-and-seek as well as any child in the parish; so off I ran to find my little one.

As winter drew on, and the days grew shorter, I was sometimes almost certain that I heard a noise as if someone was playing on the great organ in the hall. I did not hear it every evening; but, certainly, I did very often, usually when I was sitting with Miss Rosamond, after I had put her to bed, and keeping quite still and silent in the bedroom. Then I used to hear it booming and swelling away in the distance. The first night, when I went down to my supper, I asked Dorothy who had been playing music, and James said very shortly that I was a gowk to take the wind soughing among the trees for music; but I saw Dorothy look at him very fearfully, and Bessy, the kitchen-maid, said something beneath her breath, and went quite white. I saw they did not like my question, so I held my peace till I was with Dorothy alone, when I knew I could get a good deal out of her. So, the next day, I watched my time, and I coaxed and asked her who it was that played the organ; for I knew that it was the organ and not the wind well enough, for all I had kept silence before James. But Dorothy had had her lesson, I'll warrant, and never a word could I get from her. So then I tried Bessy, though I had always held my head rather above her, as I was evened to James and Dorothy, and she was little better than their servant. So she said I must never, never tell; and if ever told, I was never to say she had told me; but it was a very strange noise, and she had heard it many a time, but most of all on winter nights, and before storms; and folks did say it was the old lord playing on the great organ in the hall, just as he used to do when he was alive; but who the old lord was, or why he played, and why he played on stormy winter evenings in particular, she either could not or would not tell me. Well! I told you I had a brave heart; and I thought it was rather pleasant to have that grand music rolling about the house, let who would be the player; for now it rose above the great gusts of wind, and wailed and triumphed just like a living creature, and then it fell to a softness most complete, only it was always music, and tunes, so it was nonsense to call it the wind. I thought at first, that it might be Miss Furnivall who played, unknown to Bessy; but one day, when I was in the hall by myself, I opened the organ and peeped all about it and around it, as I had done to the organ in Crosthwaite Church once before, and I saw it was all broken and destroyed inside, though it looked so brave and fine; and then, though it was noon-day, my flesh began to creep a little, and I shut it up, and run away pretty quickly to my own bright nursery; and I did not like hearing the music for some time after that, any more than James and Dorothy did. All this time Miss Rosamond was making herself more and more beloved. The old ladies liked her to dine with them at their early dinner James stood behind Miss Furnivall's chair, and I behind Miss Rosamond's all in state; and, after dinner, she would play about in a corner of the great drawing-room as still as any mouse, while Miss Furnivall slept, and I had my dinner in the kitchen. But she was glad enough to come to me in the nursery afterwards; for, as she said Miss Furnivall was so sad, and Mrs Stark so dull; but she and I were merry enough; and, by-and-by, I got not to care for that weird rolling music, which did one no harm, if we did not know where it came from.

That winter was very cold. In the middle of October the frosts began, and lasted many, many weeks. I remember one day, at dinner, Miss Furnivall lifted up her sad, heavy eyes, and said to Mrs Stark, 'I am afraid we shall have a terrible winter,' in a strange kind of meaning way But Mrs Stark pretended not to hear, and talked very loud of something else. My little lady and I did not care for the frost; not we! As long as it was dry, we climbed up the steep brows behind the house, and went up on the Fells which were bleak and bare enough, and there we ran races in the fresh, sharp air; and once we came down by a new path, that took us past the two old gnarled holly-trees, which grew about half-way down by the east side of the house. But the days grew shorter and shorter, and the old lord, if it was he, played away, more and more stormily and sadly, on the great organ. One Sunday afternoon – it must have been towards the end of November – I asked Dorothy to take charge of little missy when she came out of the drawing-room, after Miss Furnivall had had her nap; for it was too cold to take her with me to church, and yet I wanted to go. And Dorothy was glad enough to promise and was so fond of the child, that all seemed well; and Bessy and I set off very briskly, though the sky hung heavy and black over the white earth, as if the night had never fully gone away, and the air, though still, was very biting.

'We shall have a fall of snow,' said Bessy to me. And sure enough, even while we were in church, it came down thick, in great large flakes – so thick, it almost darkened the windows. It had stopped snowing before we came out, but it lay soft, thick, and deep beneath our feet, as we tramped home. Before we got to the hall, the moon rose, and I think it was lighter then – what with the moon, and what with the white dazzling snow – than it had been when we went to church, between two and three o'clock. I have not told you that Miss Furnivall and Mrs Stark never went to church; they used to read the prayers together, in their quiet, gloomy way; they seemed to feel the Sunday very long without their tapestry-work to be busy at. So when I went to Dorothy in the kitchen, to fetch Miss Rosamond and take her upstairs with me, I did not much wonder when the old woman told me that the ladies had kept the child with them, and that she had never come to the kitchen, as I had bidden her, when she was tired of behaving pretty in the drawing-room. So I took off my things and went to find her, and bring her to her supper in the nursery. But when I went into the best drawing-room, there sat the two old ladies, very still and quiet, dropping out a word now and then, but looking as if nothing so bright and merry as Miss Rosamond had ever been near them. Still I thought she might be hiding from me; it was one of her pretty ways, – and that she had persuaded them to look as if they knew nothing about her; so I went softly peeping under this sofa and behind that chair, making believe I was sadly frightened at not finding her.

'What's the matter, Hester?' said Mrs Stark sharply. I don't know if Miss Furnivall had seen me for, as I told you, she was very deaf, and she sat quite still, idly staring into the fire, with her hopeless face. 'I'm only looking for my little Rosy Posy,' replied I, still thinking that the child was there, and near me, though I could not see her.

'Miss Rosamond is not here,' said Mrs Stark. 'She went away, more than an hour ago, to find Dorothy.' And she, too, turned and went on looking into the fire.

My heart sank at this, and I began to wish I had never left my darling. I went back to Dorothy and told her. James was gone out for the day, but she, and me, and Bessy took lights, and went up into the nursery first; and then we roamed over the great, large house, calling and entreating Miss Rosamond to come out of her hiding-place, and not frighten us to death in that way. But there was no answer; no sound.

'Oh!' said I, at last, 'can she have got into the east wing and hidden there?'

But Dorothy said it was not possible, for that she herself had never been in there; that the doors were always locked, and my lord's steward had the keys, she believed; at any rate, neither she nor James had ever seen them: so I said I would go back, and see if, after all, she was not hidden in the drawing-room, unknown to the old ladies; and if I found her there, I said, I would whip her well for the fright she had given me; but I never meant to do it. Well, I went back to the west drawing-room, and I told Mrs Stark we could not find her anywhere, and asked for leave to look all about the furniture there, for I thought now that she might have fallen asleep in some warm, hidden corner; but no! we looked – Miss Furnivall got up and looked, trembling all over – and she was nowhere there; then we set off again, everyone in the house, and looked in all the places we had searched before, but we could not find her. Miss Furnivall shivered and shook so much, that Mrs Stark took her back into the warm drawing-room; but not before they had made me promise to bring her to them when she was found. Well-a-day! I began to think she never would be found, when I bethought me to look into the great front court, all covered with snow. I was upstairs when I looked out; but, it was such clear moonlight, I could see, quite plain, two little footprints, which might be traced from the hall-door and round the corner of the east wing. I don't know how I got down, but I tugged open the great stiff hall-door, and, throwing the skirt of my gown over my head for a cloak, I ran out. I turned the east corner, and there a black shadow fell on the snow but when I came again into the moonlight, there were the little footmarks going up – up to the Fells. It was bitter cold; so cold, that the air almost took the skin off my face as I ran; but I ran on, crying to think how my poor little darling must be perished and frightened. I was within sight of the holly-trees, when I saw a shepherd coming down the hill, bearing something in his arms wrapped in his maud. He shouted to me, and asked me if I had lost a bairn; and, when I could not speak for crying, he bore towards me, and I saw my wee bairnie, lying still, and white, and stiff in his arms, as if she had been dead. He told me he had been up the Fells to gather in his sheep, before the deep cold of night came on, and that under the holly-trees (black marks on the hill-side, where no other bush was for miles around) he had found my little lady – my lamb – my queen – my darling – stiff and cold in the terrible sleep which is frost-begotten. Oh! the joy and the tears of having her in my arms once again! for I would not let him carry her; but took her, maud and all, into my own arms, and held her near my own warm neck and heart, and felt the life stealing slowly back again into her little gentle limbs. But she was still insensible when we reached the hall, and I had no breath for speech. We went in by the kitchen-door.

'Bring the warming-pan,' said I; and I carried her upstairs, and began undressing her by the nursery fire, which Bessy had kept up. I called my little lammie all the sweet and playful names I could think of, – even while my eyes were blinded by my tears; and at last, oh! at length she opened her large blue eyes. Then I put her into her warm bed, and sent Dorothy down to tell Miss Furnivall that all was well; and I made up my mind to sit by my darling's bedside the live-long night. She fell away into a soft sleep as soon as her pretty head had touched the pillow, and I watched by her till morning light; when she wakened up bright and clear – or so I thought at first – and, my dears, so I think now.

She said, that she had fancied that she should like to go to Dorothy, for that both the old ladies were asleep, and it was very dull in the drawing-room; and that, as she was going through the west lobby, she saw the snow through the high window falling – falling – soft and steady; but she wanted to see it lying pretty and white on the ground; so she made her way into the great hall: and then, going to the window, she saw it bright and soft upon the drive; but while she stood there, she saw a little girl, not so old as she was, 'but so pretty,' said my darling; 'and this little girl beckoned to me to come out; and oh, she was so pretty and so sweet, I could not choose but go.' And then this other little girl had taken her by the hand, and side by side the two had gone round the east corner.

'Now you are a naughty little girl, and telling stories,' said I. 'What would your good mamma, that is in heaven, and never told a story in her life, say to her little Rosamond, if she heard her – and I dare say she does – telling stories!'

'Indeed, Hester,' sobbed out my child, 'I'm telling you true. Indeed I am.'

'Don't tell me!' said I, very stern. 'I tracked you by your foot-marks through the snow; there were only yours to be seen: and if you had had a little girl to go hand-in-hand with you up the hill, don't you think the footprints would have gone along with yours?'

'I can't help it, dear, dear Hester,' said she, crying, 'if they did not; I never looked at her feet, but she held my hand fast and tight in her little one, and it was very, very cold. She took me up the Fell-path, up to the holly-trees; and there I saw a lady weeping and crying; but when she saw me, she hushed her weeping, and smiled very proud and grand, and took me on her knee, and began to lull me to sleep, and that's all, Hester – but that is true; and my dear mamma knows it is,' said she, crying. So I thought the child was in a fever, and pretended to believe her, as she went over her story – over and over again, and always the same. At last Dorothy knocked at the door with Miss Rosamond's breakfast; and she told me the old ladies were down in the eating parlour, and that they wanted to speak to me. They had both been into the night-nursery the evening before, but it was after Miss Rosamond was asleep; so they had only looked at her – not asked me any questions.

'I shall catch it,' thought I to myself, as I went along the north gallery. 'And yet,' I thought, taking courage, 'it was in their charge I left her; and it's they that's to blame for letting her steal away unknown and unwatched.' So I went in boldly, and told my story. I told it all to Miss Furnivall, shouting it close to her ear; but when I came to the mention of the other little girl out in the snow, coaxing and tempting her out, and wiling her up to the grand and beautiful lady by the holly-tree, she threw her arms up – her old and withered arms – and cried aloud, 'Oh! Heaven forgive! Have mercy!'

Mrs Stark took hold of her; roughly enough, I thought; but she was past Mrs Stark's management, and spoke to me, in a kind of wild warning and authority.

'Hester! keep her from that child! It will lure her to her death! That evil child! Tell her it is a wicked, naughty child.' Then, Mrs Stark hurried me out of the room; where, indeed, I was glad enough to go; but Miss Furnivall kept shrieking out, 'Oh, have mercy! Wilt Thou never forgive! It is many a long year ago' –

I was very uneasy in my mind after that. I durst never leave Miss Rosamond, night or day, for fear lest she might slip off again, after some fancy or other; and all the more, because I thought I could make out that Miss Furnivall was crazy, from their odd ways about her; and I was afraid lest something of the same kind (which might be in the family, you know) hung over my darling. And the great frost never ceased all this time; and, whenever it was a more stormy night than usual, between the gusts, and through the wind we heard the old lord playing on the great organ. But, old lord, or not, wherever Miss Rosamond went, there I followed; for my love for her, pretty, helpless orphan, was stronger than my fear for the grand and terrible sound. Besides, it rested with me to keep her cheerful and merry, as beseemed her age. So we played together, and wandered together, here and there, and everywhere; for I never dared to lose sight of her again in that large and rambling house. And so it happened, that one afternoon, not long before Christmas-day, we were playing together on the billiard-table in the great hall (not that we knew the right way of playing, but she liked to roll the smooth ivory balls with her pretty hands, and I liked to do whatever she did); and, by-and-by, without our noticing it, it grew dusk indoors, though it was still light in the open air, and I was thinking of taking her back into the nursery, when, all of a sudden, she cried out –

'Look, Hester! look! there is my poor little girl out in the snow!'

I turned towards the long narrow windows, and there, sure enough, I saw a little girl, less than my Miss Rosamond – dressed all unfit to be out-of-doors such a bitter night – crying, and beating against the window panes, as if she wanted to be let in. She seemed to sob and wail, till Miss Rosamond could bear it no longer, and was flying to the door to open it, when, all of a sudden, and close upon us, the great organ pealed out so loud and thundering, it fairly made me tremble; and all the more, when I remembered me that, even in the stillness of that dead-cold weather, I had heard no sound of little battering hands upon the window-glass, although the phantom child had seemed to put forth all its force; and, although I had seen it wail and cry, no faintest touch of sound had fallen upon my ears. Whether I remembered all this at the very moment, I do not know; the great organ sound had so stunned me into terror; but this I know, I caught up Miss Rosamond before she got the hall-door opened, and clutched her, and carried her away, kicking and screaming, into the large, bright kitchen, where Dorothy and Agnes were busy with their mince-pies.

'What is the matter with my sweet one?' cried Dorothy, as I bore in Miss Rosamond, who was sobbing as if her heart would break.

'She won't let me open the door for my little girl to come in; and she'll die if she is out on the Fells all night. Cruel, naughty Hester,' she said, slapping me; but she might have struck harder, for I had seen a look of ghastly terror on Dorothy's face, which made my very blood run cold.

'Shut the back-kitchen door fast, and bolt it well,' said she to Agnes. She said no more; she gave me raisins and almonds to quiet Miss Rosamond; but she sobbed about the little girl in the snow, and would not touch any of the good things. I was thankful when she cried herself to sleep in bed. Then I stole down to the kitchen, and told Dorothy I had made up my mind. I would carry my darling back to my father's house in Applethwaite; where, if we lived humbly, we lived at peace. I said I had been frightened enough with the old lord's organ-playing; but now that I had seen for myself this little moaning child, all decked out as no child in the neighbourhood could be, beating and battering to get in, yet always without any sound or noise – with the dark wound on its right shoulder; and that Miss Rosamond had known it again for the phantom that had nearly lured her to death (which Dorothy knew was true); I would stand it no longer.

I saw Dorothy change colour once or twice. When I had done, she told me she did not think I could take Miss Rosamond with me, for that she was my lord's ward, and I had no right over her; and she asked me would I leave the child that I was so fond of just for sounds and sights that could do me no harm; and that they had all had to get used to in their turns? I was all in a hot, trembling passion; and I said it was very well for her to talk, that knew what these sights and noises betokened, and that had, perhaps, had something to do with the spectre child while it was alive. And I taunted her so, that she told me all she knew at last; and then I wished I had never been told, for it only made me more afraid than ever.

She said she had heard the tale from old neighbours that were alive when she was first married; when folks used to come to the hall sometimes, before it had got such a bad name on the country side: it might not be true, or it might, what she had been told.

The old lord was Miss Furnivall's father – Miss Grace, as Dorothy called her, for Miss Maude was the elder, and Miss Furnivall by lights. The old lord was eaten up with pride. Such a proud man was never seen or heard of; and his daughters were like him. No one was good enough to wed them, although they had choice enough; for they were the great beauties of their day, as I had seen by their portraits, where they hung in the state drawing-room. But, as the old saying is, 'Pride will have a fall;' and these two haughty beauties fell in love with the same man, and he no better than a foreign musician, whom their father had down from London to play music with him at the Manor House. For, above all things, next to his pride, the old lord loved music. He could play on nearly every instrument that ever was heard of; and it was a strange thing it did not soften him; but he was a fierce, dour old man, and had broken his poor wife's heart with his cruelty, they said. He was mad after music, and would pay any money for it. So he got this foreigner to come; who made such beautiful music, that they said the very birds on the trees stopped their singing to listen. And, by degrees, this foreign gentleman got such a hold over the old lord, that nothing would serve him but that he must come every year; and it was he that had the great organ brought from Holland, and built up in the hall, where it stood now. He taught the old lord to play on it; but many and many a time, when Lord Furnivall was thinking of nothing but his fine organ, and his finer music, the dark foreigner was walking abroad in the woods, with one of the young ladies: now Miss Maude, and then Miss Grace.

Miss Maude won the day and carried off the prize, such as it was; and he and she were married, all unknown to anyone; and, before he made his next yearly visit, she had been confined of a little girl at a farm-house on the Moors, while her father and Miss Grace thought she was away at Doncaster Races. But though she was a wife and a mother, she was not a bit softened, but as haughty and as passionate as ever; and perhaps more so, for she was jealous of Miss Grace, to whom her foreign husband paid a deal of court – by way of blinding her – as he told his wife. But Miss Grace triumphed over Miss Maude, and Miss Maude grew fiercer and fiercer, both with her husband and with her sister; and the former – who could easily shake off what was disagreeable, and hide himself in foreign countries – went away a month before his usual time that summer, and half-threatened that he would never come back again. Meanwhile, the little girl was left at the farm-house, and her mother used to have her horse saddled and gallop wildly over the hills to see her once every week, at the very least; for where she loved she loved, and where she hated she hated. And the old lord went on playing – playing on his organ; and the servants thought the sweet music he made had soothed down his awful temper, of which (Dorothy said) some terrible tales could be told. He grew infirm too, and had to walk with a crutch; and his son – that was the present Lord Furnivall's father – was with the army in America, and the other son at sea; so Miss Maude had it pretty much her own way, and she and Miss Grace grew colder and bitterer to each other every day; till at last they hardly ever spoke, except when the old lord was by. The foreign musician came again the next summer, but it was for the last time; for they led him such a life with their jealousy and their passions, that he grew weary, and went away, and never was heard of again. And Miss Maude, who had always meant to have her marriage acknowledged when her father should be dead, was left now a deserted wife, whom nobody knew to have been married, with a child that she dared not own, although she loved it to distraction; living with a father whom she feared, and a sister whom she hated. When the next summer passed over, and the dark foreigner never came, both Miss Maude and Miss Grace grew gloomy and sad; they had a haggard look about them, though they looked handsome as ever. But, by-and-by, Miss Maude brightened; for her father grew more and more infirm, and more than ever carried away by his music, and she and Miss Grace lived almost entirely apart, having separate rooms, the one on the west side, Miss Maude on the east – those very rooms which were now shut up. So she thought she might have her little girl with her, and no one need ever know except those who dared not speak about it, and were bound to believe that it was, as she said, a cottager's child she had taken a fancy to. All this, Dorothy said, was pretty well known; but what came afterwards no one knew, except Miss Grace and Mrs Stark, who was even then her maid, and much more of a friend to her than ever her sister had been. But the servants supposed, from words that were dropped, that Miss Maude had triumphed over Miss Grace, and told her that all the time the dark foreigner had been mocking her with pretended love – he was her own husband. The colour left Miss Grace's cheek and lips that very day for ever, and she was heard to say many a time that sooner or later she would have her revenge; and Mrs Stark was for ever spying about the east rooms.

One fearful night, just after the New Year had come in, when the snow was lying thick and deep; and the flakes were still falling – fast enough to blind anyone who might be out and abroad – there was a great and violent noise heard, and the old lord's voice above all, cursing and swearing awfully, and the cries of a little child, and the proud defiance of a fierce woman, and the sound of a blow, and a dead stillness, and moans and wailings, dying away on the hill-side! Then the old lord summoned all his servants, and told them, with terrible oaths, and words more terrible, that his daughter had disgraced herself, and that he had turned her out of doors – her, and her child – and that if ever they gave her help, or food, or shelter, he prayed that they might never enter heaven. And, all the while, Miss Grace stood by him, white and still as any stone; and, when he had ended, she heaved a great sigh, as much as to say her work was done, and her end was accomplished. But the old lord never touched his organ again, and died within the year; and no wonder! for, on the morrow of that wild and fearful night, the shepherds, coming down the Fell side, found Miss Maude sitting, all crazy and smiling, under the holly-trees, nursing a dead child, with a terrible mark on its right shoulder. 'But that was not what killed it,' said Dorothy: 'it was the frost and the cold. Every wild creature was in its hole, and every beast in its fold, while the child and its mother were turned out to wander on the Fells! And now you know all! and I wonder if you are less frightened now?'

I was more frightened than ever; but I said I was not. I wished Miss Rosamond and myself well out of that dreadful house for ever; but I would not leave her, and I dared not take her away. But oh, how I watched her, and guarded her! We bolted the doors, and shut the window-shutters fast, an hour or more before dark, rather than leave them open five minutes too late. But my little lady still heard the weird child crying and mourning; and not all we could do or say could keep her from wanting to go to her, and let her in from the cruel wind and snow. All this time I kept away from Miss Furnivall and Mrs Stark, as much as ever I could; for I feared them – I knew no good could be about them, with their gray, hard faces, and their dreamy eyes, looking back into the ghastly years that were gone. But, even in my fear, I had a kind of pity for Miss Furnivall, at least. Those gone down to the pit can hardly have a more hopeless look than that which was ever on her face. At last I even got so sorry for her – who never said a word but what was quite forced from her – that I prayed for her; and I taught Miss Rosamond to pray for one who had done a deadly sin; but often, when she came to those words, she would listen, and start up from her knees, and say, 'I hear my little girl plaining and crying, very sad, – oh, let her in, or she will die!'

One night – just after New Year's Day had come at last, and the long winter had taken a turn, as I hoped – I heard the west drawing-room bell ring three times, which was the signal for me. I would not leave Miss Rosamond alone, for all she was asleep – for the old lord had been playing wilder than ever – and I feared lest my darling should waken to hear the spectre child; see her I knew she could not. I had fastened the windows too well for that. So I took her out of her bed, and wrapped her up in such outer clothes as were most handy, and carried her down to the drawing-room, where the old ladies sat at their tapestry-work as usual. They looked up when I came in, and Mrs Stark asked, quite astounded, 'Why did I bring Miss Rosamond there, out of her warm bed?' I had begun to whisper, 'Because I was afraid of her being tempted out while

I was away, by the wild child in the snow,' when she stopped me short (with a glance at Miss Furnivall), and said Miss Furnivall wanted me to undo some work she had done wrong, and which neither of them could see to unpick. So I laid my pretty dear on the sofa, and sat down on a stool by them, and hardened my heart against them, as I heard the wind rising and howling.

Miss Rosamond slept on sound, for all the wind blew so; and Miss Furnivall said never a word, nor looked round when the gusts shook the windows. All at once she started up to her full height, and put up one hand, as if to bid us listen.

'I hear voices!' said she. 'I hear terrible screams – I hear my father's voice!'

Just at that moment my darling wakened with a sudden start: 'My little girl is crying, oh, how she is crying!' and she tried to get up and go to her, but she got her feet entangled in the blanket, and I caught her up; for my flesh had begun to creep at these noises, which they heard while we could catch no sound. In a minute or two the noises came, and gathered fast, and filled our ears; we, too, heard voices and screams, and no longer heard the winter's wind that raged abroad. Mrs Stark looked at me, and I at her, but we dared not speak. Suddenly Miss Furnivall, went towards the door, out into the ante-room, through the west lobby, and opened the door into the great hall. Mrs Stark followed, and I durst not be left, though my heart almost stopped beating for fear. I wrapped my darling tight in my arms, and went out with them. In the hall the screams were louder than ever; they seemed to come from the east wing – nearer and nearer – close on the other side of the locked-up doors – close behind them. Then I noticed that the great bronze chandelier seemed all alight, though the hall was dim, and that a fire was blazing in the vast hearth-place, though it gave no heat; and I shuddered up with terror, and folded my darling closer to me. But as I did so the east door shook, and she, suddenly struggling to get free from me, cried, 'Hester! I must go. My little girl is there I hear her; she is coming! Hester, I must go!'

I held her tight with all my strength; with a set will, I held her. If I had died, my hands would have grasped her still, I was so resolved in my mind. Miss Furnivall stood listening, and paid no regard to my darling, who had got down to the ground, and whom I, upon my knees now, was holding with both my arms clasped round her neck; she still striving and crying to get free.

All at once, the east door gave way with a thundering crash, as if torn open in a violent passion, and there came into that broad and mysterious light, the figure of a tall old man, with grey hair and gleaming eyes. He drove before him, with many a relentless gesture of abhorrence, a stern and beautiful woman, with a little child clinging to her dress.

'O Hester! Hester!' cried Miss Rosamond; 'it's the lady! the lady below the holly-trees; and my little girl is with her. Hester! Hester! let me go to her; they are drawing me to them. I feel them – I feel them. I must go!'

Again she was almost convulsed by her efforts to get away; but I held her tighter and tighter, till I feared I should do her a hurt; but rather that than let her go towards those terrible phantoms. They passed along towards the great hall-door, where the winds howled and ravened for their prey; but before they reached that, the lady turned; and I could see that she defied the old man with a fierce and proud defiance; but then she quailed – and then she threw up her arms wildly and piteously to save her child – her little child – from a blow from his uplifted crutch.

And Miss Rosamond was torn as by a power stronger than mine, and writhed in my arms, and sobbed (for by this time the poor darling was growing faint).

'They want me to go with them on to the Fells – they are drawing me to them. Oh, my little girl! I would come, but cruel, wicked Hester holds me very tight.' But when she saw the uplifted crutch, she swooned away, and I thanked God for it. Just at this moment – when the tall old man, his hair streaming as in the blast of a furnace, was going to strike the little shrinking child – Miss Furnivall, the old woman by my side, cried out, 'O father! father! spare the little innocent child!' But just then I saw – we all saw – another phantom shape itself, and grow clear out of the blue and misty light that filled the hall; we had not seen her till now, for it was another lady who stood by the old man, with a look of relentless hate and triumphant scorn. That figure was very beautiful to look upon, with a soft, white hat drawn down over the proud brows, and a red and curling lip. It was dressed in an open robe of blue satin. I had seen that figure before. It was the likeness of Miss Furnivall in her youth; and the terrible phantoms moved on, regardless of old Miss Furnivall's wild entreaty, – and the uplifted crutch fell on the right shoulder of the little child, and the younger sister looked on, stony, and deadly serene. But at that moment, the dim lights, and the fire that gave no heat, went out of themselves, and Miss Furnivall lay at our feet stricken down by the palsy – death-stricken.

Yes! she was carried to her bed that night never to rise again. She lay with her face to the wall, muttering low, but muttering always: 'Alas! alas! what is done in youth can never be undone in age! What is done in youth can never be undone in age!'

The Cave of Blood

Dick Donovan

On the south-west coast of the Principality of Wales stands a romantic little village, inhabited chiefly by the poorer class of people, consisting of small farmers and oyster dredgers, whose estates are the wide ocean, and whose ploughs are the small craft in which they glide over its interminable fields in search of the treasures which they wring from its bosom. It is built on the very top of a hill, commanding on one side a view of an immense bay, and on the other of the peaceful green fields and valleys, cultivated by the greater number of its quiet inhabitants. At the period of this story distinctions were unknown in the village – every man was the equal of his neighbour.

But though rank and its unpolished distinctions were strange in the village, the superiority of talent was felt and acknowledged almost without a pause or a murmur. There was one who was as a king amongst them, by the mere force of a mightier spirit than those with whom he sojourned had been accustomed to feel among them. He was a dark and moody man – a stranger – evidently of a higher order than those around him, who had but a few months before, without any apparent object, settled among them. Where he came from no one knew. He was a mystery, and evidently knew how to keep his secrets to himself. He was not rich, but followed no occupation. He lived frugally, but quite alone, and his sole employments were to read during the day and wander out, unaccompanied, into the fields or by the beach during the night. He was a strange, silent, fearsome sort of man, with a certain uncanniness in his appearance that commanded respect no less than fear. It soon became a common belief that this man possessed miraculous powers, not only as a healer of human ailments, but as a prophet. It was, therefore, not to be wondered at that in that little community of simple fisher-folk he was looked up to as a superior being, who not only held the power of life and death in his hands, but was able to draw aside the veil that screened the future.

Sometimes he would relieve a suffering child or rheumatic old man by medicinal herbs, reprove idleness and drunkenness in the youth, and predict to all the good and evil consequences of their conduct. And in his success in some cases, his foresight in others, and his wisdom in all, won for him a high reputation among the cottagers, to which his taciturn habits contributed not a little, for, with the vulgar as with the educated, no talker was ever seriously taken for a magician, though a silent man is often decided to be a wise one.

There was but one person at all disposed to rebel against the despotic sovereignty which William Morgan – such was the name he chose to be known by – was silently establishing over the quiet village, and that was precisely the person most likely to effect a revolution. She was a beautiful young woman, the glory and boast of the village, who had been the favourite of, and to a certain degree educated by, the late lady of the manor; but the lady had died, and her protégée, with a full consciousness of her intellectual superiority, had returned to her native village, where she determined to have an empire of her own which no rival should dispute. She laughed at the girls and women folk who listened to the predictions of Morgan, and she refused her smiles to the young men who consulted him upon their affairs and their prospects; and as the beautiful Ruth was generally beloved, the silent Morgan was soon in danger of being abandoned by all save doting men and paralytic women, and feeling himself an outcast in the village.

But it was soon made clear that Morgan had no intention of allowing pretty Ruth to oust him from his position.

He had essayed to rule the village, and he was resolved to retain his hold over the people. He knew, too, that from another point of view this ascendency was necessary to his purposes, and as he had failed to establish it by wisdom and benevolence, he determined to try the effect of fear. The character of the people with whom he sojourned was admirably calculated to assist his projects. His predictions were now uttered more clearly, and his threats denounced in sterner tones and stronger and plainer words, and when he predicted that old William Williams, who had been stricken with the palsy, would die at the turn of the tide, three days from that on which he spoke, and that the light little boat of gay Griffy Morris, which sailed from the Bay on a bright winter's morning, would never again make the shore – the man died, and the storm arose, even as he said – men's hearts died within them, and they bowed down before his words, as if he had been their general fate and the individual destiny of each.

Ruth's beautiful face grew pale for a moment as she heard of these things; in the next her spirit returned, and she told some friend that she was going to Morgan to have her fortune told, and she would prove to everyone that he was an impostor. She had no difficulty in getting up a party of young men and women to accompany her, and she set off for Morgan's house with the avowed intention of 'unmasking and humiliating him.' It was rather remarkable, seeing that the man had never done her any harm, that she should have taken such a prejudice against him. When they reached his residence they made it very evident that they intended to insult him. They made jests at his expense, and rudely and satirically alluded to his professed powers of prophecy. Had Ruth been more observant and less self-conscious, she could not have failed to note that Morgan was far removed above the commonplace, and was possessed of mental powers far above anyone else in the village. He was greatly annoyed by her insulting manner and intentional rudeness, but he concealed his feelings, though he silently resolved to humble her pride. 'I will make him tell my fortune,' she said. His credit was at stake; he must daunt his enemy, or surrender to her power; he foretold sorrows and joys to the listening throng, and he made one of the young men present and Ruth herself feel exceedingly uncomfortable by revealing a secret which they themselves thought no human soul knew beside themselves. Then for the first time Ruth began to think she had made a mistake, and had underrated her opponent. Nevertheless, her self-possession did not desert her, and in an easy, flippant manner, in which there was a challenge as well as a sneer, she bade him read her future. Morgan remained silent for some moments, and steadily gazed at her. He had a large book before him, which he opened, shut, opened again, and again looked sadly and fearfully upon her; she tried to smile, but felt startled – she knew not why; the bright, inquiring glance of her dark eye could not change Morgan's manner. Her smile could not melt, nor even temper, the hardness of his deep-seated malice; he again looked sternly, and then coldly uttered these slow, soul-withering words, 'Woman, you are doomed to be a murderess!' At first she sneered at his prediction, and then laughed at him; but with greater solemnity, and speaking as if he were inspired, he exclaimed, 'I tell you, Ruth, you will become a murderess! I see blood upon your hands and blood upon your face, and the black stain of awful guilt upon your immortal soul.'

Her arrogance was subdued, her haughty spirit overcome, and with something like a groan she hurried away. But from that day she found that she was a marked woman. The superstitious villagers shunned her, and she became, as it were, an outcast.

Abhorring Morgan, she yet felt drawn towards him, and while she sat by his side felt as if he alone could avert the evil destiny which he himself had foretold. With him only was she seen to smile; elsewhere, sad, silent, stern; it seemed as if she were ever occupied in nerving her mind for that which she had to do, and she grew melancholy and morbid.

But there were moments when her naturally strong spirit, not yet wholly subdued, struggled against her conviction, and endeavoured to find modes of averting her fate; it was in one of these, perhaps, that she gave her hand to a wooer, from a distant part of the country, a mariner, who either had not heard or did not regard the prediction, upon condition that he should remove her far from her native village to the home of his family and friends, for she sometimes felt as if the decree which had gone forth against her could not be fulfilled except upon the spot where she had heard it, and that her heart would be lighter if men's eyes would again look upon her in kindliness and she no longer sat beneath the glare of those that knew so well the secret of her soul. Thus thinking, she quitted the village with her husband; and the tormentor, who had poisoned her repose, soon after her departure, left the village as secretly and as suddenly as he had entered it.

But, though Ruth could depart from his corporeal presence, and look upon his cruel visage no more, yet the eye of her soul was fixed upon his shadow, and his airy form, the creation of her sorrow, still sat by her side; the blight that he had breathed upon her peace had withered her heart, and it was in vain that she sought to forget or banish the recollection from her brain. Men and women smiled upon her as before in the days of her joy, the friends of her husband welcomed her to their bosoms, but they could give no peace to her heart; she shrunk from their friendship, she shivered equally at their neglect, she dreaded any cause that might lead to that which, it had been said, she must do; nightly she sat alone and thought, she dwelt upon the characters of those around her, and shuddered that in some she saw violence and selfishness enough to cause injury, which she might be supposed to resent to blood. Against the use of actual violence she had disabled herself; she had never struck a blow – her small hand would have suffered injury in the attempt; she did not understand the use of fire-arms, she was ignorant of what were poisons, and a knife she never allowed herself, even for the most necessary purposes. How, then, could she slay? At times she took comfort from thoughts like these, and at others she was plunged in the darkness of despair.

Her husband went forth to and returned from the voyages which made up the avocation and felicity of his life, without noticing the deep-rooted sorrow of his wife. He was a common man, and of a common mind; his eye had not seen the awful beauty of her whom he had chosen; his spirit had not felt her power; and, if he had marked, he would not have understood her grief; so she ministered to him as a duty. She was a silent and obedient wife, but she saw him come home without joy, and witnessed his departure without regret; he neither added to nor diminished her sorrow. But destiny had one solitary blessing in store for the victim of its decrees – a child was born to the hapless Ruth, a lovely little girl soon slept upon her bosom, and, coming as it did, the one lone and lovely rosebud in her desolate garden, she welcomed it with a kindlier hope.

A few years went by unsoiled by the wretchedness which had marked the preceding; the joy of the mother softened the anguish of the condemned, and sometimes when she looked upon her daughter she ceased to despair; but destiny had not forgotten its claim, and soon its hand pressed heavily upon its victim; the giant ocean rolled over the body of her husband, poverty visited the cottage of the widow, and famine's gaunt figure was visible in the distance. Oppression came with these, arrears of rent were demanded, and the landlord was brutal in his anger and harsh in his language to the sufferer.

Thus goaded, she saw but one thing that could save her – she fled from her persecutor to the home of her youth, and, leading her little Rachel by the hand, threw herself into the arms of her people. They received her with distant kindness, and assured her that she should not want. In this they kept their promise, but it was all they did for Ruth and her daughter. A miserable subsistence was given to them, and that was embittered by distrust, and the knowledge that it was yielded unwillingly. Among the villagers, although she was no longer shunned as formerly, her story was not forgotten.

If it had been, her strange beauty, her sorrow-stamped face, the flashing of her eyes, her majestic stature and solemn movements, would have recalled it to their recollections. She was a marked being, and all believed (though each would have pitied her, had they not been afraid) that her evil destiny was not to be averted. They declared that she looked like one fated to do some dreadful deed. They saw she was not one of them, and though they did not directly avoid her, yet they never threw themselves in her way, and thus the hapless Ruth had ample leisure to contemplate and grieve over her fate. One night she sat alone in her little hovel, and, with many bitter ruminations, was watching the happy sleep of her child, who slumbered tranquilly on their only bed. Midnight had long passed, yet Ruth was not disposed to rest. She trimmed her dull light, and said mentally, 'Were I not poor such a temptation might not assail me, riches would procure me deference; but poverty, or the wrongs it brings, may drive me to this evil. Were I above want it would be less likely to be. Oh, my child, for your sake would I avoid this doom more than for mine own, for if it should bring death to me, what will it not bring to you? – infamy, agony, scorn.'

She wept aloud as she spoke, and scarcely seemed to notice the singularity (at that late hour) of someone without attempting to open the door. She heard, but the circumstance made little impression. She knew that as yet her doom was unfulfilled, and that, therefore, no danger could reach her. She was no coward at any time, but now despair had made her brave. She flung the door open, a stranger entered, without either alarming or disturbing her, and it was not till he had stood face to face with Ruth, and discovered his features to be those of William Morgan, that she sprung up from her seat and gazed wildly and earnestly upon him. He gave her no time to question.

'Ruth Tudor,' said he, 'behold I come to sue for your pity and mercy. I have embittered your existence, and doomed you to a terrible lot. What first was dictated by vengeance and malice became truth as I uttered it, for what I spoke I believed. Yet, take comfort, some of my predictions have failed, and why may not this one be false? In my own fate I have ever been deceived; perhaps I may be equally so in yours. In the meantime have pity upon him who was your enemy, but who, when his vengeance was uttered, instantly became your friend. I was poor, and your seem might have robbed me of subsistence in danger, and your contempt might have given me up. Beggared by some disastrous events, hunted by creditors, I fled from my wife and son because I could no longer bear to contemplate their suffering. I have sought fortune in many ways since we parted, and always has she eluded my grasp till last night, when she rather tempted than smiled upon me. At an idle fair I met the steward of this estate drunk and stupid, but loaded with gold. He travelled towards home alone. I could not, did not, wrestle with the fiend that possessed me, but hastened to overtake him in his lonely ride. Start not! No hair of his head was harmed by me. Of his gold I robbed him, but not of his life, though, had I been the greater villain, I should now be in less danger, since he saw and marked my person. Three hundred pounds is the result of my deed, but I must keep it now or die. Ruth, you, too, are poor and forsaken, but you are faithful and kind, and will not betray me to justice. Save me, and I will not enjoy my riches alone. You know all the caves in the rocks, those hideous hiding places, where no foot, save yours, has dared to tread. Conceal me in one of these till the pursuit be passed, and I will give you one half my wealth, and return with the other to gladden my wife and son.'

The hand of Ruth was already opened, and in imagination she grasped the wealth he promised. Oppression and poverty had somewhat clouded the nobleness, but not the fierceness of her spirit. She saw that riches would save her from wrath, perhaps from blood, and as the means to escape from so mighty an evil she was not unscrupulous respecting a lesser. Independently of this, she felt a great interest in the safety of Morgan. Her own fate seemed to hang upon his. She hid the ruffian in a cave which she had known from her youth, and supplied him with light and food.

There was a happiness now in the heart of Ruth, a joy in her thoughts as she sat all the long day upon the deserted settle of her wretched fireside, to which they had, for many years, been strangers. Many times during the past years of her sorrow she had thought of Morgan, and longed to look upon his face, and sit under his shadow, as one whose presence could preserve her from the evil fate which he himself had predicted. She had long since forgiven him his prophecy. She believed he had spoken truth, and this gave her a wild confidence in his power – a confidence that sometimes thought, 'If he can foreknow, can he not also avert?'

And she thought she would deserve his confidence, and support him in his suffering. She had concealed him in a deep dark cave, hewn far in the rock, to which she alone knew the entrance from the beach. There was another (if a huge aperture in the top of the rock might be so called) which, far from attempting to descend, the peasants and seekers for the culprit had scarcely dared to look into, so perpendicular, dark, and uncertain was the hideous descent into what justly appeared to them a bottomless abyss. They passed over his head in their search through the fields above, and before the mouth of his den upon the beach below, yet they left him in safety, though incertitude and fear.

It was less wonderful, the suspicionless conduct of the villagers towards Ruth, than the calm prudence with which she conducted all the details relating to her secret. Her poverty was well known, yet she daily procured a double portion of food, which was won by double labour. She toiled in the fields for the meed of oaten cake and potatoes, or she dashed out in a crazy boat on the wide ocean, to win with the dredgers the spoils of the oyster beds that lie on its bosom. The daintier fare was for the unhappy guest, and daily did she wander among the rocks, when the tides were retiring, for the shellfish which they had flung among the fissures in their retreat, which she bore, exhausted with fatigue, to her home, and which her lovely child, now rising into womanhood, prepared for the luxurious meal. It was wonderful, too, the settled prudence of the young girl, who made no comment about the food with which she was daily supplied. If she suspected the secret of her mother she respected it too much to allow others to discover that she did so.

Many sad hours did Ruth pass in that dark cave, where the man who had blighted her life lay in hiding; and many times, by conversing with him upon the subject of her destiny, did she seek to alleviate the pangs its recollection gave her. But the result of such discussions were by no means favourable to her hopes. Morgan had acknowledged that his threat had originated in malice, and that he intended to alarm and subdue, but not to the extent that he had effected. 'I know well,' said he, 'that disgrace alone would operate upon you as I wished, for I foresaw you would glory in the thought of nobly sustaining misfortune. I meant to degrade you with the lowest. I meant to attribute to you what I now painfully experience to be the vilest of vices. I intended to tell you you were destined to be a thief, but I could not utter the words I had intended, and I was struck with horror at those I heard involuntarily proceeding from my lips. I would have recalled them, but I could not. I would have said, "Ruth, I did but jest," but there was something which seemed to withhold my speech and press upon my soul, and a dumb voice whispered in my ears, "As thou hast said shall this thing be." But take comfort, Ruth. My own fortunes have ever deceived me, and doubtlessly ever will, for I feel as if I should one day return to this cave, and make it my final home.'

He spoke solemnly, and wept; but his companion was unmoved as she looked on in wonder and contempt at his grief. 'You know not how to endure,' said she to him, 'and as soon as night shall again fall upon our mountains I will lead you forth to freedom. The danger of pursuit is now past. At midnight be ready for the journey, leave the cave, and ascend the rocks by the path I showed you, to the field in which its mouth is situated. Wait for me there a few moments, and I will bring you a fleet horse, ready saddled for the journey, for which you must pay, since I must declare to the owner that I have sold it at a distance, and for more than its rated value.'

Midnight came, and Morgan waited with trembling anxiety for the welcome step of Ruth. At length he saw her, and hastily speaking as she descended the rock:

'You must be speedy in your movements,' said she. 'When you leave me your horse waits on the other side of this field, and I would have you hasten, lest something should betray your purpose. But, before you depart, there is an account to be settled between us. I have dared danger and privation for you, that the temptations of the poor may not assail me. Give me my reward, and go.'

Morgan pressed his leather bag containing his gold to his bosom, but answered nothing. He seemed to be studying some evasion, for he looked upon the ground, and there was trouble in the working of his lip. At length he said cautiously, 'I have it not with me. I buried it, lest it should betray me, in a field some miles distant. When I leave here I will dig it up, for I know the exact spot, and send you your portion as soon as I reach a place of safety.'

Ruth gave him a glance of scorn. She had detected his meanness, and smiled at his incapacity to deceive. 'What do you press to your bosom so earnestly,' she demanded. 'Surely you are not the wise man I deemed you, thus to defraud me. Your friend alone you might cheat, and safely; but I have been made wretched by you, guilty by you, and your life is in my power. I could, as you know, easily raise the village, and win half your wealth by giving you up to justice. But I prefer reward. Give me my due, therefore, and be gone.'

But Morgan knew too well the value of the metal of sin to yield one half of it to Ruth. He tried many miserable shifts and lies, and at last, baffled by the calm penetration of his antagonist, boldly avowed his intention of keeping all the spoil he had won with so much hazard. Ruth looked at him with withering contempt. 'Keep your gold,' she said. 'If it can thus harden hearts, I covet not its possession; but there is one thing you must do, and that before you move a foot. I have supported you with hard-earned industry – that I give you; more proud, it would seem, in bestowing than I could be in receiving from such as you. But the horse that is to bear you hence to-night I borrowed for a distant journey. I must return with it, or its value. Open your bag, pay me for it, and go.'

But Morgan seemed afraid to open his bag in the presence of her he had wronged. Ruth understood his fears; but, scorning vindication of her principles, contented herself with entreating him to be honest. 'Be more just to yourself and me,' she persisted, 'the debt of gratitude I pardon; but, I beseech you, leave me not to encounter the consequence of having stolen from my friend the animal which is his only means of subsistence. I pray you not to condemn me to scorn.'

It was of no avail that Ruth humbled herself to entreaties. Morgan answered not, and while she was yet speaking cast side-long looks towards the spot where the horse was waiting, and seemed meditating whether he should not dart from Ruth and escape her entreaties and demands by dint of speed. Her stern eye detected this purpose, and, indignant at his baseness, and ashamed of her own degradation, she sprung suddenly towards him, made a desperate clutch at the leathern bag, and tore it from his grasp. He made an attempt to recover it, and a fierce struggle ensued, which drove them both back towards the yawning mouth of the cave from which he had just ascended to the world. On its very verge, on its very extreme edge, the demon who had so long ruled his spirit, now instigated him to mischief, and abandoned him to his natural brutality. He struck the unhappy Ruth a revengeful and tremendous blow. At that moment a horrible thought glanced like lightning through her soul. He was to her no longer what he had been. He was a robber, ruffian, liar – one whom to destroy was justice, and perhaps it was he—

'Villain!' she cried, 'you predicted that I was doomed to be a murderess; are you destined to be my victim?' She flung him from her with terrific force, as he stood close to the abyss, and the next instant heard him dash against its sides, as he was whirled headlong into the darkness.

It was an awful feeling, the next that passed over the soul of Ruth Tudor, as she stood alone in the pale, sorrowful moonlight, endeavouring to remember what had chanced. She gazed on the purse, on the chasm, wiped the drops of agony from her heated brow, and then, with a sudden pang of recollection, rushed down to the cavern. The light was still burning, as Morgan had left it, and served to show her the wretch extended helpless beneath the chasm. Though his body was crushed, the bones splintered, and his blood was on the cavern's sides, he was yet living, and raised his head to look upon her as she darkened the narrow entrance in her passage. He glared upon her with the visage of a demon, and spoke like a fiend in pain. 'You have murdered me!' he said, 'but I shall be avenged in all your life to come. Deem not that your doom is fulfilled, that the deed to which you are fated is done. In my dying hour I know, I feel, what is to come upon you. You are yet again to do a deed of blood!'

'Liar!' shrieked the infuriated victim.

'I tell you,' he gasped, 'your destiny is not yet fulfilled. You will yet commit another deed of horror. You will slay your own daughter. You are yet doomed to be a double murderess!' She rushed to him, but he was dead.

Ruth Tudor stood for a moment by the corpse, blind, stupefied, deaf, and dumb. In the next she laughed aloud, till the cavern rang with her ghastly mirth, and many voices mingled with and answered it. But the voices scared her, and in an instant she became stolidly grave. She threw back her dark locks with an air of offended dignity, and walked forth majestically from the cave. She took the horse by his rein, and led him back to the stable. With the same unvarying calmness she entered her cottage, and listened to the quiet breathings of her sleeping daughter. She longed to approach her nearer, but some new and horrid fear restrained her, and held her in check. Suddenly, remembrance and reason returned, and she uttered a shriek so loud and shrill that her daughter sprung from her bed, and threw herself into her arms.

It was in vain that the gentle Rachel supplicated her mother to find rest in sleep.

'Not here,' she muttered, 'it must not be here; the deep cave and the hard rock, these shall be my resting place; and the bed-fellow, lo! now he awaits my coming.' Then she would cry aloud, clasp her Rachel to her beating heart, and as suddenly, in horror, thrust her from it.

The next midnight beheld Ruth Tudor in the cave, seated upon a point of rock, at the head of the corpse, her chin resting upon her hands, gazing earnestly upon the distorted face. Decay had already begun its work, and Ruth sat there watching the progress of mortality, as if she intended that her stern eye should quicken and facilitate its operation. The next night also beheld her there, but the current of her thoughts had changed, and the dismal interval which had passed appeared to be forgotten. She stood with her basket of food.

'Will you not eat!' she demanded; 'arise, strengthen yourself for your journey; eat, eat, sleeper; will you never awaken? Look, here is the meat you love'; and as she raised his head and put the food to his lips the frail remnant of mortality remained dumb and rigid, and again she knew that he was dead.

It was evident to all that a shadow and a change was over the senses of Ruth; till this period she had been only wretched, but now madness was mingled with her grief. It was in no instance more apparent than in her conduct towards her beloved child; indulgent to all her wishes, ministering to all her wants with a liberal hand, till men wondered from whence she derived the means of indulgence, she yet seized every opportunity to send her from her presence. The gentle-hearted Rachel wept at her conduct, yet did not complain, for she believed it the effect of the disease that had for so many years been preying upon her soul. Ruth's nights were passed in roaming abroad, her days in the solitude of her hut; and even this became painful when the step of her child broke upon it. At length she signified that a relative of her husband had died and left her wealth, and that it would enable her to dispose of herself as she had long wished; so, leaving Rachel with her relatives, she retired to a hut upon a lonely heath, where she was less wretched, because there were none to observe her awful grief.

In many of her ravings she had frequently spoken darkly of her crime, and her nightly visits to the cave; and more frequently still she addressed some unseen thing, which she asserted was for ever at her side. But few heard these horrors, and those who did called to mind the early prophecy and deemed them the workings of insanity in a fierce and imaginative mind. So thought also the beloved Rachel, who hastened daily to visit her mother, but not now alone, as formerly. A youth of the village was her companion and protector, one who had offered her worth and love, and whose gentle offers were not rejected. Ruth, with a hurried gladness, gave her consent, and a blessing to her child; and it was remarked that she received her daughter more kindly and detained her longer at the Cottage when Evan was by her side than when she went to the gloomy heath alone. Rachel herself soon made this observation, and as she could depend upon the honesty and prudence of him she loved, she felt less fear at his being a frequent witness of her mother's terrific ravings. Thus all that human consolation was capable to afford was offered to the sufferer by her sympathising children.

But the delirium of Ruth Tudor appeared to increase with every nightly visit to the secret cave of blood; some hideous shadow seemed to follow her steps in the darkness and sit by her side in the light. Sometimes she held strange parley with this creation of her frenzy, and at others smiled upon it in scornful silence; now her language was in the tones of entreaty, pity, and forgiveness; anon it was the burst of execration, curses, and scorn. To the gentle listeners her words were blasphemy; and, shuddering at her boldness, they deemed, in the simple holiness of their own hearts, that the Evil One was besetting her, and that religion alone could banish him. Possessed by this idea, Evan one day suddenly interrupted her tremendous denunciations upon her fate and him who, she said, stood over her to fulfil it, with imploring her to open the book which he held in his hand, and seek consolation from its words and its promises. She listened, and grew calm in a moment; with an awful smile she bade him open and read at the first place which should meet his eye: 'From that, the word of truth, as thou sayest, I shall know my fate; what is there written I will believe.' He opened the book and read: '"Whither shall I go from Thy spirit, or whither shall I flee from Thy presence? If I go up into heaven, Thou art there; if I make my bed in hell, Thou art there; if I take the wings of the morning, and dwell in the uttermost parts of the sea, even there shall Thy hand lead me, and Thy right hand shall hold me."'

Ruth laid her hand upon the book. 'It is enough; its words are truth; it has said there is no hope, and I find comfort in my despair. I have already spoken thus in the secrecy of my heart, and I know that He will be obeyed; the unnamed sin must be—'

Evan knew not how to comfort, so he shut up his Bible and retired; and Rachel kissed the cheek of her mother as she bade her a tender good-night. Another month, and she was to be the bride of Evan, and she passed over the heath with a light step, for the thought of her bridal seemed to give joy to her mother. 'We shall all be happy then,' said the smiling girl, as the youth of her heart parted from her hand for the night; 'and heaven kindly grant that happiness may last.'

The time appointed for the marriage of Rachel Tudor and Evan Edwards had long passed away, and winter had set in with unusual sternness, even on that stormy coast, when, during a land tempest, on a dark November afternoon, a stranger to the country, journeying on foot, lost his way in endeavouring to find a short route to his destination, over stubble fields and meadow lands, by following the footmarks of those who had preceded him. The stranger was a young man, of a bright eye and a hardy look, and he went on buffeting the elements, and buffeted by them, without a thought of weariness or a single expression of impatience. Night descended upon him as he walked, and the snowstorm came down with unusual violence, as if to try the temper of his mind, a mind cultivated and enlightened, though cased in a frame accustomed to hardships, and veiled by a plain, almost rustic exterior. The storm roared loudly above him, the wind blowing tremendously, raising the new-fallen snow from the earth, which mingling with that which fell, raised a shroud about his head which bewildered and blinded the traveller, who, finding himself near some leafless brambles and a few clustered bushes of the mountain broom, took shelter under them to recover his senses and reconnoitre his position. 'This storm cannot last long,' he mused, 'and when it slackens I shall hope to find my way to shelter and comfort.' In this hope he was not mistaken. The tempest abated, and, starting once more on his journey, he saw some distance ahead what looked like a white-washed cottage, standing solitary and alone on the miserable heath which he was now traversing. Full of hope of a shelter from the storm, and lit onwards by a light that gleamed like a beacon from the cottage window, the stranger trod cheerily forwards, and in less than half an hour arrived at the white cottage, which, from the low wall of loose limestones by which it was surrounded, he judged to be, as he had already imagined, the humble residence of some poor tenant of the manor. He opened the little gate, and was proceeding to knock at the door, when his steps were arrested by a singular and unexpected sound. It was a choral burst of many voices, singing slowly and solemnly that magnificent dirge of the Church of England, the 104th Psalm. The stranger loved music, and the touching melody of that beautiful air had an instant effect upon his feelings. He lingered in solemn and silent admiration till the strains had ceased; he then knocked gently at the door, which was instantly and courteously opened to his inquiry.

On entering, he found himself in a cottage of a more respectable interior than from its outward appearance he had been led to expect; but he had little leisure or inclination for the survey of its effects, for his senses and imagination were immediately and entirely occupied by the scene which presented itself on his entrance. In the centre of the room into which he had been so readily admitted stood, on its trestles, an open coffin; lights were at its head and foot, and on each side sat many persons of both sexes, who appeared to be engaged in the customary ceremony of watching the corpse previous to its interment in the morning. There were many who appeared to the stranger to be watchers, but there were but two who, in his eye, bore the appearance of mourners, and they had faces of grief which spoke too plainly of the anguish that was reigning within. At the foot of the coffin was a pale youth just blooming into manhood, who covered his eyes with trembling fingers that ill-concealed the tears which trickled down his wan cheeks; the other – but why should we again describe that still unbowed and lofty form? The awful marble brow upon which the stranger gazed was that of Ruth Tudor.

There was much whispering and quiet talk among the people while refreshments were handed to them; and so little curiosity was excited by the appearance of the traveller that he naturally concluded that it must be no common loss that could deaden a feeling usually so intense in the bosoms of Welsh peasants. He was even checked from an attempt to question; but one man – he who had given him admittance, and seemed to possess authority in the circle – informed the traveller that he would answer his questions when the guests should depart, but till then he must keep silence. The traveller endeavoured to obey, and sat down in quiet contemplation of the figure who most interested his attention, and who sat at the coffin's head. Ruth Tudor spoke nothing, nor did she appear to heed aught of the business that was passing around her. Absorbed by reflection, her eyes were generally cast to the ground; but when they were raised, the traveller looked in vain for that expression of grief which had struck him so forcibly on his entrance; there was something wonderfully strange in the character of her perfect features. Could he have found words for his thoughts, and might have been permitted the expression, he would have called it triumphant despair, so deeply agonised, so proudly stern, looked the mourner who sat by the dead.

The interest which the traveller took in the scene became more intense the longer he gazed upon its action; unable to resist the anxiety which had begun to prey upon his spirit, he arose and walked towards the coffin, with the purpose of contemplating its occupant. A sad explanation was given, by its appearance, of the grief and the anguish he had witnessed. A beautiful girl was reposing in the narrow box, with a face as calm and lovely as if she was sleeping a deep and refreshing sleep, and the morning sun would again smile upon her awakening; salt, the emblem of an immortal soul, was placed upon her breast; and in her pale and perishing fingers a branch of living flowers were struggling for life in the grasp of death, and diffusing their sweet and gracious fragrance over the cold odour of mortality. These images, so opposite, yet so alike, affected the spirit of the gazer, and he almost wept as he continued looking upon them, till he was aroused from his trance by the strange conduct of Ruth Tudor, who had caught a glimpse of his face as he bent in sorrow over the coffin. She sprang up from her seat, and, darting at him a terrible glance of recognition, pointed down to the corpse, and then, with a hollow burst of frantic laughter, shouted:

'Behold, you double-dyed liar!'

The startled stranger was relieved from the necessity of speaking by someone taking his arm and gently leading him to the farther end of the cottage. The eyes of Ruth followed him, and it was not till he had done violence to himself in turning from her to his conductor that he could escape their singular fascination. When he did so, he beheld a venerable man, the pastor of a distant village, who had come that night to speak comfort to the mourners, and perform the last sad duty to the dead on the morrow. 'Be not alarmed at what you have witnessed, my young friend,' said he; 'these ravings are not uncommon. This unhappy woman, at an early period of her life, gave ear to the miserable superstitions of her country, and a wretched pretender to wisdom predicted that she should become a shedder of blood. Madness has been the inevitable consequence in an ardent spirit, and in its ravings she dreams she has committed one sin, and is still tempted to add to it another.'

'You may say what you please, parson,' said the old man who had given admittance to the stranger, and who now, after dismissing all the guests save the youth, joined the talkers, and seated himself on the settle by their side. 'You may say what you please about madness and superstition, but I know Ruth Tudor was a fated woman, and the deed that was to be I believe she has done. Aye, aye, her madness is conscience; and if the deep sea and the jagged rocks could speak, they might tell us a tale of other things than that. But she is judged now; her only child is gone – her pretty Rachel. Poor Evan! he was her suitor. Ah! he little thought two months ago, when he was preparing for a gay bridal, that her slight sickness would end thus. He does not deserve it; but for her – God forgive me if I do her wrong, but I think it is the hand of God, and it lies heavy, as it should.' And the grey-haired old man hobbled away, satisfied that in thus thinking he was showing his zeal for virtue.

'Alas! that so white a head should acknowledge so hard a heart!' said the pastor. 'Ruth is condemned, according to his system, for committing that which a mightier hand compelled her to do. How harsh and misjudging is age! But we must not speak so loud,' continued he; 'for see, the youth Evan is retiring for the night, and the miserable mother has thrown herself on the floor to sleep. The sole domestic is rocking on her stool, and therefore I will do the honours of this poor cottage to you. There is a chamber above this containing the only bed in the hut; thither you may go and rest, for otherwise it will certainly be vacant to-night. I shall find a bed in the village, and Evan sleeps near you with some of the guests in the barn. But, before I go, if my question be not unwelcome and intrusive, tell me who you are, and whither you are bound.'

'I was ever somewhat of a subscriber to the old man's creed of fatalism,' said the stranger, smiling, 'and I believe I am more confirmed in it by the singular events of this day. My father was of a certain rank in society, but of selfish and disorderly habits. A course of extravagance and idleness was succeeded by difficulties and distress. Instead of exertion, he had recourse to flight, and left us to face the difficulties from which he shrunk. He was absent for years, while his family toiled and struggled with success. Suddenly we heard that he was concealed in this part of the coast. The cause which made that concealment necessary I forbear to mention; but he suddenly disappeared from the eyes of men, though we never could trace him beyond this part of the country. I have always believed that I should one day find my father, and have lately, though with difficulty, prevailed upon my mother to allow me to make my residence in this neighbourhood. But my search is at an end today. I believe that I have found my father. Roaming along the beach, I penetrated into several of those dark caverns. Through the fissures of one I discovered, in the interior, a light. Surprised, I penetrated to its concealment, and discovered a man sleeping on the ground. I advanced to awake him, and found but a fleshless skeleton, cased in tattered and decaying garments. He had probably met his death by accident, for exactly over the corpse I observed, at a great height, the daylight, as if streaming down from an aperture above. Thus the wretched man must have fallen, but how long since, or who had discovered his body, and left the light which I beheld, I knew not, though I cannot help cherishing a strong conviction that it was the body of William Morgan that I saw.'

'Who talks of William Morgan?' demanded a stern voice near the coffin, 'and of the cave where the outcast rots?' They turned quickly at the sound, and beheld Ruth Tudor standing up, as if she had been intently listening to the story.

'It was I who spoke,' said the stranger, gently, 'and I spoke of my father – of William Morgan. I am Owen, his son.'

'Son! Owen Morgan!' said the bewildered Ruth, passing her hand over her forehead, as if to enable her to recover the combination of these names. 'Why speak you of living things as pertaining to the dead? Father! He is father to nought save sin, and murder is his only begotten!'

She advanced to the traveller as she spoke, and again caught a view of his face. Again he saw the wild look of recognition, and an unearthly shriek followed the convulsive horror of her face. 'There! there!' she said, 'I knew it must be. Once before to-night have I beheld you. Yet what can your coming bode? Back with you, ruffian, for is not your dark work done!'

'Let us leave her,' said the good pastor, 'to the care of her attendant. 'Do not continue to meet her gaze. Your presence may increase, but cannot allay her malady. Go up to your bed and rest.'

He retired as he spoke, and Owen, in compliance with his wish, ascended the rickety stair which led to his chamber, after he had beheld Ruth Tudor quietly place herself in her seat at the open coffin's head. The room to which he mounted was not of the most cheering aspect, yet he felt he had often slept soundly in a worse. It was a gloomy, unfinished chamber, and the wind was whistling coldly and drearily through the uncovered rafters above his head. Like many of the cottages in that part of the country, it appeared to have grown old and ruinous before it had been finished, for the flooring was so crazy as scarcely to support the huge wooden bedstead, and in many instances the boards were entirely separated from each other; and in the centre, time, or the rot, had so completely devoured the larger half of one that through the gaping aperture Owen had an entire command of the room and the party below, looking down immediately above the coffin. Ruth was in the same attitude as when he left her. Owen threw himself upon his hard couch, and endeavoured to compose himself to rest for the night. His thoughts, however, still wandered to the events of the day, and he felt there was some strange connection between the scene he had just witnessed and the darker one of the secret cave. He grew restless, and watched, and amidst the tossings of impatient anxiety fatigue overpowered him, and he sunk into a perturbed and heated sleep. His slumber was broken by dreams that might well be the shadows of his waking reveries. He was alone – as in reality – upon his humble bed, when imagination brought to his ear the sound of many voices again singing the slow and monotonous psalm. It was interrupted by the outcries of some unseen things who attempted to enter his chamber, and, amid yells of fear and execrations of anger, bade him 'Arise, and come forth, and aid.' Then the coffined form which slept so quietly below stood by his side, and, in beseeching accents, bade him 'Arise and save her.' In his sleep he attempted to spring up, but a horrid fear restrained him, a fear that he should be too late. Then he crouched like a coward beneath his coverings, to hide from the reproaches of the spectre, while shouts of laughter and shrieks of agony were poured like a tempest around him. He sprung from his bed, and awoke.

It was some moments before he could recover himself, or shake off the horror which had seized upon his soul. He listened, and with infinite satisfaction observed an unbroken silence throughout the house. He smiled at his own terrors, attributed them to the events of the day or the presence of the corpse, and determined not to look down into the lower room till he should be summoned thither in the morning. He walked to the casement, and peered through at the night. The clouds were many, black, and lowering, and the face of the sky looked angry, while the wind moaned with a strange and eerie sound. He turned from the window, with the intention of again trying to sleep, but the light from below attracted his eye, and he could not pass the aperture without taking one glance at the coffin and its lonely watcher.

Ruth was earnestly gazing at the lower end of the room upon something without the sight of Owen. His attention was next fixed upon the corpse, and he thought he had never seen any living thing so lovely; and so calm was the aspect of her repose that it more resembled a temporary suspension of the faculties than the eternal stupor of death. Her features were pale, but not distorted, and there was none of the livid hue of death in her beautiful mouth and lips; but the flowers in her hand gave stronger demonstration of the presence of the power before whose potency their little strength was fading – drooping with a mortal sickness, they bowed down their heads in submission, as one by one they dropped from her pale and perishing fingers. Owen gazed till he thought he saw the grasp of her hand relapse, and a convulsive smile pass over her cold and rigid features. He looked again. The eyelids shook and vibrated like the string of some fine-strung instrument; the hair rose, and the head cloth moved. He started up ashamed.

'Does the madness of this woman affect all who would sleep beneath her roof?' he thought. 'What is this that disturbs me, or am I yet in a dream? Hark!' he muttered aloud. 'What is that!'

It was the voice of Ruth. She had risen from her seat, and was standing near the coffin, apparently addressing someone who stood at the lower end of the room.

'To what purpose is your coming now!' she asked in a low and melancholy voice, 'and at what do you laugh and gibe? Lo! behold. She is here, and the sin you know of cannot be. How can I take the life which another has already withdrawn? Go, go, hence, to your cave of night, for this is no place of safety for you.' Her thoughts now took another turn. She seemed as if trying to hide someone from the pursuit of others. 'Lie still! Lie still!' she whispered. 'Put out your light! So, so, they pass by, and do not see you. You are safe; good night, good night. Now will I home to sleep,' and she seated herself in her chair, as if composing her senses to rest.

Owen was again bewildered in the chaos of thought, but for the time he determined to subdue his imagination, and, throwing himself upon his bed, again gave himself up to sleep. But the images of his former dreams still haunted him, and their hideous phantasms were more powerfully renewed. Again he heard the solemn psalm of death, but unsung by mortals. It was pealed through earth up to the high heaven by myriads of the viewless and the mighty. Again he heard the execrations of millions for some unremembered sin, and the wrath and hatred of a world was rushing upon him.

'Come forth! Come forth!' was the cry, and amid yells and howls they were darting upon him, when the pale form of the beautiful dead arose between them and shielded him from their malice. But he heard her say aloud:

'It is for this that thou wilt not save me. Arise, arise, and help!'

He sprang up as he was commanded. Sleeping or waking he never knew, but he started from his bed to look down into the chamber, as he heard the voice of Ruth loud in terrific denunciation. He looked. She was standing, uttering yells of madness and rage, and close to her was a well-known form of appalling recollection – his father, as he had seen him last. He darted to the door.

'I am mad!' said he. 'I am surely mad, or this is still a continuation of my dream.'

Some strange and unholy fascination drew him back again to the aperture, and he looked down once more. Ruth was still there, though alone.

But though no visible form stood by the maniac, some fiend had entered her soul and mastered her spirit. She had armed herself with an axe, and, shouting, 'Liar! liar! hence!' pursued an imaginary foe to the darker side of the cottage. Owen strove hard to trace her motions, but as she had retreated to the space occupied by his bed he could no longer see her, and his eyes involuntarily fastened themselves upon the coffin. There a new horror met them. The corpse had risen, and with wild and glaring eyes was watching the scene before her. Owen distrusted his senses till he heard the terrific voice of Ruth, as she marked the miracle he had witnessed.

'The fiend, the robber!' she yelled, 'it is he who hath entered the pure body of my child. Back to your cave of blood, you lost one! Back to your own dark hell!'

Owen flew to the door. It was too late. He heard the shriek, the blow. He rushed into the room, but only in time to hear the second blow, and see the cleft head of the hapless Rachel fall back upon its bloody pillow. His terrible cries brought in the sleepers from the barn, headed by the wretched Evan, and for a time the roar of the storm was drowned in the clamorous grief of those present. No one dared to approach the miserable Ruth, who now, in utter frenzy, strode round the room, brandishing, with diabolical laughter, the bloody axe. Then she broke into a wild song of triumph and fierce joy. All fell back, appalled with horror, and the wild screeching of the wind was like the exultant cry of the damned. Then an extraordinary thing happened – a blinding flash of lightning, as if the heavens themselves had burst into flame, illuminated every nook and cranny, and imparted an awful, ghastly, and weird effect to the dramatic scene. In a few seconds the lightning was followed by a terrific peal of thunder. The house seemed to rock to its foundations. The inmates were blinded and stunned, and, moved by some strange impulse, they all fell upon their knees and murmured a prayer. Presently, as their self-possession returned, they rose one by one, and then a feeling of unutterable horror held them spellbound. Ruth Tudor lay stretched upon the floor, half of her body under the coffin, her face distorted and horrible, while hanging half out of the coffin was the now dead body of her resuscitated daughter, a stream of hot blood flowing from an awful wound in the skull. Ruth Tudor was also stone dead, and in her hand she still grasped the axe with which she had battered out the life of her child, who had awakened from a trance to meet death at the hands of her maniac mother.

The predictions of William Morgan had been literally fulfilled.

The Yellow Wall-paper

Charlotte Perkins Gilman

It is very seldom that mere ordinary people like John and myself secure ancestral halls for the summer.

A colonial mansion, a hereditary estate, I would say a haunted house, and reach the height of romantic felicity—but that would be asking too much of fate!

Still I will proudly declare that there is something queer about it.

Else, why should it be let so cheaply? And why have stood so long untenanted?

John laughs at me, of course, but one expects that in marriage.

John is practical in the extreme. He has no patience with faith, an intense horror of superstition, and he scoffs openly at any talk of things not to be felt and seen and put down in figures.

John is a physician, and *perhaps*—(I would not say it to a living soul, of course, but this is dead paper and a great relief to my mind)—*perhaps* that is one reason I do not get well faster.

You see, he does not believe I am sick!

And what can one do?

If a physician of high standing, and one's own husband, assures friends and relatives that there is really nothing the matter with one but temporary nervous depression—a slight hysterical tendency—what is one to do?

My brother is also a physician, and also of high standing, and he says the same thing.

So I take phosphates or phosphites—whichever it is, and tonics, and journeys, and air, and exercise, and am absolutely forbidden to "work" until I am well again.

Personally, I disagree with their ideas.

Personally, I believe that congenial work, with excitement and change, would do me good.

But what is one to do?

I did write for a while in spite of them; but it *does* exhaust me a good deal—having to be so sly about it, or else meet with heavy opposition.

I sometimes fancy that in my condition if I had less opposition and more society and stimulus—but John says the very worst thing I can do is to think about my condition, and I confess it always makes me feel bad.

So I will let it alone and talk about the house.

The most beautiful place! It is quite alone, standing well back from the road, quite three miles from the village. It makes me think of English places that you read about, for there are hedges and walls and gates that lock, and lots of separate little houses for the gardeners and people.

There is a *delicious* garden! I never saw such a garden—large and shady, full of box bordered paths, and lined with long grape-covered arbors with seats under them.

There were greenhouses, too, but they are all broken now.

There was some legal trouble, I believe, something about the heirs and co-heirs; anyhow, the place has been empty for years.

That spoils my ghostliness, I am afraid, but I don't care—there is something strange about the house—I can feel it.

I even said so to John one moonlight evening, but he said what I felt was a *draught*, and shut the window.

I get unreasonably angry with John sometimes. I'm sure I never used to be so sensitive. I think it is due to this nervous condition.

But John says if I feel so, I shall neglect proper self-control; so I take pains to control myself—before him, at least, and that makes me very tired.

I don't like our room a bit. I wanted one downstairs that opened on the piazza and had roses all over the window, and such pretty, old-fashioned chintz hangings! but John would not hear of it.

He said there was only one window and not room for two beds, and no near room for him if he took another.

He is very careful and loving, and hardly lets me stir without special direction.

I have a schedule prescription for each hour in the day; he takes all care from me, and so I feel basely ungrateful not to value it more.

He said we came here solely on my account, that I was to have perfect rest and all the air I could get. "Your exercise depends on your strength, my dear," said he, "and your food somewhat on your appetite; but air you can absorb all the time." So we took the nursery, at the top of the house.

It is a big, airy room, the whole floor nearly, with windows that look all ways, and air and sunshine galore. It was nursery first and then playground and gymnasium, I should judge; for the windows are barred for little children, and there are rings and things in the walls.

The paint and paper look as if a boys' school had used it. It is stripped off—the paper—in great patches all around the head of my bed, about as far as I can reach, and in a great place on the other side of the room low down. I never saw a worse paper in my life.

One of those sprawling flamboyant patterns committing every artistic sin.

It is dull enough to confuse the eye in following, pronounced enough to constantly irritate and provoke study, and when you follow the lame uncertain curves for a little distance they suddenly commit suicide—plunge off at outrageous angles, destroy themselves in unheard-of contradictions.

The color is repellant, almost revolting; a smoldering, unclean yellow, strangely faded by the slow-turning sunlight.

It is a dull yet lurid orange in some places, a sickly sulphur tint in others.

No wonder the children hated it! I should hate it myself if I had to live in this room long.

There comes John, and I must put this away,—he hates to have me write a word.

We have been here two weeks, and I haven't felt like writing before, since that first day.

I am sitting by the window now, up in this atrocious nursery, and there is nothing to hinder my writing as much as I please, save lack of strength.

John is away all day, and even some nights when his cases are serious.

I am glad my case is not serious!

But these nervous troubles are dreadfully depressing.

John does not know how much I really suffer. He knows there is no *reason* to suffer, and that satisfies him.

Of course it is only nervousness. It does weigh on me so not to do my duty in any way!

I meant to be such a help to John, such a real rest and comfort, and here I am a comparative burden already!

Nobody would believe what an effort it is to do what little I am able,—to dress and entertain, and order things.

It is fortunate Mary is so good with the baby. Such a dear baby!

And yet I *cannot* be with him, it makes me so nervous.

I suppose John never was nervous in his life. He laughs at me so about this wall-paper!

At first he meant to repaper the room, but afterwards he said that I was letting it get the better of me, and that nothing was worse for a nervous patient than to give way to such fancies.

He said that after the wall-paper was changed it would be the heavy bedstead, and then the barred windows, and then that gate at the head of the stairs, and so on.

"You know the place is doing you good," he said, "and really, dear, I don't care to renovate the house just for a three months' rental."

"Then do let us go downstairs," I said, "there are such pretty rooms there."

Then he took me in his arms and called me a blessed little goose, and said he would go down to the cellar, if I wished, and have it whitewashed into the bargain.

But he is right enough about the beds and windows and things.

It is an airy and comfortable room as any one need wish, and, of course, I would not be so silly as to make him uncomfortable just for a whim.

I'm really getting quite fond of the big room, all but that horrid paper.

Out of one window I can see the garden, those mysterious deep-shaded arbors, the riotous old-fashioned flowers, and bushes and gnarly trees.

Out of another I get a lovely view of the bay and a little private wharf belonging to the estate. There is a beautiful shaded lane that runs down there from the house. I always fancy I see people walking in these numerous paths and arbors, but John has cautioned me not to give way to fancy in the least. He says that with my imaginative power and habit of story-making, a nervous weakness like mine is sure to lead to all manner of excited fancies, and that I ought to use my will and good sense to check the tendency. So I try.

I think sometimes that if I were only well enough to write a little it would relieve the press of ideas and rest me.

But I find I get pretty tired when I try.

It is so discouraging not to have any advice and companionship about my work. When I get really well, John says we will ask Cousin Henry and Julia down for a long visit; but he says he would as soon put fireworks in my pillow-case as to let me have those stimulating people about now.

I wish I could get well faster.

But I must not think about that. This paper looks to me as if it *knew* what a vicious influence it had!

There is a recurrent spot where the pattern lolls like a broken neck and two bulbous eyes stare at you upside down.

I got positively angry with the impertinence of it and the everlastingness. Up and down and sideways they crawl, and those absurd, unblinking eyes are everywhere. There is one place where two breadths didn't match, and the eyes go all up and down the line, one a little higher than the other.

I never saw so much expression in an inanimate thing before, and we all know how much expression they have! I used to lie awake as a child and get more entertainment and terror out of blank walls and plain furniture than most children could find in a toy-store.

I remember what a kindly wink the knobs of our big old bureau used to have, and there was one chair that always seemed like a strong friend.

I used to feel that if any of the other things looked too fierce I could always hop into that chair and be safe.

The furniture in this room is no worse than inharmonious, however, for we had to bring it all from downstairs. I suppose when this was used as a playroom they had to take the nursery things out, and no wonder! I never saw such ravages as the children have made here.

The wall-paper, as I said before, is torn off in spots, and it sticketh closer than a brother—they must have had perseverance as well as hatred.

Then the floor is scratched and gouged and splintered, the plaster itself is dug out here and there, and this great heavy bed which is all we found in the room, looks as if it had been through the wars.

But I don't mind it a bit—only the paper.

There comes John's sister. Such a dear girl as she is, and so careful of me! I must not let her find me writing.

She is a perfect and enthusiastic housekeeper, and hopes for no better profession. I verily believe she thinks it is the writing which made me sick!

But I can write when she is out, and see her a long way off from these windows.

There is one that commands the road, a lovely shaded winding road, and one that just looks off over the country. A lovely country, too, full of great elms and velvet meadows.

This wall-paper has a kind of sub-pattern in a different shade, a particularly irritating one, for you can only see it in certain lights, and not clearly then.

But in the places where it isn't faded, and where the sun is just so—I can see a strange, provoking, formless sort of figure, that seems to sulk about behind that silly and conspicuous front design.

There's sister on the stairs!

Well, the Fourth of July is over! The people are all gone and I am tired out. John thought it might do me good to see a little company, so we just had mother and Nellie and the children down for a week.

Of course I didn't do a thing. Jennie sees to everything now.

But it tired me all the same.

John says if I don't pick up faster he shall send me to Weir Mitchell in the fall.

But I don't want to go there at all. I had a friend who was in his hands once, and she says he is just like John and my brother, only more so!

Besides, it is such an undertaking to go so far.

I don't feel as if it was worthwhile to turn my hand over for anything, and I'm getting dreadfully fretful and querulous.

I cry at nothing, and cry most of the time.

Of course I don't when John is here, or anybody else, but when I am alone.

And I am alone a good deal just now. John is kept in town very often by serious cases, and Jennie is good and lets me alone when I want her to.

So I walk a little in the garden or down that lovely lane, sit on the porch under the roses, and lie down up here a good deal.

I'm getting really fond of the room in spite of the wall-paper. Perhaps *because* of the wall-paper.

It dwells in my mind so!

I lie here on this great immovable bed—it is nailed down, I believe—and follow that pattern about by the hour. It is as good as gymnastics, I assure you. I start, we'll say, at the bottom, down in the corner over there where it has not been touched, and I determine for the thousandth time that I *will* follow that pointless pattern to some sort of a conclusion.

I know a little of the principles of design, and I know this thing was not arranged on any laws of radiation, or alternation, or repetition, or symmetry, or anything else that I ever heard of.

It is repeated, of course, by the breadths, but not otherwise.

Looked at in one way each breadth stands alone, the bloated curves and flourishes—a kind of "debased Romanesque" with *delirium tremens*—go waddling up and down in isolated columns of fatuity.

But, on the other hand, they connect diagonally, and the sprawling outlines run off in great slanting waves of optic horror, like a lot of wallowing seaweeds in full chase.

The whole thing goes horizontally, too, at least it seems so, and I exhaust myself in trying to distinguish the order of its going in that direction.

They have used a horizontal breadth for a frieze, and that adds wonderfully to the confusion.

There is one end of the room where it is almost intact, and there, when the crosslights fade and the low sun shines directly upon it, I can almost fancy radiation after all,—the interminable grotesque seem to form around a common center and rush off in headlong plunges of equal distraction.

It makes me tired to follow it. I will take a nap, I guess.

I don't know why I should write this.

I don't want to.

I don't feel able.

And I know John would think it absurd. But I *must* say what I feel and think in some way—it is such a relief!

But the effort is getting to be greater than the relief.

Half the time now I am awfully lazy, and lie down ever so much.

John says I mustn't lose my strength, and has me take cod liver oil and lots of tonics and things, to say nothing of ale and wine and rare meat.

Dear John! He loves me very dearly, and hates to have me sick. I tried to have a real earnest reasonable talk with him the other day, and tell him how I wished he would let me go and make a visit to Cousin Henry and Julia.

But he said I wasn't able to go, nor able to stand it after I got there; and I did not make out a very good case for myself, for I was crying before I had finished.

It is getting to be a great effort for me to think straight. Just this nervous weakness, I suppose.

And dear John gathered me up in his arms, and just carried me upstairs and laid me on the bed, and sat by me and read to me till it tired my head.

He said I was his darling and his comfort and all he had, and that I must take care of myself for his sake, and keep well.

He says no one but myself can help me out of it, that I must use my will and self-control and not let any silly fancies run away with me.

There's one comfort, the baby is well and happy, and does not have to occupy this nursery with the horrid wall-paper.

If we had not used it, that blessed child would have! What a fortunate escape! Why, I wouldn't have a child of mine, an impressionable little thing, live in such a room for worlds.

I never thought of it before, but it is lucky that John kept me here, after all, I can stand it so much easier than a baby, you see.

Of course I never mention it to them any more—I am too wise,—but I keep watch of it all the same.

There are things in that paper that nobody knows but me, or ever will.

Behind that outside pattern the dim shapes get clearer every day.

It is always the same shape, only very numerous.

And it is like a woman stooping down and creeping about behind that pattern. I don't like it a bit. I wonder—I begin to think—I wish John would take me away from here!

It is so hard to talk with John about my case, because he is so wise, and because he loves me so.

But I tried it last night.

It was moonlight. The moon shines in all around just as the sun does.

I hate to see it sometimes, it creeps so slowly, and always comes in by one window or another.

John was asleep and I hated to waken him, so I kept still and watched the moonlight on that undulating wall-paper till I felt creepy.

The faint figure behind seemed to shake the pattern, just as if she wanted to get out.

I got up softly and went to feel and see if the paper *did* move, and when I came back John was awake.

"What is it, little girl?" he said. "Don't go walking about like that—you'll get cold."

I thought it was a good time to talk, so I told him that I really was not gaining here, and that I wished he would take me away.

"Why, darling!" said he, "our lease will be up in three weeks, and I can't see how to leave before.

"The repairs are not done at home, and I cannot possibly leave town just now. Of course if you were in any danger, I could and would, but you really are better, dear, whether you can see it or not. I am a doctor, dear, and I know. You are gaining flesh and color, your appetite is better, I feel really much easier about you."

"I don't weigh a bit more," said I, "nor as much; and my appetite may be better in the evening when you are here, but it is worse in the morning when you are away!"

"Bless her little heart!" said he with a big hug, "she shall be as sick as she pleases! But now let's improve the shining hours by going to sleep, and talk about it in the morning!"

"And you won't go away?" I asked gloomily.

"Why, how can I, dear? It is only three weeks more and then we will take a nice little trip of a few days while Jennie is getting the house ready. Really dear you are better!"

"Better in body perhaps—" I began, and stopped short, for he sat up straight and looked at me with such a stern, reproachful look that I could not say another word.

"My darling," said he, "I beg of you, for my sake and for our child's sake, as well as for your own, that you will never for one instant let that idea enter your mind! There is nothing so dangerous, so fascinating, to a temperament like yours. It is a false and foolish fancy. Can you not trust me as a physician when I tell you so?"

So of course I said no more on that score, and we went to sleep before long. He thought I was asleep first, but I wasn't, and lay there for hours trying to decide whether that front pattern and the back pattern really did move together or separately.

On a pattern like this, by daylight, there is a lack of sequence, a defiance of law, that is a constant irritant to a normal mind.

The color is hideous enough, and unreliable enough, and infuriating enough, but the pattern is torturing.

You think you have mastered it, but just as you get well underway in following, it turns a back-somersault and there you are. It slaps you in the face, knocks you down, and tramples upon you. It is like a bad dream.

The outside pattern is a florid arabesque, reminding one of a fungus. If you can imagine a toadstool in joints, an interminable string of toadstools, budding and sprouting in endless convolutions—why, that is something like it.

That is, sometimes!

There is one marked peculiarity about this paper, a thing nobody seems to notice but myself, and that is that it changes as the light changes.

When the sun shoots in through the east window—I always watch for that first long, straight ray—it changes so quickly that I never can quite believe it.

That is why I watch it always.

By moonlight—the moon shines in all night when there is a moon—I wouldn't know it was the same paper.

At night in any kind of light, in twilight, candlelight, lamplight, and worst of all by moonlight, it becomes bars! The outside pattern I mean, and the woman behind it is as plain as can be.

I didn't realize for a long time what the thing was that showed behind, that dim sub-pattern, but now I am quite sure it is a woman.

By daylight she is subdued, quiet. I fancy it is the pattern that keeps her so still. It is so puzzling. It keeps me quiet by the hour.

I lie down ever so much now. John says it is good for me, and to sleep all I can.

Indeed, he started the habit by making me lie down for an hour after each meal.

It is a very bad habit, I am convinced, for, you see, I don't sleep.

And that cultivates deceit, for I don't tell them I'm awake—O no!

The fact is I am getting a little afraid of John.

He seems very queer sometimes, and even Jennie has an inexplicable look.

It strikes me occasionally, just as a scientific hypothesis,—that perhaps it is the paper!

I have watched John when he did not know I was looking, and come into the room suddenly on the most innocent excuses, and I've caught him several times *looking at the paper!* And Jennie too. I caught Jennie with her hand on it once.

She didn't know I was in the room, and when I asked her in a quiet, a very quiet voice, with the most restrained manner possible, what she was doing with the paper—she turned around as if she had been caught stealing, and looked quite angry—asked me why I should frighten her so!

Then she said that the paper stained everything it touched, that she had found yellow smooches on all my clothes and John's, and she wished we would be more careful!

Did not that sound innocent? But I know she was studying that pattern, and I am determined that nobody shall find it out but myself!

Life is very much more exciting now than it used to be. You see I have something more to expect, to look forward to, to watch. I really do eat better, and am more quiet than I was.

John is so pleased to see me improve! He laughed a little the other day, and said I seemed to be flourishing in spite of my wall-paper.

I turned it off with a laugh. I had no intention of telling him it was *because* of the wall-paper—he would make fun of me. He might even want to take me away.

I don't want to leave now until I have found it out. There is a week more, and I think that will be enough.

I'm feeling ever so much better! I don't sleep much at night, for it is so interesting to watch developments; but I sleep a good deal in the daytime.

In the daytime it is tiresome and perplexing.

There are always new shoots on the fungus, and new shades of yellow all over it. I cannot keep count of them, though I have tried conscientiously.

It is the strangest yellow, that wall-paper! It makes me think of all the yellow things I ever saw—not beautiful ones like buttercups, but old foul, bad yellow things.

But there is something else about that paper—the smell! I noticed it the moment we came into the room, but with so much air and sun it was not bad. Now we have had a week of fog and rain, and whether the windows are open or not, the smell is here.

It creeps all over the house.

I find it hovering in the dining-room, skulking in the parlor, hiding in the hall, lying in wait for me on the stairs.

It gets into my hair.

Even when I go to ride, if I turn my head suddenly and surprise it—there is that smell!

Such a peculiar odor, too! I have spent hours in trying to analyze it, to find what it smelled like.

It is not bad—at first, and very gentle, but quite the subtlest, most enduring odor I ever met.

In this damp weather it is awful, I wake up in the night and find it hanging over me.

It used to disturb me at first. I thought seriously of burning the house—to reach the smell.

But now I am used to it. The only thing I can think of that it is like is the *color* of the paper! A yellow smell.

There is a very funny mark on this wall, low down, near the mopboard. A streak that runs round the room. It goes behind every piece of furniture, except the bed, a long, straight, even *smooch,* as if it had been rubbed over and over.

I wonder how it was done and who did it, and what they did it for. Round and round and round—round and round and round—it makes me dizzy!

I really have discovered something at last.

Through watching so much at night, when it changes so, I have finally found out.

The front pattern *does* move—and no wonder! The woman behind shakes it!

Sometimes I think there are a great many women behind, and sometimes only one, and she crawls around fast, and her crawling shakes it all over.

Then in the very bright spots she keeps still, and in the very shady spots she just takes hold of the bars and shakes them hard.

And she is all the time trying to climb through. But nobody could climb through that pattern—it strangles so; I think that is why it has so many heads.

They get through, and then the pattern strangles them off and turns them upside down, and makes their eyes white!

If those heads were covered or taken off it would not be half so bad.

I think that woman gets out in the daytime!

And I'll tell you why—privately—I've seen her!

I can see her out of every one of my windows!

It is the same woman, I know, for she is always creeping, and most women do not creep by daylight.

I see her in that long shaded lane, creeping up and down. I see her in those dark grape arbors, creeping all around the garden.

I see her on that long road under the trees, creeping along, and when a carriage comes she hides under the blackberry vines.

I don't blame her a bit. It must be very humiliating to be caught creeping by daylight!

I always lock the door when I creep by daylight. I can't do it at night, for I know John would suspect something at once.

And John is so queer, now, that I don't want to irritate him. I wish he would take another room! Besides, I don't want anybody to get that woman out at night but myself.

I often wonder if I could see her out of all the windows at once.

But, turn as fast as I can, I can only see out of one at one time.

And though I always see her she *may* be able to creep faster than I can turn!

I have watched her sometimes away off in the open country, creeping as fast as a cloud shadow in a high wind.

If only that top pattern could be gotten off from the under one! I mean to try it, little by little.

I have found out another funny thing, but I shan't tell it this time! It does not do to trust people too much.

There are only two more days to get this paper off, and I believe John is beginning to notice. I don't like the look in his eyes.

And I heard him ask Jennie a lot of professional questions about me. She had a very good report to give.

She said I slept a good deal in the daytime.

John knows I don't sleep very well at night, for all I'm so quiet!

He asked me all sorts of questions, too, and pretended to be very loving and kind.

As if I couldn't see through him!

Still, I don't wonder he acts so, sleeping under this paper for three months.

It only interests me, but I feel sure John and Jennie are secretly affected by it.

Hurrah! This is the last day, but it is enough. John is to stay in town overnight, and won't be out until this evening.

Jennie wanted to sleep with me—the sly thing! But I told her I should undoubtedly rest better for a night all alone.

That was clever, for really I wasn't alone a bit! As soon as it was moonlight, and that poor thing began to crawl and shake the pattern, I got up and ran to help her.

I pulled and she shook, I shook and she pulled, and before morning we had peeled off yards of that paper.

A strip about as high as my head and half around the room.

And then when the sun came and that awful pattern began to laugh at me I declared I would finish it today!

We go away tomorrow, and they are moving all my furniture down again to leave things as they were before.

Jennie looked at the wall in amazement, but I told her merrily that I did it out of pure spite at the vicious thing.

She laughed and said she wouldn't mind doing it herself, but I must not get tired.

How she betrayed herself that time!

But I am here, and no person touches this paper but me,—not *alive!*

She tried to get me out of the room—it was too patent! But I said it was so quiet and empty and clean now that I believed I would lie down again and sleep all I could; and not to wake me even for dinner—I would call when I woke.

So now she is gone, and the servants are gone, and the things are gone, and there is nothing left but that great bedstead nailed down, with the canvas mattress we found on it.

We shall sleep downstairs tonight, and take the boat home tomorrow.

I quite enjoy the room, now it is bare again.

How those children did tear about here!

This bedstead is fairly gnawed!

But I must get to work.

I have locked the door and thrown the key down into the front path.

I don't want to go out, and I don't want to have anybody come in, till John comes.

I want to astonish him.

I've got a rope up here that even Jennie did not find. If that woman does get out, and tries to get away, I can tie her!

But I forgot I could not reach far without anything to stand on!

This bed will *not* move!

I tried to lift and push it until I was lame, and then I got so angry I bit off a little piece at one corner—but it hurt my teeth.

Then I peeled off all the paper I could reach standing on the floor. It sticks horribly and the pattern just enjoys it! All those strangled heads and bulbous eyes and waddling fungus growths just shriek with derision!

I am getting angry enough to do something desperate. To jump out of the window would be admirable exercise, but the bars are too strong even to try.

Besides, I wouldn't do it. Of course not. I know well enough that a step like that is improper and might be misconstrued.

I don't like to *look* out of the windows even—there are so many of those creeping women, and they creep so fast.

I wonder if they all come out of that wall-paper, as I did?

But I am securely fastened now by my well-hidden rope—you don't get *me* out in the road there!

I suppose I shall have to get back behind the pattern when it comes night, and that is hard!

It is so pleasant to be out in this great room and creep around as I please!

I don't want to go outside. I won't, even if Jennie asks me to.

For outside you have to creep on the ground, and everything is green instead of yellow.

But here I can creep smoothly on the floor, and my shoulder just fits in that long smooch around the wall, so I cannot lose my way.

Why, there's John at the door!

It is no use, young man, you can't open it!

How he does call and pound!

Now he's crying for an axe.

It would be a shame to break down that beautiful door!

"John, dear!" said I in the gentlest voice, "the key is down by the front steps, under a plantain leaf!"

That silenced him for a few moments.

Then he said—very quietly indeed, "Open the door, my darling!"

"I can't," said I. "The key is down by the front door, under a plantain leaf!"

And then I said it again, several times, very gently and slowly, and said it so often that he had to go and see, and he got it, of course, and came in. He stopped short by the door.

"What is the matter?" he cried. "For God's sake, what are you doing?"

I kept on creeping just the same, but I looked at him over my shoulder.

"I've got out at last," said I, "in spite of you and Jane! And I've pulled off most of the paper, so you can't put me back!"

Now why should that man have fainted? But he did, and right across my path by the wall, so that I had to creep over him every time!

The Spectre Bridegroom

Washington Irving

A Traveller's Tale[3]

He that supper for is dight,
He lyes full cold, I trow, this night!
Yestreen to chamber I him led,
This night Gray-Steel has made his bed!
SIR EGER, SIR GRAHAME, AND SIR GRAY-STEEL.

On the summit of one of the heights of the Odenwald, a wild and romantic tract of Upper Germany that lies not far from the confluence of the Main and the Rhine, there stood many, many years since the castle of the Baron Von Landshort. It is now quite fallen to decay, and almost buried among beech trees and dark firs; above which, however, its old watch-tower may still be seen struggling, like

3 The erudite reader, well versed in good-for-nothing lore, will perceive that the above Tale must have been suggested to the old Swiss by a little French anecdote, a circumstance said to have taken place in Paris.

the former possessor I have mentioned, to carry a high head and look down upon the neighboring country.

The baron was a dry branch of the great family of Katzenellenbogen,[4] and inherited the relics of the property and all the pride, of his ancestors. Though the warlike disposition of his predecessors had much impaired the family possessions, yet the baron still endeavored to keep up some show of former state. The times were peaceable, and the German nobles in general had abandoned their inconvenient old castles, perched like eagles' nests among the mountains, and had built more convenient residences in the valleys; still, the baron remained proudly drawn up in his little fortress, cherishing with hereditary inveteracy all the old family feuds, so that he was on ill terms with some of his nearest neighbors, on account of disputes that had happened between their great-great-grandfathers.

The baron had but one child, a daughter, but Nature, when she grants but one child, always compensates by making it a prodigy; and so it was with the daughter of the baron. All the nurses, gossips, and country cousins assured her father that she had not her equal for beauty in all Germany; and who should know better than they? She had, moreover, been brought up with great care under the superintendence of two maiden aunts, who had spent some years of their early life at one of the little German courts, and were skilled in all branches of knowledge necessary to the education of a fine lady. Under their instructions she became a miracle of accomplishments. By the time she was eighteen she could embroider to admiration, and had worked whole histories of the saints in tapestry with such strength of expression in their countenances that they looked like so many souls in purgatory. She could read without great difficulty, and had spelled her way through several Church legends and almost all the chivalric wonders of the Heldenbuch. She had even made considerable proficiency in writing; could sign her own name without missing a letter, and so legibly that her aunts could read it without spectacles. She excelled in making little elegant good-for-nothing, lady-like knicknacks of all kinds, was versed

4 i.e., Cat's Elbow—the name of a family of those parts, and very powerful in former times. The appellation, we are told, was given in compliment to a peerless dame of the family, celebrated for a fine arm.

in the most abstruse dancing of the day, played a number of airs on the harp and guitar, and knew all the tender ballads of the Minnelieders by heart.

Her aunts, too, having been great flirts and coquettes in their younger days, were admirably calculated to be vigilant guardians and strict censors of the conduct of their niece; for there is no duenna so rigidly prudent and inexorably decorous as a superannuated coquette. She was rarely suffered out of their sight; never went beyond the domains of the castle unless well attended, or rather well watched; had continual lectures read to her about strict decorum and implicit obedience; and, as to the men—pah!—she was taught to hold them at such a distance and in such absolute distrust that, unless properly authorized, she would not have cast a glance upon the handsomest cavalier in the world—no, not if he were even dying at her feet.

The good effects of this system were wonderfully apparent. The young lady was a pattern of docility and correctness. While others were wasting their sweetness in the glare of the world, and liable to be plucked and thrown aside by every hand, she was coyly blooming into fresh and lovely womanhood under the protection of those immaculate spinsters, like a rosebud blushing forth among guardian thorns. Her aunts looked upon her with pride and exultation, and vaunted that, though all the other young ladies in the world might go astray, yet thank Heaven, nothing of the kind could happen to the heiress of Katzenellenbogen.

But, however scantily the Baron Von Landshort might be provided with children, his household was by no means a small one; for Providence had enriched him with abundance of poor relations. They, one and all, possessed the affectionate disposition common to humble relatives—were wonderfully attached to the baron, and took every possible occasion to come in swarms and enliven the castle. All family festivals were commemorated by these good people at the baron's expense; and when they were filled with good cheer they would declare that there was nothing on earth so delightful as these family meetings, these jubilees of the heart.

The baron, though a small man, had a large soul, and it swelled with satisfaction at the consciousness of being the greatest man in the little world about him. He loved to tell long stories about the stark old warriors whose portraits looked grimly down from the walls around, and he found no listeners equal to those who fed at his expense. He was much given to the marvellous and a firm believer in all those supernatural tales with which every mountain and valley in Germany abounds. The faith of his guests exceeded even his own: they listened to every tale of wonder with open eyes and mouth, and never failed to be astonished, even though repeated for the hundredth time. Thus lived the Baron Von Landshort, the oracle of his table, the absolute monarch of his little territory, and happy, above all things, in the persuasion that he was the wisest man of the age.

At the time of which my story treats there was a great family gathering at the castle on an affair of the utmost importance: it was to receive the destined bridegroom of the baron's daughter. A negotiation had been carried on between the father and an old nobleman of Bavaria to unite the dignity of their houses by the marriage of their children. The preliminaries had been conducted with proper punctilio. The young people were betrothed without seeing each other, and the time was appointed for the marriage ceremony. The young Count Von Altenburg had been recalled from the army for the purpose, and was actually on his way to the baron's to receive his bride. Missives had even been received from him from Würtzburg, where he was accidentally detained, mentioning the day and hour when he might be expected to arrive.

The castle was in a tumult of preparation to give him a suitable welcome. The fair bride had been decked out with uncommon care. The two aunts had superintended her toilet, and quarreled the whole morning about every article of her dress. The young lady had taken advantage of their contest to follow the bent of her own taste; and fortunately it was a good one. She looked as lovely as a youthful bridegroom could desire; and the flutter of expectation heightened the lustre of her charms.

The suffusions that mantled her face and neck, the gentle heaving of the bosom, the eye now and then lost in reverie, all betrayed the soft tumult that was going on in her little heart. The aunts were continually hovering around her, for maiden aunts are apt to take great interest in affairs of this nature. They were giving her a world of staid counsel in how to deport herself, what to say, and in what manner to receive the expected lover.

The baron was no less busied in preparations. He had, in truth, nothing exactly to do; but he was naturally a fuming, bustling little man, and could not remain passive when all the world was in a hurry. He worried from top to bottom of the castle with an air of infinite anxiety; he continually called the servants from their work to exhort them to be diligent; and buzzed about every hall and chamber, as idly restless and importunate as a blue-bottle fly on a warm summer's day.

In the mean time the fatted calf had been killed; the forests had rung with the clamor of the huntsmen; the kitchen was crowded with good cheer; the cellars had yielded up whole oceans of *Rhein-wein* and *Ferne-wein;* and even the great Heidelberg tun had been laid under contribution. Everything was ready to receive the distinguished guest with *Saus und Braus* in the true spirit of German hospitality; but the guest delayed to make his appearance. Hour rolled after hour. The sun, that had poured his downward rays upon the rich forest of the Odenwald, now just gleamed along the summits of the mountains. The baron mounted the highest tower and strained his eyes in hopes of catching a distant sight of the count and his attendants. Once he thought he beheld them; the sound of horns came floating from the valley, prolonged by the mountain echoes. A number of horsemen were seen far below slowly advancing along the road; but when they had nearly reached the foot of the mountain they suddenly struck off in a different direction. The last ray of sunshine departed, the bats began to flit by in the twilight, the road grew dimmer and dimmer to the view, and nothing appeared stirring in it but now and then a peasant lagging homeward from his labor.

While the old castle of Landshort was in this state of perplexity a very interesting scene was transacting in a different part of the Odenwald.

The young Count Von Altenburg was tranquilly pursuing his route in that sober jog-trot way in which a man travels toward matrimony when his friends have taken all the trouble and uncertainty of courtship off his hands and a bride is waiting for him as certainly as a dinner at the end of his journey. He had encountered at Würtzburg a youthful companion-in-arms with whom he had seen some service on the frontiers—Herman Von Starkenfaust, one of the stoutest hands and worthiest hearts of German chivalry—who was now returning from the army. His father's castle was not far distant from the old fortress of

Landshort, although an hereditary feud rendered the families hostile and strangers to each other.

In the warm-hearted moment of recognition the young friends related all their past adventures and fortunes, and the count gave the whole history of his intended nuptials with a young lady whom he had never seen, but of whose charms he had received the most enrapturing descriptions.

As the route of the friends lay in the same direction, they agreed to perform the rest of their journey together, and that they might do it the more leisurely, set off from Würtzburg at an early hour, the count having given directions for his retinue to follow and overtake him.

They beguiled their wayfaring with recollections of their military scenes and adventures; but the count was apt to be a little tedious now and then about the reputed charms of his bride and the felicity that awaited him.

In this way they had entered among the mountains of the Odenwald, and were traversing one of its most lonely and thickly wooded passes. It is well known that the forests of Germany have always been as much infested by robbers as its castles by spectres; and at this time the former were particularly numerous, from the hordes of disbanded soldiers wandering about the country. It will not appear extraordinary, therefore, that the cavaliers were attacked by a gang of these stragglers, in the midst of the forest. They defended themselves with bravery, but were nearly overpowered when the count's retinue arrived to their assistance. At sight of them the robbers fled, but not until the count had received a mortal wound. He was slowly and carefully conveyed back to the city of Würtzburg, and a friar summoned from a neighboring convent who was famous for his skill in administering to both soul and body; but half of his skill was superfluous; the moments of the unfortunate count were numbered.

With his dying breath he entreated his friend to repair instantly to the castle of Landshort and explain the fatal cause of his not keeping his appointment with his bride. Though not the most ardent of lovers, he was one of the most punctilious of men, and appeared earnestly solicitous that his mission should be speedily and courteously executed. "Unless this is done," said he, "I shall not sleep quietly in my grave." He repeated these last words with peculiar solemnity. A request at a moment so impressive admitted no hesitation. Starkenfaust endeavored to soothe him to calmness, promised faithfully to execute his wish, and gave him his hand in solemn pledge. The dying man pressed it in acknowledgment, but soon lapsed into delirium—raved about his bride, his engagements, his plighted word—ordered his horse, that he might ride to the castle of Landshort, and expired in the fancied act of vaulting into the saddle.

Starkenfaust bestowed a sigh and a soldier's tear on the untimely fate of his comrade and then pondered on the awkward mission he had undertaken. His heart was heavy and his head perplexed; for he was to present himself an unbidden guest among hostile people, and to damp their festivity with tidings fatal to their hopes. Still, there were certain whisperings of curiosity in his bosom to see this far-famed beauty of Katzenellenbogen, so cautiously shut up from the world; for he was a passionate admirer of the sex, and there was a dash of eccentricity and enterprise in his character that made him fond of all singular adventure.

Previous to his departure he made all due arrangements with the holy fraternity of the convent for the funeral solemnities of his friend, who was to be buried in the cathedral of Würtzburg near some of his illustrious relatives, and the mourning retinue of the count took charge of his remains.

It is now high time that we should return to the ancient family of Katzenellenbogen, who were impatient for their guest, and still more for their dinner, and to the worthy little baron, whom we left airing himself on the watch-tower.

Night closed in, but still no guest arrived. The baron descended from the tower in despair. The banquet, which had been delayed from hour to hour, could no longer be postponed. The meats were already overdone, the cook in an agony, and the whole household had the look of a garrison, that had been reduced by famine. The baron was obliged reluctantly to give orders for the feast without the presence of the guest. All were seated at table, and just on the point of commencing, when the sound of a horn from without the gate gave notice of the approach of a stranger. Another long blast filled the old courts of the castle with its echoes, and was answered by the warder from the walls. The baron hastened to receive his future son-in-law.

The drawbridge had been let down, and the stranger was before the gate. He was a tall gallant cavalier, mounted on a black steed. His countenance was pale, but he had a beaming, romantic eye and an air of stately melancholy. The baron was a little mortified that he should have come in this simple, solitary style. His dignity for a moment was ruffled, and he felt disposed to consider it a want of proper respect for the important occasion and the important family with which he was to be connected. He pacified himself, however, with the conclusion that it must have been youthful impatience which had induced him thus to spur on sooner than his attendants.

"I am sorry," said the stranger, "to break in upon you thus unseasonably—"

Here the baron interrupted him with a world of compliments and greetings, for, to tell the truth, he prided himself upon his courtesy and eloquence. The stranger attempted once or twice to stem the torrent of words, but in vain, so he bowed his head and suffered it to flow on. By the time the baron had come to a pause they had reached the inner court of the castle, and the stranger was again about to speak, when he was once more interrupted by the appearance of the female part of the family, leading forth the shrinking and blushing bride. He gazed on her for a moment as one entranced; it seemed as if his whole soul beamed forth in the gaze and rested upon that lovely form. One of the maiden aunts whispered something in her ear; she made an effort to speak; her moist blue eye was timidly raised, gave a shy glance of inquiry on the stranger, and was cast again to the ground. The words died away, but there was a sweet smile playing about her lips, and a soft dimpling of the cheek that showed her glance had not been unsatisfactory. It was impossible for a girl of the fond age of eighteen, highly predisposed for love and matrimony, not to be pleased with so gallant a cavalier.

The late hour at which the guest had arrived left no time for parley. The baron was peremptory, and deferred all particular conversation until the morning, and led the way to the untasted banquet.

It was served up in the great hall of the castle. Around the walls hung the hard-favored portraits of the heroes of the house of Katzenellenbogen, and the trophies which they had gained in the field, and in the chase. Hacked corselets, splintered jousting spears, and tattered banners were mingled with the spoils of sylvan warfare: the jaws of the wolf and the tusks of the boar grinned horribly among crossbows and battle-axes, and a huge pair of antlers branched immediately over the head of the youthful bridegroom.

The cavalier took but little notice of the company or the entertainment. He scarcely tasted the banquet, but seemed absorbed in admiration of his bride. He conversed in a low tone that could not be overheard, for the language of love is never loud; but where is the female ear so dull that it cannot catch the softest whisper of the lover? There was a mingled tenderness and gravity in his manner that appeared to have a powerful effect upon the young lady. Her color came and went as she listened with deep attention. Now and then she made some blushing reply, and when his eye was turned away she would steal a sidelong glance at his romantic countenance, and heave a gentle sigh of tender happiness. It was evident that the young couple were completely enamored. The aunts, who were deeply versed in the mysteries of the heart, declared that they had fallen in love with each other at first sight.

The feast went on merrily, or at least noisily, for the guests were all blessed with those keen appetites that attend upon light purses and mountain air. The baron told his best and longest stories, and never had he told them so well or with such great effect. If there was anything marvellous, his auditors were lost in astonishment; and if anything facetious, they were sure to laugh exactly in the right place. The baron, it is true, like most great men, was too dignified to utter any joke but a dull one; it was always enforced, however, by a bumper of excellent Hockheimer, and even a dull joke at one's own table, served up with jolly old wine, is irresistible. Many good things were said by poorer and keener wits that would not bear repeating, except on similar occasions; many sly speeches whispered in ladies' ears that almost convulsed them with suppressed laughter; and a song or two roared out by a poor but merry and broad-faced cousin of the baron that absolutely made the maiden aunts hold up their fans.

Amidst all this revelry the stranger guest maintained a most singular and unseasonable gravity. His countenance assumed a deeper cast of dejection as the evening advanced, and, strange as it may appear, even the baron's jokes seemed only to render him the more melancholy. At times he was lost in thought, and at times there was a perturbed and restless wandering of the eye that bespoke a mind but ill at ease.

His conversations with the bride became more and more earnest and mysterious. Lowering clouds began to steal over the fair serenity of her brow, and tremors to run through her tender frame.

All this could not escape the notice of the company. Their gayety was chilled by the unaccountable gloom of the bridegroom; their spirits were infected; whispers and glances were interchanged, accompanied by shrugs and dubious shakes of the head. The song and the laugh grew less and less frequent: there were dreary pauses in the conversation, which were at length succeeded by wild tales and supernatural legends. One dismal story produced another still more dismal, and the baron nearly frightened some of the ladies into hysterics with the history of the goblin horseman that carried away the fair Leonora—a dreadful story which has since been put into excellent verse, and is read and believed by all the world.

The bridegroom listened to this tale with profound attention. He kept his eyes steadily fixed on the baron, and, as the story drew to a close, began gradually to rise from his seat, growing taller and taller, until in the baron's entranced eye he seemed almost to tower into a giant. The moment the tale was finished he heaved a deep sigh and took a solemn farewell of the company. They were all amazement. The baron was perfectly thunderstruck.

"What! Going to leave the castle at midnight? Why, everything was prepared for his reception; a chamber was ready for him if he wished to retire."

The stranger shook his head mournfully and mysteriously: "I must lay my head in a different chamber to-night."

There was something in this reply and the tone in which it was uttered that made the baron's heart misgive him; but he rallied his forces and repeated his hospitable entreaties.

The stranger shook his head silently, but positively, at every offer, and, waving his farewell to the company, stalked slowly out of the hall. The maiden aunts were absolutely petrified; the bride hung her head and a tear stole to her eye.

The baron followed the stranger to the great court of the castle, where the black charger stood pawing the earth and snorting with impatience. When they had reached the portal, whose deep archway was dimly lighted by a cresset, the stranger paused, and addressed the baron in a hollow tone of voice, which the vaulted roof rendered still more sepulchral.

"Now that we are alone," said he, "I will impart to you the reason of my going. I have a solemn, an indispensable engagement—"

"Why," said the baron, "cannot you send some one in your place?"

"It admits of no substitute—I must attend it in person; I must away to Würtzburg cathedral—"

"Ay," said the baron, plucking up spirit, "but not until to-morrow—to-morrow you shall take your bride there."

"No! no!" replied the stranger, with tenfold solemnity, "my engagement is with no bride—the worms! The worms expect me! I am a dead man—I have been slain by robbers—my body lies at Würtzburg—at midnight I am to be buried—the grave is waiting for me—I must keep my appointment!"

He sprang on his black charger, dashed over the drawbridge, and the clattering of his horse's hoofs was lost in the whistling of the night blast.

The baron returned to the hall in the utmost consternation, and related what had passed. Two ladies fainted outright, others sickened at the idea of having banqueted with a spectre. It was the opinion of some that this might be the wild huntsman, famous in German legend. Some talked of mountain sprites, of wood-demons, and of other supernatural beings with which the good people of Germany have been so grievously harassed since time immemorial. One of the poor relations ventured to suggest that it might be some sportive evasion of the young cavalier, and that the very gloominess of the caprice seemed to accord with so melancholy a personage. This, however, drew on him, the indignation of the whole company, and especially of the baron, who looked upon him as little better than an infidel; so that he was fain to abjure his heresy as speedily as possible and come into the faith of the true believers.

But, whatever may have been the doubts entertained, they were completely put to an end by the arrival next day of regular missives confirming the intelligence of the young count's murder and his interment in Würtzburg cathedral.

The dismay at the castle may well be imagined. The baron shut himself up in his chamber. The guests, who had come to rejoice with him, could not think of abandoning him in his distress. They wandered about the courts or collected in groups in the hall, shaking their heads and shrugging their shoulders at the troubles of so good a man, and sat longer than ever at table, and ate and drank more stoutly than ever, by way of keeping up their spirits. But the situation of the widowed bride was the most pitiable. To have lost a husband before she had even embraced him—and such a husband! If the very spectre could be so gracious and noble, what must have been the living man? She filled the house with lamentations.

On the night of the second day of her widowhood she had retired to her chamber, accompanied by one of her aunts, who insisted on sleeping with her. The aunt, who was one of the best tellers of ghost-stories in all Germany, had just been recounting one of her longest, and had fallen asleep in the very midst of it. The chamber was remote and overlooked a small garden. The niece lay pensively gazing at the beams of the rising moon as they trembled on the leaves of an aspen tree before the lattice. The castle clock had just tolled midnight when a soft strain of music stole up from the garden. She rose hastily from her bed and stepped lightly to the window. A tall figure stood among the shadows of the trees. As it raised its head a beam of moonlight fell upon the countenance. Heaven and earth! She beheld the Spectre Bridegroom! A loud shriek at that moment burst upon her ear, and her aunt, who had been awakened by the music and had followed her silently to the window, fell into her arms. When she looked again the spectre had disappeared.

Of the two females, the aunt now required the most soothing, for she was perfectly beside herself with terror. As to the young lady, there was something even in the spectre of her lover that seemed endearing. There was still the semblance of manly beauty, and, though the shadow of a man is but little calculated to satisfy the affections of a lovesick girl, yet where the substance is not to be had even that is consoling. The aunt declared she would never sleep in that chamber again; the niece, for once, was refractory, and declared as strongly that she would sleep in no other in the castle: the consequence was, that she had to sleep in it alone; but she drew a promise from her aunt not to relate the story of the spectre, lest she should be denied the only melancholy pleasure left her on earth—that of inhabiting the chamber over which the guardian shade of her lover kept its nightly vigils.

How long the good old lady would have observed this promise is uncertain, for she dearly loved to talk of the marvellous, and there is a triumph in being the first to tell a frightful story; it is, however, still quoted in the neighborhood as a memorable instance of female secrecy that she kept it to herself for a whole week, when she was suddenly absolved from all further restraint by intelligence brought to the breakfast-table one morning that the young lady was not to be found. Her room was empty—the bed had not been slept in—the window was open and the bird had flown!

The astonishment and concern with which the intelligence was received can only be imagined by those who have witnessed the agitation which the mishaps of a great man cause among his friends. Even the poor relations paused for a moment from the indefatigable labors of the trencher, when the aunt, who had at first been struck speechless, wrung her hands and shrieked out, "The goblin! The goblin! She's carried away by the goblin!"

In a few words she related the fearful scene of the garden, and concluded that the spectre must have carried off his bride. Two of the domestics corroborated the opinion, for they had heard the clattering of a horse's hoofs down the mountain about midnight, and had no doubt that it was the spectre on his black charger bearing her away to the tomb. All present were struck with the direful probability for events of the kind are extremely common in Germany, as many well-authenticated histories bear witness.

What a lamentable situation was that of the poor baron! What a heartrending dilemma for a fond father and a member of the great family of Katzenellenbogen! His only daughter had either been rapt away to the grave, or he was to have some wood-demon for a son-in-law, and perchance a troop of goblin grandchildren. As usual, he was completely bewildered, and all the castle in an uproar. The men were ordered to take horse and scour every road and path and glen of the Odenwald. The baron himself had just drawn on his jack-boots, girded on his sword, and was about to mount his steed to sally forth on the doubtful quest, when he was brought to a pause by a new apparition. A lady was seen approaching the castle mounted on a palfrey, attended by a cavalier on horseback. She galloped up to the gate, sprang from her horse, and, falling at the baron's feet, embraced his knees. It was his lost daughter, and her companion—the Spectre Bridegroom! The baron was astounded. He looked at his daughter, then at the spectre, and almost doubted the evidence of his senses. The latter, too, was wonderfully improved in his appearance since his visit to the world of spirits. His dress was splendid, and set off a noble figure of manly symmetry. He was no longer pale and melancholy. His fine countenance was flushed with the glow of youth, and joy rioted in his large dark eye.

The mystery was soon cleared up. The cavalier (for, in truth, as you must have known all the while, he was no goblin) announced himself as Sir Herman Von Starkenfaust. He related his adventure with the young count. He told how he had hastened to the castle to deliver the unwelcome tidings, but that the eloquence of the baron had interrupted him in every attempt to tell his tale. How the sight of the bride had completely captivated him and that to pass a few hours near her he had tacitly suffered the mistake to continue. How he had been sorely perplexed in what way to make a decent retreat, until the baron's goblin stories had suggested his eccentric exit. How, fearing the feudal hostility of the family, he had repeated his visits by stealth—had haunted the garden beneath the young lady's window—had wooed—had won—had borne away in triumph—and, in a word, had wedded the fair.

Under any other circumstances the baron would have been inflexible, for he was tenacious of paternal authority and devoutly obstinate in all family feuds; but he loved his daughter; he had lamented her as lost; he rejoiced to find her still alive; and, though her husband was of a hostile house, yet, thank heaven, he was not a goblin. There was something, it must be acknowledged, that did not exactly accord with his notions of strict veracity in the joke the knight had passed upon him of his being a dead man; but several old friends present, who had served in the wars, assured him that every stratagem was excusable in love, and that the cavalier was entitled to especial privilege, having lately served as a trooper.

Matters, therefore, were happily arranged. The baron pardoned the young couple on the spot. The revels at the castle were resumed. The poor relations overwhelmed this new member of the family with loving-kindness; he was so gallant, so generous—and so rich. The aunts, it is true, were somewhat scandalized that their system of strict seclusion and passive obedience should be so badly exemplified, but attributed it all to their negligence in not having the windows grated. One of them was particularly mortified at having her marvellous story marred, and that the only spectre she had ever seen should turn out a counterfeit; but the niece seemed perfectly happy at having found him substantial flesh and blood. And so the story ends.

The Room in the Tower

Edward Frederic Benson

It is probable that everybody who is at all a constant dreamer has had at least one experience of an event or a sequence of circumstances which have come to his mind in sleep being subsequently realized in the material world. But, in my opinion, so far from this being a strange thing, it would be far odder if this fulfilment did not occasionally happen, since our dreams are, as a rule, concerned with people whom we know and places with which we are familiar, such as might very naturally occur in the awake and daylit world. True, these dreams are often broken into by some absurd and fantastic incident, which puts them out of court in regard to their subsequent fulfilment, but on the mere calculation of chances, it does not appear in the least unlikely that a dream imagined by anyone who dreams constantly should occasionally come true. Not long ago, for instance, I experienced such a fulfilment of a dream which seems to me in no way remarkable and to have no kind of psychical significance. The manner of it was as follows.

A certain friend of mine, living abroad, is amiable enough to write to me about once in a fortnight. Thus, when fourteen days or thereabouts have elapsed since I last heard from him, my mind, probably, either consciously or subconsciously, is expectant of a letter from him. One night last week I dreamed that as I was going upstairs to dress for dinner I heard, as I often heard, the sound of the postman's knock on my front door, and diverted my direction downstairs instead. There, among other correspondence, was a letter from him. Thereafter the fantastic entered, for on opening it I found inside the ace of diamonds, and scribbled across it in his well-known handwriting, 'I am sending you this for safe custody, as you know it is running an unreasonable risk to keep aces in Italy.' The next evening I was just preparing to go upstairs to dress when I heard the postman's knock, and did precisely as I had done in my dream. There, among other letters, was one from my friend. Only it did not contain the ace of diamonds. Had it done so, I should have attached more weight to the matter, which, as it stands, seems to me a perfectly ordinary coincidence. No doubt I consciously or subconsciously expected a letter from him, and this suggested to me my dream. Similarly, the fact that my friend had not written to me for a fortnight suggested to him that he should do so. But occasionally it is not so easy to find such an explanation, and for the following story I can find no explanation at all. It came out of the dark, and into the dark it has gone again.

All my life I have been a habitual dreamer: the nights are few, that is to say, when I do not find on awaking in the morning that some mental experience has been mine, and sometimes, all night long, apparently, a series of the most dazzling adventures befall me. Almost without exception these adventures are pleasant, though often merely trivial. It is of an exception that I am going to speak.

It was when I was about sixteen that a certain dream first came to me, and this is how it befell. It opened with my being set down at the door of a big red-brick house, where, I understood, I was going to stay. The servant who opened the door told me that tea was being served in the garden, and led me through a low dark-panelled hall, with a large open fireplace, on to a cheerful green lawn set round with flower beds. There were grouped about the tea-table a small party of people, but they were all strangers to me except one, who was a schoolfellow called Jack Stone, clearly the son of the house, and he introduced me to his mother and father and a couple of sisters. I was, I remember, somewhat astonished to find myself here, for the boy in question was scarcely known to me, and I rather disliked what I knew of him; moreover, he had left school nearly a year before. The afternoon was very hot, and an intolerable oppression reigned. On the far side of the lawn ran a red-brick wall, with an iron gate in its centre, outside which stood a walnut tree. We sat in the shadow of the house opposite a row of long windows, inside which I could see a table with cloth laid, glimmering with glass and silver. This garden front of the house was very long, and at one end of it stood a tower of three storeys, which looked to me much older than the rest of the building.

Before long, Mrs Stone, who, like the rest of the party, had sat in absolute silence, said to me, 'Jack will show you your room: I have given you the room in the tower.'

Quite inexplicably my heart sank at her words. I felt as if I had known that I should have the room in the tower, and that it contained something dreadful and significant. Jack instantly got up, and I understood that I had to follow him. In silence we passed through the hall, and mounted a great oak staircase with many corners, and arrived at a small landing with two doors set in it. He pushed one of these open for me to enter, and without coming in himself, closed it after me. Then I knew that my conjecture had been right: there was something awful in the room, and with the terror of nightmare growing swiftly and enveloping me, I awoke in a spasm of terror.

Now that dream or variations on it occurred to me intermittently for fifteen years. Most often it came in exactly this form, the arrival, the tea laid out on the lawn, the deadly silence succeeded by that one deadly sentence, the mounting with Jack Stone up to the room in the tower where horror dwelt, and it always came to a close in the nightmare of terror at that which was in the room, though I never saw what it was. At other times I experienced variations on this same theme. Occasionally, for instance, we would be sitting at dinner in the dining-room, into the windows of which I had looked on the first night when the dream of this house visited me, but wherever we were, there was the same silence, the same sense of dreadful oppression and foreboding. And the silence I knew would always be broken by Mrs Stone saying to me, 'Jack will show you your room: I have given you the room in the tower.' Upon which (this was invariable) I had to follow him up the oak staircase with many corners, and enter the place that I dreaded more and more each time that I visited it in sleep. Or, again, I would find myself playing cards still in silence in a drawing-room lit with immense chandeliers, that gave a blinding illumination. What the game was I have no idea; what I remember, with a sense of miserable anticipation, was that soon Mrs Stone would get up and say to me, 'Jack will show you your room: I have given you the room in the tower.' This drawing room where we played cards was next to the dining room, and, as I have said, was always brilliantly illuminated, whereas the rest of the house was full of dusk and shadows. And yet, how often, in spite of those bouquets of lights, have I not pored over the cards that were dealt me, scarcely able for some reason to see them. Their designs, too, were strange: there were no red suits, but all were black, and among them there were certain cards which were black all over. I hated and dreaded those.

As this dream continued to recur, I got to know the greater part of the house. There was a smoking room beyond the drawing room, at the end of a passage with a green baize door. It was always very dark there, and as often as I went there I passed somebody whom I could not see in the doorway coming out. Curious developments, too, took place in the characters that peopled the dream as might happen to living persons. Mrs Stone, for instance, who, when I first saw her, had been black-haired, became grey, and instead of rising briskly, as she had done at first when she said, 'Jack will show you your room: I have given you the room in the tower,' got up very feebly, as if the strength was leaving her limbs. Jack also grew up, and became a rather ill-looking young man, with a brown moustache, while one of the sisters ceased to appear, and I understood she was married.

Then it so happened that I was not visited by this dream for six months or more, and I began to hope, in such inexplicable dread did I hold it, that it had passed away for good. But one night after this interval I again found myself being shown out onto the lawn for tea, and Mrs Stone was not there, while the others were all dressed in black. At once I guessed the reason, and my heart leaped at the thought that perhaps this time I should not have to sleep in the room in the tower, and though we usually all sat in silence, on this occasion the sense of relief made me talk and laugh as I had never yet done. But even then matters were not altogether comfortable, for no one else spoke, but they all looked secretly at each other. And soon the foolish stream of my talk ran dry, and gradually an apprehension worse than anything I had previously known gained on me as the light slowly faded.

Suddenly a voice which I knew well broke the stillness, the voice of Mrs Stone, saying, 'Jack will show you your room: I have given you the room in the tower.' It seemed to come from near the gate in the red-brick wall that bounded the lawn, and looking up, I saw that the grass outside was sown thick with gravestones. A curious greyish light shone from them, and I could read the lettering on the grave nearest me, and it was, 'In evil memory of Julia Stone.' And as usual Jack got up, and again I followed him through the hall and up the staircase with many corners. On this occasion it was darker than usual, and when I passed into the room in the tower I could only just see the furniture, the position of which was already familiar to me. Also there was a dreadful odour of decay in the room, and I woke screaming.

The dream, with such variations and developments as I have mentioned, went on at intervals for fifteen years. Sometimes I would dream it two or three nights in succession; once, as I have said, there was an intermission of six months, but taking a reasonable average, I should say that I dreamed it quite as often as once in a month. It had, as is plain, something of nightmare about it, since it always ended in the same appalling terror, which so far from getting less, seemed to me to gather fresh fear every time that I experienced it. There was, too, a strange and dreadful consistency about it. The characters in it, as I have mentioned, got regularly older, death and marriage visited this silent family, and I never in the dream, after Mrs Stone had died, set eyes on her again. But it was always her voice that told me that the room in the tower was prepared for me, and whether we had tea out on the lawn, or the scene was laid in one of the rooms overlooking it, I could always see her gravestone standing just outside the iron gate. It was the same, too, with the married daughter; usually she was not present, but once or twice she returned again, in company with a man, whom I took to be her husband. He, too, like the rest of them, was always silent. But, owing to the constant repetition of the dream, I had ceased to attach, in my waking hours, any significance to it. I never met Jack Stone again during all those years, nor did I ever see a house that resembled this dark house of my dream. And then something happened.

I had been in London in this year, up till the end of the July, and during the first week in August went down to stay with a friend in a house he had taken for the summer months, in the Ashdown Forest district of Sussex. I left London early, for John Clinton was to meet me at Forest Row Station, and we were going to spend the day golfing, and go to his house in the evening. He had his motor with him, and we set off, about five of the afternoon, after a thoroughly delightful day, for the drive, the distance being some ten miles. As it was still so early we did not have tea at the club house, but waited till we should get home. As we drove, the weather, which up till then had been, though hot, deliciously fresh, seemed to me to alter in quality, and become very stagnant and oppressive, and I felt that indefinable sense of ominous apprehension that I am accustomed to before thunder. John, however, did not share my views, attributing my loss of lightness to the fact that I had lost both my matches. Events proved, however, that I was right, though I do not think that the thunderstorm that broke that night was the sole cause of my depression.

Our way lay through deep high-banked lanes, and before we had gone very far I fell asleep, and was only awakened by the stopping of the motor. And with a sudden thrill, partly of fear but chiefly of curiosity, I found myself standing in the doorway of my house of dream. We went, I half wondering whether or not I was dreaming still, through a low oak-panelled hall, and out onto the lawn, where tea was laid in the shadow of the house. It was set in flower beds, a red-brick wall, with a gate in it, bounded one side, and out beyond that was a space of rough grass with a walnut tree. The facade of the house was very long, and at one end stood a three-storeyed tower, markedly older than the rest.

Here for the moment all resemblance to the repeated dream ceased. There was no silent and somehow terrible family, but a large assembly of exceedingly cheerful persons, all of whom were known to me. And in spite of the horror with which the dream itself had always filled me, I felt nothing of it now that the scene of it was thus reproduced before me. But I felt intensest curiosity as to what was going to happen.

Tea pursued its cheerful course, and before long Mrs Clinton got up. And at that moment I think I knew what she was going to say. She spoke to me, and what she said was:

'Jack will show you your room: I have given you the room in the tower.'

At that, for half a second, the horror of the dream took hold of me again. But it quickly passed, and again I felt nothing more than the most intense curiosity. It was not very long before it was amply satisfied.

John turned to me.

'Right up at the top of the house,' he said, 'but I think you'll be comfortable. We're absolutely full up. Would you like to go and see it now? By Jove, I believe that you are right, and that we are going to have a thunderstorm. How dark it has become.'

I got up and followed him. We passed through the hall, and up the perfectly familiar staircase. Then he opened the door, and I went in. And at that moment sheer unreasoning terror again possessed me. I did not know what I feared: I simply feared. Then like a sudden recollection, when one remembers a name which has long escaped the memory, I knew what I feared. I feared Mrs Stone, whose grave with the sinister inscription, 'In evil memory,' I had so often seen in my dream, just beyond the lawn which lay below my window. And then once more the fear passed so completely that I wondered what there was to fear, and I found myself, sober and quiet and sane, in the room in the tower, the name of which I had so often heard in my dream, and the scene of which was so familiar.

I looked around it with a certain sense of proprietorship, and found that nothing had been changed from the dreaming nights in which I knew it so well. Just to the left of the door was the bed, lengthways along the wall, with the head of it in the angle. In a line with it was the fireplace and a small bookcase; opposite the door the outer wall was pierced by two lattice-paned windows, between which stood the dressing-table, while ranged along the fourth wall was the washing-stand and a big cupboard. My luggage had already been unpacked, for the furniture of dressing and undressing lay orderly on the wash-stand and toilet-table, while my dinner clothes were spread out on the coverlet of the bed. And then, with a sudden start of unexplained dismay, I saw that there were two rather conspicuous objects which I had not seen before in my dreams: one a life-sized oil painting of Mrs Stone, the other a black-and-white sketch of Jack Stone, representing him as he had appeared to me only a week before in the last of the series of these repeated dreams, a rather secret and evil-looking man of about thirty. His picture hung between the windows, looking straight across the room to the other portrait, which hung at the side of the bed. At that I looked next, and as I looked I felt once more the horror of nightmare seize me.

It represented Mrs Stone as I had seen her last in my dreams: old and withered and white-haired. But in spite of the evident feebleness of body, a dreadful exuberance and vitality shone through the envelope of flesh, an exuberance wholly malign, a vitality that foamed and frothed with unimaginable evil. Evil beamed from the narrow, leering eyes; it laughed in the demon-like mouth. The whole face was instinct with some secret and appalling mirth; the hands, clasped together on the knee, seemed shaking with suppressed and nameless glee. Then I saw also that it was signed in the left-hand bottom corner, and wondering who the artist could be, I looked more closely, and read the inscription, 'Julia Stone by Julia Stone.'

There came a tap at the door, and John Clinton entered.

'Got everything you want?' he asked.

'Rather more than I want,' said I, pointing to the picture.

He laughed.

'Hard-featured old lady,' he said. 'By herself, too, I remember. Anyhow she can't have flattered herself much.'

'But don't you see?' said I. 'It's scarcely a human face at all. It's the face of some witch, of some devil.'

He looked at it more closely.

'Yes; it isn't very pleasant,' he said. 'Scarcely a bedside manner, eh? Yes; I can imagine getting the nightmare if I went to sleep with that close by my bed. I'll have it taken down if you like.'

'I really wish you would,' I said. He rang the bell, and with the help of a servant we detached the picture and carried it out onto the landing, and put it with its face to the wall.

'By Jove, the old lady is a weight,' said John, mopping his forehead. 'I wonder if she had something on her mind.'

The extraordinary weight of the picture had struck me too. I was about to reply, when I caught sight of my own hand. There was blood on it, in considerable quantities, covering the whole palm.

'I've cut myself somehow,' said I.

John gave a little startled exclamation.

'Why, I have too,' he said.

Simultaneously the footman took out his handkerchief and wiped his hand with it. I saw that there was blood also on his handkerchief.

John and I went back into the tower room and washed the blood off; but neither on his hand nor on mine was there the slightest trace of a scratch or cut. It seemed to me that, having ascertained this, we both, by a sort of tacit consent, did not allude to it again. Something in my case had dimly occurred to me that I did not wish to think about. It was but a conjecture, but I fancied that I knew the same thing had occurred to him.

The heat and oppression of the air, for the storm we had expected was still undischarged, increased very much after dinner, and for some time most of the party, among whom were John Clinton and myself, sat outside on the path bounding the lawn, where we had had tea. The night was absolutely dark, and no twinkle of star or moon ray could penetrate the pall of cloud that overset the sky. By degrees our assembly thinned, the women went up to bed, men dispersed to the smoking or billiard room, and by eleven o'clock my host and I were the only two left. All the evening I thought that he had something on his mind, and as soon as we were alone he spoke.

'The man who helped us with the picture had blood on his hand, too, did you notice?' he said.

'I asked him just now if he had cut himself, and he said he supposed he had, but that he could find no mark of it. Now where did that blood come from?'

By dint of telling myself that I was not going to think about it, I had succeeded in not doing so, and I did not want, especially just at bedtime, to be reminded of it.

'I don't know,' said I, 'and I don't really care so long as the picture of Mrs Stone is not by my bed.'

He got up.

'But it's odd,' he said. 'Ha! Now you'll see another odd thing.'

A dog of his, an Irish terrier by breed, had come out of the house as we talked. The door behind us into the hall was open, and a bright oblong of light shone across the lawn to the iron gate which led on to the rough grass outside, where the walnut tree stood. I saw that the dog had all his hackles up, bristling with rage and fright; his lips were curled back from his teeth, as if he was ready to spring at something, and he was growling to himself. He took not the slightest notice of his master or me, but stiffly and tensely walked across the grass to the iron gate. There he stood for a moment, looking through the bars and still growling. Then of a sudden his courage seemed to desert him: he gave one long howl, and scuttled back to the house with a curious crouching sort of movement.

'He does that half-a-dozen times a day,' said John. 'He sees something which he both hates and fears.'

I walked to the gate and looked over it. Something was moving on the grass outside, and soon a sound which I could not instantly identify came to my ears. Then I remembered what it was: it was the purring of a cat. I lit a match, and saw the purrer, a big blue Persian, walking round and round in a little circle just outside the gate, stepping high and ecstatically, with tail carried aloft like a banner. Its eyes were bright and shining, and every now and then it put its head down and sniffed at the grass.

I laughed.

'The end of that mystery, I am afraid,' I said. 'Here's a large cat having Walpurgis night all alone.'

'Yes, that's Darius,' said John. 'He spends half the day and all night there. But that's not the end of the dog mystery, for Toby and he are the best of friends, but the beginning of the cat mystery. What's the cat doing there? And why is Darius pleased, while Toby is terror-stricken?'

At that moment I remembered the rather horrible detail of my dreams when I saw through the gate, just where the cat was now, the white tombstone with the sinister inscription. But before I could answer the rain began, as suddenly and heavily as if a tap had been turned on, and simultaneously the big cat squeezed through the bars of the gate, and came leaping across the lawn to the house for shelter. Then it sat in the doorway, looking out eagerly into the dark. It spat and struck at John with its paw, as he pushed it in, in order to close the door.

Somehow, with the portrait of Julia Stone in the passage outside, the room in the tower had absolutely no alarm for me, and as I went to bed, feeling very sleepy and heavy, I had nothing more than interest for the curious incident about our bleeding hands, and the conduct of the cat and dog. The last thing I looked at before I put out my light was the square empty space by my bed where the portrait had been. Here the paper was of its original full tint of dark red: over the rest of the walls it had faded. Then I blew out my candle and instantly fell asleep.

My awaking was equally instantaneous, and I sat bolt upright in bed under the impression that some bright light had been flashed in my face, though it was now absolutely pitch dark. I knew exactly where I was, in the room which I had dreaded in dreams, but no horror that I ever felt when asleep approached the fear that now invaded and froze my brain. Immediately after a peal of thunder crackled just above the house, but the probability that it was only a flash of lightning which awoke me gave no reassurance to my galloping heart. Something I knew was in the room with me, and instinctively I put out my right hand, which was nearest the wall, to keep it away. And my hand touched the edge of a picture-frame hanging close to me.

I sprang out of bed, upsetting the small table that stood by it, and I heard my watch, candle, and matches clatter onto the floor. But for the moment there was no need of light, for a blinding flash leaped out of the clouds, and showed me that by my bed again hung the picture of Mrs Stone. And instantly the room went into blackness again. But in that flash I saw another thing also, namely a figure that leaned over the end of my bed, watching me. It was dressed in some close-clinging white garment, spotted and stained with mould, and the face was that of the portrait.

Overhead the thunder cracked and roared, and when it ceased and the deathly stillness succeeded, I heard the rustle of movement coming nearer me, and, more horrible yet, perceived an odour of corruption and decay. And then a hand was laid on the side of my neck, and close beside my ear I heard quick-taken, eager breathing. Yet I knew that this thing, though it could be perceived by touch, by smell, by eye and by ear, was still not of this earth, but something that had passed out of the body and had power to make itself manifest. Then a voice, already familiar to me, spoke.

'I knew you would come to the room in the tower,' it said. 'I have been long waiting for you. At last you have come. Tonight I shall feast; before long we will feast together.'

And the quick breathing came closer to me; I could feel it on my neck.

At that the terror, which I think had paralysed me for the moment, gave way to the wild instinct of self-preservation. I hit wildly with both arms, kicking out at the same moment, and heard a little animal-squeal, and something soft dropped with a thud beside me. I took a couple of steps forward, nearly tripping up over whatever it was that lay there, and by the merest good-luck found the handle of the door. In another second I ran out on the landing, and had banged the door behind me. Almost at the same moment I heard a door open somewhere below, and John Clinton, candle in hand, came running upstairs.

'What is it?' he said. 'I sleep just below you, and heard a noise as if – Good heavens, there's blood on your shoulder.'

I stood there, so he told me afterwards, swaying from side to side, white as a sheet, with the mark on my shoulder as if a hand covered with blood had been laid there.

'It's in there,' I said, pointing. 'She, you know. The portrait is in there, too, hanging up on the place we took it from.'

At that he laughed.

'My dear fellow, this is mere nightmare,' he said.

He pushed by me, and opened the door, I standing there simply inert with terror, unable to stop him, unable to move.

'Phew! What an awful smell,' he said.

Then there was silence; he had passed out of my sight behind the open door. Next moment he came out again, as white as myself, and instantly shut it.

'Yes, the portrait's there,' he said, 'and on the floor is a thing – a thing spotted with earth, like what they bury people in. Come away, quick, come away.'

How I got downstairs I hardly know. An awful shuddering and nausea of the spirit rather than of the flesh had seized me, and more than once he had to place my feet upon the steps, while every now and then he cast glances of terror and apprehension up the stairs. But in time we came to his dressing-room on the floor below, and there I told him what I have here described.

The sequel can be made short; indeed, some of my readers have perhaps already guessed what it was, if they remember that inexplicable affair of the churchyard at West Fawley, some eight years ago, where an attempt was made three times to bury the body of a certain woman who had committed suicide. On each occasion the coffin was found in the course of a few days again protruding from the ground. After the third attempt, in order that the thing should not be talked about, the body was buried elsewhere in unconsecrated ground. Where it was buried was just outside the iron gate of the garden belonging to the house where this woman had lived. She had committed suicide in a room at the top of the tower in that house. Her name was Julia Stone.

Subsequently the body was again secretly dug up, and the coffin was found to be full of blood.

Strange Event in the Life of Schalken the Painter

Sheridan Le Fanu

Being a Seventh Extract from the Legacy of the late Francis Purcell, P. P. of Drumcoolagh

You will no doubt be surprised, my dear friend, at the subject of the following narrative. What had I to do with Schalken, or Schalken with me? He had returned to his native land, and was probably dead and buried, before I was born; I never visited Holland nor spoke with a native of that country. So much I believe you already know. I must, then, give you my authority, and state to you frankly the ground upon which rests the credibility of the strange story which I am about to lay before you.

I was acquainted, in my early days, with a Captain Vandael, whose father had served King William in the Low Countries, and also in my own unhappy land during the Irish campaigns. I know not how it happened that I liked this man's society, spite of his politics and religion: but so it was; and it was by means of the free intercourse to which our intimacy gave rise that I became possessed of the curious tale which you are about to hear.

I had often been struck, while visiting Vandael, by a remarkable picture, in which, though no connoisseur myself, I could not fail to discern some very strong peculiarities, particularly in the distribution of light and shade, as also a certain oddity in the design itself, which interested my curiosity. It represented the interior of what might be a chamber in some antique religious building – the foreground was occupied by a female figure, arrayed in a species of white robe, part of which is arranged so as to form a veil. The dress, however, is not strictly that of any religious order. In its hand the figure bears a lamp, by whose light alone the form and face are illuminated; the features are marked by an arch smile, such as pretty women wear when engaged in successfully practising some roguish trick; in the background, and, excepting where the dim red light of an expiring fire serves to define the form, totally in the shade, stands the figure of a man equipped in the old fashion, with doublet and so forth, in an attitude of alarm, his hand being placed upon the hilt of his sword, which he appears to be in the act of drawing.

'There are some pictures,' said I to my friend, 'which impress one, I know not how, with a conviction that they represent not the mere ideal shapes and combinations which have floated through the imagination of the artist, but scenes, faces, and situations which have actually existed. When I look upon that picture, something assures me that I behold the representation of a reality.'

Vandael smiled, and, fixing his eyes upon the painting musingly, he said:

'Your fancy has not deceived you, my good friend, for that picture is the record, and I believe a faithful one, of a remarkable and mysterious occurrence. It was painted by Schalken, and contains, in the face of the female figure, which occupies the most prominent place in the design, an accurate portrait of Rose Velderkaust, the niece of Gerard Douw, the first and, I believe, the only love of Godfrey Schalken. My father knew the painter well, and from Schalken himself he learned the story of the mysterious drama, one scene of which the picture has embodied. This painting, which is accounted a fine specimen of Schalken's style, was bequeathed to my father by the artist's will, and, as you have observed, is a very striking and interesting production.'

I had only to request Vandael to tell the story of the painting in order to be gratified; and thus it is that I am enabled to submit to you a faithful recital of what I heard myself, leaving you to reject or to allow the evidence upon which the truth of the tradition depends, with this one assurance, that Schalken was an honest, blunt Dutchman, and, I believe, wholly incapable of committing a flight of imagination; and further, that Vandael, from whom I heard the story, appeared firmly convinced of its truth.

There are few forms upon which the mantle of mystery and romance could seem to hang more ungracefully than upon that of the uncouth and clownish Schalken – the Dutch boor – the rude and dogged, but most cunning worker in oils, whose pieces delight the initiated of the present day almost as much as his manners disgusted the refined of his own; and yet this man, so rude, so dogged, so slovenly, I had almost said so savage, in mien and manner, during his after successes, had been selected by the capricious goddess, in his early life, to figure as the hero of a romance by no means devoid of interest or of mystery.

Who can tell how meet he may have been in his young days to play the part of the lover or of the hero – who can say that in early life he had been the same harsh, unlicked, and rugged boor that, in his maturer age, he proved – or how far the neglected rudeness which afterwards marked his air, and garb, and manners, may not have been the growth of that reckless apathy not unfrequently produced by bitter misfortunes and disappointments in early life?

These questions can never now be answered.

We must content ourselves, then, with a plain statement of facts, or what have been received and transmitted as such, leaving matters of speculation to those who like them.

When Schalken studied under the immortal Gerard Douw, he was a young man; and in spite of the phlegmatic constitution and unexcitable manner which he shared, we believe, with his countrymen, he was not incapable of deep and vivid impressions, for it is an established fact that the young painter looked with considerable interest upon the beautiful niece of his wealthy master.

Rose Velderkaust was very young, having, at the period of which we speak, not yet attained her seventeenth year, and, if tradition speaks truth, possessed all the soft dimpling charms of the fair, light-haired Flemish maidens. Schalken had not studied long in the school of Gerard Douw, when he felt this interest deepening into something of a keener and intenser feeling than was quite consistent with the tranquillity of his honest Dutch heart; and at the same time he perceived, or thought he perceived, flattering symptoms of a reciprocity of liking, and this was quite sufficient to determine whatever indecision he might have heretofore experienced, and to lead him to devote exclusively to her every hope and feeling of his heart. In short, he was as much in love as a Dutchman could be. He was not long in making his passion known to the pretty maiden herself, and his declaration was followed by a corresponding confession upon her part.

Schalken, however, was a poor man, and he possessed no counter-balancing advantages of birth or position to induce the old man to consent to a union which must involve his niece and ward in the strugglings and difficulties of a young and nearly friendless artist. He was, therefore, to wait until time had furnished him with opportunity, and accident with success; and then, if his labours were found sufficiently lucrative, it was to be hoped that his proposals might at least be listened to by her jealous guardian. Months passed away, and, cheered by the smiles of the little Rose, Schalken's labours were redoubled, and with such effect and improvement as reasonably to promise the realisation of his hopes, and no contemptible eminence in his art, before many years should have elapsed.

The even course of this cheering prosperity was, however, destined to experience a sudden and formidable interruption, and that, too, in a manner so strange and mysterious as to baffle all investigation, and throw upon the events themselves a shadow of almost supernatural horror.

Schalken had one evening remained in the master's studio considerably longer than his more volatile companions, who had gladly availed themselves of the excuse which the dusk of evening afforded, to withdraw from their several tasks, in order to finish a day of labour in the jollity and conviviality of the tavern.

But Schalken worked for improvement, or rather for love. Besides, he was now engaged merely in sketching a design, an operation which, unlike that of colouring, might be continued as long as there was light sufficient to distinguish between canvas and charcoal. He had not then, nor, indeed, until long after, discovered the peculiar powers of his pencil, and he was engaged in composing a group of extremely roguish-looking and grotesque imps and demons, who were inflicting various ingenious torments upon a perspiring and pot-bellied St Anthony, who reclined in the midst of them, apparently in the last stage of drunkenness.

The young artist, however, though incapable of executing, or even of appreciating, anything of true sublimity, had nevertheless discernment enough to prevent his being by any means satisfied with his work; and many were the patient erasures and corrections which the limbs and features of saint and devil underwent, yet all without producing in their new arrangement anything of improvement or increased effect.

The large, old-fashioned room was silent, and, with the exception of himself, quite deserted by its usual inmates. An hour had passed – nearly two – without any improved result. Daylight had already declined, and twilight was fast giving way to the darkness of night. The patience of the young man was exhausted, and he stood before his unfinished production, absorbed in no very pleasing ruminations, one hand buried in the folds of his long dark hair, and the other holding the piece of charcoal which had so ill executed its office, and which he now rubbed, without much regard to the sable streaks which it produced, with irritable pressure upon his ample Flemish inexpressibles.

'Pshaw!' said the young man aloud, 'would that picture, devils, saint, and all, were where they should be – in hell!'

A short, sudden laugh, uttered startlingly close to his ear, instantly responded to the ejaculation.

The artist turned sharply round, and now for the first time became aware that his labours had been overlooked by a stranger.

Within about a yard and a half, and rather behind him, there stood what was, or appeared to be, the figure of an elderly man: he wore a short cloak, and broad-brimmed hat with a conical crown, and in his hand, which was protected with a heavy, gauntlet-shaped glove, he carried a long ebony walking-stick, surmounted with what appeared, as it glittered dimly in the twilight, to be a massive head of gold, and upon his breast, through the folds of the cloak, there shone what appeared to be the links of a rich chain of the same metal.

The room was so obscure that nothing further of the appearance of the figure could be ascertained, and the face was altogether overshadowed by the heavy flap of the beaver which overhung it, so that not a feature could be discerned. A quantity of dark hair escaped from beneath this sombre hat, a circumstance which, connected with the firm, upright carriage of the intruder, proved that his years could not yet exceed threescore or thereabouts.

There was an air of gravity and importance about the garb of this person, and something indescribably odd, I might say awful, in the perfect, stone-like movelessness of the figure, that effectually checked the testy comment which had at once risen to the lips of the irritated artist. He therefore, as soon as he had sufficiently recovered the surprise, asked the stranger, civilly, to be seated, and desired to know if he had any message to leave for his master.

'Tell Gerard Douw,' said the unknown, without altering his attitude in the smallest degree, 'that Mynher Vanderhauseny of Rotterdam, desires to speak with him to-morrow evening at this hour, and, if he please, in this room, upon matters of weight – that is all. Good-night.'

The stranger, having finished this message, turned abruptly, and, with a quick but silent step, quitted the room, before Schalken had time to say a word in reply.

The young man felt a curiosity to see in what direction the burgher of Rotterdam would turn on quitting the studio, and for that purpose he went directly to the window which commanded the door.

A lobby of considerable extent intervened between the inner door of the painter's room and the street entrance, so that Schalken occupied the post of observation before the old man could possibly have reached the street.

He watched in vain, however. There was no other mode of exit.

Had the old man vanished, or was he lurking about the recesses of the lobby for some bad purpose? This last suggestion filled the mind of Schalken with a vague horror, which was so unaccountably intense as to make him alike afraid to remain in the room alone and reluctant to pass through the lobby.

However, with an effort which appeared very disproportioned to the occasion, he summoned resolution to leave the room, and, having double-locked the door and thrust the key in his pocket, without looking to the right or left, he traversed the passage which had so recently, perhaps still, contained the person of his mysterious visitant, scarcely venturing to breathe till he had arrived in the open street.

'Mynher Vanderhausen,' said Gerard Douw within himself, as the appointed hour approached, 'Mynher Vanderhausen of Rotterdam! I never heard of the man till yesterday. What can he want of me? A portrait, perhaps, to be painted; or a younger son or a poor relation to be apprenticed; or a collection to be valued; or – pshaw! there's no one in Rotterdam to leave me a legacy. Well, whatever the business may be, we shall soon know it all.'

It was now the close of day, and every easel, except that of Schalken, was deserted. Gerard Douw was pacing the apartment with the restless step of impatient expectation, every now and then humming a passage from a piece of music which he was himself composing; for, though no great proficient, he admired the art; sometimes pausing to glance over the work of one of his absent pupils, but more frequently placing himself at the window, from whence he might observe the passengers who threaded the obscure by-street in which his studio was placed.

'Said you not, Godfrey,' exclaimed Douw, after a long and fruitless gaze from his post of observation, and turning to Schalken – 'said you not the hour of appointment was at about seven by the clock of the Stadhouse?'

'It had just told seven when I first saw him, sir,' answered the student.

'The hour is close at hand, then,' said the master, consulting a horologe as large and as round as a full-grown orange. 'Mynher Vanderhausen, from Rotterdam – is it not so?'

'Such was the name.'

'And an elderly man, richly clad?' continued Douw.

'As well as I might see,' replied his pupil; 'he could not be young, nor yet very old neither, and his dress was rich and grave, as might become a citizen of wealth and consideration.'

At this moment the sonorous boom of the Stadhouse clock told, stroke after stroke, the hour of seven; the eyes of both master and student were directed to the door; and it was not until the last peal of the old bell had ceased to vibrate, that Douw exclaimed:

'So, so; we shall have his worship presently – that is, if he means to keep his hour; if not, thou mayst wait for him, Godfrey, if you court the acquaintance of a capricious burgomaster. As for me, I think our old Leyden contains a sufficiency of such commodities, without an importation from Rotterdam.'

Schalken laughed, as in duty bound; and after a pause of some minutes, Douw suddenly exclaimed:

'What if it should all prove a jest, a piece of mummery got up by Vankarp, or some such worthy! I wish you had run all risks, and cudgelled the old burgomaster, stadholder, or whatever else he may be, soundly. I would wager a dozen of Rhenish, his worship would have pleaded old acquaintance before the third application.'

'Here he comes, sir,' said Schalken, in a low admonitory tone; and instantly, upon turning towards the door, Gerard Douw observed the same figure which had, on the day before, so unexpectedly greeted the vision of his pupil Schalken.

There was something in the air and mien of the figure which at once satisfied the painter that there was no mummery in the case, and that he really stood in the presence of a man of worship; and so, without hesitation, he doffed his cap, and courteously saluting the stranger, requested him to be seated.

The visitor waved his hand slightly, as, if in acknowledgment of the courtesy, but remained standing.

'I have the honour to see Mynher Vanderhausen, of Rotterdam?' said Gerard Douw.

'The same,' was the laconic reply of his visitant.

'I understand your worship desires to speak with me,' continued Douw, 'and I am here by appointment to wait your commands.'

'Is that a man of trust?' said Vanderhausen, turning towards Schalken, who stood at a little distance behind his master.

'Certainly,' replied Gerard.

'Then let him take this box and get the nearest jeweller or goldsmith to value its contents, and let him return hither with a certificate of the valuation.'

At the same time he placed a small case, about nine inches square, in the hands of Gerard Douw, who was as much amazed at its weight as at the strange abruptness with which it was handed to him.

In accordance with the wishes of the stranger, he delivered it into the hands of Schalken, and repeating *his* directions, despatched him upon the mission.

Schalken disposed his precious charge securely beneath the folds of his cloak, and rapidly traversing two or three narrow streets, he stopped at a corner house, the lower part of which was then occupied by the shop of a Jewish goldsmith.

Schalken entered the shop, and calling the little Hebrew into the obscurity of its back recesses, he proceeded to lay before him Vanderhausen's packet.

On being examined by the light of a lamp, it appeared entirely cased with lead, the outer surface of which was much scraped and soiled, and nearly white with age. This was with difficulty partially removed, and disclosed beneath a box of some dark and singularly hard wood; this, too, was forced, and after the removal of two or three folds of linen, its contents proved to be a mass of golden ingots, close packed, and, as the Jew declared, of the most perfect quality.

Every ingot underwent the scrutiny of the little Jew, who seemed to feel an epicurean delight in touching and testing these morsels of the glorious metal; and each one of them was replaced in the box with the exclamation:

'Mein Gott, how very perfect! not one grain of alloy – beautiful, beautiful!'

The task was at length finished, and the Jew certified under his hand the value of the ingots submitted to his examination to amount to many thousand rix-dollars.

With the desired document in his bosom, and the rich box of gold carefully pressed under his arm, and concealed by his cloak, he retraced his way, and entering the studio, found his master and the stranger in close conference.

Schalken had no sooner left the room, in order to execute the commission he had taken in charge, than Vanderhausen addressed Gerard Douw in the following terms:

'I may not tarry with you tonight more than a few minutes, and so I shall briefly tell you the matter upon which I come. You visited the town of Rotterdam some four months ago, and then I saw in the church of St Lawrence your niece, Rose Velderkaust. I desire to marry her, and if I satisfy you as to the fact that I am very wealthy – more wealthy than any husband you could dream of for her – I expect that you will forward my views to the utmost of your authority. If you approve my proposal, you must close with it at once, for I cannot command time enough to wait for calculations and delays.'

Gerard Douw was, perhaps, as much astonished as anyone could be by the very unexpected nature of Mynher Vanderhausen's communication; but he did not give vent to any unseemly expression of surprise, for besides the motives supplied by prudence and politeness, the painter experienced a kind of chill and oppressive sensation, something like that which is supposed to affect a man who is placed unconsciously in immediate contact with something to which he has a natural antipathy – an undefined horror and dread while standing in the presence of the eccentric stranger, which made him very unwilling to say anything which might reasonably prove offensive.

'I have no doubt,' said Gerard, after two or three prefatory hems, 'that the connection which you propose would prove alike advantageous and honourable to my niece; but you must be aware that she has a will of her own, and may not acquiesce in what *we* may design for her advantage.'

'Do not seek to deceive me, Sir Painter,' said Vanderhausen; 'you are her guardian – she is your ward. She is mine if *you* like to make her so.'

The man of Rotterdam moved forward a little as he spoke, and Gerard Douw, he scarce knew why, inwardly prayed for the speedy return of Schalken.

'I desire,' said the mysterious gentleman, 'to place in your hands at once an evidence of my wealth, and a security for my liberal dealing with your niece. The lad will return in a minute or two with a sum in value five times the fortune which she has a right to expect from a husband. This shall lie in your hands, together with her dowry, and you may apply the united sum as suits her interest best; it shall be all exclusively hers while she lives. Is that liberal?'

Douw assented, and inwardly thought that fortune had been extraordinarily kind to his niece. The stranger, he thought, must be both wealthy and generous, and such an offer was not to be despised, though made by a humourist, and one of no very prepossessing presence.

Rose had no very high pretensions, for she was almost without dowry; indeed, altogether so, excepting so far as the deficiency had been supplied by the generosity of her uncle. Neither had she any right to raise any scruples against the match on the score of birth, for her own origin was by no means elevated; and as to other objections, Gerard resolved, and, indeed, by the usages of the time was warranted in resolving, not to listen to them for a moment.

'Sir,' said he, addressing the stranger, 'your offer is most liberal, and whatever hesitation I may feel in closing with it immediately, arises solely from my not having the honour of knowing anything of your family or station. Upon these points you can, of course, satisfy me without difficulty?'

'As to my respectability,' said the stranger, drily, 'you must take that for granted at present; pester me with no inquiries; you can discover nothing more about me than I choose to make known. You shall have sufficient security for my respectability – my word, if you are honourable: if you are sordid, my gold.'

'A testy old gentleman,' thought Douw; 'he must have his own way. But, all things considered, I am justified in giving my niece to him. Were she my own daughter, I would do the like by her. I will not pledge myself unnecessarily, however.'

'You will not pledge yourself unnecessarily,' said Vanderhausen, strangely uttering the very words which had just floated through the mind of his companion; 'but you will do so if it *is* necessary, I presume; and I will show you that I consider it indispensable. If the gold I mean to leave in your hands satisfy you, and if you desire that my proposal shall not be at once withdrawn, you must, before I leave this room, write your name to this engagement.'

Having thus spoken, he placed a paper in the hands of Gerard, the contents of which expressed an engagement entered into by Gerard Douw, to give to Wilken Vanderhausen, of Rotterdam, in marriage, Rose Velderkaust, and so forth, within one week of the date hereof.

While the painter was employed in reading this covenant, Schalken, as we have stated, entered the studio, and having delivered the box and the valuation of the Jew into the hands of the stranger, he was about to retire, when Vanderhausen called to him to wait; and, presenting the case and the certificate to Gerard Douw, he waited in silence until he had satisfied himself by an inspection of both as to the value of the pledge left in his hands. At length he said:

'Are you content?'

The painter said he would fain have another day to consider.

'Not an hour,' said the suitor, coolly.

'Well, then,' said Douw, 'I am content; it is a bargain.'

'Then sign at once,' said Vanderhausen; 'I am weary.'

At the same time he produced a small case of writing materials, and Gerard signed the important document.

'Let this youth witness the covenant,' said the old man; and Godfrey Schalken unconsciously signed the instrument which bestowed upon another that hand which he had so long regarded as the object and reward of all his labours.

The compact being thus completed, the strange visitor folded up the paper, and stowed it safely in an inner pocket.

'I will visit you tomorrow night, at nine of the clock, at your house, Gerard Douw, and will see the subject of our contract. Farewell.' And so saying, Wilken Vanderhausen moved stiffly, but rapidly out of the room.

Schalken, eager to resolve his doubts, had placed himself by the window in order to watch the street entrance; but the experiment served only to support his suspicions, for the old man did not issue from the door. This was very strange, very odd, very fearful. He and his master returned together, and talked but little on the way, for each had his own subjects of reflection, of anxiety, and of hope.

Schalken, however, did not know the ruin which threatened his cherished schemes.

Gerard Douw knew nothing of the attachment which had sprung up between his pupil and his niece; and even if he had, it is doubtful whether he would have regarded its existence as any serious obstruction to the wishes of Mynher Vanderhausen.

Marriages were then and there matters of traffic and calculation; and it would have appeared as absurd in the eyes of the guardian to make a mutual attachment an essential element in a contract of marriage, as it would have been to draw up his bonds and receipts in the language of chivalrous romance.

The painter, however, did not communicate to his niece the important step which he had taken on her behalf, and his resolution arose not from any anticipation of opposition on her part, but solely from a ludicrous consciousness that if his ward were, as she very naturally might do, to ask him to describe the appearance of the bridegroom whom he destined for her, he would be forced to confess that he had not seen his face, and, if called upon, would find it impossible to identify him.

Upon the next day, Gerard Douw having dined, called his niece to him, and having scanned her person with an air of satisfaction, he took her hand, and looking upon her pretty, innocent face with a smile of kindness, he said:

'Rose, my girl, that face of yours will make your fortune.' Rose blushed and smiled. 'Such faces and such tempers seldom go together, and, when they do, the compound is a love-potion which few heads or hearts can resist. Trust me, thou wilt soon be a bride, girl. But this is trifling, and I am pressed for time, so make ready the large room by eight o'clock tonight, and give directions for supper at nine. I expect a friend tonight; and observe me, child, do thou trick thyself out handsomely. I would not have him think us poor or sluttish.'

With these words he left the chamber, and took his way to the room to which we have already had occasion to introduce our readers – that in which his pupils worked.

When the evening closed in, Gerard called Schalken, who was about to take his departure to his obscure and comfortless lodgings, and asked him to come home and sup with Rose and Vanderhausen.

The invitation was of course accepted, and Gerard Douw and his pupil soon found themselves in the handsome and somewhat antique-looking room which had been prepared for the reception of the stranger.

A cheerful wood-fire blazed in the capacious hearth; a little at one side an old-fashioned table, with richly-carved legs, was placed – destined, no doubt, to receive the supper, for which preparations were going forward; and ranged with exact regularity, stood the tall-backed chairs, whose ungracefulness was more than counterbalanced by their comfort.

The little party, consisting of Rose, her uncle, and the artist, awaited the arrival of the expected visitor with considerable impatience.

Nine o'clock at length came, and with it a summons at the street-door, which, being speedily answered, was followed by a slow and emphatic tread upon the staircase; the steps moved heavily across the lobby, the door of the room in which the party which we have described were assembled slowly opened, and there entered a figure which startled, almost appalled, the phlegmatic Dutchmen, and nearly made

Rose scream with affright; it was the form, and arrayed in the garb, of Mynher Vanderhausen; the air, the gait, the height was the same, but the features had never been seen by any of the party before.

The stranger stopped at the door of the room, and displayed his form and face completely. He wore a dark-coloured cloth cloak, which was short and full, not falling quite to the knees; his legs were cased in dark purple silk stockings, and his shoes were adorned with roses of the same colour. The opening of the cloak in front showed the under-suit to consist of some very dark, perhaps sable material, and his hands were enclosed in a pair of heavy leather gloves which ran up considerably above the wrist, in the manner of a gauntlet. In one hand he carried his walking-stick and his hat, which he had removed, and the other hung heavily by his side. A quantity of grizzled hair descended in long tresses from his head, and its folds rested upon the plaits of a stiff ruff, which effectually concealed his neck.

So far all was well; but the face! – all the flesh of the face was coloured with the bluish leaden hue which is sometimes produced by the operation of metallic medicines administered in excessive quantities; the eyes were enormous, and the white appeared both above and below the iris, which gave to them an expression of insanity, which was heightened by their glassy fixedness; the nose was well enough, but the mouth was writhed considerably to one side, where it opened in order to give egress to two long, discoloured fangs, which projected from the upper jaw, far below the lower lip; the hue of the lips themselves bore the usual relation to that of the face, and was consequently nearly black. The character of the face was malignant, even satanic, to the last degree; and, indeed, such a combination of horror could hardly be accounted for, except by supposing the corpse of some atrocious malefactor, which had long hung blackening upon the gibbet, to have at length become the habitation of a demon – the frightful sport of Satanic possession.

It was remarkable that the worshipful stranger suffered as little as possible of his flesh to appear, and that during his visit he did not once remove his gloves.

Having stood for some moments at the door, Gerard Douw at length found breath and collectedness to bid him welcome, and, with a mute inclination of the head, the stranger stepped forward into the room.

There was something indescribably odd, even horrible, about all his motions, something undefinable, that was unnatural, un-human – it was as if the limbs were guided and directed by a spirit unused to the management of bodily machinery.

The stranger said hardly anything during his visit, which did not exceed half an hour; and the host himself could scarcely muster courage enough to utter the few necessary salutations and courtesies: and, indeed, such was the nervous terror which the presence of Vanderhausen inspired, that very little would have made all his entertainers fly bellowing from the room.

They had not so far lost all self-possession, however, as to fail to observe two strange peculiarities of their visitor.

During his stay he did not once suffer his eyelids to close, nor even to move in the slightest degree; and further, there was a death-like stillness in his whole person, owing to the total absence of the heaving motion of the chest, caused by the process of respiration.

These two peculiarities, though when told they may appear trifling, produced a very striking and unpleasant effect when seen and observed. Vanderhausen at length relieved the painter of Leyden of his inauspicious presence; and with no small gratification the little party heard the street-door close after him.

'Dear uncle,' said Rose, 'what a frightful man! I would not see him again for the wealth of the States!'

'Tush, foolish girl!' said Douw, whose sensations were anything but comfortable. 'A man may be as ugly as the devil, and yet if his heart and actions are good, he is worth all the pretty-faced, perfumed puppies that walk the Mall. Rose, my girl, it is very true he has not thy pretty face, but I know him to be wealthy and liberal; and were he ten times more ugly—'

'Which is inconceivable,' observed Rose.

'These two virtues would be sufficient,' continued her uncle, 'to counterbalance all his deformity; and if not of power sufficient actually to alter the shape of the features, at least of efficacy enough to prevent one thinking them amiss.'

'Do you know, uncle,' said Rose, 'when I saw him standing at the door, I could not get it out of my head that I saw the old, painted, wooden figure that used to frighten me so much in the church of St Laurence of Rotterdam.'

Gerard laughed, though he could not help inwardly acknowledging the justness of the comparison. He was resolved, however, as far as he could, to check his niece's inclination to ridicule the ugliness of her intended bridegroom, although he was not a little pleased to observe that she appeared totally exempt from that mysterious dread of the stranger which, he could not disguise it from himself, considerably affected him, as also his pupil Godfrey Schalken.

Early on the next day there arrived, from various quarters of the town, rich presents of silks, velvets, jewellery, and so forth, for Rose; and also a packet directed to Gerard Douw, which, on being opened, was found to contain a contract of marriage, formally drawn up, between Wilken Vanderhausen of the Boom-quay, in Rotterdam, and Rose Velderkaust of Leyden, niece to Gerard Douw, master in the art of painting, also of the same city; and containing engagements on the part of Vanderhausen to make settlements upon his bride, far more splendid than he had before led her guardian to believe likely, and which were to be secured to her use in the most unexceptionable manner possible – the money being placed in the hands of Gerard Douw himself.

I have no sentimental scenes to describe, no cruelty of guardians, or magnanimity of wards, or agonies of lovers. The record I have to make is one of sordidness, levity, and interest. In less than a week after the first interview which we have just described, the contract of marriage was fulfilled, and Schalken saw the prize which he would have risked anything to secure, carried off triumphantly by his formidable rival.

For two or three days he absented himself from the school; he then returned and worked, if with less cheerfulness, with far more dogged resolution than before; the dream of love had given place to that of ambition.

Months passed away, and, contrary to his expectation, and, indeed, to the direct promise of the parties, Gerard Douw heard nothing of his niece, or her worshipful spouse. The interest of the money, which was to have been demanded in quarterly sums, lay unclaimed in his hands. He began to grow extremely uneasy.

Mynher Vanderhausen's direction in Rotterdam he was fully possessed of. After some irresolution he finally determined to journey thither – a trifling undertaking, and easily accomplished – and thus to satisfy himself of the safety and comfort of his ward, for whom he entertained an honest and strong affection.

His search was in vain, however. No one in Rotterdam had ever heard of Mynher Vanderhausen.

Gerard Douw left not a house in the Boom-quay untried; but all in vain. No one could give him any information whatever touching the object of his inquiry; and he was obliged to return to Leyden, nothing wiser than when he had left it.

On his arrival he hastened to the establishment from which Vanderhausen had hired the lumbering though, considering the times, most luxurious vehicle which the bridal party had employed to convey them to Rotterdam. From the driver of this machine he learned, that having proceeded by slow stages, they had late in the evening approached Rotterdam; but that before they entered the city, and while yet nearly a mile from it, a small party of men, soberly clad, and after the old fashion, with peaked beards and moustaches, standing in the centre of the road, obstructed the further progress of the carriage. The driver reined in his horses, much fearing, from the obscurity of the hour, and the loneliness of the road, that some mischief was intended.

His fears were, however, somewhat allayed by his observing that these strange men carried a large litter, of an antique shape, and which they immediately set down upon the pavement, whereupon the bridegroom, having opened the coach-door from within, descended, and having assisted his bride to do likewise, led her, weeping bitterly and wringing her hands, to the litter, which they both entered. It was then raised by the men who surrounded it, and speedily carried towards the city, and before it had proceeded many yards the darkness concealed it from the view of the Dutch charioteer.

In the inside of the vehicle he found a purse, whose contents more than thrice paid the hire of the carriage and man. He saw and could tell nothing more of Mynher Vanderhausen and his beautiful lady. This mystery was a source of deep anxiety and almost of grief to Gerard Douw.

There was evidently fraud in the dealing of Vanderhausen with him, though for what purpose committed he could not imagine. He greatly doubted how far it was possible for a man possessing in his countenance so strong an evidence of the presence of the most demoniac feelings, to be in reality anything but a villain; and every day that passed without his hearing from or of his niece, instead of inducing him to forget his fears, on the contrary tended more and more to exasperate them.

The loss of his niece's cheerful society tended also to depress his spirits; and in order to dispel this despondency, which often crept upon his mind after his daily employment was over, he was wont frequently to prevail upon Schalken to accompany him home, and by his presence to dispel, in some degree, the gloom of his otherwise solitary supper.

One evening, the painter and his pupil were sitting by the fire, having accomplished a comfortable supper, and had yielded to that silent pensiveness sometimes induced by the process of digestion, when their reflections were disturbed by a loud sound at the street-door, as if occasioned by some person rushing forcibly and repeatedly against it. A domestic had run without delay to ascertain the cause of the disturbance, and they heard him twice or thrice interrogate the applicant for admission, but without producing an answer or any cessation of the sounds.

They heard him then open the hall-door, and immediately there followed a light and rapid tread upon the staircase. Schalken laid his hand on his sword, and advanced towards the door. It opened before he reached it, and Rose rushed into the room. She looked wild and haggard, and pale with exhaustion and terror; but her dress surprised them as much even as her unexpected appearance. It consisted of a kind of white woollen wrapper, made close about the neck, and descending to the very ground. It was much deranged and travel-soiled. The poor creature had hardly entered the chamber when she fell senseless on the floor. With some difficulty they succeeded in reviving her, and on recovering her senses she instantly exclaimed, in a tone of eager, terrified impatience:

'Wine, wine, quickly, or I'm lost!'

Much alarmed at the strange agitation in which the call was made, they at once administered to her wishes, and she drank some wine with a haste and eagerness which surprised them. She had hardly swallowed it, when she exclaimed, with the same urgency:

'Food, food, at once, or I perish!'

A considerable fragment of a roast joint was upon the table, and Schalken immediately proceeded to cut some, but he was anticipated; for no sooner had she become aware of its presence than she darted at it with the rapacity of a vulture, and, seizing it in her hands she tore off the flesh with her teeth and swallowed it.

When the paroxysm of hunger had been a little appeased, she appeared suddenly to become aware how strange her conduct had been, or it may have been that other more agitating thoughts recurred to her mind, for she began to weep bitterly and to wring her hands.

'Oh! send for a minister of God,' said she; 'I am not safe till he comes; send for him speedily.'

Gerard Douw despatched a messenger instantly, and prevailed on his niece to allow him to surrender his bedchamber to her use; he also persuaded her to retire to it at once and to rest; her consent was extorted upon the condition that they would not leave her for a moment.

'Oh that the holy man were here!' she said; 'he can deliver me. The dead and the living can never be one – God has forbidden it.'

With these mysterious words she surrendered herself to their guidance, and they proceeded to the chamber which Gerard Douw had assigned to her use.

'Do not – do not leave me for a moment,' said she. 'I am lost for ever if you do.'

Gerard Douw's chamber was approached through a spacious apartment, which they were now about to enter. Gerard Douw and Schalken each carried a wax candle, so that a sufficient degree of light was cast upon all surrounding objects. They were now entering the large chamber, which, as I have said, communicated with Douw's apartment, when Rose suddenly stopped, and, in a whisper which seemed to thrill with horror, she said:

'O God! he is here – he is here! See, see – there he goes!'

She pointed towards the door of the inner room, and Schalken thought he saw a shadowy and ill-defined form gliding into that apartment. He drew his sword, and raising the candle so as to throw its light with increased distinctness upon the objects in the room, he entered the chamber into which the shadow had glided. No figure was there – nothing but the furniture which belonged to the room, and yet he could not be deceived as to the fact that something had moved before them into the chamber.

A sickening dread came upon him, and the cold perspiration broke out in heavy drops upon his forehead; nor was he more composed when he heard the increased urgency, the agony of entreaty, with which Rose implored them not to leave her for a moment.

'I saw him,' said she. 'He's here! I cannot be deceived – I know him. He's by me – he's with me – he's in the room. Then, for God's sake, as you would save, do not stir from beside me!'

They at length prevailed upon her to lie down upon the bed, where she continued to urge them to stay by her. She frequently uttered incoherent sentences, repeating again and again, 'The dead and the living cannot be one – God has forbidden it!' and then again, 'Rest to the wakeful – sleep to the sleep-walkers.'

These and such mysterious and broken sentences she continued to utter until the clergyman arrived.

Gerard Douw began to fear, naturally enough, that the poor girl, owing to terror or ill-treatment, had become deranged; and he half suspected, by the suddenness of her appearance, and the unseasonableness of the hour, and, above all, from the wildness and terror of her manner, that she had made her escape from some place of confinement for lunatics, and was in immediate fear of pursuit. He resolved to summon medical advice as soon as the mind of his niece had been in some measure set at rest by the offices of the clergyman whose attendance she had so earnestly desired; and until this object had been attained, he did not venture to put any questions to her, which might possibly, by reviving painful or horrible recollections, increase her agitation.

The clergyman soon arrived – a man of ascetic countenance and venerable age – one whom Gerard Douw respected much, forasmuch as he was a veteran polemic, though one, perhaps, more dreaded as a combatant than beloved as a Christian – of pure morality, subtle brain, and frozen heart. He entered the chamber which communicated with that in which Rose reclined, and immediately on his arrival she requested him to pray for her, as for one who lay in the hands of Satan, and who could hope for deliverance – only from heaven.

That our readers may distinctly understand all the circumstances of the event which we are about imperfectly to describe, it is necessary to state the relative position of the parties who were engaged in it. The old clergyman and Schalken were in the anteroom of which we have already spoken; Rose lay in the inner chamber, the door of which was open;

and by the side of the bed, at her urgent desire, stood her guardian; a candle burned in the bedchamber, and three were lighted in the outer apartment.

The old man now cleared his voice, as if about to commence; but before he had time to begin, a sudden gust of air blew out the candle which served to illuminate the room in which the poor girl lay, and she, with hurried alarm, exclaimed:

'Godfrey, bring in another candle; the darkness is unsafe.'

Gerard Douw, forgetting for the moment her repeated injunctions in the immediate impulse, stepped from the bedchamber into the other, in order to supply what she desired.

'O God! do not go, dear uncle!' shrieked the unhappy girl; and at the same time she sprang from the bed and darted after him, in order, by her grasp, to detain him.

But the warning came too late, for scarcely had he passed the threshold, and hardly had his niece had time to utter the startling exclamation, when the door which divided the two rooms closed violently after him, as if swung to by a strong blast of wind.

Schalken and he both rushed to the door, but their united and desperate efforts could not avail so much as to shake it.

Shriek after shriek burst from the inner chamber, with all the piercing loudness of despairing terror. Schalken and Douw applied every energy and strained every nerve to force open the door; but all in vain.

There was no sound of struggling from within, but the screams seemed to increase in loudness, and at the same time they heard the bolts of the latticed window withdrawn, and the window itself grated upon the sill as if thrown open.

One *last* shriek, so long and piercing and agonised as to be scarcely human, swelled from the room, and suddenly there followed a death-like silence.

A light step was heard crossing the floor, as if from the bed to the window; and almost at the same instant the door gave way, and, yielding to the pressure of the external applicants, they were nearly precipitated into the room. It was empty. The window was open, and Schalken sprang to a chair and gazed out upon the street and canal below. He saw no form, but he beheld, or thought he beheld, the waters of the broad canal beneath settling ring after ring in heavy circular ripples, as if a moment before disturbed by the immersion of some large and heavy mass.

No trace of Rose was ever after discovered, nor was anything certain respecting her mysterious wooer detected or even suspected; no clue whereby to trace the intricacies of the labyrinth and to arrive at a distinct conclusion was to be found. But an incident occurred, which, though it will not be received by our rational readers as at all approaching to evidence upon the matter, nevertheless produced a strong and a lasting impression upon the mind of Schalken.

Many years after the events which we have detailed, Schalken, then remotely situated, received an intimation of his father's death, and of his intended burial upon a fixed day in the church of Rotterdam. It was necessary that a very considerable journey should be performed by the funeral procession, which, as it will readily be believed, was not very numerously attended. Schalken with difficulty arrived in Rotterdam late in the day upon which the funeral was appointed to take place. The procession had not then arrived. Evening closed in, and still it did not appear.

Schalken strolled down to the church – he found it open – notice of the arrival of the funeral had been given, and the vault in which the body was to be laid had been opened. The official who corresponds to our sexton, on seeing a well-dressed gentleman, whose object was to attend the expected funeral, pacing the aisle of the church, hospitably invited him to share with him the comforts of a blazing wood fire, which, as was his custom in winter time upon such occasions, he had kindled on the hearth of a chamber which communicated, by a flight of steps, with the vault below.

In this chamber Schalken and his entertainer seated themselves, and the sexton, after some fruitless attempts to engage his guest in conversation, was obliged to apply himself to his tobacco-pipe and can to solace his solitude.

In spite of his grief and cares, the fatigues of a rapid journey of nearly forty hours gradually overcame the mind and body of Godfrey Schalken, and he sank into a deep sleep, from which he was awakened by someone shaking him gently by the shoulder. He first thought that the old sexton had called him, but *he* was no longer in the room.

He roused himself, and as soon as he could clearly see what was around him, he perceived a female form, clothed in a kind of light robe of muslin, part of which was so disposed as to act as a veil, and in her hand she carried a lamp. She was moving rather away from him, and towards the flight of steps which conducted towards the vaults.

Schalken felt a vague alarm at the sight of this figure, and at the same time an irresistible impulse to follow its guidance. He followed it towards the vaults, but when it reached the head of the stairs, he paused; the figure paused also, and, turning gently round, displayed, by the light of the lamp it carried, the face and features of his first love, Rose Velderkaust. There was nothing horrible, or even sad, in the countenance. On the contrary, it wore the same arch smile which used to enchant the artist long before in his happy days.

A feeling of awe and of interest, too intense to be resisted, prompted him to follow the spectre, if spectre it were. She descended the stairs – he followed; and, turning to the left, through a narrow passage, she led him, to his infinite surprise, into what appeared to be an old-fashioned Dutch apartment, such as the pictures of Gerard Douw have served to immortalise.

Abundance of costly antique furniture was disposed about the room, and in one corner stood a four-post bed, with heavy black-cloth curtains around it; the figure frequently turned towards him with the same arch smile; and when she came to the side of the bed, she drew the curtains, and by the light of the lamp which she held towards its contents, she disclosed to the horror-stricken painter, sitting bolt upright in the bed, the livid and demoniac form of Vanderhausen. Schalken had hardly seen him when he fell senseless upon the floor, where he lay until discovered, on the next morning, by persons employed in closing the passages into the vaults. He was lying in a cell of considerable size, which had not been disturbed for a long time, and he had fallen beside a large coffin which was supported upon small stone pillars, a security against the attacks of vermin.

To his dying day Schalken was satisfied of the reality of the vision which he had witnessed, and he has left behind him a curious evidence of the impression which it wrought upon his fancy, in a painting executed shortly after the event we have narrated, and which is valuable as exhibiting not only the peculiarities which have made Schalken's pictures sought after, but even more so as presenting a portrait, as close and faithful as one taken from memory can be, of his early love, Rose Velderkaust, whose mysterious fate must ever remain matter of speculation.

The picture represents a chamber of antique masonry, such as might be found in most old cathedrals, and is lighted faintly by a lamp carried in the hand of a female figure, such as we have above attempted to describe; and in the background, and to the left of him who examines the painting, there stands the form of a man apparently aroused from sleep, and by his attitude, his hand being laid upon his sword, exhibiting considerable alarm: this last figure is illuminated only by the expiring glare of a wood or charcoal fire.

The whole production exhibits a beautiful specimen of that artful and singular distribution of light and shade which has rendered the name of Schalken immortal among the artists of his country. This tale is traditionary, and the reader will easily perceive, by our studiously omitting to heighten many points of the narrative, when a little additional colouring might have added effect to the recital, that we have desired to lay before him, not a figment of the brain, but a curious tradition connected with, and belonging to, the biography of a famous artist.

The Romance of Certain Old Clothes

Henry James

Towards the middle of the eighteenth century there lived in the Province of Massachusetts a widowed gentlewoman, the mother of three children, by name Mrs. Veronica Wingrave. She had lost her husband early in life, and had devoted herself to the care of her progeny. These young persons grew up in a manner to reward her tenderness and to gratify her highest hopes. The first-born was a son, whom she had called Bernard, after his father. The others were daughters—born at an interval of three years apart. Good looks were traditional in the family, and this youthful trio were not likely to allow the tradition to perish. The boy was of that fair and ruddy complexion and that athletic structure which in those days (as in these) were the sign of good English descent—a frank, affectionate young fellow, a deferential son, a patronizing brother, a steadfast friend. Clever, however, he was not; the wit of the family had been apportioned chiefly to his sisters. The late Mr. Wingrave had been a great reader of Shakespeare, at a time when this pursuit implied more freedom of thought than at the present day, and in a community where it required much courage to patronize the drama even in the closet: and he had wished to call attention to his admiration of the great poet by calling his daughters out of his favorite plays.

Upon the elder he had bestowed the romantic name of Rosalind, and the younger he had called Perdita, in memory of a little girl born between them, who had lived but a few weeks.

When Bernard Wingrave came to his sixteenth year his mother put a brave face upon it and prepared to execute her husband's last injunction. This had been a formal command that, at the proper age, his son should be sent out to England, to complete his education at the university of Oxford, where he himself had acquired his taste for elegant literature. It was Mrs. Wingrave's belief that the lad's equal was not to be found in the two hemispheres, but she had the old traditions of literal obedience. She swallowed her sobs, and made up her boy's trunk and his simple provincial outfit, and sent him on his way across the seas. Bernard presented himself at his father's college, and spent five years in England, without great honor, indeed, but with a vast deal of pleasure and no discredit. On leaving the university he made the journey to France.

In his twenty-fourth year he took ship for home, prepared to find poor little New England (New England was very small in those days) a very dull, unfashionable residence. But there had been changes at home, as well as in Mr. Bernard's opinions. He found his mother's house quite habitable, and his sisters grown into two very charming young ladies, with all the accomplishments and graces of the young women of Britain, and a certain native-grown originality and wildness, which, if it was not an accomplishment, was certainly a grace the more.

Bernard privately assured his mother that his sisters were fully a match for the most genteel young women in the old country; whereupon poor Mrs. Wingrave, you may be sure, bade them hold up their heads. Such was Bernard's opinion, and such, in a tenfold higher degree, was the opinion of Mr. Arthur Lloyd. This gentleman was a college-mate of Mr. Bernard, a young man of reputable family, of a good person and a handsome inheritance; which latter appurtenance he proposed to invest in trade in the flourishing colony. He and Bernard were sworn friends; they had crossed the ocean together, and the young American had lost no time in presenting him at his mother's house, where he had made quite as good an impression as that which he had received and of which I have just given a hint.

The two sisters were at this time in all the freshness of their youthful bloom; each wearing, of course, this natural brilliancy in the manner that became her best. They were equally dissimilar in appearance and character. Rosalind, the elder—now in her twenty-second year—was tall and white, with calm gray eyes and auburn tresses; a very faint likeness to the Rosalind of Shakespeare's comedy, whom I imagine a brunette (if you will), but a slender, airy creature, full of the softest, quickest impulses. Miss Wingrave, with her slightly lymphatic fairness, her fine arms, her majestic height, her slow utterance, was not cut out for adventures. She would never have put on a man's jacket and hose; and, indeed, being a very plump beauty, she may have had reasons apart from her natural dignity. Perdita, too, might very well have exchanged the sweet melancholy of her name against something more in consonance with her aspect and disposition.

She had the cheek of a gypsy and the eye of an eager child, as well as the smallest waist and lightest foot in all the country of the Puritans. When you spoke to her she never made you wait, as her handsome sister was wont to do (while she looked at you with a cold fine eye), but gave you your choke of a dozen answers before you had uttered half your thought.

The young girls were very glad to see their brother once more; but they found themselves quite able to spare part of their attention for their brother's friend. Among the young men their friends and neighbors, the belle jeunesse of the Colony, there were many excellent fellows, several devoted swains, and some two or three who enjoyed the reputation of universal charmers and conquerors. But the homebred arts and somewhat boisterous gallantry of these honest colonists were completely eclipsed by the good looks, the fine clothes, the punctilious courtesy, the perfect elegance, the immense information, of Mr. Arthur Lloyd. He was in reality no paragon; he was a capable, honorable, civil youth, rich in pounds sterling, in his health and complacency and his little capital of uninvested affections. But he was a gentleman; he had a handsome person; he had studied and traveled; he spoke French, he played the flute, and he read verses aloud with very great taste. There were a dozen reasons why Miss Wingrave and her sister should have thought their other male acquaintance made but a poor figure before such a perfect man of the world. Mr. Lloyd's anecdotes told our little New England maidens a great deal more of the ways and means of people of fashion in European capitals than he had any idea of doing. It was delightful to sit by and hear him and Bernard talk about the fine people and fine things they had seen. They would all gather round the fire after tea, in the little wainscoted parlor, and the two young men would remind each other, across the rug, of this, that and the other adventure. Rosalind and Perdita would often have given their ears to know exactly what adventure it was, and where it happened, and who was there, and what the ladies had on; but in those days a well-bred young woman was not expected to break into the conversation of her elders, or to ask too many questions; and the poor girls used therefore to sit fluttering behind the more languid—or more discreet—curiosity of their mother.

That they were both very fine girls Arthur Lloyd was not slow to discover; but it took him some time to make up his mind whether he liked the big sister or the little sister best. He had a strong presentiment—an emotion of a nature entirely too cheerful to be called a foreboding—that he was destined to stand up before the parson with one of them; yet he was unable to arrive at a preference, and for such a consummation a preference was certainly necessary, for Lloyd had too much young blood in his veins to make a choice by lot and be cheated of the satisfaction of falling in love. He resolved to take things as they came—to let his heart speak. Meanwhile he was on very pleasant footing. Mrs. Wingrave showed a dignified indifference to his "intentions," equally remote from a carelessness of her daughter's honor and from that sharp alacrity to make him come to the point, which, in his quality of young man of property, he had too often encountered in the worldly matrons of his native islands. As for Bernard, all that he asked was that his friend should treat his sisters as his own; and as for the poor girls themselves, however each may have secretly longed that their visitor should do or say something "marked," they kept a very modest and contented demeanor.

Towards each other, however, they were somewhat more on the offensive. They were good friends enough, and accommodating bed-fellows (they shared the same four-poster), betwixt whom it would take more than a day for the seeds of jealousy to sprout and bear fruit; but they felt that the seeds had been sown on the day that Mr. Lloyd came into the house. Each made up her mind that, if she should be slighted, she would bear her grief in silence, and that no one should be any the wiser; for if they had a great deal of ambition, they had also a large share of pride. But each prayed in secret, nevertheless, that upon her the selection, the distinction, might fall. They had need of a vast deal of patience, of self-control, of dissimulation. In those days a young girl of decent breeding could make no advances whatever, and barely respond, indeed, to those that were made. She was expected to sit still in her chair, with her eyes on the carpet, watching the spot where the mystic handkerchief should fall. Poor Arthur Lloyd was obliged to carry on his wooing in the little wainscoted parlor, before the eyes of Mrs. Wingrave, her son, and his prospective sister-in-law. But youth and love are so cunning that a hundred signs and tokens might travel to and fro, and not one of these three pairs of eyes detect them in their passage. The two maidens were almost always together, and had plenty of chances to betray themselves. That each knew she was being watched, made not a grain of difference in the little offices they mutually rendered, or in the various household tasks they performed in common.

Neither flinched nor fluttered beneath the silent battery of her sister's eyes. The only apparent change in their habits was that they had less to say to each other. It was impossible to talk about Mr. Lloyd, and it was ridiculous to talk about anything else. By tacit agreement they began to wear all their choice finery, and to devise such little implements of conquest, in the way of ribbons and top-knots and kerchiefs, as were sanctioned by indubitable modesty. They executed in the same inarticulate fashion a contract of fair play in this exciting game. "Is it better so?" Rosalind would ask, tying a bunch of ribbons on her bosom, and turning about from her glass to her sister. Perdita would look up gravely from her work and examine the decoration. "I think you had better give it another loop," she would say, with great solemnity, looking hard at her sister with eyes that added, "upon my honor!" So they were for ever stitching and turning their petticoats, and pressing out their muslins, and contriving washes and ointments and cosmetics, like the ladies in the household of the vicar of Wakefield. Some three or four months went by; it grew to be midwinter, and as yet Rosalind knew that if Perdita had nothing more to boast of than she, there was not much to be feared from her rivalry. But Perdita by this time—the charming Perdita—felt that her secret had grown to be tenfold more precious than her sister's.

One afternoon Miss Wingrave sat alone—that was a rare accident—before her toilet-glass, combing out her long hair. It was getting too dark to see; she lit the two candles in their sockets, on the frame of her mirror, and then went to the window to draw her curtains. It was a gray December evening; the landscape was bare and bleak, and the sky heavy with snowclouds. At the end of the large garden into which her window looked was a wall with a little postern door, opening into a lane. The door stood ajar, as she could vaguely see in the gathering darkness, and moved slowly to and fro, as if someone were swaying it from the lane without. It was doubtless a servant-maid who had been having a tryst with her sweetheart. But as she was about to drop her curtain Rosalind saw her sister step into the garden and hum along the path which led to the house. She dropped the curtain, all save a little crevice for her eyes. As Perdita came up the path she seemed to be examining something in her hand, holding it close to her eyes. When she reached the house she stopped a moment, looked intently at the object, and pressed it to her lips.

Poor Rosalind slowly came back to her chair and sat down before her glass where, if she had looked at it less abstractly, she would have seen her handsome features sadly disfigured by jealousy. A moment afterwards the door opened behind her and her sister came into the room, out of breath, her cheeks aglow with the chilly air.

Perdita started. "Ah," said she, "I thought you were with our mother." The ladies were to go to a tea-party, and on such occasions it was the habit of one of the girls to help their mother to dress.

Instead of coming in, Perdita lingered at the door.

"Come in, come in," said Rosalind. "We have more than an hour yet. I should like you very much to give a few strokes to my hair." She knew that her sister wished to retreat, and that she could see in the glass all her movements in the room. "Nay, just help me with my hair," she said, "and I will go to mamma."

Perdita came reluctantly, and took the brush. She saw her sister's eyes, in the glass, fastened hard upon her hands. She had not made three passes when Rosalind clapped her own right hand upon her sister's left, and started out of her chair. "Whose ring is that?" she cried, passionately, drawing her towards the light.

On the young girl's third finger glistened a little gold ring, adorned with a very small sapphire.

Perdita felt that she need no longer keep her secret, yet that she must put a bold face on her avowal. "It's mine," she said proudly.

"Who gave it to you?" cried the other.

Perdita hesitated a moment. "Mr. Lloyd."

"Mr. Lloyd is generous, all of a sudden."

"Ah no," cried Perdita, with spirit, "not all of a sudden! He offered it to me a month ago."

"And you needed a month's begging to take it?" said Rosalind, looking at the little trinket, which indeed was not especially elegant, although it was the best that the jeweler of the Province could furnish. "I wouldn't have taken it in less than two."

"It isn't the ring," Perdita answered, "it's what it means!"

"It means that you are not a modest girl!" cried Rosalind. "Pray, does your mother know of your intrigue? does Bernard?"

"My mother has approved my 'intrigue,' as you call it. Mr. Lloyd has asked for my hand, and mamma has given it. Would you have had him apply to you, dearest sister?"

Rosalind gave her companion a long look, full of passionate envy and sorrow. Then she dropped her lashes on her pale cheeks and turned away. Perdita felt that it had not been a pretty scene; but it was her sister's fault. However, the elder girl rapidly called back her pride, and turned herself about again. "You have my very best wishes," she said, with a low curtsey. "I wish you every happiness, and a very long life."

Perdita gave a bitter laugh. "Don't speak in that tone!" she cried. "I would rather you should curse me outright. Come, Rosy," she added, "he couldn't marry both of us."

"I wish you very great joy," Rosalind repeated, mechanically, sitting down to her glass again, "and a very long life, and plenty of children." There was something in the sound of these words not at all to Perdita's taste, "Will you give me a year to live at least?" she said. "In a year I can have one little boy—or one little girl at least.

If you will give me your brush again I will do your hair."

"Thank you," said Rosalind. "You had better go to mamma. It isn't becoming that a young lady with a promised husband should wait on a girl with none."

"Nay," said Perdita good-humoredly, "I have Arthur to wait upon me. You need my service more than I need yours."

But her sister motioned her away, and she left the room. When she had gone poor Rosalind fell on her knees before her dressing-table, buried her head in her arms, and poured out a flood of tears and sobs. She felt very much the better for this effusion of sorrow. When her sister came back she insisted on helping her to dress—on her wearing her prettiest things. She forced upon her acceptance a bit of lace of her own, and declared that now that she was to be married she should do her best to appear worthy of her lover's choice. She discharged these offices in stern silence; but, such as they were, they had to do duty as an apology and an atonement; she never made any other.

Now that Lloyd was received by the family as an accepted suitor nothing remained but to fix the wedding-day. It was appointed for the following April, and in the interval preparations were diligently made for the marriage. Lloyd, on his side, was busy with his commercial arrangements, and with establishing a correspondence with the great mercantile house to which he had attached himself in England. He was therefore not so frequent a visitor at Mrs. Wingrave's as during the months of his diffidence and irresolution, and poor Rosalind had less to suffer than she had feared from the sight of the mutual endearments of the young lovers. Touching his future sister-in-law Lloyd had a perfectly clear conscience. There had not been a particle of love-making between them, and he had not the slightest suspicion that he had dealt her a terrible blow. He was quite at his ease; life promised so well, both domestically and financially. The great revolt of the Colonies was not yet in the air, and that his connubial felicity should take a tragic turn it was absurd, it was blasphemous, to apprehend. Meanwhile, at Mrs. Wingrave's, there was a greater rustling of silks, a more rapid clicking of scissors and flying of needles, than ever. The good lady had determined that her daughter should carry from home the genteelest outfit that her money could buy or that the country could furnish. All the sage women in the Province were convened, and their united taste was brought to bear on Perdita's wardrobe. Rosalind's situation, at this moment, was assuredly not to be envied. The poor girl had an inordinate love of dress, and the very best taste in the world, as her sister perfectly well knew. Rosalind was tall, she was stately and sweeping, she was made to earn stiff brocade and masses of heavy lace, such as belong to the toilet of a rich man's wife. But Rosalind sat aloof with her beautiful arms folded and her head averted, while her mother and sister and the venerable women aforesaid worried and wondered over their materials, oppressed by the multitude of their resources. One day there came in a beautiful piece of white silk, brocaded with heavenly blue and silver sent by the bridegroom himself—it not being thought amiss in those days that the husband-elect should contribute to the bride's trousseau. Perdita could think of no form or fashion which would do sufficient honor to the splendor of the material.

"Blue's your color, sister, more than mine," she said, with appealing eyes. "It is a pity it's not for you. You would know what to do with it."

Rosalind got up from her place and looked at the great shining fabric, as it lay spread over the back of a chair. Then she took it up in her hands and felt it—lovingly, as Perdita could see—and turned about towards the mirror with it. She let it roll down to her feet, and flung the other end over her shoulder, gathering it in about her waist with her white arm, which was bare to the elbow. She threw back her head, and looked at her image, and a hanging tress of her auburn hair fell upon the gorgeous surface of the silk. It made a dazzling picture. The women standing about uttered a little "Look, look!" of admiration. "Yes, indeed," said Rosalind, quietly, "blue is my color." But Perdita could see that her fancy had been stirred, and that she would now fall to work and solve all their silken riddles. And indeed she behaved very well, as Perdita, knowing her insatiable love of millinery, was quite ready to declare. Innumerable yards of lustrous silk and satin, of muslin, velvet and lace, passed through her cunning hands, without a jealous word coming from her lips. Thanks to her industry, when the wedding-day came Perdita was prepared to espouse more of the vanities of life than any fluttering young bride who had yet received the sacramental blessing of a New England divine.

It had been arranged that the young couple should go out and spend the first days of their wedded life at the country-house of an English gentleman—a man of rank and a very kind friend to Arthur Lloyd. He was a bachelor; he declared he should be delighted to give up the place to the influence of Hymen. After the ceremony at church—it had been performed by an English clergyman—young Mrs. Lloyd hastened back to her mother's house to change her nuptial robes for a riding-dress. Rosalind helped her to effect the change, in the little homely room in which they had spent their undivided younger years. Perdita then hurried off to bid farewell to her mother, leaving Rosalind to follow. Then parting was short; the horses were at the door, and Arthur was impatient to start. But Rosalind had not followed, and Perdita hastened back to her room, opening the door abruptly. Rosalind, as usual, was before the glass, but in a position which caused the other to stand still, amazed. She had dressed herself in Perdita's cast-off wedding veil and wreath, and on her neck she had hung the full string of pearls which the young girl had received from her husband as a wedding-gift. These things had been hastily laid aside, to await their possessor's disposal on her return from the country. Bedizened by this unnatural garb Rosalind stood before the mirror, plunging a long look into its depths and reading heaven knows what audacious visions. Perdita was horrified. It was a hideous image of their old rivalry come to life again. She made a step towards her sister, as if to pull off the veil and the flowers. But catching her eyes in the glass, she stopped.

"Farewell, sweetheart," she said. "You might at least have waited till I had got out of the house!" And she hurried away from the room.

Mr. Lloyd had purchased in Boston a house which to the taste of those days appeared as elegant as it was commodious; and here he very soon established himself with his young wife. He was thus separated by a distance of twenty miles from the residence of his mother-in-law. Twenty miles, in that primitive era of roads and conveyances, were as serious a matter as a hundred at the present day, and Mrs. Wingrave saw but little of her daughter during the first twelvemonth of her marriage. She suffered in no small degree from Perdita's absence; and her affliction was not diminished by the fact that Rosalind had fallen into terribly low spirits and was not to be roused or cheered but by change of air and company. The real cause of the young lady's dejection the reader will not be slow to suspect. Mrs. Wingrave and her gossips, however, deemed her complaint a mere bodily ill, and doubted not that she would obtain relief from the remedy just mentioned. Her mother accordingly proposed, on her behalf, a visit to certain relatives on the paternal side, established in New York, who had long complained that they were able to see so little of their New England cousins. Rosalind was despatched to these good people, under a suitable escort, and remained with them for several months. In the interval her brother Bernard, who had begun the practice of the law, made up his mind to take a wife. Rosalind came home to the wedding, apparently cured of her heartache, with bright roses and lilies in her face and a proud smile on her lips. Arthur Lloyd came over from Boston to see his brother-in-law married, but without his wife, who was expecting very soon to present him with an heir. It was nearly a year since Rosalind had seen him. She was glad—she hardly knew why—that Perdita had stayed at home. Arthur looked happy, but he was more grave and important than before his marriage.

She thought he looked "interesting"—for although the word, in its modern sense, was not then invented, we may be sure that the idea was. The truth is, he was simply anxious about his wife and her coming ordeal. Nevertheless, he by no means failed to observe Rosalind's beauty and splendor, and to note how she effaced the poor little bride. The allowance that Perdita had enjoyed for her dress had now been transferred to her sister, who turned it to wonderful account.

On the morning after the wedding he had a lady's saddle put on the horse of the servant who had come with him from town, and went out with the young girl for a ride. It was a keen, clear morning in January; the ground was bare and hard, and the horses in good condition—to say nothing of Rosalind, who was charming in her hat and plume, and her dark blue riding coat, trimmed with fur. They rode all the morning, lost their way and were obliged to stop for dinner at a farmhouse. The early winter dusk had fallen when they got home. Mrs. Wingrave met them with a long face. A messenger had arrived at noon from Mrs. Lloyd; she was beginning to be ill, she desired her husband's immediate return. The young man, at the thought that he had lost several hours, and that by hard riding he might already have been with his wife, uttered a passionate oath. He barely consented to stop for a mouthful of supper, but mounted the messenger's horse and started off at a gallop.

He reached home at midnight. His wife had been delivered of a little girl. "Ah, why weren't you with me?" she said, as he came to her bedside.

"I was out of the house when the man came. I was with Rosalind," said Lloyd, innocently.

Mrs. Lloyd made a little moan, and turned away. But she continued to do very well, and for a week her improvement was uninterrupted. Finally, however, through some indiscretion in the way of diet or exposure, it was checked, and the poor lady grew rapidly worse. Lloyd was in despair. It very soon became evident that she was breathing her last. Mrs. Lloyd came to a sense of her approaching end, and declared that she was reconciled with death. On the third evening after the change took place she told her husband that she felt she should not get through the night. She dismissed her servants, and also requested her mother to withdraw—Mrs. Wingrave having arrived on the preceding day. She had had her infant placed on the bed beside her, and she lay on her side, with the child against her breast, holding her husband's hands. The night-lamp was hidden behind the heavy curtains of the bed, but the room was illuminated with a red glow from the immense fire of logs on the hearth.

"It seems strange not to be warmed into life by such a fire as that," the young woman said, feebly trying to smile. "If I had but a little of it in my veins! But I have given all my fire to this little spark of mortality." And she dropped her eyes on her child. Then raising them she looked at her husband with a long, penetrating gaze. The last feeling which lingered in her heart was one of suspicion. She had not recovered from the shock which Arthur had given her by telling her that in the hour of her agony he had been with Rosalind. She trusted her husband very nearly as well as she loved him; but now that she was called away forever she felt a cold horror of her sister. She felt in her soul that Rosalind had never ceased to be jealous of her good fortune; and a year of happy security had not effaced the young girl's image, dressed in her wedding-garments, and smiling with simulated triumph. Now that Arthur was to be alone, what might not Rosalind attempt? She was beautiful, she was engaging; what arts might she not use, what impression might she not make upon the young man's saddened heart? Mrs. Lloyd looked at her husband in silence. It seemed hard, after all, to doubt of his constancy. His fine eyes were filled with tears; his face was convulsed with weeping; the clasp of his hands was warm and passionate. How noble he looked, how tender, how faithful and devoted! "Nay," thought Perdita, "he's not for such a one as Rosalind. He'll never forget me. Nor does Rosalind truly care for him; she cares only for vanities and finery and jewels." And she lowered her eyes on her white hands, which her husband's liberality had covered with rings, and on the lace ruffles which trimmed the edge of her nightdress. "She covets my rings and my laces more than she covets my husband."

At this moment the thought of her sister's rapacity seemed to cast a dark shadow between her and the helpless figure of her little girl. "Arthur," she said, "you must take off my rings. I shall not be buried in them. One of these days my daughter shall wear them—my rings and my laces and silks. I had them all brought out and shown me today. It's a great wardrobe—there's not such another in the Province; I can say it without vanity, now that I have done with it. It will be a great inheritance for my daughter when she grows into a young woman. There are things there that a man never buys twice, and if they are lost you will never again see the like. So you will watch them well. Some dozen things I have left to Rosalind: I have named them to my mother. I have given her that blue and silver; it was meant for her; I wore it only once, I looked ill in it.

But the rest are to be sacredly kept for this little innocent. It's such a providence that she should be my color; she can wear my gowns; she has her mother's eyes. You know the same fashions come back even twenty years. She can wear my gowns as they are. They will lie there quietly waiting till she grows into them—wrapped in camphor and rose-leaves, and keeping their colors in the sweetscented darkness. She shall have black hair, she shall wear my carnation satin. Do you promise me, Arthur?"

"Promise you what, dearest?"

"Promise me to keep your poor little wife's old gowns."

"Are you afraid I shall sell them?"

"No, but that they may get scattered. My mother will have them properly wrapped up, and you shall lay them away under a double-lock. Do you know the great chest in the attic, with the iron bands? There is no end to what it will hold. You can put them all there. My mother and the housekeeper will do it, and give you the key. And you will keep the key in your secretary, and never give it to anyone but your child. Do you promise me?"

"Ah, yes, I promise you," said Lloyd, puzzled at the intensity with which his wife appeared to cling to this idea.

"Will you swear?" repeated Perdita.

"Yes, I swear."

"Well—I trust you—I trust you," said the poor lady, looking into his eyes with eyes in which, if he had suspected her vague apprehensions, he might have read an appeal quite as much as an assurance.

Lloyd bore his bereavement rationally and manfully. A month after his wife's death, in the course of business, circumstances arose which offered him an opportunity of going to England.

He took advantage of it, to change the current of his thoughts. He was absent nearly a year, during which his little girl was tenderly nursed and guarded by her grandmother. On his return he had his house again thrown open, and announced his intention of keeping the same state as during his wife's lifetime. It very soon came to be predicted that he would marry again, and there were at least a dozen young women of whom one may say that it was by no fault of theirs that, for six months after his return, the prediction did not come true. During this interval he still left his little daughter in Mrs. Wingrave's hands, the latter assuring him that a change of residence at so tender an age would be full of danger for her health. Finally, however, he declared that his heart longed for his daughter's presence and that she must be brought up to town. He sent his coach and his housekeeper to fetch her home. Mrs. Wingrave was in terror lest something should befall her on the road; and, in accordance with this feeling, Rosalind offered to accompany her.

She could return the next day. So she went up to town with her little niece, and Mr. Lloyd met her on the threshold of his house, overcome with her kindness and with paternal joy. Instead of returning the next day Rosalind stayed out the week; and when at last she reappeared, she had only come for her clothes. Arthur would not hear of her coming home, nor would the baby. That little person cried and choked if Rosalind left her; and at the sight of her grief Arthur lost his wits, and swore that she was going to die. In fine, nothing would suit them but that the aunt should remain until the little niece had grown used to strange faces.

It took two months to bring this consummation about; for it was not until this period had elapsed that Rosalind took leave of her brother-in-law. Mrs. Wingrave had shaken her head over her daughter's absence; she had declared that it was not becoming, that it was the talk of the whole country. She had reconciled herself to it only because, during the girl's visit, the household enjoyed an unwonted term of peace. Bernard Wingrave had brought his wife home to live, between whom and her sister-in-law there was as little love as you please. Rosalind was perhaps no angel; but in the daily practice of life she was a sufficiently good-natured girl, and if she quarreled with Mrs. Bernard, it was not without provocation. Quarrel, however, she did, to the great annoyance not only of her antagonist, but of the two spectators of these constant altercations. Her stay in the household of her brother-in-law, therefore, would have been delightful, if only because it removed her from contact with the object of her antipathy at home.

It was doubly—it was ten times—delightful, in that it kept her near the object of her early passion. Mrs. Lloyd's sharp suspicions had fallen very far short of the truth. Rosalind's sentiment had been a passion at first, and a passion it remained—a passion of whose radiant heat, tempered to the delicate state of his feelings, Mr. Lloyd very soon felt the influence. Lloyd, as I have hinted, was not a modern Petrarch; it was not in his nature to practice an ideal constancy. He had not been many days in the house with his sister-in-law before he began to assure himself that she was, in the language of that day, a devilish fine woman. Whether Rosalind really practiced those insidious arts that her sister had been tempted to impute to her it is needless to enquire. It is enough to say that she found means to appear to the very best advantage. She used to seat herself every morning before the big fireplace in the dining-room, at work upon a piece of tapestry, with her little niece disporting herself on the carpet at her feet, or on the train of her dress, and playing with her woollen balls. Lloyd would have been a very stupid fellow if he had remained insensible to the rich suggestions of this charming picture. He was exceedingly fond of his little girl, and was never weary of taking her in his arms and tossing her up and down, and making her crow with delight. Very often, however, he would venture upon greater liberties than the young lady was yet prepared to allow, and then she would suddenly vociferate her displeasure.

Rosalind, at this, would drop her tapestry, and put out her handsome hands with the serious smile of the young girl whose virgin fancy has revealed to her all a mother's healing arts. Lloyd would give up the child, their eyes would meet, their hands would touch, and Rosalind would extinguish the little girl's sobs upon the snowy folds of the kerchief that crossed her bosom. Her dignity was perfect, and nothing could be more discreet than the manner in which she accepted her brother-in-law's hospitality. It may almost be said, perhaps, that there was something harsh in her reserve. Lloyd had a provoking feeling that she was in the house and yet was unapproachable. Half-an-hour after supper, at the very outset of the long winter evenings, she would light her candle, make the young man a most respectful curtsey, and march off to bed. If these were arts, Rosalind was a great artist. But their effect was so gentle, so gradual, they were calculated to work upon the young widower's fancy with a crescendo so finely shaded, that, as the reader has seen, several weeks elapsed before Rosalind began to feel sure that her returns would cover her outlay. When this became morally certain she packed up her trunk and returned to her mother's house. For three days she waited: on the fourth Mr. Lloyd made his appearance—a respectful but pressing suitor, Rosalind heard him to the end, with great humility, and accepted him with infinite modesty. It is hard to imagine that Mrs. Lloyd would have forgiven her husband; but if anything might have disarmed her resentment it would have been the ceremonious continence of this interview. Rosalind imposed upon her lover but a short probation. They were married, as was becoming, with great privacy—almost with secrecy—in the hope perhaps, as was waggishly remarked at the time, that the late Mrs. Lloyd wouldn't hear of it.

The marriage was to all appearance a happy one, and each party obtained what each had desired—Lloyd "a devilish fine woman," and Rosalind—but Rosalind's desires, as the reader will have observed, had remained a good deal of a mystery. There were, indeed, two blots upon their felicity, but time would perhaps efface them. During the first three years of her marriage Mrs. Lloyd failed to become a mother, and her husband on his side suffered heavy losses of money.

This latter circumstance compelled a material retrenchment in his expenditure, and Rosalind was perforce less of a fine lady than her sister had been. She contrived, however, to carry it like a woman of considerable fashion. She had long since ascertained that her sister's copious wardrobe had been sequestrated for the benefit of her daughter, and that it lay languishing in thankless gloom in the dusty attic. It was a revolting thought that these exquisite fabrics should await the good pleasure of a little girl who sat in a high chair and ate bread-and-milk with a wooden spoon. Rosalind had the good taste, however, to say nothing about the matter until several months had expired. Then, at last, she timidly broached it to her husband. Was it not a pity that so much finery should be lost?—for lost it would be, what with colors fading, and moths eating it up, and the change of fashions. But Lloyd gave her so abrupt and peremptory a refusal, that she saw, for the present, her attempt was vain. Six months went by, however, and brought with them new needs and new visions. Rosalind's thoughts hovered lovingly about her sister's relics. She went up and looked at the chest in which they lay imprisoned. There was a sullen defiance in its three great padlocks and its iron bands which only quickened her cupidity.

There was something exasperating in its incorruptible immobility. It was like a grim and grizzled old household servant, who locks his jaws over a family secret. And then there was a look of capacity in its vast extent, and a sound as of dense fullness, when Rosalind knocked its side with the toe of her little shoe, which caused her to flush with baffled longing. "It's absurd," she cried; "it's improper, it's wicked;" and she forthwith resolved upon another attack upon her husband.

On the following day, after dinner, when he had had his wine, she boldly began it. But he cut her short with great sternness.

"Once for all, Rosalind," said he, "it's out of the question. I shall be gravely displeased if you return to the matter."

"Very good," said Rosalind. "I am glad to learn the esteem in which I am held. Gracious heaven," she cried, "I am a very happy woman! It's an agreeable thing to feel one's self sacrificed to a caprice!" And her eyes filled with tears of anger and disappointment.

Lloyd had a good-natured man's horror of a woman's sobs, and he attempted—I may say he condescended—to explain. "It's not a caprice, dear, it's a promise," he said—"an oath."

"An oath? It's a pretty matter for oaths! and to whom, pray?"

"To Perdita," said the young man, raising his eyes for an instant, and immediately dropping them.

"Perdita—ah, Perdita!" and Rosalind's tears broke forth. Her bosom heaved with stormy sobs—sobs which were the long-deferred sequel of the violent fit of weeping in which she had indulged herself on the night when she discovered her sister's betrothal. She had hoped, in her better moments, that she had done with her jealousy; but her temper, on that occasion, had taken an ineffaceable hold, "And pray, what right had Perdita to dispose of my future?" she cried.

"What right had she to bind you to meanness and cruelty? Ah, I occupy a dignified place, and I make a very fine figure! I am welcome to what Perdita has left! And what has she left? I never knew till now how little! Nothing, nothing, nothing."

This was very poor logic, but it was very good as a "scene." Lloyd put his arm around his wife's waist and tried to kiss her, but she shook him off with magnificent scorn. Poor fellow! he had coveted a "devilish fine woman," and he had got one. Her scorn was intolerable. He walked away with his ears tingling—irresolute, distracted. Before him was his secretary, and in it the sacred key which with his own hand he had turned in the triple lock. He marched up and opened it, and took the key from a secret drawer, wrapped in a little packet which he had sealed with his own honest bit of glazonry. Je garde, said the motto—"I keep." But he was ashamed to put it back. He flung it upon the table beside his wife.

"Put it back!" she cried. "I want it not. I hate it!"

"I wash my hands of it," cried her husband. "God forgive me!"

Mrs. Lloyd gave an indignant shrug of her shoulders, and swept out of the room, while the young man retreated by another door. Ten minutes later Mrs. Lloyd returned, and found the room occupied by her little stepdaughter and the nursery-maid. The key was not on the table. She glanced at the child. Her little niece was perched on a chair, with the packet in her hands. She had broken the seal with her own small fingers. Mrs. Lloyd hastily took possession of the key.

At the habitual supper-hour Arthur Lloyd came back from his counting-room. It was the month of June, and supper was served by daylight. The meal was placed on the table, but Mrs. Lloyd failed to make her appearance. The servant whom his master sent to call her came back with the assurance that her room was empty, and that the women informed him that she had not been seen since dinner. They had, in truth, observed her to have been in tears, and, supposing her to be shut up in her chamber, had not disturbed her. Her husband called her name in various parts of the house, but without response. At last it occurred to him that he might find her by taking the way to the attic. The thought gave him a strange feeling of discomfort, and he bade his servants remain behind, wishing no witness in his quest. He reached the foot of the staircase leading to the topmost flat, and stood with his hands on the banisters, pronouncing his wife's name. His voice trembled. He called again louder and more firmly. The only sound which disturbed the absolute silence was a faint echo of his own tones, repeating his question under the great eaves.

He nevertheless felt irresistibly moved to ascend the staircase. It opened upon a wide hall, lined with wooden closets, and terminating in a window which looked westward, and admitted the last rays of the sun. Before the window stood the great chest. Before the chest, on her knees, the young man saw with amazement and horror the figure of his wife. In an instant he crossed the interval between them, bereft of utterance. The lid of the chest stood open, exposing, amid their perfumed napkins, its treasure of stuffs and jewels. Rosalind had fallen backward from a kneeling posture, with one hand supporting her on the floor and the other pressed to her heart.

On her limbs was the stiffness of death, and on her face, in the fading light of the sun, the terror of something more than death. Her lips were parted in entreaty, in dismay, in agony; and on her blanched brow and cheeks there glowed the marks of ten hideous wounds from two vengeful ghostly hands.